Wrightsville Beach

Wrightsville Beach

Robert B. Corbett

E-BookTime, LLC
Montgomery, Alabama

Wrightsville Beach

ISBN: 978-1-60862-036-4

First Edition
Published May 2009
E-BookTime, LLC
6598 Pumpkin Road
Montgomery, AL 36108
www.e-booktime.com

Dedication

I dedicate this book to the celebration of life. I am not talking about such functions and obligations as eating, breathing, going to school, or the drudge of having to get up early and go to work five or more days a week. You have heard the term, "the working stiff?" Life is much deeper, broader, and higher than that. Looks or appearances can be deceiving. You can even fool yourself. My mother has some beautiful artificial flowers displayed in her yard and on her back porch. Neighbors have often commented on the beautiful flowers. They are especially amazed and want to know how she is able to keep them looking so fresh and beautiful in cold weather. Are you like my mother's flowers?

Jesus Christ once said that a man's life must consist of more than bread alone. I will allow you to look up the passage and get the point. What are you living for? Is it for real or are you sustaining yourself with artificial food and drink and not the real thing? People are so good at putting on masks now days. We have all kinds of masks we pull out of our actor's bag to fool others and even ourselves occasionally. That bag of masks was purchased with no money downtown on Main Street at the junction of Hypocrisy Street and Going Along With The Crowd Avenue.

Do you remember or have you seen the movie, *The Awakening?* If you have not seen the movie, I recommend it. Robin Williams plays the part of a young doctor who finds a temporary solution for a terrible disease that the patients in the facility he works at have come down with. I will allow you to look up the disease that is often transmitted by the Tsetse Fly, Herpes cold sores, or Herpes genital sores that can turn people into living statues. The name of the disease is called on the street, Sleeping Sickness, and in the doctor's office, Post-Encephalitis. The results are that the patients are paralyzed by Parkinson's disease. The doctor in the movie finds a way, a medium, to put the drug into so that the "sleepers'" bodies could accept the drug. The effect was a miracle! The victims of this disease became "alive" and they realized that they had missed out on a lot of years of living. They celebrated life to its fullness to the best of their ability! I will not share the end of the movie because that is not my point.

Dedication

Are you really awake or are you like those unfortunate victims of the disease in the movie? You have heard of the living dead? They are all around you practically speaking. Get a life! Wake up or you are going to be off the train of life before you realize that you were ever on it! Find something to do besides your normal duties. Find a good healthy hobby, read a good book occasionally, take a walk to the park. I would just not recommend that you do it late at night. You know how things are now days. Go fishing or take yourself or your family to a museum. You might actually learn something and have fun doing it all at the same time. I used to love to walk to the beautiful swamp that is located across the road in front of our farm house. The huge cypress trees in the swamp are now considered part of the largest and oldest living cypress tree grove in the world. I still enjoy going into the country and walking down the old mill road dam located in Colly Swamp and look at the pond the old Colly Veneer Plant once stood about a century ago. This swamp almost reminds me of a tropical jungle.

I am not poking fun or trying to insult you. I want you to see life from a different prospective, an adventure, a great privilege. Give it your best shot. After all, it is your Act. The curtain is up and I want you to be at your best so that you can get your Oscar.

One

Leaving Boston

Our story begins in the driveway of David Smith's parents' home as they bid their son, daughter-in-law, and their two grandchildren goodbye. David's father, Doctor Daniel Smith Senior, is a prominent physician who lives with his wife Patsy in a very large home in an upper class neighborhood in the city of Boston. Doctor Smith's people have been part of Boston's prominent families for nearly three hundred years. Brenda, Doctor David Smith Junior's wife, moved to Boston thirteen years ago to go to school there. It was in Boston that she met David. Two years later, they were married. Brenda's parents attended the wedding that was held at the church David's people had been attending for nearly three hundred years. Brenda's father, and old Southern boy living at the junction of, Pender County, Sampson, and Bladen Counties, North Carolina, was not overly pleased by the marriage, but was kept in check by his wife Lillian.

"David might be a D Yankee from Boston, but he was their daughter's husband and he was the father of their grandchildren."

"But why marry a Yankee from all places, Boston? Those high browed people with their fancy ways think that they are better than everyone else!" Mrs. Pridgen, Brenda's mother, would always say to her husband when he would start acting up.

"Now, Beard, the Good Lord works in marvelous ways his wonders to perform. At least that boy has a good job and is making good money. You should be proud of him! Our daughter could have married mostly any fellow in these woods, but what kind of future would she have or our grandkids?"

"Well, at least he would know how to skin a deer or plow a straight furrow."

"Beard, now everyone does not live like us. Brenda tells me that David is a geologist and an oceanographer."

"Yea, and I bet he does not even know how to catch a fish!"

"Oh, I don't know about that, Beard. Brenda tells me that they love to fish."

"Just wait and see; I can't wait to carry that boy down the river one nice cold day and see what he is made of. Shucks, I bet he will be crying before the day is done!"

Our conversation now goes back to Boston. Neither, David, nor his children had visited North Carolina before; except, David, who once worked off Wrightsville Beach for a few weeks while on vacation in an underwater laboratory named the Sea Wise. The wedding twelve years ago as stated earlier had taken place in Boston. Brenda's parents had visited Boston several times in the past. Brenda's parents were not much for fancy city life, especially her father. The only thing that kept them there was the desire to be with their daughter and the opportunity to get acquainted with their grandchildren, Dan and Betty.

After about an hour of travel, the children wanted to know about where they were going. Dan their son, who is ten, was the first to ask questions.

"Mother, how long will it take for us to get to Grandfather and Grandmother Pridgen's house?"

"Son, we are probably going to stay in Rocky Mount before we go to my parents' house."

"Why do we need to do that?"

"The trip is too far to make in one day." Betty who is eight years old decides to get into the conversation.

"Mother, could you tell me where our grandparents live?"

"Honey, they live at the junction of Pender, Sampson, and Bladen Counties in the State of North Carolina and up and down on both sides of the Black River. They live about three miles outside of a little village called Atkinson."

"Are there a lot of houses there?"

"No, I am afraid not, there are only about one hundred or so. Your grandfather tells me that it has been about the same size for over forty years." Betty speaks once again:

"Mother, are there going to be a lot of kids there to play with? I will miss all of my friends in Boston!"

"There will be plenty of children to play with. Not as many as in Boston, but you will learn to enjoy them just like you enjoyed your friends in Boston." Dan questions his mother:

"Mother, what can kids do in a small place like Atkinson?" Dan's mother pauses a moment and speaks:

"Well, it has been awhile since I was a kid." David looks over at his wife with a smile and speaks:

"Not that long." Brenda smiles back at David and continues her conversation with her son. David speaks to his children after his wife ends her conversation with her son.

"Now, children, we will not be living at your grandparents permanently. We will live there eight month or so until we can find a house." Dan speaks up:

"Daddy, where are we going to find a house?"

"I am not sure, but I would like to see if we could move to a small town on the ocean called Wrightsville Beach. It is a very beautiful town." The children in the back are all excited because they love to fish, swim, and be near the water. Dan asks his mother a question:

"Mother, what did you and your friends do when you played? Did you play with dinosaurs or something?" David could see an amused smile on his wife's face the moment his son asked the question that was obviously hatched up as a form of amusement. His mother answered back without falling into the dinosaurs trap kids like to setup for their parents.

"No, not exactly. We did not play with dinosaurs when I was your age. I guess that your grandfather had shot all of them. There were all kinds of things to keep us busy and entertained when I was a child."

"Like what?"

"Now, I didn't have someone to carry me to a big city mall, a fancy toy store, or a big city park. I didn't get to take ballet classes or singing lessons like big city kids, but I made out all right. I would not trade my life as a kid for all of the limelight of the big city. We had fun back in those days and you usually did not have to pay for it. We had our imaginations and the whole world before us so to speak as a play pen." David had by then become interested in the conversation between his wife and son so he spoke up:

"Honey, by all means get on with it! What exactly did you kids do in the middle of nowhere?" Betty looks back toward her husband with a, how dare you frown, and then smiles.

"Well, let's see, what did we do? I guess for starters we would all get into our bathing suits and go down to the swimming hole."

"Betty, their daughter, looks up from her computer game and speaks:

"Swimming hole, what is a swimming hole, Mother?"

"It is a deep round hole off the banks of Buzzard Creek. It has a white sandy bottom that allowed us to see all the way to the bottom." Dan speaks up:

"How deep is it? Is it dangerous?"

"It is about ten feet deep at its deepest point and about the size of a house. There are some large trees near the shore and we kids would take turns jumping off a huge limb that stuck out above the water. Sometimes we would get on a rope and see how far we could swing out before we let go." Dan once again speaks up:

"Did anyone ever get hurt?"

"No, not that I am aware of. Kids back in those days could be trusted. I guess that the only trouble, if it could be called trouble, was when Tommy Cobb jumped in and snagged his pants on a small limb. We were a little older in those days. We were all in our mid-teens. Dan speaks up:

"Hey, what did he do?"

"What do you mean by what did he do? He lost his pants. What could he do? We teased him for a while, but when he threatened to tell our parents, we threw his shorts back to him and turned our heads while he put them back on. When we finished swimming, we would all go up to my parents' big house and eat cold watermelons and have cake or cookies Mama baked." Betty spoke up:

"Mother, where did all of those kids come from?"

"Most of them would come from Atkinson. Tommy had a horse and he would hitch it up to a wagon. Six or seven kids came from Atkinson to join the fun. They would come almost every week. Often several of our cousins would spend the summer with us."

"Wow that sounds like fun!"

"It was son. The creek was nice and cold on a hot summer day. There was no one to bother us. No pollution and the water was clean enough to drink. The scenery around there is unrivaled. Moss hangs from huge trees that stop at the water's edge. Huge cypress trees over a thousand years old add beauty and mystery to the swamp. One huge cypress tree is so large that several of us could get inside a hollow in its side that reminded us of a small cave. Beautiful wild flowers are everywhere to look at and fill the air with their fragrances. We would see and hear all kinds of birds. Squirrels would chatter and jump from one tree to another. Huge red headed woodpeckers would create a primitive, but wonderful noise as they hammered away at the trees. You could hear them for miles! Up ahead huge turkey buzzards would circle. Occasionally one would flap its wings a few times to gain altitude. Butterflies showed off their beautiful wings as they circled us. If you held your hand out, they would often land on it and you could talk to them.

"I remember that there was a huge alligator snapping turtle that lived nearby. As long as we did not disturb him he would sit on an old log and sun. Occasionally he would slide off to catch a fish or something. Daddy told us that that same old snapper was there when he was a boy. He told us to respect it and that it would respect us. I believe that Daddy called him Old Hard Head." Dan speaks up:

"Mama, are there any dangerous snakes around there?"

"Sure, we would see an occasional water moccasin or a rattlesnake."

"You guys were not afraid?"

"No, no more than we are afraid when we go to the beach. Everyone knows that there are sharks in the ocean, but that does not stop us from enjoying the ocean. We were not careless. Most of the time snakes will leave if a crowd of people comes walking up. I don't believe we ever had to kill a snake. We came close one time." Dan speaks:

"What happened, Mother?"

"Well, we walked down to the swimming hole and to our surprise a huge water moccasin was on a log not far from where we were planning to swim. Your Uncle Gregg threw a large stick at it to scare it away and it became angry and started swimming toward us on the shore. Believe me, we moved about as fast as we could. All of a sudden we heard a noise like someone was shaking the top of a bush and out comes a huge black King snake." Betty listens with great interest and speaks:

"Mother, what did you kids do?"

"We just stood there looking in shock because that huge black King snake took off after that water moccasin like he owned him!" Dan with eyes wide open speaks with excitement:

"Boy, I bet there was a bad fight! What happened?" While Brenda continued to talk to her children about her childhood, David, her husband, once again turned his attention to what his wife was sharing with the kids about her childhood near and around Buzzard Creek.

"What else did you do for excitement?" Brenda was amused and pleased that David would be as interested as the kids were about her unusual childhood. David grew up in the big city of Boston. His children would get to experience some of the childhood his wife had experienced. They would leave big city life and enter this strange and exciting world his wife described. Brenda continues to give an account of her childhood.

"I don't know where to begin! There was always something to do and it seemed that the days were always too short. I loved to help build playhouses high up in the branches of huge live oak trees. Some of the houses were as large as a living room in a regular sized house. They had porches, windows, and doors with handmade furniture inside. We built a dozen of them up in those trees by the time we all grew up and left the area. We made walkways up in the trees that joined hundreds of trees together. One boardwalk allowed us to cross Buzzard Creek high in the sky. Often we would be walking to a favorite spot up there and meet an

Opossum with her little ones on her back hitching a free ride." Betty speaks:

"What did you guys do then?"

"Oh, nothing, we would leave the mama Opossum to her business and continue our walk. We saw raccoons, squirrels, and rats on our boardwalk in the sky. Below we would often see deer, especially at night, if there was a full Moon. An old sow bear lived in one area. We would sometimes tease her by throwing small sticks at her." Dan spoke:

"Wasn't that dangerous?"

"No, son, we were about forty feet up. Besides, the bear was too big to climb up and follow us on our boardwalk. We were not worried." David speaks:

"What did you guys do for fishing?"

"We did a lot of fishing. Papa would carry us two or three times a month. We did a lot of creek fishing, but we usually caught a lot more fish while fishing with him in Black River or the lake." David continues to ask questions to his wife:

"What kind of boat did he have?"

"Oh just a homemade boat that he and Great Uncle Roy Hilburn made. It was a nice twenty foot boat that was about six feet wide. Daddy always kept two paddles and a long pole in the boat just in case the old Johnson motor he used conked out. The motor only caused him trouble one time if I remember correctly, but we were prepared!" Dan questions his mother:

"Mother, was there a bait and tackle shop nearby?"

"No, dear, we provided our own bait. We usually had plenty of red worms available in an old bathtub where we raised them. Mama threw table scraps in the tub to feed them. We also carried crickets with us. What we did was to get a bunch of cloth feed sacks from the barn. Next we would sprinkle cornmeal on the grass and cover the meal with the sacks. The next morning we would surround the sacks with small wire cages in our hands. The sacks were quickly removed from the ground to reveal hundreds of hungry crickets dining on the cornmeal. We quickly picked up the crickets and put them into the cages. If the fish were not biting worms that day, we would provide them with the crickets we had captured." Dan questions his mother:

"Mother, how far is it to Atkinson from Boston?"

"Son, according to the computer it is about eight hundred and forty miles."

"Mother, that is a long way for Daddy to drive!"

"Dan, we are not going to drive the entire distance in one day. Like I said, we will be stopping at a motel in Rocky Mount. I believe that your father will want me to drive from Rocky Mount to Atkinson. I will be entering my territory." After many hours, the Smith family drives into the city of Rocky Mount, N.C., and spends the night there. The next morning Brenda is behind the wheel. While traveling on the road after their night's rest in Rocky Mount, the Smith family focused their attention on the new state they were going to live in. The Smith's eight-year-old daughter, Betty, questions her father, David:

"Daddy, where are you going to work when we live in our new home?"

"Honey, I am going to work at the University of North Carolina at Wilmington." Dan, the Smith's ten year old son joins the questioning.

"Father, what will you teach?"

"Well, son, unless things change, I will teach and help run the science department just like I did at the University of Boston. I am sure that you know what your old man teaches."

"Yes, sir, you will teach oceanography and geology. Are you still going to be using those submarines like you did at the University of Boston?"

"Yes, son, I worked out a deal with the University of Boston and got a government grant that will allow the new school I will be teaching at to buy one of the exploration submarines the University of Boston was planning on replacing in a few years. It will help both institutions meet their goals."

"What is a government grant?"

"Son, the Federal Government gives money away to institutions like colleges to be used to buy equipment and to sometime hire teachers. Often all of the grant will be free. In other words, it will not have to be paid back."

"Is this the reason they hired you?" Smith looks at his wife and smiles surprised at his son's bold question.

"No, son, I don't believe that was the reason, but I am sure that it didn't hurt my chances of being hired."

"Daddy, are we going to live in Wilmington?"

"We might live there, but we are going to try to buy a house at or near the beach." Betty next speaks to her mother who is doing the driving:

"Mother, have you ever been to Wrightsville Beach?"

"Sure, I didn't get to go often. Your grandparents do not travel a lot. We probably got to go there two or three times a year. Most of our trips were with other young people from church. Once in awhile I would go with a family in our neighborhood. Neighbors would call our house a week or two in advance and invite us kids. Occasionally our parents would go along as well." Dan speaks:

"I bet you were upset when they said no!"

"Not always, son. When I was your age, I would be very disappointed, but when I became a little older and wiser, I realized that my parents needed me on the plantation. We always had a lot of things to do. We did have plenty of help and Mattie."

"What kind of work did you guys do?"

"Well, son, we had to help milk the cows and make butter. Mama would sell most of it at the flea market in Atkinson."

"Do our grandparents still make butter?"

"Yes, son, as far as I know they do. I promise you that Grandmother Pridgen will allow you kids to help her make butter. It takes a lot of work, but the butter has a flavor no store brought butter has. There are no artificial additives. Your grandmother puts the butter in all kinds of molds to make it pretty. She owns about twelve different kinds of molds. Most of the molds imprint the images of pretty flowers on the butter cakes. Other molds imprint images of cats, dogs, and birds." Betty speaks:

"Mother, what else did you kids do?"

"Well, let me see. The time of the year usually determined what kind of things we did."

"I don't understand." Brenda heard a small disturbance in the backseat and realized that Dan was questioning the intellect of his sister based on her question.

"Your sister has asked a good question. What time of the year does your father mow grass, Betty?"

"Daddy mows the grass in hot weather."

"Yes, in the warmer months."

"Oh, I understand what you are saying!"

"In the fall of the year, we would shuck the newly dried corn. So that you can understand for now, we were removing the shucks, the outer layer of each ear of corn. You kids know what shucks are as many times as you guys have helped your father and me remove them before we roasted fresh corn on the grill. When we removed the shucks, we would have other people to put the corn into hand powered shellers. We dropped ears of dried corn into the sheller's mouth while someone turned the handle. The machine would take all of the kernels off each shucked ear. The loose corn would pour down into a bucket or bag. The corncobs are thrown out of the way by the machine. Daddy would get several hundred pounds of shelled corn and carry it to the mill that is on the plantation. The corn is ground into fine cornmeal that your grandmother makes into the best cornbread, flapjacks, and corncakes you have ever tried! Part of the meal is given away to family members or Uncle Preston who runs the mill for our family." Dan questions his mother:

"Mother, who is Uncle Preston?" Is he one of Grandfather Pridgen's brothers that we don't know about?" Brenda pauses a second and then answers her young son:

"Your grandfather treats him almost like a brother, but he is not physically akin to us. His fourth-great grandfather was a slave on the plantation before the Civil War. You know about the Civil War?" Dan once again speaks up:

"I know a little about the Civil War, but not much."

"Well, don't worry about it. When you get a little older, you will take U.S. History. I will be home schooling you kids part of the time. I will find other qualified people to teach subjects I am not an expert in." Betty speaks:

"Mother, does this mean that we will not have friends?"

"No, I will offer almost free schooling for qualified kids. Before you guys even ask, let me reveal my plans. Your father and I have plans to purchase a large house of seven or eight bedrooms. We are going to convert four of the bedrooms into classrooms. When you kids finish school, we will turn the rooms back into bedrooms." Betty speaks:

"Mother, how many kids are you going to try to get?"

"Your father and I believe that we should have about fifteen kids for each class not counting you two. Fifteen kids will be your age Betty and the other fifteen will be Dan's age. We are going to try to get qualified parents to help teach. We are also going to hire students who have at least a Master of education." Dan once again speaks to his mother:

"Mother, don't you have a PD in education?"

"Yea, son, that is what kind of degree your mother has!"

"No, son, your father is being silly. I have a Ph.D. in education. Now until you get into high school, I would not worry about what kind of degree your mother has. By then, you will be old enough to appreciate your mother's education." Betty now typically pursues the same line of questioning.

"Mother, what kind of degree does Father have?"

"Honey, he is right in front of you, why don't you ask him?"

"I guess that I am just being silly. Father, what kind of degree do you have? Do you have a degree like Mother has?"

"No, Betty, one Ph.D. in education is enough for our family. I have two degrees. I have a doctorate in Oceanography and a doctorate in Geology."

"Why do you need two degrees, Father?"

"I guess that I really need only one degree, but I have made good use of both of them. I have opportunity to explore and learn about the oceans and the structure of the land below and above them. The degrees complement each other. I will try to explain by this illustration. I could paddle a small rowboat by one good paddle. A paddle represents one of my degrees. It is much easier; however, to paddle a small boat with double paddles that are attached to the sides of the boat. That away, I can go almost twice as fast with not a lot of extra work involved." Dan starts talking:

"Father, we all paddled around in those kinds of boats at the park we went to about a year ago!"

"Yes, I know, son. This is the reason I explained myself by speaking about a boat with two paddles. Like two paddles, two degrees help me understand and get a lot more work done than I could with only one degree. Brenda, you spoke about two people named Mattie and Uncle Preston. What else should we know about these characters?"

"Mattie lives in a kind of suite of her own in my parents' home. The suite was originally built to house servants. Mattie's rooms can be reached from the back bottom porch. A porch surrounds each of the first two floors. Mattie is a little slow, but she is a dear. I love her like family. She can't read or write, but she keeps her rooms clean and neat."

"How long has she lived in that apartment?"

"As long as I can remember she has lived there, David. I understand that she came from a dysfunctional family in the country about fifteen miles from Atkinson. My father would go to Berry Hill to recruit help for tobacco season. Mattie would ask him to let her work for him. Father always said no because he realized that Mattie was mentally and socially challenged. Every time Father showed up she would beg him."

"What made him change his mind about her?"

"I don't know. I guess a combination of things. Father called the local sheriff about Mattie and her family and learned that her father was as bad as they get. Mattie seldom had enough to eat. They would eat anything. I am sure that you would not want to learn more."

"Why, not?"

"OK, I understand that they cooked their food in a big black pot that was outside in the yard. Mostly everything was cooked with water and stirred with a wooden paddle. Mattie said that one day while she was watching her mother stir the contents of the pot, a cat's head popped up in the rice."

"That is sick and disgusting, how terrible!"

"Mattie told us kids that when she was about fourteen years old, they had nothing to cook for Christmas Dinner. Mattie told me that her father went to an elderly white preacher's house and stole his old red rooster for their Christmas."

"Did the preacher find out?"

"Yes, I understand that he saw Mattie's Pa leaving the chicken house at about eleven o'clock at night with something in his hands that was putting up a fight."

"What did the preacher do?"

"He called out his name when he recognized him, but I understand that he did not call the law."

"That was mighty nice of him!"

"Well, I am sure that old preacher was aware of the struggle Mattie's family had. He was aware that the father was a no good drunk who did not work. The good preacher knew the children could use a heavy meal. Mattie also told my parents that her family would go to newly cut ditches and gather white mineral clay."

"What on earth for?"

"I understand that the stuff has certain nutritional benefits to it. I read something about that in a newspaper article when I was in high school."

"Really, I might have to check on this, there might be something worth knowing about."

"Now, they also cooked collards, Opossums, and if they were lucky a raccoon."

"So, Mattie's father was a hunter!"

"No, I don't think so. I would suspect that most of everything was road kill. There is always an Opossum on the road. Often they are not torn up all over the road way."

"I bet they also had venison."

"Yes, David, I have not thought about deer. Actually, I would imagine that they would have been able to harvest deer off the road in front of their house. I believe one or two a year." Dan speaks:

"Mother, you did not finish telling us about Uncle Preston. Exactly who is he?"

"Like I said, his fourth-great grandfather was a slave on the Pridgen plantation." Your sixth-great grandfather thought so much of his fourth-great grandfather that he asked him to continue to live on the plantation."

"Why in the world would a freed slave want to continue to live on the plantation, Honey?" Brenda turns her head toward her husband for a split second and muses.

"He had a good job as a slave and wanted to keep it. If he left, where was he to go? My fifth-great grandfather built a better house for him and allowed him to use two hundred acres of land free of charge. He started planting corn and he sold it on the market as whole corn or as cornmeal. Today his fourth-great grandson, whom we call, Uncle Preston, sells corn called *Uncle Preston's Corn Meal* all over the South and many places up North. Uncle Preston grinds up my father's corn into meal and once for my grandfather when he farmed." David questions his wife Brenda:

"Honey, who is the owner of the Pridgen plantation?"

"My grandparents still own the plantation. My parents will be given the property at the death of my grandparents."

"I don't understand why your grandparents don't go ahead and give the property to their son. He is over sixty years old!"

"I don't know the answer. I guess it is family tradition. My parents run the huge place and receive all of the money. My grandparents are well taken care of and still live in their old mansion along with my parents. I guess that Grandfather Pridgen is like a CEO of a corporation. He probably still gives Daddy advice when he either asks for it or when Grandfather Pridgen feels he needs to be heard. I have never heard my parents complain. My Mother loves Daddy's parents with all of her heart. Anyway, back to Uncle Preston and the mill. Uncle Preston fixes up blends of animal feed for Daddy's horses, cows, and the catfish pond. Most of the rest is sold on the market."

"How many horses do your father own?"

"I believe about twelve or fourteen hundred. He uses about four hundred and thirty two at a time when he has the fields plowed and when the fall harvest is gathered. Believe me two hundred and sixteen teams of heavy plow horses can cover a lot of territory in a good day! We tend about eight thousand acres. We could tend several times more, but we would have to hire outside help. We don't need the money and want to preserve our old growth trees. It takes us a week or two to handle such a big operation. Sometimes the weather slows us down."

"How many acres of land do you think can be plowed by a team of horses, Honey?"

"I believe about five acres a day can be plowed by a team."

"Honey, that means that about one thousand and eighty acres can be worked a day by his horses. That is not bad!" Brenda continues to talk:

"I realize that thirty or forty heavy tractors can do the same thing, but my family has always used animals. If one gets sick, the horse is checked out of service and cared for. We have many extra horses that are constantly rotated so that they are not overworked. There is little diesel fuel to buy or need for huge tanks to store the thousands of gallons of fuel tractors would need on such a huge farm. We seldom have expensive mechanical jobs to pay for. Tractors can't duplicate themselves. Our horses have babies every year."

"What would concern me is the cost of the human labor. It would take a large crew to manage your family's plantation. I don't see how they can pay so many people!"

"Most of the people, which make up about a hundred and fifty families, actually live on the plantation. The plantation is almost totally self sustaining. I understand that most of the families living on the plantation have been living there long before the Civil War. Each family has been assigned a twenty-five acre plot. These people can use this land as they see fit. Almost all of the twenty-five acre farms are modeled after the plantation. These people grow, raise, or make almost everything they need or want. They all get to fish in the plantation's huge lake, which is constantly stocked. Uncle Preston, the mill operator, has tons of fish food prepared each month to feed the fish and other creatures living in the lake."

"What other creatures are you referring to, dear?"

"One of my grandfathers had miles of ditches dug on three corners of the lake. They were created to provide a home or estuary for crayfish or freshwater shrimp, bullfrogs, and baby fish that are born in the lake, or the ones that are put in the lake to replenish the fish population called stockfish."

"Why would it be necessary to dig ditches when there is a 150 square mile lake available?" Betty smiles before she answers:

"Come now, Doctor Smith, you are supposed to be the expert."

"Yes, in my field I am considered a minor expert, but this is a little different!" Brenda speaks:

"The ditches are about fifteen feet wide and the water in them is about two and a half feet deep. The ditches are kept clear of trees and excess growth of any kind. You can paddle a boat in them to gig frogs or catch the crayfish."

"I did not realize that Southern people in North Carolina ate crayfish!"

"My people have been eating them for over two hundred and fifty years. I understand that an old slave purchased from New Orleans convinced one of my great-grandfathers to add crayfish to his diet."

"I didn't realize that slave owners listened to their slaves!"

"I guess it is no different than today. A worker or employee presents an idea to his boss or the owner of the factory or office he works in. Once in awhile the boss is smart enough to recognize value in what an employee or a person under them offers by way of a suggestion. In the case of the slave from New Orleans, I am sure that he benefited also because he loved crayfish and was also put in charge of the project for life."

"That is cool! In other words, that slave created his own job."

"Yes, I have not thought of it that way, David. I am sure you will get a chance to gig for bullfrogs. I know that you love frog legs. Now back to the miles of wide shallow ditches. The ditches also provide sanctuary for baby fish to grow up before they venture into the much deeper lake. Bullfrogs do better in ditches than deep lakes that house large aggressive fish. The same can be said for the tiny crayfish that hide in the waterweeds that grow in the ditches.

"Now back to the plantation, David. The people who live on the plantation use Daddy's horses for free. They check them out at one of the stables. There is always someone at the stables to keep account of who is checking out horses or bringing them back. In the fall of the year, each family can gather a hundred pounds of pecans in the four hundred acre pecan orchard. My family uses the rest of the pecans or they are sold on the market. Our pecans are sold locally and by scores of stores in the several states that surround North Carolina. My mother and grandmother bake pecan pies and cakes. When I was a child, my mother would fill a long pan with a layer of salted buttered pecans and roast them. When our family has family reunions or church reunions, homemade pecan ice cream is always served." Dan questions his mother:

"Mother, I now understand where you got all of those pecans every year that were delivered by UPS, cool! Mother, what else is grown on that plantation?"

"Son, there is more going on that plantation than I have time or the strength to tell. You will get a chance to fill your eyes and ears up when you get there. It takes years of living and working there to see all."

"How many acres do your family own?"

"I am not sure, David, but I believe that Daddy once said over one hundred thousand acres not counting the area occupied by the great fishing lake, the catfish pond, or the small farms people live on. I do know that that plantation is the most organized and productive place I believe that I have ever seen. Oh, I can't wait until you get to fish for catfish!" Dan speaks up:

"I love catfish! They serve them at restaurants now days." Brenda speaks to her family.

"Once in awhile, Daddy will get my three brothers and go catfish fishing at the huge pond. The catfish pond is about two miles from the lake." David is keen with interest and speaks to Brenda:

"Honey, how large is the catfish pond?"

"I understand that the pond is about eight hundred acres in size. The fish are fed tons of fishmeal that is prepared on the plantation a month. Fish have been caught that are over seventy pounds. Daddy has people on the plantation who do nothing day and night, but to assure that no unauthorized people fish. My grandfather always sold catfish on the market, but Daddy has expanded and sells fish as far away as New York City. Who knows, we might have eaten some of those fish when we ordered catfish at fine restaurants in Boston. I know that the fish markets want fish that are ten or fifteen pounds at most. Sometimes folks order an extra large catfish if they are having a large get together." David speaks:

"Brenda, I can't wait to go fishing with your father and brothers!" Dan in the back expresses the same desire. Dan is compelled to question his mother:

"Mother, you didn't finish telling us about Mattie!" Brenda looks over to her husband with an amused smile on her face.

"I didn't, well excuse me. Remember that Mattie moved into her suite before I was born. I understand that Daddy told my mother about Mattie and expressed his concern for her. Mother at first did not go along with Daddy's wish to put her in the old servants' suite. Mother said that Mattie would be an extra burden that she didn't need.

"One morning during breakfast, Mattie showed up at the house. Mama had prepared a big breakfast and everyone was hungry. There was a lot of work to be done in the garden. Peas, butter beans, tomatoes, and all kinds of vegetables needed to be harvested. Your great Aunt Dorothy and four cousins were going to help Mama with the harvest for several days. While everyone was in the kitchen eating, they all heard someone just outside one of the doors that goes into the kitchen. Daddy got up to see who was making the fuss and opened one of the doors and walked out onto the porch.

"Mattie had been beaten up and she was weeping. Her clothes were torn and Mama told me that Mattie was a sight to be seen. Daddy asked Mama to step out onto the porch and she was asked to close the door so that others would not stare at Mattie. Mama was shocked and angered when Mattie revealed to my parents that she had been badly beaten by her crazy drunk father. Mama got Mattie to wash up and she got Mattie a nice pair of work pants and a shirt. Mama insisted that the law be called. I believe that old Sheriff Ralph Croom showed up with a deputy. Mama told him about the incident and insisted that Mattie's sorry father be arrested for assault and battery. The sheriff told her that it would do no good that his people could only hold him for no more than a few months. He would be soon out and back to his sorry ways again.

"I understand that this is when Mama agreed that Mattie would live on the plantation. The sheriff warned both of my parents that they were taking on a responsibility that could backfire. As we all know now, the old sheriff was wrong and my parents and later us children have been blessed so much with Mattie around! It is true that she is very slow when it comes to book learning, but she has made up for this shortage. Mattie has been in her suite every since then. Mama tells me that she does not know how they made it before Mattie arrived. Mattie helps Mama cook and wash the dishes. She helps with keeping wood in the fireplaces during the cold weather. Mattie helps keep the yard around the house and has picked and shelled more beans and peas than anyone Mama knows. My parents have purchased both life and health insurance for Mattie. When she dies, which I hope is a long time away, she will be buried in our family's cemetery."

"Honey, are you sure that Mattie is not just a glorified slave on that plantation?" Brenda looks at her husband with a little disappointment and speaks:

"No, David, Mattie is not a glorified slave. It is true that she works hard. We all do on the plantation. Mattie has never complained. She works with more enthusiasm than anyone I have ever known! She has a nice place to stay in. She has her own big screen plasma television and her own fancy stereo system that is loaded with features and functions. I guarantee you that her suite is as nice as a five star hotel suite. Mattie keeps it spotless. She does not work all of the time on the plantation. She is allowed to help local farmers in their tobacco and their blueberry fields. These are folks that my parents have known or done business with all their lives practically. Mama does not allow Mattie to work with just anyone. The farmers pay Mattie just like they pay all of their help. Mama puts a lot of the money Mattie makes into a savings account setup for her. When Mattie wants to buy something, which is not too often, Mama allows her to spend her money as she pleases." Betty the Smith's eight-year old daughter questions her mother.

"Mother, what sort of things does Mattie purchase?"

"Well, I know that she purchased that new sixty-four inch television last year for herself. Mama called me and told me about the purchase. I know that Mama carries Mattie shopping with her when she goes to Burgaw. When I was a kid, I would also go with Mama. Mattie would usually buy chewing gum, a little candy, and drinks. Oh, she also buys peach flavored snuff. Mama complains about Mattie's habit of using tobacco, but has learned to live with it. Mama just shakes her head and says:

"No one is perfect. Everyone has at least one weakness. If it keeps her happy, it is well worth it!" Dan's curiosity has now been stimulated.

"Mother, what is snuff?"

"Honey, snuff is grounded up tobacco. The manufacturers add different flavors to the powder."

"Have you ever tried snuff?" David, Brenda's husband, looks at his wife with a silly smile that borders on being a little sarcastic and speaks.

"Yea, Honey, have you ever dipped snuff?" Brenda looks at her teasing husband with a half smile while she rolls her eyes a little that speak as clear as good English without finding it necessary to vocalize her thoughts to David. Those words spoken would say:

"Please, I don't need two kids asking questions at the same time, especially you, dear!" The two adults could hear suppressed giggles by the two children at the question their father asked their mother.

"OK, I will admit that I tried the peach flavored tobacco once; all of us kids did. I tried it and became sick at the stomach for about twenty minutes. Mama saw it all over my mouth and realized that I was whiter than usual and what I had done. I had accidentally swallowed a mouth full of the snuff! Mama took advantage of the situation to teach me a lesson and told me that I deserved my temporary sick feeling. She made me wash my mouth out and gave me a cold Coca Cola to make my stomach better. I will assure you all that I learned my lesson! That stuff is not intended for most folks!" Brenda speaks with grave conviction resonating in her voice! Dan speaks to his mother:

"Mother, when we get to where we are going, and settle in, what are we going to do for fun?"

"Dan, the trip we are now on should be fun enough. The excitement of moving into a new neighborhood and getting to be with your grandparents should satisfy you." Eight year old Betty speaks:

"I will miss Grandfather and Grandmother Smith! When are we going to see them again?"

"Your grandparents have promised to visit us twice a year. They will probably wait until we find a permanent place to live. I am sure that we will also visit them three times a year. Your father will still do work at his old job." David speaks to his son:

"Yes, son, we will visit my parents two or three times a year in addition to our regular visits. I am going to be working on forming a working relationship between UNCW and the University of Boston. Oceanography students and faculty from both institutions will be able to learn from each other and share their resources. People from the University of Boston will travel to UNCW and will take classes there for a semester. People from the University of Boston will do the same thing at UNCW." Dan speaks:

"Why are they going to do that, Father?"

"Well, son, no school can afford all of the things they would like to have. The University of Boston has a larger program with more money to work with than UNCW in large exploration submarines. UNCW, on the other hand, has an extra laboratory named the Sea Wise that can house over ten scientists underwater. The submarine I have in mind can dive much deeper and has much more equipment on board to help us explore and document the ocean off the coast of North Carolina. There are a lot of things that we would like to look at and check out. UNCW obtained a huge underwater living complex from a Japanese firm about fifteen years ago. When the hundred foot plus facility is delivered to the University of Boston from UNCW, the University of Boston will have it placed just off the waters of Massachusetts. Senior students and instructors will have the opportunity to live year round underwater. The unit is a hundred and twenty feet long. The University of Boston has permission from the State of Massachusetts to move the facility every time it is important to study at a different location." Betty questions her father:

"Father, how are they going to move that thing to the University of Boston?"

"You have seen barges?"

"Yes, you told me that those huge flat boats were barges."

"You know what a crane is, right?"

"I believe so."

"Let me explain. A crane is a big machine that lifts heavy things up high off the ground." Betty speaks:

"Like the one that was downtown Boston when we drove by?"

"Yes, dear, very similar to that one. A large ocean going barge will have a crane on it. The barge will carry the living complex we have been talking about to the location the University of Boston's science department wants it to be. The Sea Wise will be picked up by the large crane and lowered to the ocean bottom the moment the engineers give the OK. Now I know that you probably don't know what an engineer is, that is all right, one day you will." Betty continues to ask away:

"Father, have you ever lived in that underwater complex?"

"Yes, Honey. Don't you remember the trip I took to North Carolina about two years ago?"

"I think so."

"Well, it does not matter. I was invited by the chairman of the department of science to live in the complex with fellow scientist and students for about three weeks." Betty once again questions her father:

"What did you do?"

"I did a lot of looking at fish and other sea creatures. The underwater complex was a few hundred feet from a reef. We got to study the sharks that live there. We saw an occasional stingray."

"Father, can we visit the Sea Wise when it is moved to Massachusetts?"

"No, son, only students in oceanography and related fields from universities and colleges can do that. If you decide to go into oceanography when you are in college, I am sure you will get a chance to visit the Sea Wise or another facility like it." Brenda who had been listening questions her husband:

"Honey, where did they purchase the Sea Wise from?"

"From Japan, dear. The unit did not come from the government, but a large private company that owns underwater oyster farms. They also harvest pearls. Some of the underwater fields leased to them by the Japanese Government are a thousand acres or more."

"Why would they need something like the Sea Wise?"

"There are a lot of reasons. The company houses hundreds of workers in such underwater farms. One complex may house security. They are, of course, there to protect the property. These people get into small, but armed submarines and patrol each farm. Some of the complexes house underwater engineers and farmers. The engineers maintain huge soundtronic holding pens for giant tuna and other fish. Oysters are seeded for pearls and huge racks are designed to hold individual oysters so that they will reach their maximum size and to make it easy for them to be harvested when full size. The oysters are actually vibrated from the gripers that hold them when they reach maximum size. Computers control this part of the process. The oysters actually fall down into stainless steel holding baskets where they are collected for market. For fish farming, new high tech holding pens have been designed that have no walls. These facilities are many square miles in size. The fish are not held inside of four walls or huge nets like traditional holding pens, but are kept in certain areas of the ocean where they can be fed and harvested with ease. Now before you ask, I will try to explain this new technology. I know that you know about invisible fences to keep our pets in our yards so that we will not have to put up traditional fences constructed of wood or metal. Engineers now maintain sound barriers to keep fish in certain areas of the ocean. Fish will not venture outside of these invisible barriers because the sound will stun them. Fish like most creatures have the good sense to not challenge these unseen barriers. I have been told that hogs and cows will not usually challenge electrical fences because they sense the electrical current several yards before they actually touch the hot fence." Brenda speaks:

"David, I have never heard of sound barriers to keep fish corralled like cattle. I am aware of huge nets and ponds on land to raise fish. I have read about these facilities and have seen programs on television designed to entice people to turn some of their farmland into fishponds so that fish can be commercially harvested. I understand that already nearly half of all our fish come from fish farms because the oceans have been over fished." David speaks:

"It is true that the fish in our oceans have been overfished. It is also true that a lot of countries do not have the land to convert into fishponds. Japan is now using giant sound devices to section off huge areas around their coastline for the so called holding pens. Huge machines that create bubbles of air are also used in conjunction with the sound waves. The bubble makers suck in millions of cubic feet of air a minute from the surface to create bubble barriers. The sound machines are in the same alignment so that the sound will resonate off the trillions of bubbles that are continually forming a type of barrier around the fish. Some of these areas are many square miles in diameter. All of this machinery can be moved to different locations. For example, the scientist and fish farmers know when huge schools of certain species of fish are on the move. The sound and bubble fences are positioned in areas of the ocean the fish will pass through. When the fish swim through a particular location, they find a wall of bubbles and sound in front of them. When the fish attempt to escape and go another way, other devices that produce bubbles and sound are dropped in place, thus surrounding the fish. Scientists are learning that this is a better way than the traditional holding nets because the fish are allowed to move on once a certain percentage of the fish are harvested. The rest are allowed to continue on their migration so that the fish population will be healthy and will be able to maintain their natural habitats. Fish enclosed in large nets or in ponds are not as healthy nor do they taste as good as fish that are allowed to live life nature intends them to live. Large companies are giving the opportunity to harvest from and maintain these sites. I was instrumental in designing these sound devices." Brenda speaks:

"David, you have not said a word about your work in this area!" David speaks:

"That is true, Brenda, but I work on so many projects that I would not have time to explain or talk about everything I am doing. I, as you know, work with my computers all of the time. I design and experiment on dozens of things all of the time. Most of my work is not public knowledge because I don't want to be troubled by a hundred phone calls a week from companies from all over the world wanting to know what I can do for them. I usually offer my inventions to governments that will share this knowledge to companies that will use them for the greater good of all mankind. These governments buy my patens from me." Brenda speaks:

"David, I assume that most of your inventions are computer software programs that you come up with." David speaks:

"This is true. I usually do not have access to a laboratory or a factory where I can physically make new devices or machines. I design things and provide the so called blueprints for others to assemble together my inventions." Brenda speaks:

"David, I did not realize that such complicated facilities exist. What you have described reminds me of an old movie I watched when I was a child called *Ten Thousand Leagues under the Sea.*"

"I understand what you are saying, Brenda. The big difference, of course, is that the movie entitled, *Ten Thousand Leagues under the Sea*, was taken from a novel written by a famous science fiction writer named Julies Vern. The huge underwater farms I refer to are very real and represent advanced technology Mr. Julies Vern could only dream about."

"Look, look, the sign says that Atkinson is only six miles from here!" Betty, the Smith's daughter, wakes up from her sleep when she hears her brother's excited voice. Betty questions her Mother:

"Mother, how long will it be before we see Grandfather and Grandmother Pridgen?"

"Honey, we are only about fifteen or twenty minutes from the plantation. The plantation starts about three and a half miles outside of Atkinson and follows Black River nearly to Harrell's. The land goes from Highway 210 West to a few miles outside of Maple hill on the other side of the North East Cape Fear River. It is a nice piece of land." David turns his head toward his wife who is driving and questions her.

"Honey, are there any secondary roads crossing all that land?"

"Yes, but originally these roads were little more than trails carved out by people going from one part of the county to the other. Time went by and the small paths were widened to accommodate more traffic. Eventually the state suggested very strongly that my father's fourth-great grandfather keep the roads up for a fee paid to him by the state. He went along with this so called proposal, but later decided that it was not worth it. When the state agreed to take care of the roads, they demanded more road way and sent in surveyors to map out the right of ways. Eventually the state simply took the property. No one really cared because roads are necessary for everyone's benefit."

Our story temporarily leaves the Smith family as they continue to travel down highway 53 bound for the small town of Atkinson. Brenda will drive the car down the main street of Atkinson to show off the place to her family and turn around and make a right turn onto Beatty's Bridge Road, which will eventually cross Beatty's Bridge across Black River.

We now turn our attention to the hallowed halls of the science department at the University of North Carolina at Wilmington, one of the South's most prestigious Universities with over seventy majors. The year is 2030 and the school has acquired thousands of more students that it could not boast about in the early years of the Twenty First Century. The school has aged gracefully both in the ornate Southern style buildings and gardens that delight the eyes and hearts of many a Southern born and bred lady or gentleman. UNCW is a school that is now recognized all over the nation for its academic weight and athletic achievements.

Back in 1947, when UNCW first opened its doors, it was only a small business college called Wilmington College located in a large town name Wilmington. Southern as the buildings and the landscape are, they no longer represent the heritage of most of the faculty or the student body. Most of the scholars who attend this once truly Southern School are now from the Northern regions of our fair country. Some of the older professors who were locally born and reared secretly hate the change, but they cannot deny that this northern wind has prospered the school in more ways than one. New buildings are going up all of the time. More money is available for equipment, faculty, and staff. Most Northern professors and staff are politically sensitive to the feelings they sense from some of the old Southern boys and girls who have taught in the same departments for many decades. Many were far beyond normal retirement age, but they needed something to live for. It must also be noted, to be honest about the situation, is that the chancellor is an old Southern Aristocrat whose proud Southern heritage goes back to Colonial days. Doctor Julia DeVann Corbett was no one to trifle with! Doctor Corbett had gilded the so called mountain climbing career of many a young professor or administrator born north of the Mason Dixon Line who displayed what she coined *Northern Academic Aggression* on her own turf.

In an adjacent hall near their offices four seasoned members of the science department are having a little get together. All of them appear to be around sixty years old. One of the scientists, who is a woman, starts the conversation just to see how her male counterpart, who has been teaching at UNCW for over twenty years, would react to her comment. This small herd of faculty looked around themselves careful lest a student or subordinate over hear their conversation. Little birds that hear the wrong things could cause even long termed faculty a lot of grief if whispered into the wrong ears!

Professor Joyce Brown acting as innocently as she could while holding her morning coffee in an impressive coffee mug with the words UNCW across its top in bold display looks up at Professor Sam Hardin and speaks:

"I understand that our illustrious department head has decided to pass you up on the promotion we thought you were getting." Doctor Hardin had expected to be promoted as the assistant to the department of science. He had worked long and hard for the opportunity to fill the seat vacated by the famous Professor Doctor Tommy Carr an old local boy who felt that he should retire and let another have his office. Doctor Carr had been at the school for over forty years, a record for almost any school. He had once been chairman of the department of science, but poor health had encouraged him to give up his once cherished chair to a younger and healthier man.

Doctor Hardin looked down at Doctor Joyce Brown from his six foot four inch frame with some irritation noted on his face. He could not hide his disappointment. Doctor Hardin, while speaking with his volume low, looked around for listening uninvited ears and spoke:

"That is right. I have worked here for a long time. I am confident that Doctor Fletcher will regret his decision! It just does not make sense to hire an outsider who is not even forty years old." Doctor Brown speaks again:

"No, you are wrong, I believe. I have the newspaper on my desk. It says that Doctor Smith is forty one." Doctor Hardin looks at Doctor Brown with a little flush noted on his face and speaks:

"Doctor Brown, I was teaching when he was in grammar school!" Doctor Brown replies:

"So was I and so were the rest of us Professor." Doctor Brown looks around at the other instructors who appear amused and indifferent to Doctor Hardin who was known more as a politician than as a professor. One of the male professors who did not particularly like Doctor Hardin, but stayed out of his way most of the time was compelled to speak:

"Well now my good fellow, don't feel too sorely about the results. Every politician is bound to lose an election once in awhile." Doctor Hardin looks at his colleague with some surprise and angry at his bold statement.

"What damn election are you talking about? How dare you!" Our good professor turns around rather quickly for a man of his girth and marches back to his office. Doctor Brown looks up at the man who made the smart comment to Hardin and speaks while shaking her head with a look on her face that bordered somewhere between a smile and a suppressed laugh. Doctor Brown speaks:

"I can't believe that you had the nerve to say that!" Doctor Jerry Skinner smiled as proudly as a kid who had just gotten away with pulling a nasty little prank on a less than loved high school teacher.

"I know; I just could not help it. I could see it coming." One of the other instructors quickly spoke and then left for his first class that morning.

"Yes, my fellow instructors, I also read the newspaper article about Doctor David Smith. He was a child prodigy. He finished both doctorates by the time he was twenty three. I understand that he has already rightly predicted several hundred earthquakes and is responsible for saving over a million people's lives in a large Indian city by convincing the Government of India and the mayor of Sopara to evacuate the city. I understand that this is only the tip of the iceberg of the accomplishments and discoveries and inventions this young man has credited to his name! I just hope that the rest of us will not be completely forgotten about!" Doctor Joyce Brown speaks just before they all depart to a classroom or an office:

"No, I don't expect trouble. I have an old classmate who used to work for Doctor Smith. I understand from her that David Smith is really a very nice young man who likes to share his knowledge with his colleagues. She also tells me that he is too smart to be for real, but otherwise, a nice young man." While our professors split up, one man walks toward his office with his assistant who was one of our original four in the hallway.

"I hope that guy will be as nice as Doctor Brown's friend says. We sure as hell don't need a super Hardin around here! I don't believe that I could take it." The other man nods his head in firm affirmation.

We now once again join the Smith family as they enter the big city of Atkinson, NC, population three hundred and sixty-five people. The kids are all excited and David asks his wife where the town was as a form of light humor.

"Honey, I saw the sign back there that reads, 'Welcome to Atkinson: Speed limit thirty-five MPH,' "but where is the town?"

"Funny, you are really a barrel of monkeys today, I see! I will have you know that this is a very proud community. Their crime rate is almost zero." David still in a silly mode interrupts his wife.

"I guess so, it takes two to tangle! I understand why the crime rate is so low around here!" Brenda defends Atkinson:

"This is really a very nice little village. I have not lived here, but a lot of my best friends grew up here. I am sure that you will get to meet many of them as soon as word is out that I am living back on the plantation. I love Boston too, David." David realizes that he should not have teased so much.

"I am sorry, Honey. I really meant nothing by what I said. I do appreciate the fact that you love Boston. We both have a lot of good friends there that we will always remember!" Brenda continues to talk about Atkinson. She now addresses her children:

"Children, you will get to meet a lot of the kids your mother grew up with. Folks around here stay near home after they grow up. Many of them run or help run businesses their grandparents and now parents are associated with." David once again speaks to his wife:

"Brenda, don't take this the wrong way, remember that I am a big city boy. Exactly what businesses are you referring to here?"

"I am not talking about large factories or corporate headquarters for major firms. I am referring to well established small family owned and operated businesses. Look to your left, there is a small branch bank. Farmers all over this part of the county deposit their money there. I know several farmers worth five or ten million dollars. Look to your right, there is Woodcock's full service station." David speaks:

"Yes, he does have four ports in the building and six gas pumps. Not bad, dear!" Brenda continues:

"That is true. Mr. Woodcock and family have a good name all over this part of Pender County. His son Ronnie used to play with us kids on the plantation. Look on your left; I am sure all of you noticed that there is a fish market. The owner has his own boat on the sound near Wrightsville Beach. The next business beside the fish market is a nice restaurant." Dan who has been listening to his mother speaks:

"Mother, can we go to the restaurant?"

"As far as I know we can visit that restaurant, son." Dan once again questions his mother:

"Mother, what kind of restaurant is it?"

"They serve country food there. I know that catfish is served there. They batter it and fry it. Sometimes they serve catfish stew." Dan and his sister both say the same thing.

"Mother, we have never tried catfish stew before, is it good?"

"Well, I think so. Of course, I grew up around here. Frog legs, crab, shrimp, and fried oysters are also served. When in season, they will serve specials like, Shad, Herring or Spots there." David speaks:

"I am aware of Shad. I know that they swim up rivers in the spring to spawn. They are caught in the months of March or April. I have never tried Shad as a meal. I look forward to a Shad on my plate!" While talking to his wife, David notices a sign on the front of a country hardware store.

"Pridgen's Hardware"

"Honey, do your parents own that store?"

"Yes, my parents own it." David looks at his wife with a look of surprise.

"I was under the impression that your family devoted all of its energy to that plantation it lives on!"

"David, that is a general hardware store. My father sells animal food there too. Daddy is thinking about opening up about three or four stores in the Wilmington area. The plantation can supply all of the animal feed, lumber, and all kinds of products. You will learn about Daddy's plans, I am sure. Various people make furniture such as swings, gliders, outdoor furniture, picnic tables, handles for axes, hatchets, hammers and other tools. Daddy says that he has received offers from all over to sell his high quality furniture, but he had rather open up his own stores and sell direct to the public."

"Your father is an amazing man! I did not realize he was such an entrepreneur!"

"Well, David, just take a look at the plantation. It is one big business from morning to night." When the Smiths drive into the road that leads into the plantation, there is a large fenced in area with an outdoor stadium. Here the public is invited. The Pridgens offer the facility for singing groups, preaching, and horse shows." David questions his wife about the outdoor market in Atkinson.

"Brenda, where is the outdoor market?"

"It is off of East Henry Street where the old public school is located. Do you want to see it?" David speaks:

"Why, not? Let's turn around and go back to Atkinson!" The kids in the back are all eyes beholding the old school building. Dan speaks to his mother:

"Mother, did you go to school there?"

"No, dear, this place was closed almost sixty years ago. I believe that your great grandfather attended school here. The old school has served as a flea market for many decades. I see that the farmers market is held outside in the field that surrounds the old school. I believe that those tables that go from one end of the field to the other are where the farmers display their produce." David speaks:

"I see that the owner of this place had the good sense to have provided covers for the tables! Do your parents come here, Brenda?"

"I believe, that Mama told me that she sells butter and other farm produce here."

"I can't believe that your mother needs the money!"

"No, I would imagine that she does a lot of socializing here. She probably gets to talk to a lot of her old friends. Mama tells me that the market has been good for the community. Folks around here are usually so busy that they can't socialize like in the big cities. Now everyone can talk and make money at the same time."

"Does your father sell his furniture here?"

"No, I don't think so, he might. I would imagine that he prefers to sell furniture at the general hardware store he owns. I feel that we have seen enough of Atkinson for now. I will now turn around and drive back toward the plantation. The children in the back are so excited that their parents have to ask them to hold it down. Brenda makes a left turn onto Beatty's Bridge Road and some miles later drives over the Black River bridge called Beatty's Bridge. While they are crossing the river, they all notice several small fishing boats in the river. Up farther on their left and extending along the bank for about three hundred feet is a boat pier. Tied to the pier are about seven small yachts. On the bank they see a large blue building that is surrounded by a parking lot. Still further down on the same bank are boat ramps. A large boat crane is being used to pick up a fifty foot boat and is about to place it on the back of a large trailer. Huge letters are written on the side of the blue building that say, "Croom's Marina." The large sign facing the road also says the same thing with added information. The sign reports that boats can be stored, sandblasted, and painted, motors serviced, and repaired. Brenda speaks to David:

"Honey, that place has been here for about ten years." David replies:

"I would imagine people take advantage of this place. I realize that everyone can't afford a house on Black River with a private boat ramp. This facility houses your boat in the winter months and launches it upon request by the owner."

"Yes, I saw the sign. I understand that my grandfather is not thrilled about this place."

"Why, what is wrong with this place?"

"He says that it will open up the river to every Yankee in the country." David looks at his wife like he is a little annoyed and speaks.

"Well, excuse me for being a Yankee!"

"David, let's look at things from his prospective for awhile. Grandfather has seen the damage done to the environment down here by the huge influx of people from up North. For centuries the people down here were mostly isolated from big city ways and life. Things have been basically the same since people first settled here from such places as Ireland, Scotland, Wales, and England. Grandfather says that you did not see trash on the river floating. The fish were abundant and all manner of wildlife. Now older folks born in this part of the country are fearful that they will not only lose the rivers and the once abundant forest, but their sense of identity and way of life.

"These people are very proud and have noted that the people up North have destroyed the land their ancestors had. Now the ancient forest has been cut down. Huge buildings and factories are everywhere. There are so many foreigners from other countries coming in that in a hundred years people will be speaking English as a second language. Grandfather and his generation feel that everything truly worth having is being destroyed by this cultural invasion. I am sure that this is the reason my people and many of the families around here have worked so hard to protect their identity. I also believe that this is the reason why most of the young people around here remain here. They feel that there is something special about their little part of paradise. My parents could sell their land off in lots. I am sure they would sell like hot cakes. They would make hundreds of millions of dollars. Offers have been made and there have even been attempts by large real estate companies to force our family to sell off part of their property.

"I have heard several people say that if the Pridgen Plantation gives in to the demands of land hungry vultures, the entire territory will be up for the taking. Daddy tells me that you can't push an old bear, but so far before he turns around and uses his natural abilities to defend his territory." David sits amazed not fully realizing how strong his wife stood on her Southern Roots.

"Honey, I guess the American Indians felt the same way your folks and neighbors feel. Look at what happened to them. They helped the early white settlers make it. If they had not taught them survival skills they would have never made it. Yet, the great grandchildren of many of these people and other people from Europe and England took land from the Indians." Brenda is so emotional that she cannot help the tears that are dropping from her eyes.

"Yes, David, the white man raped the land and destroyed the lives of millions of native people. Now that same spirit is trying to take away our culture. When my people settled here, the Indians were still here," David looks at Brenda and smiles.

"Like they say, you can take an old country girl to the big city, but you can't take the country out of the girl."

"That is right, Honey! I will always carry a part of my country up bringing with me wherever I might have to live. I am not like Grandfather. He is all country. He has no desire to go up North and experience big city life. It would be too big a cultural shock. I on the other hand have learned to live in both worlds. I have learned to accept what I can't change and have learned to appreciate other ways of thinking and doing things. I realize that things will not be like they are right now in my neck of the woods in a hundred years or so from now. Our plantation may only be part of the history people will read about. Slowly, but surely things will change. Not necessarily for the best, but people will do what they have to do to survive and create their own identity. In the mean while, I believe that we are about to enter the plantation road." David noted that there was no grand entrance road leading to the estate. There was a small three by four foot hand written sign with letters that appeared to have been created by a blowtorch and black paint that says, "Pridgen Property, No trespassing." David speaks:

"I can't believe that there is not a huge boulevard with enormous oak trees on each side leading to the house!"

"My family does not want to advertise its plantation to the world. My grandfather came close to shooting some foreigners from some Middle Eastern country who did not understand the English word (NO)." David frowns a little and speaks:

"I don't understand, dear!"

"The men wanted to buy the plantation."

"You are joking. Why would some foreigners from the Middle EAST want to buy the property?"

"They felt that it would make a good investment."

"How did they learn about the plantation?"

"I understand that someone put information about the plantation in a trade journal magazine. I believe it was intended as a joke, but grandfather was not happy about the affair!"

"Did he ever learn who put the information in that magazine?"

"He couldn't prove it, but he felt that he knew who did it. He approached old man Jimmy Jones about it. He denied knowing anything about it."

"So you say he had to get out his old shotgun? Unbelievable, sounds like something I would see in the movies or read in an old novel!"

"Yes, Daddy said that between the shotgun and the yard dogs the thick headed men eventually got into their limousine and drove off."

"How many years ago did this all take place?"

"It happened when Daddy was about twelve years old. He told me that he realized they had company and saw the huge car and the four or five strange looking gentlemen. He became alarmed when he realized that his father was holding a double barrel shotgun. The three yard dogs were growling with their fur bristled back and their huge teeth showing ready to spring into action the moment Grandfather gave them the attack signal. Daddy says that his father is a patience man, but those guys didn't want to take no for an answer."

"I guess or hope that was the end of that!"

"Actually, believe it or not, it wasn't. About a year later the foreigners tried to once again buy the property. Grandfather received an official letter from a law firm from New York City. The firm represented the gentlemen. The letter expressed concern that there was such a big misunderstanding. The offer was once again voiced by the foreigners through their attorneys."

"What did your grandfather do then?"

"I am sure that he fussed about the letter for days. I was told that he called up an old school buddy who was a prominent lawyer and asked him to write the New York lawyer firm for him. I understand that Grand-father's friend was able to make it abundantly clear that Pridgen property was not for sale."

"Mother, what is that big thing?"

"You have been to ball games, son. It is not as big as Yankee Stadium, but it serves its purpose. My father built it with the help of a lot of plantation help. My family invites Country and Western singers to perform there. Sometimes Gospel Singers are called in to perform. Daddy also lets local preachers hold area revivals there. My parents charge a small fee to use the facility. The money is used to upkeep the place and to help pay the performing artist. We will get to attend some of the events that will take place there. Once in awhile, a political candidate will make speeches there. When I was about sixteen years old, a man running for governor used the stadium. Mama told me that about three thousand people were in attendance. I would suspect that was the largest crowd in history to get together in this neck of the woods."

Two

Plantation Life

The Smiths drove for about a mile into the woods. David and his children had never seen so many trees before. This was truly a new world for them. Everywhere huge oak, sweet gum, dogwood, popular, maple, ash, hickory, and pine trees dominated the road next to the river. In fact, the trees are so thick that they could see only glimpses of the river on their right. The dirt road is as wide as a two lane paved highway. Occasionally the Smiths would cross a heavy wooden bridge. These bridges were built to cross several creeks that flow to the river. One bridge they had to cross was lined on both sides with black boys in their early or mid teens. They all had straw hats on or caps on their heads. Brenda slowed the SUV down and lowered the window on her side. She recognized one youth and asked him if he was catching anything. He told her that he had caught a few perch, a large black fish, and an old shoe. While he conversed with Brenda, the young man recognized who she was and his expression was filled with excitement and pleasure.

"Miss Brenda, I can't believe that it is you! Are you really going to stay here for real?"

"I will be staying for eight or nine months, John Henry, until my family can find a house to live in."

"You can move to the plantation house. I know there are lots of empty bedrooms. I went upstairs there a few weeks ago helping your mother."

"Like I said, we will be moving in for eight or nine months. My husband is not a farmer, or logger. He will be working at the university in Wilmington. He wants to live near his job."

"I can understand that, Miss Brenda. When I grow up, I don't believe that I want to live with my parents. I love them, but they would not let me be me."

"I understand you perfectly, John Henry." The other kids were standing back and side of Henry with the look of curiosity all over their young faces. Brenda recognized another young fellow.

"George Hawes, is that you, son?"

"Yes, ma'am, Miss Brenda."

"I can't believe how much you have grown! It is a miracle! The last time I saw you, you could not have been much over five feet tall. How tall are you now?"

"I am six foot two, Miss Brenda." Brenda looks at her amused husband and introduces her family to the young people who were fishing on the bridge.

"I will see you fellows later. I need to drive to the house." The boys all wave goodbye and went back to their fishing.

"Mother, can I fish off that bridge?"

"I don't see a problem with that, son. You will need to get a cane pole, bait, and tackle. I am sure that your grandfather or someone can help you with that." From the backseat the children practically stand up at the sight of the huge ornate Southern Plantation house. The house is on a bluff facing Black River. Surrounding the twenty eight bedroom mega mansion is a tall white fence, a left over tradition that was once necessary in this part of the country over a hundred and thirty years ago. The law allowed back then what is called open range on farm animals. Animals roamed freely and people had to fence in their property.

The house represents three stories of grand Southern style planning. Huge brick chimneys were everywhere to accommodate the eighty eight room house. The double story porch wrapped around the complex in grand style. There are no huge white columns at the front of the mansion, only scores of large skillfully designed post holding up the twenty foot deep and eighteen foot high porches. Huge magnolia trees that average about three hundred years old surround the mansion. The first floor of the great house is over twelve feet above the surrounding yard. Huge brick steps that are decorated on each side by massive male African lions serve the four corners of the house.

Beautiful colonial style windows and doors that are over ten feet high serve to give the house the look of a Southern Queen. On the porches above on the ceilings hang scores of huge ceiling fans designed exclusively for this house. Wooden swings are seen in various places on the two porches. Each swing is large enough to accommodate eight people. Flowerpots enough to fill a large florist shop hang from the two porches.

"Mother, it is huge! Do our grandparents really live in that house?" Betty could not believe the size and grandeur of the house.

"The last time I talked to your grandmother she indicated that they still lived here, honey." David is also overwhelmed by the rich splendor of one of the largest and finest homes of the South.

"Oh; my word, what a grand house your people live in! Brenda, your parents truly live in a beautiful house! I am truly impressed!" Brenda cannot help, but to chuckle a little, surprised at her husband's reaction the first few moments of looking at her old family home. Dan who is looking for all he is worth blurts out:

"Look, Father, horses! They are so beautiful!" What Dan was seeing were scores of large plow horses standing in a large white fenced in area next to the stable complex about half a mile away. Beyond the horse pasture and the stables twelve huge grain silos stand guard over the yard. Even farther back a creek runs into Black River. The swift current of the creek is arrested by a dam and a holding pond that feed thousands of gallons of water a minute to two huge water wheels that were constructed on either side of the millhouse. Brenda called her parents by her cell phone and let them know that they had arrived.

The moment Brenda steps out of her family's SUV, she is surrounded by the excited arms of her mother Lillian Pridgen. Dan and Betty dash out of the large vehicle into the awaiting arms of their grandfather, Beard Pridgen. Mr. Pridgen is a very rugged built man about six foot three with dark brown hair. His beard and mustache have started to turn a little gray. Beard had the appearance of a lumberjack in his long sleeved shirt that had pictures of wolves and log cabins all over it. Mrs. Pridgen was still a very beautiful Southern lady in her late fifties with black hair that was complemented with a little natural curl in it. She was a descendant of good Scotch Irish stock. Mrs. Pridgen wore a beautiful cameo around her neck that her great grandmother passed down to her daughter, Lillian's mother. Around her dress was a very fancy apron tied around her waist to protect her dress from last minute work performed in the kitchen. David patiently watched his children with his father-in-law. He was thankful that his in-laws had made an effort to visit the grandchildren often enough that the love cords were strong and healthy. After about ten minutes, Beard turns his attention to his son-in-law while the grandchildren ran around the SUV to their grandmother who showed them love and affection that only a good Godly grandmother could.

"Well, David, how have you been, son?"

"I have been doing good; thank you, sir!" It was a long trip, but I am sure Brenda told you that we spent the night in Rocky Mount."

"Yes, Lillian kept me informed." While David and his father-in-law spoke, Beard held out his huge right hand for David to shake. David was not comfortable placing his hand into Beard's bear like hand. He realized that his father-in-law was a man of steel. Beard on the other hand enjoyed humbling other men with his handgrip, but Lillian knowing her husband's nature had already warned her husband to not crush her son-in-law's hand. Standing thirty feet away from David and his family, a nervous excited black woman with a straw hat on her head, work pants, and a bright colored shirt stood watching. Lillian smiles and turns toward Mattie:

"Mattie, come on now, don't be shy! Folks, this is Mattie; she has been living here for a long time. I don't know what we would do without her!" Dan and Betty surprise Mattie by going up to her and insisting that they give her a big hug each. David walks up to Mattie and extends his right hand to Mattie for a handshake.

"Mattie, Brenda has told me a lot about you. My name is David." Mattie was a bit too nervous and not used to formal greetings, but managed to hold out her hand so that she could shake David's hand. Mattie immediately started helping the Smiths with their luggage and baggage, which was considerable. After six trips back and forth from SUV to porch, the personal belongings of the Smiths were placed on the porch.

Mattie seemed a bit impatient wanting to immediately carry the last of the luggage inside the mansion. Brenda's mother realized that Mattie is over excited and not focused.

"Mattie, now do you remember where this luggage is supposed to go?" Mattie redeems herself by controlling her excitement a bit.

"Yes, the first three bedrooms on the right upstairs on the second floor." David realized that Mattie is trying to carry too much at a time.

"No, Mattie, I can help too! Let me take the large suite case." In the main while, Brenda and Lillian grab what they can carry and go up the grand staircase to the first three rooms on the right. David looks around as he walks up the huge staircase. He cannot believe the beauty and size of the place. He sees scores of rooms and many hallways filled with beautiful furniture that would be worthy of a palace. He looks up at the ceiling and estimates them to be about twenty three feet high. The ceiling itself was not a disappointment and was expected in a great house. Molded plaster had been cunningly designed into patterns to please the eyes of even the critical. Large circular patterns surrounded smaller circles that are decorated with what looks like carved pinecones. Around each pinecone are dozens of little flowers.

In the middle of each pattern is a circle that is decorated with leaf design. The entire ceiling with its many sculptured circles within circles reminded David of beautifully decorated wedding cakes he had seen in fancy Boston shops. Huge chandeliers hung from the ceiling of every major room he could see as he continued to walk upstairs. On the right of the stairway are huge mahogany panels rich with carvings. The first panel is a beautiful depiction of homemade bread loafs of various shapes, natural colors, and grains. The next panel is beautiful masterfully carved fruit baskets to please the eye. The fruit appeared real. David felt that the artist used no paint, or artificial color. He later learned that the artist used woods from all over the world to create the colors and textures required to represent each kind of fruit.

David continued to admire the mansion as he quickly climbed the stairs. Beautiful molding decorated the ceiling. He estimated that the strips are about a foot wide. In each corner at ceiling level he was delighted to notice carvings that he was sure represented Magnolia flowers. When everyone had climbed the staircase with luggage in hand, David and the children walked across the eighteen foot wide hall to admire a huge vanity cabinet standing against the wall at the head of the stairs. Inside the massive cabinet a display of almost unrivaled antique crystal glass adored the vanity.

"Oh, my, where did all of this beautiful crystal come from? It is worthy of a palace!" Mrs. Pridgen smiled and spoke:

"No, I didn't buy this stuff. This vanity with its content has been handed down over the years. Some of the crystal came from my side of the family, the Moores. The rest came from Beard's family. We also have a vanity cabinet in the main living room that is filled full of antiques from China. We have Ming Chinese porcelain made to serve kings and nobles with centuries ago. I understand it was shipped from China on a Clipper ship back about one hundred and sixty years ago. Beard's seventh great grandfather did not order the China created to be used by the Chinese Nobility. The china was a gift from the shipping company to make up for valuable merchandise that was lost by the sinking of the ship during a huge storm." David speaks:

"You mean to tell me that you have real Ming Dynasty porcelain that is probably worth millions of dollars?"

"I wouldn't doubt it, but who is selling? I plan to pass the china down to the next line of Pridgens just like it was handed down to us." Before David opened the bedroom door, he noticed an unusual looking lantern on the wall about fifteen feet on the other side of the hall. He turns to Mr. Pridgen with a questioning look on his face and speaks:

"So you use gas lanterns in this house. I didn't think anyone in the country used gas in their homes for lighting." Beard speaks:

"David, we use carbide gas in a few places." David speaks:

"I believe that I have heard of the stuff in chemistry class."

"One day I will carry you on a tour of the grounds around here. I will show you how we make the carbide for the lantern. The company that sold the last of these units went out of business in the nineteen thirties, but we keep them in repair." Dan, David's son, pushes opens the bedroom door and exclaims:

"Wow, this thing is heavy. Why is this door so heavy, Grandfather?"

"Well, Grandson, things were made a lot better two hundred and seventy five years ago when this house was built." David also feels the weight and thickness of the door.

"This is indeed a heavy door. It is probably three inches thick!" In the meanwhile little Betty is about to be shown her bedroom or at least she thinks the bedroom will be hers.

"What a huge bedroom! I will need a small ladder to get into my bed Mother!"

"No, Honey, I have a feeling that you will not be sleeping in here. I believe that this is your father and mother's bedroom." Brenda looks at her mother, Mrs. Pridgen.

"Yes, your mother is right, be patient and we will show you your bedroom in just a few minutes." The children's luggage and other personal items were separated from their parents' luggage. David looks into his bedroom and is amazed.

"This is truly a magnificent room. It must be twenty feet wide and over thirty feet long." Brenda speaks:

"Honey, on the other side of that door there is a large walk-in closet and a bathroom included in this suite." David comments:

"Surely the bathroom was not here when the house was first built?"

"No, David, in those days I am afraid that the bathroom was outside. However; this bathroom has been here about a hundred years." Brenda looks over to her mother with a little stress on her face.

"Mama, do you mind if we go ahead and show the children their rooms? They will calm down a little." Mrs. Pridgen scans the room with her eyes and realizes that her grandchildren are in overdrive intoxicated with excitement. Lillian Pridgen speaks:

"Betty, Dan, let's get your things and go to your bedrooms. Your Mother is a little tired." Betty is the first child to enter her bedroom.

The children are introduced to their bedrooms. When Betty enters her bedroom, she realizes that it is identical to her parents' bedroom except for the size of the furniture. Over on the wall is a huge painting by one of Beard's aunts of a large fishpond on a beautiful and stately Southern

Plantation. The theme of the painting is children fishing. About ten boys and girls are dressed in Nineteenth Century vintage clothing. The children are preparing to fish at the pond. All of the children have straw hats on. The girls have flowers woven into their hats to give them a feminine character. The boys' hats are not decorated with flowers. Some of the hats the boys wear have embossed fish on their front sides. One boy has a catfish embossed on the front of his straw cap. Another child has a pretty Cracker Jack knife attached to the front of his hat.

Everyone is dressed for hot weather. A large willow tree stands about twenty feet from the pond. Leaning against the tree are a half dozen extra cane fishing poles. Near the kids is a large bucket filled half full of rich black soil that is impregnated with hundreds of crawling red worms placed in the container the day before. Beside the bucket is a large lunch basket filled with ham sandwiches, potato salad, and cookies. A large brown apple cider jug filled with fresh homemade lemonade is tied to a rope and is being lowered into the pond by one boy to keep the precious content nice and cool. Sunlight is bouncing off of the surface of the pond making the picture look almost like a scene from a mythical land. Lilies with their beautiful white flowers adore the pond on the other side across from the children. On top of a broad Lilly leaf is a small green frog with its red tongue lashing out at a passing fly. Here and there large Dragonflies are on patrol ready to swoop down upon flies and other insects brave enough to cross their territory. Across the pond perched on a small branch of a pecan tree several blue birds show off their beauty. One girl has already caught a fish and has it dangling on her line. The picture is so inspirational to the kids that they beg their grandmother for the opportunity to go fishing one day.

In front of the bed is a large wooden chest with brass handles and screws. Lighthouses are painted all over the chest.

"Mother, what is that huge thing? It is so pretty!"

"Betty, your grandmother keeps homemade quilts in it. Make sure that you do not take the quilts out because they need to be kept clean for cold weather." Near one of the windows was another chest. It was obvious what it contained. Betty runs over to the large wooden box that was painted all over with dolls and toys and strains to get it opened. Her little blue eyes sparkled with pleasure and wonder as she sees the beautiful dolls and the huge foldaway dollhouse.

"Oh, Grandmother, they are so beautiful! Can I play with them?" Mrs. Pridgen looks at her daughter Brenda before answering Betty.

"Betty, you can play with them. Just be careful with them because they belong to your mother."

"Mother, I never realized that you played with dolls!" Mrs. Pridgen speaks again:

"Yes, your Mother was a little girl just like you are. Believe it or not, a long time ago, I was once a little girl. I even have old photos to prove it." Brenda speaks to her daughter:

"Honey, I don't mind you playing with the dolls. Just be careful with them. Do not take them out of the room. One day you might want to show them to your little girl if you have one."

In the main time, Mr. Beard and his son-in-law David are in Dan's room. Everything has been stepped down size wise for a young boy. Dan is impressed with the miniature King George's bed. A large wooden chest sits at the foot of this bed also filled with homemade quilts carefully folded inside. Over against the wall is a huge chest with trains painted all over it.

"Grandfather, what is in that huge box?"

"Open it up and find out!" Dan opens the box and discovers to his delight a train set.

"Can I play with it?" Beard answers his grandson:

"Son, you can play with it, but you will probably need to get your father to help you assemble it. That is a rather large project for a boy your age. Just be careful with it. Your Uncle John Wesley got that train set for Christmas when he was about fourteen years old."

"So this was Uncle John's room at one time?"

"Yes it was, and I would imagine he will make sure you take care of the train set. He will most likely marry one day and pass the train set down to his son if he has one."

"I understand, Grandfather, I will take real good care of it." Mrs. Pridgen tells everyone that dinner is ready. Dinner time for Southern folk means that it is twelve o'clock during the day or high noon. Everyone quickly washes up and goes into the kitchen for dinner. The main dining room is not used for many practical reasons. One reason is that it was designed for very large formal occasions. The dining area included in the kitchen is more practical. Overhead above the table, which can seat twelve people, are two small beaten brass chandelles. A massive cupboard stands against the wall. In it are scores of neatly stacked dishes. The drawers below contain the utensils. David notes the weight of the silverware, twice as heavy as modern utensils. They are not the fancies that David has seen, but they are made of pure silver. No doubt they are the handy-work of a silversmith several centuries before our story.

"Be careful with that pot, Mattie." Mrs. Pridgen cautions Mattie as she brings the last heavy pot to the table. After Mr. Pridgen says the grace, covers are taken off of the pots and pans to reveal a simple, but delicious meal. One large black pot is steaming with a beautiful Brunswick stew. The aroma fills the dining room. Inside everyone sees strips of pork, chicken, potatoes, corn, beans, carrots, onions, and tomato juice surrounding the meat. Dan could not help but ask to be served as soon as possible. One large plate was piled high with homemade biscuits while another was loaded down with slices of farm fresh cornbread. One medium size dish was filled with cabbage that was flavored with small pieces of pork and seasoning salt. Stir fry potatoes, golden brown fried okra, butter beans, and stewed squash surrounded the Brunswick stew in various containers. No good Southern table would be complete without a sweet potato pie and a pound cake that Great Grandmother Lilly had fixed for the occasion.

Over on the wall are two large boxed in pictures of farm life. Each was about a yard square. One picture, which is actually a hand carving, shows the inside of a well made chicken house. Rows of middle aged looking hens dressed like women with bonnets on their heads, aprons tied around their waist, and wire rimmed glasses are standing to attention. In front of the hens is a large commanding figure of an old red rooster. The rooster has a cane in one of its wings that he claps like he has human hands. He wears a single eyeglass in his right eye. Looking every bit a Southern Aristocrat, the old boy is giving the hens a pep talk before they go to the barnyard. The second shadow box shows the porch and steps of a rather modest country dwelling. On the porch is a young boy of about thirteen years old. On either side of the boy lay two hound dogs. The dogs give the boy their full attention waiting for the boy to get up and go with them on a country adventure. Most likely something important like chasing cats, finding and rescuing turtles on the highway, and throwing sticks into the creek for the dogs to retrieve. Brenda notices the shadow boxes and speaks:

"Mother, where did you get those lovely shadow boxes?"

"Oh, I got them at the flea market in Atkinson. I purchased them from old man Johnny Horrell. You know that he loves to make pretty things out of wood."

"Yes, Daddy here told me that he loved to make paddles out of oak for the school teachers and the principal." Mr. Beard chuckled listening to his wife and daughter go on.

"No, dear, Mr. Horrell's grandfather old man Johnny Horrell Senior made the paddles. That was before my day in school. I remember him, but Daddy here benefited from Mr. Horrell's handy work." Zeb Pridgen patriarch of the Pridgen clan who has not been introduced speaks up:

"Shucks, I believe that the only one that benefited was old man Horrell. He made a little extra cash making those things." Dan speaks up:

"Great Grandfather, did you ever get a paddling?"

"Of, course not, why your great grandfather was as nice as an angel!" It was all he could do to keep a straight face. Lilly Pridgen, Zeb's wife, speaks up:

"Zeb, you must be getting ready for the old folks home making a statement like that to your great grandson. I recall things a bit different. I remember you taking several hikes down to the principal's office for a tanning. Remember that you had to walk pass my room to get there!"

"How do you know I was going to the principal's office for a paddling? I could have been going to see the old man to say good morning to him!" Lilly started laughing out loud:

"Ha, ha, to tell him good morning did you. Ha ha, bless my soul, I could hear that educational board being applied to your backside loud and clear thank you!" Zeb realized it was no use lying and spoke.

"Well, at least I finished high school and I believe that I turned out to be an outstanding gentleman despite my occasional run-ins with the old man at school." Everyone started laughing amused that they would learn about something so long ago. Lillian speaks:

"I can say one thing about those paddles. We didn't have paddling when I was in school. Kids were not disciplined and many a boy or girl who could have been straightened out early in life ended up doing time in the pen." David her son-in-law speaks:

"You all know that I teach school. Now I don't advocate paddling college students, but I agree that teachers should have the right to paddle younger kids in certain situations." Brenda speaks:

"I agree with you, David. Of course, paddling has been out a long time ago, but I believe children should be aware that school officials could apply corporal punishment if it is necessary. I don't believe that it should happen often. Most likely one or two incidents with a paddle would steer a child in the right direction. Once a tree matures it is too late to straighten it out.

"Enough of this paddling business, now who wants some of my pound cake?" Mrs. Lilly, the great grandmother looks over to the Smiths. Brenda helps her grandmother cut the cake. She quickly gives vanilla ice cream to the kids along with the pound cake. An hour later dinner is over and David speaks:

"Mrs. Pridgen, you and your mother-in-law cooked a wonderful meal!"

"David, thank you so much! Mother here baked the pound cake."

"Yes, ma'am, I know. I will try some later if that is alright. I ate so much that I don't have room right now for desert." The kids beg permission to leave, but before they leave their mother wants to know where they are going.

"Where are you guys going? I don't need you two to get hurt or lost!" Dan speaks up:

"Mother, we want to go on the porch and swing."

"Sounds great, now don't go anywhere else except the porch unless someone is with you two." Dan and Betty get up quickly from the table and find a large swing to swing in on the huge porch. Zeb Pridgen, Brenda's grandfather, asks David to go on the porch with him. The rest of the adults remain in the dining area to talk and clean up. Mr. Zeb is an older gentleman about eighty five years old. He is about six feet tall and still has some brown streaks in his white hair, a left over from earlier years. He walks firm and still can grip impressively strong for a man of any age. He wears blue work pants and a rugged country styled brown shirt with two pockets. One pocket holds his reading glasses and the other pocket holds several Tamper Nugget cigars and a lighter. The men walk out onto the porch and sit down onto two porch couches made out of expensive wicker.

"Well, son, how do you like it so far in these here woods?"

"Mr. Zeb, I believe that *Paradise Found* could be written while describing your plantation! I am thankful there are still places like this in this country!"

"I am glad that you feel that away! I seldom travel far from this place. I am a simple man of the earth. I have spent most of my life turning the good earth with a plow to prepare it for a fall harvest. We are almost totally self sufficient around here. We grow all our food. There are not many things we need from the outside. Lilly and Lillian even make their own mayonnaise, ketchup, and mustard. We grow our own sugarcane here. I raise bees that supply us with more than enough honey. We sell that stuff by the barrels. Lilly and Lillian make most all the cloths we wear around here. Shucks, I don't even go to the store to buy belts or shoes. We have always made our own. One member of the families that have lived here for over two hundred years does that for us. His name is Jackson Corbett. He even captures snakes around the lake and the catfish pond. We have a blacksmith around here and his four sons who help him. We even have our own gristmill. A man name Preston runs that place." David speaks:

"Yes, I know about the gristmill. Brenda told us about it."

"Did Brenda tell you about the lake and the catfish pond?"

"Yes, sir, I would love to fish. I have fished all of my life, but not for catfish. Most of my fishing has been in the ocean or the sound.

"What kind of fish are up your way, David?"

"We catch such fish as the Atlantic halibut, cod, hake, haddock, and flounder." David looks up at the porch ceiling. Hanging down from the eighteen foot ceiling is a huge fan turning at medium speed.

"Mr. Zeb, where did you get these huge fans?"

"We made them on the plantation. We ordered the two horsepower motors in a machine shop magazine and the rest we were able to make here. The blades are made out of white oak wood. The blades are twelve feet long each. These fans will not go very fast, but there are twenty four of them on each porch."

"They sure make a nice breeze!" Mattie comes out on the porch smiling with a platter with some ice cream, pound cake, and a glass of tea for David. She just stands side of him without saying a word. Zeb tells David to take the cake and ice cream to keep the ladies happy.

"Thank you, Mattie. Mr. Zeb, I believe they are trying to fatten me up!"

"There is enough work around here to burn all of that cake off. I will assure you! David, I don't do much catfish fishing like I used to, but Beard and his boys will take you fishing. They also do a lot of frog gigging. Roy Henry, one of the black gentlemen who lives on the plantation manages the crawdad fishing. You would have to go with him to learn about that."

"Do you eat crawdads, Mr. Zeb?"

"Why sure, they are similar to freshwater shrimp. Of course, I am aware that you realize that. We have crawdad parties around here several times a year. Beard and I invite our friends and kinfolk over for the occasion."

"Where do you have it?"

"Oh, we go over to one of the barns. We set up tables and chairs. I get some of the fellows around here to help Roy cook them for us."

"Do you have to pay them?"

"No, that is Henry's job, but he and the boys that help him are rewarded with two hundred or more pounds of crawdads when we finish our meal."

"Sounds like a good bargain to me!" Mr. Zeb takes a cigar out of a pocket and places it into his mouth. He has a look of satisfaction on his face. He lights the cigar and a wonderful rich smell surrounds the area. He takes the cigar out of his mouth and offers David one.

"David, care for a smoke? They have a mild rich flavor. I never got into cigarettes, they burn my throat."

"What kind of cigar are you smoking?"

"They are Tamper Nugget Sweets. I am sure I smoke them because my grandfather smoked them around me when I was a lad. They are not very expensive, under fifty cents apiece, but a fine cigar!"

"I have never smoked, sir, in my life. You would not want to get a young man started on a habit now would you?" David smiles as he spoke:

"Oh, no, I would not want to start a habit for you that might lead to your moral downfall. I am sure you would be better off not tasting the apple if you know what I refer to."

"Oh, I believe I do, sir! I have gone to church all my life." Zeb comments:

"What religions practice are you in, David?"

"My family has been going to a certain Presbyterian church for nearly three hundred years."

"Well, I am a Baptist. I have also heard the old joke that Baptists are Presbyterian also; they just can't read as well."

"I don't know about that, sir! I am aware that the Baptists are not as formal in their worship services. Sir, I believe I will try one of your cigars before Brenda comes out here just for fun." Zeb speaks:

"That a boy; I love a little adventure myself! Just don't draw too much in at a time and you will be just fine. I really do not smoke that many, about one a day. The smoke from them does help keep the biting bugs off me most of the time." The shrill screams of delight by the children playing on the swing could be heard despite the fact they were on one side of the porch over one hundred and fifty feet from David and Mr. Zeb. David takes a deep breath and considers the symmetry of the beautiful landscape that could be seen from where he sat.

"Mr. Zeb, I have seldom seen a place so splendidly manicured! Someone must be spending a lot of time keeping up this huge yard." Zeb answers:

"Yes, it is a sight, I must admit. My ninth great grandfather was a man of refinement and rich taste. He was the Southern Planter who built the place. He was a man of considerable wealth and hired one of the best architects and landscaper in the world. His wife was from France. I understand that she was from a long line of wealthy nobles. I guess you might say that he married high on the hog. Many of the gardens and fancy enclosed areas were designed to match the way it was back in France. I have always left the grounds and flower gardens to Lilly to take care of.

Of course, Lillian has taken up most of that responsibility now. Lilly and I are getting along in age now."

"I assume that they have plenty of help."

"Oh, yes, they do indeed! A crew of about thirty young men who live on the plantation maintain this two hundred acres yard. None of the families here pay to stay here with greenbacks. We have always traded labor and goods produced here on the plantation. It has worked out well for all of us. No one has to worry about finding a job or a place to stay or something to eat."

"Excuse me, I am going to go check on the children for a few minutes before I come back here to continue our conversation." David checks on the children and is delighted to see his children having so much fun on the big swing. He is also pleased to see that there are seat belts on the swing to prevent people from falling out when the swing is swung high. Ten minutes later David sees Brenda and Great Grandmother Pridgen walking down the front steps. He realizes from their conversation that they are going to look at some new shrubs and flowers Brenda has not seen before. When David walks back to where Mr. Zeb is sitting, Zeb decides to take David on a little tour. Beard, David's father-in-law, needs to go to Atkinson to check on his hardware store. He realizes that his father is getting ready to show David something on the grounds so he does not offer David a chance to go with him.

"David, I will be leaving for Atkinson. I will be back in about three or four hours. I am sure that Pa here will keep you entertained while I am gone." Beard goes to the carport and gets into one of his pickup trucks and heads for Atkinson. David and Zeb walk down the twelve foot high steps that are adorned with huge male lions on each side and go to the south side of the mansion. After walking about three hundred feet from the house, David notices a large walled in area just ahead of them. A better description would be a thick four sided enclosure that has a huge black wrought iron gate at the front entrance. On top of the red brick wall are dozens of what appeared to be human babies with angel wings. The babies or little angels have watering spouts in their hands that are turned downward and toward the inside of the enclosure. In other words, it appears that the little angels are busy watering the herb garden, which David is about to visit.

On the outside complimenting the heavy brick walls are granite inserts embedded into the brick. The inserts or slabs of granite begin at the ground and are about seven feet high and about thirty- four feet long. Both of the longer sidewalls are decorated with these inserts. The inserts are skillfully carved to depict famous palaces, and public works in Paris, and other famous places in Eighteenth Century France. When they arrive at the huge ornate Iron Gate, Mr. Zeb Pridgen directs David to one of the sidewalls so that he can see the beautiful inserts.

"David, before we go into the herb garden, why don't you walk over here so I can show you something."

"Mr. Zeb, this is unbelievable! I feel like I am at the French National Museum in Paris! This is truly a work of art. How long has this place been here?"

"It was completed sometime after the house was built by my ninth great grandfather. His wife was from France. The garden is modeled after one that was in Paris, France, centuries ago. Back in those days, herbs were more valuable than they are today. Almost every family had a small herb garden to provide needed medical treatments for their ailments and to enhance the quality of their lives. Remember, that back in those days, most people could not just walk into a drug store or buy the many spices, teas, room deodorizers, and medicine like we can today. A lot of time was spent in these places. People would often work these gardens year around. Of course, back in those days there was plenty of help available in the Old South."

"Yes, sir, I believe I understand."

"David, let's go inside and we will learn about these places." One side of the gate was pushed open and our party walks inside.

"Mr. Zeb, what are the dimensions of this garden?"

"The garden is one hundred and eighty feet long and one hundred feet wide." David's eyes sparkle with delight as he enters the enclosure. Beautiful hanging baskets hung from ornate hangers that hung from the sides of the enclosure. A hundred and eighty feet away at the back of the garden David noticed a small brick building and a fancy green house that was about the size of a large living room in a large house. The entire floor of the garden was paved with multicolored granite slabs of different shapes and sizes. The granite was not a solid covering for the floor of the garden, but each tile was spaced two inches apart from each other to allow for drainage when it rained or when the place was watered by Mr. Zeb. The floor of the herb garden is truly beautiful with its many shapes and colors.

"David, the greenhouse is for seeding the herbs that come from seed. Cuttings best propagate some of the herbs. For example, the Lavender, Winter Savory, Sage, Rosemary and the Thyme. Of course, there are many others available."

"Mr. Zeb, I love how these paved boxed in areas are arranged. They are a delight to see!" What David was seeing on the floor of the garden were forty feet long by three feet wide rectangular shaped cement planters that are raised two feet off of the floor so that gardener would not have to get on his knees or strain his back to work the beds.

"David, I work the soil with a small tiller that only weights about fifteen pounds. It has a powerful motor that allows the tines to move very fast."

"What kind of soil do you use in these enclosures?"

"We make up our own compost for all gardening on the plantation. I make up Lilly and Lillian's compost also. They have their own greenhouse and vegetable garden. If you want to see a botanical wonder, go by their garden and greenhouse one day. We even have guided tours once in awhile on site. The state sends 4H students and aspiring botanist by here every year so that the young people can see how we do it."

"I am truly impressed. Most people are delighted just to keep their plants reasonably healthy."

"David, those large drums between the greenhouse and the drying building are for making the compost."

"Exactly how large is their greenhouse?"

"I believe it is about three hundred feet long and about a hundred and forty wide. There are some very unusual and rare plants growing around here. Some are experimental varieties of common plants. Other plants or flowers are simply grown in the greenhouse so that we can have them year round. When in season, most common plants are grown outside in the regular garden. Let's go to the compost bins a few minutes. We can go inside my little greenhouse or the drying shed as I call it. As you can see for yourself, there are twenty four compost drums or bins, twelve to a row. Each drum is twelve feet long and holds about half a ton of compost. Naturally they hold less weight when the waste is first put into them. Each bin is rotated once a day by an electrical motor. I can rotate one at a time or this switch will turn all of the drums at once. We have water sprayed into the compost to keep it moist and alive with good germs."

"I am very impressed! I am going to probably ask a stupid question, but how do you get the mix out once it is ready?"

"There is a flap on the back of each bin. We have a nice motorized cart that is positioned at the rear of a bin. The flap or door is raised and locked into place. We use rakes to pull the material into the cart. Look over there and you will see one of those rakes. As you can see, the rakes have extra long handles for reaching. The leavers on the sides of the bins tilt the bins about twenty two degrees. Your father-in-law came up with that idea. The bins being tilted require less effort too empty.

"Now you may think that we just mix up leaves and animal waste and that is that, but we have a lot of different kinds of vegetables, flowers, and herbs around here. They all do not use the same kind of compost. Some require more acid as an example. David, we have found out that it is best to grind up the leaves, pine straw, grass, or whatever before we put it into the bins. We also add cotton seed meal. We have plenty of it here because we grow two thousand acres of cotton around here."

"Mr. Zeb, do you make up compost for the orchards?"

"No, that is too big of a project for me. I let Preston take care of that for me. Our chickens, hogs, cows, and horses produce enough natural compost to keep him busy. I believe that Beard told me that Preston's oldest son will take charge of that operation. Preston is our general manager. He has a big responsibility and is one of the finest black people I have ever met!" Zeb gave David a quick tour of the greenhouse and the drying shed where various herbs and roots are dried and stored. That night, after supper, David and Brenda go upstairs to be with each other while Lillian and her mother-in-law Mrs. Lilly take little Betty on a tour of the mansion. Dan in the mean while goes out on the porch to be with his great grandfather. Mattie has just fed the three yard dogs and Percy the family's large male Main Coon house cat. Old Percy actually spends as much time outdoors exploring the plantation as he does inside. Weighing in at over thirty pounds, he has won the respect of the dogs that are several years Percy's junior.

Three

A Junior Astronomer

There is a nice breeze blowing on the porch and the air is filled with the fragrance of the great magnolia trees and the acres upon acres of flower gardens and shrubs that surround the house. Little Dan is sitting across from his great grandfather. His legs are too short to touch the floor with his feet. In the not too far distance a Bob White Dove is calling out to his mate. Fast moving shadows of bats darting here and there capturing bugs that dare fly at night are seen. An old owl starts to hoot. The great bird takes flight and moves closer to the old mansion and finds a more suitable perch to give him the opportunity to swoop down on varmints that roam around at night. Dan could hear the voices of tens of thousands of frogs out at the catfish pond and the lake some miles away. Once in awhile the deep voice of a male bullfrog would be heard. There was no Moon overhead and only the stars above to light the night sky.

"Great Grandfather, I have never seen so many stars before. Where did they all come from?"

"Son, they have been there all along. You just could not see them. There are too many lights in big cities like Boston to be able to see nature in its full glory."

"It is so beautiful, Great Grandfather, it is so beautiful! Grandfather, why do you suppose that God put all of those lights up there? So he can see or something?"

"No, son, I don't believe that the Almighty needs lights like us mortals down here to see with. Dan, I have been a Sunday School teacher at my church for nearly fifty years. I have had thousands of questions addressed to me about God and his creation. I believe that I just might be able to find a few verses about the stars and other things we see up there in the sky." Zeb walks to an old shelf that is standing against the porch wall and gets out an oversized print study Bible. He reaches over and pulls the cord of a goose necked reading lamp and turns to the Book of Psalms in the Bible.

Son, we have plenty of time and we might as well spend it wisely. Let me read some Bible passages and see if they can shed light on why God created all of those things we see up there in the night sky. Zeb finds Psalms nineteen and reads several verses.

The heavens declare the glory of God; and the
Firmament showeth his handiwork
Day unto day uttereth speech, and night unto
Night showeth knowledge.
There is no speech nor language where their
Voice is not heard.
Their line is gone out through all the earth,
And their words to the end of the world. In them
Hath he set a tabernacle for the sun,
Which is as a bridegroom coming out of his
Chamber, and rejoiceth as a strong man to run a race.
His going forth is from the end of the heaven, and his circuit unto the ends
of it: and there is
Nothing hid from the heat thereof.

"That is beautiful Great Grandfather! What does glory mean?"

"It is something like praise. When someone does something very brave or creates something very useful or beautiful, we say good things about that person. In other words, a person is honored for his or her achievements. Have you ever been to a fair and noticed a blue ribbon on a cake or pie or maybe something that has been canned?"

"Yes, sir, father carried us several times to a county fair. I believe I understand you, Great Grandfather. God gets praise and honor for the beautiful things he has made."

"I could not have said it better myself! Dan, when God creates something, it usually has a purpose. Things may be beautiful, but there is more to it than making our eyes happy. Look at the Moon for example. It is very beautiful to look at. People look at it every night through telescopes just to admire its mystery and beauty."

"Great Grandfather, I have a six inch telescope. I believe it is upstairs in my bedroom."

"Now that is just dandy! Why don't you get it out one clear night and we will look at the Moon and stars together?"

"Oh, I would love to do that!"

"Dan, as I was saying, everything God has up there has more than one purpose for it being around. Look at the Moon for example. It is a light at night most of the time. I can still see to get around this great big yard with a full Moon high in the sky. The Moon also causes the tides to rise and fall."

"Yes, sir, Father told me that life on Earth would not be possible if the tides stopped."

"Yes, the tides help regulate water quality in our rivers."

"Great, grandfather, look, look, what are those tiny lights flying around? I have never seen anything like that before. It is like magic is in the air!" What Dan saw were fireflies flying around in the darkness near the porch. The child's statement took his elder by surprise, but then he was amazed and delighted the moment he realized that this child who had never experienced life in the country had never seen one of the most common delights Southern kids have always known about. Zeb chuckled and speaks:

"Son, they are called fireflies. We see them down South this time of the year. Just wait another month and you will see a lot more of them when the weather is warmer." Dan runs off the porch and down the stairs and dashes into the yard attempting to capture one of the bugs as it blinked its amber light off and on.

"Son, just be still and directly one of them will land on some shrubbery out there. When he lands, use both hands. Clasp your hands around it, but be careful not to hurt it." After several desperate attempts, Dan succeeds in capturing a firefly. He is overcome by this strange new delight and runs up the huge set of steps to where his amused great grandfather watches with pleasure.

"Look, I have got him!" Dan cracks open his fingers a little so that he could show the family's patriarch his newfound delight. The boy is so excited that he crushes the insect. While touched with a slight feeling of guilt and disappointment at his carelessness, he was amazed that the glowing light was on his fingers. He stood amazed at this almost unprecedented discovery of his young life. His great grandfather's eyes were moistened a bit because it reminded him of another little boy so long ago who captured his first firefly. My, how the years had gone by, as swift as a fast horse. The incident made Zeb remember a Bible passage his grandfather had once read to him about the brevity of life and the awesome responsibility each of us have to use it wisely as possible while it remains ours.

Man that is born of a woman is of few days and
And full of trouble.
He cometh forth like a flower and is cut down,

He fleeth also as a shadow, and continueth not

Dan in his haste to get the firefly's body parts off his hands quickly rubs his hands on his jeans and is amazed to see streaks of glowing stuff all over the front of his pants.

"Son, the light will go away. Just enjoy it while it last. Your mama can wash your pants later." That night after supper, everyone disappears to his or her bedroom or to a favorite recluse. The children were in their bedrooms playing with the toys. Brenda had helped little Betty assemble the dollhouse that Betty discovered in the large wooden box in her room. The house is nine feet long and looks like a two story Southern Mansion. Betty is busy arranging fancy dollhouse furniture in each of the dozens of rooms available. The dining room table even has real tiny plates and silverware and everything expected on a fancy table setting. The house is even wired like a real house and an electrical cord is plugged into the wall receptacle. Real miniature chandeliers hang from the ceilings. Miniature stoves can heat up little containers of food. Brenda told Betty that when she got older, she could cook some of the food. There are also things like a real working refrigerator in the kitchen. Even small appliances expected in a kitchen work. The living areas of the house and bedrooms have working radios, and television sets.

A family of lifelike dolls came with the house. The dolls have lifetime rechargeable batteries in them and computer chips that control tiny electrical motors that allow them to talk to each other and move about as if they are actually alive. The dolls are even installed with sensor devices that allow them to recognize each other's presence. Heads move, mouths move, and limbs appear to be real.

Betty puts the dolls in the starting position, the dining room table, and watched them talk to each other and lift forks, spoons, cups, and glasses to their tiny mouths. The program allows the dolls to hold conversations with each other. The computer program is constantly updated via the Internet. The miniatures represent characters in a television show of a well to do businessman who has a wife who is a psychologist. They have three children, two girls, and a teenager boy. Betty sat amazed watching these lifelike dolls move around the house acting out the hour long programs.

Dan, the Smith's only son, was also in his bedroom watching the action of a very sophisticated computer controlled train set. The sixty foot track had over five thousand action figures moving around. The three Big Boy locomotives pulled over a hundred cars that represented all kinds of industry. There are cars that are filled with cows looking out cattle cars.

The cows actually move their heads about and make cow noises as they gaze out the sides of the stock cars. Flatbed cars are loaded with lumber and steam engines that look like giant pumps designed to pump water out of mine shafts. Coal cars are filled to the maximum. A large workable crane is on one specially designed car. Streets and roads are included with the set. Early model cars and trucks drive around the streets with their miniature people inside. Out on the streets and yards, miniature people are moving around at work or play. Cars and trucks are stopping at the railroad crossing while the lights flash and the bells are heard. The arm to block traffic from trying to cross the tracks is lowered before the train passes a street and is raised after the train passed on by. Beautiful houses line neighborhoods streets and department stores line the streets of the business district of *Middle Town* on both sides. Out much farther from downtown are docks with goods piled up and factories with steam pouring out of tall stacks. The train makes stops at the factories and docks to deliver or receive its cargo. The train even stops for real water, which automatically poured down a spout into the water tanks of the engines. The three electrical locomotives turn the water into steam to make it all realistic. The whistles sound off and steam comes out of the whistles and sides of the locomotives when they are operating. Electrical lights that look like gas lanterns are installed on the front of each locomotive. This action is only a glimpse of the activity taking place before the amazed ten year old boy.

While the children are at play, David and Brenda are in bed talking. They are almost sitting in bed with pillows high behind their backs. David has his right arm back of Brenda's neck and his left hand rest on Brenda's left hand. Brenda speaks first:

"Well, David, I trust that you did not get bored today. I know that it must be a culture shock to one who has lived in the grand City of Boston. Now you are out in the woods basically in the middle of nowhere on a Southern Plantation." David realizes that Brenda was teasing him a bit.

"Yes, you are right, Brenda. I definitely am under the influence of a cultural shock. I almost feel like I have walked back two hundred years in time. This place is an inspiration to behold, and to think that it is all for real. No wonder your grandfather did not want to sell this place! At the going price of fifty thousand dollars an acre on a hundred thousand plus acre plantation not counting the huge fishing lake's many square miles of territory with the mansion and other buildings makes this place worth billions!"

"Yes, David, I am thankful that my folks have kept our heritage intact. I can't imagine this place not being here for future generations. It represents far more than wealth. The wealth is only the icing on the top of the cake. The plantation represents a way of life and values we live by. Everyone who lives on these grounds does so of their own volition; no one is forced to live here. Folks around here, hunt, fish, learn crafts and skills that have long been forgotten by most people. The beautiful thing about it is that we here all depend on these skills. We are not a tourist museum showing people how things once were. What did you do today?"

"Well, Brenda, I went to the herb garden with your grandfather. That place is amazing! I learned about all kinds of herbs and how they are used for teas, spices, and medicine. Your grandfather showed me the greenhouse and the drying barn. It smells wonderful in there with all of those herbs drying out. He let me try out several kinds of teas. He boiled a kettle of hot water out there and poured the water on top of the herbs to make tea. He offered plantation honey to sweeten up the tea. I never realized that so many different kinds of teas existed." Brenda speaks:

"Mama and Grandmother use herbs all of the time in the kitchen and almost everywhere else. Grandfather brings the herbs in the house for their use. I know they use Bouguetgarni in their water when they cook."

"What is Bouguetgarni, Honey?"

"Oh, it is just a bunch of finely chopped herbs. Usually Grandfather gets, tarragon, bay, parsley, and other herbs and places them into little bags made of something like cheesecloth. The little bags of herbs are tied with strings and dropped into the water while the cooking takes place."

"No wonder your parents' house smells so good! I am sure there are bushels of potpourri in fancy hanging baskets in this mansion."

"I had potpourri at our home in Boston, but they were not as fresh as these herbs straight from the herb garden. David, we also depend on these herbs for medicine."

"Brenda, isn't that dangerous to prescribe drugs for human illness?"

"If it is, I would not have made it."

"You have a point there."

"Grandmother and Mother mix most of the herbs around here for the medicine. That knowledge has been passed down for generations. One day you should ask Grandmother about herbs and their medicinal powers."

"I believe, I will take you up on that. Does your grandmother grow these herbs?"

"No, Grandfather grows them. He makes the herbs available. I have seen my grandmother go to the woods and come back with a plant or root that she wants Grandfather to grow for her."

"Brenda, do you want to go over to UNCW tomorrow about ten o'clock?"

"Who is going to take care of the children while we are absent?"

"Your mother said that she would handle the kids for us. I believe that she is going to ask everyone to watch them."

"I have a feeling that Mother will know how to take care of our children's excess energy!"

"What are you talking about, Brenda?"

"She told me that she is going to pick green peas, gather turnips, mustard greens, and young onions out of the garden. The kids can help her. While she cleans and prepares the vegetables, I would imagine she will have the kids to help Mattie make butter." David speaks:

"I can't imagine our kids making butter." Brenda speaks:

"Betty will enjoy putting the butter into mother's molds and creating beautiful imprints on the soft butter. Mother will have everything organized so everyone will know just what to do."

The next morning after a classic great Southern breakfast with their family, Brenda and David get into their SUV and travel to UNCW. After crossing Beatty's Bridge and traveling down Beatty's Bridge Road from the Pridgen Plantation, Brenda turns left onto Highway 53 which divides the small town of Atkinson into half. Our couple drives down highway 53 through Atkinson, which is Church Street while in Atkinson, and turns right onto Highway 117 in Burgaw the county seat. Fifteen miles outside of Burgaw they enter the town of Rocky Point. Brenda turns left at the light and momentarily used Highway 210 to turn right onto Interstate 140. Large buildings were seen on both sides of I40. Brenda has a concerned frown on her face as she sees the huge factories and warehouses just outside of Rocky Point.

"David, Daddy tells me that when he was a boy none of this existed. In fact, there was no I40. What concerns him and my grandparents even more is that Pender County citizens will stop fighting their county's officials and let all this human activity spill into Pender Count and neighboring counties destroying what is left of the natural environment. Officials want the taxes. The average citizen in general wants to preserve the neighborhoods from the invasion from up North."

"I guess that I can understand the citizens. I have only known about big city life myself. As you know, Brenda, outside and surrounding Boston is one solid complex of industry now. Half of the companies are now foreign owned; now that concerns me." The Smith's turn right off of College Road into the beautiful UNCW campus.

Four

Brenda and David Visit UNCW and Later Wrightsville Beach

"Well, Brenda, we are back at your old Alma Mater. I hope that you recognize the place."

"I don't believe that I will have any problem getting around here. I, after all, spent six years here getting my master's in education. I lived in a dorm my last two years. The round trips from here back to the plantation every day were just too much."

"I don't know how you did it for four years! I would hate to drive back and forth from the plantation myself." Brenda speaks:

"It was not easy for me to live in Wilmington. I did not want to stay away from my family and the plantation. When I stayed on the plantation, Mama would help me by making sure my clothes were washed and ironed. My breakfast was always ready before I left for school and supper was ready when I got back from school. Of course, there were times I had to stay in Wilmington. I often stayed with my friends in their dorms or at their parents' houses. There were ball games to attend and other activity that occasionally caused me to come home late. David, if you don't mind, I believe that I would like to visit the educational department while you go to the science complex." David looked over at Brenda with a smile.

"You mean that I will not have the distinguished pleasure of introducing my lovely wife?"

"Now, David, if you insist, I will go along with you. I just thought that you would be better off not having to introduce me to every person you come across."

"OK, Brenda, we will meet again in two hours at the SUV. I will see you then, dear." David and Brenda kiss and depart to the places of their choosing.

David knocks on the door of the head secretary and no one answers. He walks inside and sits down on a fancy sofa while waiting for someone to show up. While he sits, he picks up a magazine about the oceans. The magazine has a special report in it about the discovery of dozens of unknown fish and crustacean, which includes shrimp, crabs, lobsters, and other creatures with hard outer bodies and limbs. After about fifteen minutes of waiting, a tall rather thin older woman dressed in a very formal business suit wearing wire rimmed glasses and a short haircut comes into the office and notices David.

"Yes, sir, young man, may I help you? I am Doris Blankenship, secretary and part time receptionist for Doctor Fletcher." David's face turns a little red not accustomed to being addressed as young man on college campuses.

"Yes, ma'am, Mrs. Blankenship."

"Call me Miss Blankenship, I have never married. It is probably a little too late now." Miss Blankenship smiles while extending her large thin hand to David.

"I am Doctor David Smith. I thought that I would pay Doctor Fletcher a visit."

"Oh, my, you are the new scientist who will be Doctor Fletcher's assistant! I apologize for not recognizing you, sir! I was out the first week you were here on vacation. I hope you take no offence!" David smiles and answers her:

"I would not worry, Miss Blankenship. I realize that I am new around here. Most of the department staff and faculty have not been introduced to me. I also realize that I look rather young even for a forty one year old. My wife likes to tease me about my appearance."

"Doctor Smith, pardon my humble opinion, but I believe that we need some more young instructors around here. Most of us are showing our age around here. Age has its rewards because most of us will be retiring in ten years or less. Doctor Fletcher should be here any minute. He is now finishing up a class."

"How many classes does he teach?"

"He teaches two a day. The rest of his time is spent with his duties as the department head. I am sure that you know about that!"

"Yes, ma'am, I do. I was assistant head at the science department at the University of Boston for ten years. When my boss resigned, I took his place." Miss Blankenship speaks:

"I believe that is Doctor Fletcher walking down the hall. I recognize his walking pattern." When Doctor Fletcher walked into the office, he was delighted that Doctor Smith had dropped by.

"Doctor Smith, it is a real pleasure to have you here! I assume that you are living on that big plantation right now."

"Yes, sir, and the key word is big!"

"Well, I am glad that you have honored us with your presence. Come right on into my office and please be seated. I believe that it will be the end of next month before you go back up North and arrange for that exploration submarine to be shipped here."

"Yes, I look forward to using it, sir. I am sure that there are a lot of interesting things just waiting for us to learn about." Doctor Fletcher speaks to David about the underwater living facility UNCW owns.

"We will have the Sea Wise ready for shipment in about two months. We have to finish up our classroom credits aboard her and to tidy up a small dispute about raising her onto a sea going barge. I do not trust tugboats pulling or pushing a motor-less barge with cargo that precious. The barge we are going to raise and transport the Sea Wise on has its own power."

"Yes, sir, I have seen a few vessels like the one you are talking about. The operators of the vessel will flood the barge and it will sink about twenty five feet below the ocean. The Sea Wise will be floated back to the surface and be winched onto the barge deck. The barge will then have its ballast emptied so that its deck will rise about ten feet above the ocean." Doctor Fletcher speaks:

"Yes, you have got the idea! I just believe this will be a lot safer than a conventional barge and a hoisting crane. There will be less chance for any structural damage." David notices about six photos on the wall of distinguished looking men and women.

"Doctor Fletcher, I assume that these photos are the pictures of past department heads."

"Yes, this first one here is Doctor Charles Blankenship. This last photo is Doctor Tommy Carr. His bust stands out in the junction of the halls. He, of course, was not the first to chair the department, but he had a very distinguished career here." David speaks:

"I assume that Doctor Tommy Carr is still alive then?"

"Yes, very much so. He has had some health problems for a number of years. He lives here in Wilmington on Fourth Street. He lives in a very large old historical home that I believe was passed down to him."

"So he is a local."

"Oh, yes, and he is not bashful about that! Most of the instructors who started working here when he came on board are history or they will retire in a few years. All of them could retire today, but they continue to teach here. Oh course, I am not a spring chicken myself. I will be sixty five this fall."

"I hope you will not retire then, sir!"

"No, I am still in great shape. I will try to hang on until I am seventy. My wife and I have plans to go back up North and be with the rest of our siblings. When we were young, we all went to college. We got our degrees and departed from one another. I only get to see my family about twice a year."

"Well, sir, I hope you and your wife's family will continue to have good health and fortune so that you can all enjoy each other's company for many years after all of you guys retire."

"David, please forgive me. I have a son nearly your age, but around here I will need to call you, Doctor Smith. I want you to meet some of the people who will be working under you. Now, even though you will not be teaching here until next January, there are plenty of things I am sure you could do if you want to. Your office, as you know, is across the hall from this office. You can bring your books and anything else you want to. That away, you will be setup and will not have to worry about such when January comes around." David speaks:

"I believe I could go ahead and move most of my things into my office suite. I will, of course, be setting up the new program and work on getting the classes started for the exploration submarine I will be getting from the University of Boston."

"I look forward to a trip or two myself in that exploration submarine! I believe that it seats eight people. That vessel will add a new dimension to our practical studies around here."

"Yes, sir, the students will learn how to operate the submarine. It will greatly enhance their opportunities getting future jobs in the marine science industry."

"David, let's take a walk and meet some people."

"The two men worked their way down the hall to where most of the offices are located. After a brief knock on Doctor Hardin's door, a voice from inside asks the knocker to enter the room. When Doctor Hardin saw his department head walk in with a young man who looked important, he immediately got up from the desk chair and waited to be introduced to the visitor. Quicker than a speeding bullet, Doctor Hardin realizes who the young man is. The person who would have the office he coveted so badly! It was all he could do to hold back his true feelings, but Doctor Hardin was very good at putting on a smiling face. Doctor Fletcher the department head paused a moment before he introduced the two men. He was taking a moment to inventory Doctor Hardin's reaction to being introduced to his new boss. He failed to detect any resentment, but he realized that Doctor Hardin could smile after he broke one of his big toes if the right people were watching. Doctor Hardin speaks as excited as a used car dealer who is about to close a deal.

"Doctor Smith, it is such a pleasure to have the opportunity to meet you! I have heard so many positive things about you! Would you please sit down; I have about twenty minutes before my next class." Doctor Fletcher speaks:

"Doctor, Hardin, I am afraid that we will have to go. I don't mean to rush things, but I would like Doctor Smith to meet as many of our people as possible. You will have plenty of time to get acquainted. He will be moving his books and things into his office suite." Doctor Hardin answers back:

"I understand. Step by now when you have opportunity. Once again, it is such a pleasure making your acquaintance." David speaks:

"The same here, sir. I will be back within a week. I have my wife with me. She is to meet me at our SUV after her visit to the department of education." Doctor Hardin speaks almost silly:

"Well, is she going to sign up for classes?"

"No, Doctor Hardin, she received her first two degrees here about fourteen years ago. Brenda earned her doctorate at Boston University about seven years ago."

Doctor Hardin calmed down a bit. He was almost acting like a clown who realized that his mask had just fallen off. Doctor Hardin picks up a pen after David and Doctor Fletcher leave his office. He holds the pen by both hands and just stares at the wall on the other side of his desk. He breaks the pen into and throws it into a corner of the room while voicing his opinion of the situation out loud to himself. David and Brenda later meet at their SUV.

"Brenda, we have plenty of time. In fact, why don't we call your parents' house and see if your people will look out for our kids while we visit Wrightsville Beach today and part of tomorrow."

"Are you saying that you want to stay the night at the beach?"

"Why not, while we are in Wilmington? We might as well take advantage of our close proximity to the beach." The Smith's drive to the Wrightsville Beach Museum of History on 303 West Salisbury Street and get out. It is May the first and the sun is shining brightly overhead, but the temperature is only about sixty five degrees. The cry of Sea Gulls circling overhead is a pleasant and expected natural sound to David and Brenda. The air smells fresh and clean and both our subjects breathe deep and slowly take in the pure air. A small private plane flies high in the sky and David glances up at it for a second and notices that there are a few small white clouds in the sky. David speaks:

"Nice place!"

"Yes, I believe that a lot of what we are looking at was added in 2020, David."

"Brenda, I did not realize that there was a yacht club on this beach this early!" Brenda walks over to the display and speaks:

"I believe that I heard something about that, but I didn't realize that it was founded in 1853. The Carolina Yacht Club held dozens of races every year and is considered the third oldest yacht club in the United States." David speaks:

"Unfortunately, this fine club had its activities curtailed by the Civil War. That is so amazing! Those fellows did not realize that their fine yachts would be used by the Confederate Military." Brenda speaks:

"How about this, it says here that three blockade runners are believed to have been sunk on this beach and that one ship could have carried a valuable sword on board with a handle covered with expensive jewels. Can you imagine finding that sword today?" David speaks:

"Unless it was made of a good alloy, I doubt there is anything left of that sword. I don't believe stainless steel was used back in those days. I guess it is possible for that valuable thing to be around." David looks at the hurricane history and speaks:

"Lots of hurricanes have hit this beach. I remember them from my education. Just look at them, Bertha, Fran, Irene, Bonnie, Dennis, and Floyd in the 1990's. In the 2000's Wrightsville Beach was visited by Charlie and Ophelia." Brenda speaks:

"Grandfather told me that he remembers Hurricane Hazel. I understand that was a very bad storm."

"Yes, Brenda, I have some old film and still pictures of before and after Hazel. The entire area including Wrightsville Beach was a disaster zone. This storm did not stop people from building again on this beach. As long as there is a strip of land here to build on, people will build." David and Brenda continued to look and listen to the information about the storms." Brenda speaks:

"The folks who live here have accepted that Mother Nature will always throw them a curve ball. When I think about the struggle people here have, it reminds me of some of the documentations I have seen about areas of the world where there is a lot of volcanic activity. People often lose houses and their farms to incoming lava. Folks just can't give up. We have to be like the ants. When a human walks on an ant castle and crushes it, the ants don't pack and go somewhere else. They usually start all over again. In a way, people are like ants." David does not make a comment, but realizes that Brenda is really thinking out loud about the ebb and flow of life.

While their parents take a nice walk on the beautiful beach, Dan and Betty are learning about plantation life. Bushels of sweet peas, turnips, squash, mustard, and green onions are carried to the house. The grandparents with the help of Mattie are busy cleaning and preparing the vegetables for cooking or storage. Sweet peas are being shelled by everyone, including the children. Little Betty's small hands and finger dexterity is not up to the task and she is having a hard time. She has peas going all over the place until her grandmother gives her a larger plastic pan to work with. Dan who is ten years old is doing a fair job. Great Grandmother Lilly places a large piece of smoked country ham into a large pot on a stove. The ham, which will flavor the vegetables, is cooked for about fifteen minutes before the vegetables are put in. Fresh turnip tops and bottoms and mustard will cook in the pot. The air is filled with the smell of the vegetables. Cornbread is almost ready in one of the ovens. On the top of the stove is a large heavy duty iron pot on low heat. In the pot is a large roast with onions, carrots, and fresh red potatoes from the garden. Almost ready to serve is a cooker filled with moist rice flavored with the herbs from the herb garden. Beside the cornbread in the oven is a heavy duty glass dish with a lid on top. Inside the dish is split sweet potatoes garnished with farm fresh butter, brown sugar, raisings, black walnut bits, and slices of pineapple.

Fifteen minutes later, everyone washes up and sits down to a first class meal. The children eat like ravished dogs they're so hungry! The food was no doubt from Heaven! Great Grandmother Lilly chuckles and speaks:

"You kids act like you are starving. I don't believe that I have ever seen people enjoy food like you kids!" Lillian, their grandmother, speaks to her mother-in-law:

"Well, Mama, I don't believe that Boston restaurants can compete with our farm fresh food. When you kids finish eating, I will get you started helping me make butter." The children have been told about the butter and were excited. The Pridgens have a large commercial size walk-in cooler and freezer combo on the porch used to keep food like milk, butter, and ice cream nice and cold or cool. Mattie and Mrs. Lillian get several large churns out of the cooler and placed them in front of the stools they intend to sit on. The children sat on shorter stools. Brenda and her siblings used these same stools when they were children helping make butter. Lillian speaks to the children:

"Now children, the clabbered milk is already in the churns. All we have to do is go up and down with the dashers until the cream turns to butter." Mrs. Lilly Pridgen made up a little chant to make it easier for the children and to pretend they were not really working. Five minutes into the song everyone was enjoying the little diversion.

> Come Peter Cotton Tail
> Come down the trail
> Up comes Brea Fox
> Looking for Brea Rabbit
> Come to dinner friend
> Oh no Mr. Fox
> I know your scheme
> You'll not have rabbit
> I'll jump into the
> Briar patch my friend

It was such a pleasure for the adults to sing along with the children as they poured their hearts into their work. Farm folks had learned centuries ago that work and pleasure are good companions creating an atmosphere that makes life an enjoyable and productive experience.

In the main time back at the beach, David and his lovely young wife Brenda are taking a scroll near Johnny Mercers Pier, which is in the middle of Wrightsville Beach. There is a slight chill from the air, but they are dressed to stay awhile. Locked hand in hand they walk the beach. A few young people are having a kite party. Brenda and David are amazed at the large beautifully decorated kites. These were not ordinary kites, but represented advancement in the sport that allowed the operators of the kites more speed, coordination, and height control.

Several people wearing rubber boots stood knee deep in water fishing and lucking up once in awhile on a catch. Several young women who were apparently die hard sun lovers were in swimming suits lying down on expensive cushions with sowed in pillows at one end. David looks over at them and smiles before making a comment:

"Looks like these girls are desperate to get a tan." Brenda shakes her head in disapproval and speaks:

"I believe that I can wait until the weather is warmer, that is ridiculous!" After walking for a couple of miles, the Smiths turn around and walk back toward the pier. When they get to the pier, David wants to walk onto it. Brenda tells David that she had not had the privilege to walk on the pier since she had moved to Boston years ago. The pier's store, restaurant, and game-room had been made much larger and nicer than ever. Nice tables were available for customers to sit and order a meal. Beautiful mounted fish were everywhere on the walls for the public to admire. Photos of fishing trips, friends, and patrons were proudly displayed on one wall. The game machines were very advanced virtual reality projectors that were as real as it gets. The game machines of the nineties and early two thousands would be considered primitive in comparison. One or more players can play against other people from locations worldwide. One of the most popular is the World War II series focused on the battles in the Pacific Ocean. Helmets with computer controlled visors and sound effects are worn by the players creating a sensation on the thresh hold of actually participating in the battles.

David and Brenda order a wonderful oyster and crab dinner with slaw, potato fries, and hush puppies. After the meal, they take a walk on the pier, which is twice as long as it was back in the Twentieth Century. The big difference is that the entire pier is made completely of steel and high grade concrete. People were catching Mullets, Croaker, Spot, and Spanish mackerel. One young lad had a large Cobia on a line. The fish was pulling steady with no relief in sight for the boy. Later that night, our couple goes to the famous Holiday Inn Sun Spree Resort and have a wonderful time.

Back on the plantation, the Smith children are having the time of their lives. Little Betty is content to be upstairs with the dollhouse while Dan has just found his telescope and has walked out into the porch. The sky is clear as a crystal and the Moon is only a thin yellow smile in the sky. The Moon being not very bright in the night sky allowed a host of stars and planets to show off their stuff. The night air was still and just perfect for a young astronomer. Dan speaks:

"Great Grandfather, I guess that God is getting glory tonight!" Mr. Zeb who was on a porch easy chair with a cigar in his mouth hears his great grandson speak, but did not answer him immediately. It then dawns upon him that the boy was referring to the Bible verses he had read to his great grandson.

"Yes, Grandson, that he is! I see that you have brought your telescope down from that bedroom!"

"Great Grandfather, have you ever used a telescope?"

"Well, yes, but I have never owned one. I have gone across from the Battleship the USS North Carolina and used that telescope. You have to put change in a coin receiver to use the telescope. A friend of mine brought one to my old high school years ago. The science teacher allowed us time to look at the Moon with it. I believe that it was about half the size of yours."

"Great Grandfather, how many stars are up there?"

"Let me ask you a question, Great Grandson. How many grains of sand are on all of the beaches of the world?"

"I don't know; there are too many to tell!"

"I have been told, Dan, that if all of the grains of sand on all of the beaches of the world would represent one star or planet each, there would not be near enough grains of sand to take the place of what is up there."

"Great Grandfather, why did God make so many stars?"

"I don't know, Great Grandson, but God is a very big God and when he does something he does it very big!"

"Great Grandfather, if we had a really fast rocket ship could we go to the stars?"

"No, I am afraid that we can get there only with our imaginations. Do you remember how long your trip from Boston took?"

"Yes, sir, we traveled all day and spent the night in Rocky Mount."

"I am sure you already know, but what is earth's nearest neighbor in space?"

"Oh, everyone knows that it is the Moon."

"Well, then tell me how far the Moon is from us. Suppose we could build a highway all the way to the Moon; how long would it take for us going seventy miles an hour to get there?"

"I guess many days, Great Grandfather, I am not sure."

"Son, it would take over four months nonstop to get there. I am talking about a car that would not need to ever stop for gas and people who would not have to eat or go to the bathroom."

"Great Grandfather, I have a feeling that we will never travel to the stars."

"Son, the Book of Job says:"

> Behold the height of the stars
> How high they are

"Great Grandfather, how can God keep up with all those stars?"

"Great Grandson, our God is a very big God. He keeps up with all of his creation better than I know this here plantation. There is nothing that is hid or unknown to the Almighty. I believe that I just might be able to quote a few verses that tell us mortals about God's ability to keep up with even the smallest details. Let's see, oh, yes, I do remember where, Psalms 147:4-5." 'He counts the number of the stars; he gives names to all of them. Great is our Lord, and abundant in strength; His understanding is infinite.'" Dan looks toward the Moon with his telescope.

"Great Grandfather, look, I see a tiny bright light moving away from the Moon!" Zeb looks hard and guesses what the light is all about.

"Son, I suspect that it's that huge spaceship coming back from the Moon. I believe I heard the newsman on Channel 6 say that they were suppose to come back this way tonight. The first people to travel to the Moon did it when I was a young man in my mid-twenties. I saw it on television July 20, 1969. That event was the biggest technological thing that we had done as a nation, but then the enthusiasm died down for several decades until President Bush gave us the new vision to start building up there. That was way back in 2005. It is hard for a fellow my age to imagine us going back there again. I suspect that your generation will build factories of some kind up there. My generation dropped the torch so to speak."

"I think I understand, Great Grandfather."

"Don't worry, you will understand and much more than I will one of these days. Yes, I look up there and see all of that creation and I wonder how God even notices us little creatures down here. When I was your age, we had to memorize a lot of Bible verses. We had contest at church as to how many verses a person could memorize. The winner would go to a regional contest and then go to the convention headquarters in Tennessee."

"Did you ever win, Great Grandfather?"

"Yes and no. I won a few regional contests, but there was simply too much work around here for me to spend the time some of the kids had on their hands. Oh, I memorized several thousand verses by the time I was about sixteen years old. I still can quote a passel of them now, but I am not as sharp as I use to be. I am eighty six years old now! The Good Lord has blessed me mightily. I can't complain. Even if I did, it would not help. Now let's see. I do recall an appropriate verse in Psalms 8:3-4:

> When I consider thy heavens, the work
> Of thy fingers, the Moon and the
> Stars, which thy hath ordained; what
> Is man, that thou are mindful of him?

"Now, Dan, a lot of things we see up there can probably be best observed by the naked eye. Look at all of these stars. If you look at them through a telescope, it will not change things that much unless you are looking through the world's most powerful telescopes."

"Why is that, Great Grandfather?"

"It has to do with distance. Those stars are so far away. Now some of the new telescopes I hear about can actually make a big difference. I understand that even the planets around other stars can be detected. I watched a science program that presented the new thousand foot diameter telescope on the Moon. Of course, they are making telescopes out of some kind of new material that is very hard and light." Zeb points up at the sky.

"Son, do you see that group of stars that look like a water dipper with a handle on it?"

"I am not sure, do you mean that one?"

"No, Son, the one below that one?"

"Oh, I see it." Dan counted seven stars."

"I see seven stars, cool!"

"Son, they call that Ursa Major. Before you ask me, I will tell you that means Big Dipper."

"Look there is another smaller one!"

"Yes, that is called Ursa Minor which means Little Dipper. Now that long string of stars between the Big Dipper and the Little Dipper is called Draco. Let's go back to the Big Dipper. Use your fingers to point at the bucket end on the opposite side of the handle. There are two stars. At the bottom of the bucket we see Merak and the other star is called Dubhe. Point your finger up past Dubhe right there. Do you see that bright star?"

"Yes, sir, but that star is the last star on the handle of the Little Dipper!"

"Indeed it is, and that star is called Polaris, which is the North Star."

"Great Grandfather, why is it important to study the stars?" Mr. Zeb reached to his head and gently scratched it as he contemplates giving the boy a proper answer.

"Well, son, I reckon there are lots of reasons. I suspect some of the reasons are not as important as they were years ago. However, we will always depend on those stars up there and the Moon. I again refer to the Bible by quoting Genesis."

And the evening and the morning were the third day.
And God said, Let there be lights in the
Firmament of the heaven to divide the day from
The night, and let them be for signs and for
Seasons and for days, and years;
And God made two great lights; the greater
To rule the day, and the lesser light to rule the
Night: he made the stars also
And God set them in the firmament of the

Heaven to give light upon the earth
And to rule over the day and over the night
And God saw that it was good.

"If you ask most scientists why it is important to study all that stuff up there, I am sure they would tell you that it is important for mankind to understand how everything got started. I am sure you have heard people on science programs tell their audiences that the future of mankind lies in our ability to understand and conquer all those worlds up there."

"Yes, sir, Great Grandfather, my science teacher at school told us that one day the sun was going to explode and would destroy the Earth and all of the other planets. He said that it would probably be millions of years from now. He told us that we would need to develop spaceships that can carry tens of millions of people far away to a solar system like ours."

"I am not a scientist Great Grandson, but I don't believe we will ever have to worry about the sun blowing up. I firmly believe that the Good Lord is in control of his creation. It is getting late. You probably should be getting on to bed before your grandmother comes out here."

"Good night, Great Grandfather."

"Good night, Great Grandson. I will see you at the breakfast table if I live the night through."

The next morning, everyone, including Brenda and David, sat at the breakfast table. Naturally questions were asked about the visit to UNCW and the trip to the beach. The children wanted to go visit the beach and their parents promised to take them there. Brenda wanted to visit Fort Fisher and the aquarium near there. Dan asks his father a question:

"Father, can we go fishing too?"

"Son, fishing is an all day adventure. We can't do everything in one day. I am sure that there are plenty of places around here you can go fishing. We will have to wait and do our salt water fishing when we move near the ocean." Betty their daughter speaks:

"Father, when are we going to move to the beach?"

"I cannot say. We have just arrived in North Carolina a few days ago. It will take time. My new job basically starts next year. We are not in a hurry. I would like to enjoy the plantation before thinking about leaving so soon." Brenda speaks:

"David, we could get a realtor to start looking for us."

"I would like for us to look ourselves before we hire someone just to get a mental picture of the possibilities." Great Grandmother Lilly frowned and shook her head a little and spoke out loud.

"People are always moving around it seems. I made one move in my life and that was a long time ago. That was when I married Zeb here and moved from the Moore farm to the Pridgen Plantation. A good move, I made, I might add. I don't believe I would have the energy to move again. My old bones will be planted on the hill with the rest of the Pridgens I believe." Great Grandfather speaks:

"Yes, Lilly, there is plenty of room up on that hill for all of us and a lot more! I plan to delay my visit there as long as I can. I kind of like living. I find that life is a wonderful adventure. Now that the Great Grandkids are staying here with us, I am ready for a new world to open up!" Lillian speaks:

"Yes, not many great grandparents get to be with their great grandkids. I believe that you two will make a deep impression in their lives and will be remembered with fond affection." Betty speaks:

"I will always remember you, Great Grandfather and Great Grandmother. I will remember you forever!" Zeb speaks:

"Well, it is nice to know that we will always be remembered." Zeb winks at his wife Lilly and speaks again in a louder and sterner voice.

Five

Brenda's Three Brothers Visit

"What in the tar nation is all that noise out there? Sounds like the Hells Angels have just arrived! Beard, you need to talk to those boys about that! They are going to run over one of us one of these days!" Beard Junior, Gregg, and John had just arrived on the scene driving three super duty four by four pickup trucks. The fellows had just come from the plantation logging camp located just off Black River about fifteen miles from the big house. Beard Junior is Beard's and Lillian's second child, Gregg is the third child, and John Wesley Pridgen is the fourth child. Beard Junior is thirty three years old, Gregg is twenty seven years old, and John Wesley Pridgen is twenty one. Lilly tries to defend her grandsons to put a damper on Zeb's temper.

"Now, Zeb, boys will be boys. I am sure that you had your wild moments when you were young enough to be wild!" Zeb looks over at Lilly with a challenging look.

"Lilly, I am not dead yet, but when I was young, I had the good sense to let my steam off in more positive ways!"

"And what are you talking about, Zeb Pridgen?"

"It took about half of my steam just courting you. You were a hard catch!"

"Well, Zeb, if you want something worth having you have to pay more for it!" Even the children realized what the old folks were talking about. Everyone was laughing and cracking remarks to his or her mate. Brenda chuckles and shakes her head slightly as she looks over across the table at her mother.

"Well, here come the elephants. I hope there is enough breakfast or we might be eaten." Lillian speaks:

"Oh, I am sure there is plenty. I was kind of expecting your brothers. They couldn't break from the logging camp until today." It sounded almost like a herd of large animals as Brenda's brothers quickly walked down the huge porch toward the doors of the large foyer that leads into the kitchen dining area. The children were quickly grabbed up into the arms of their uncles for their hugs. The guys shook David's hand and they all wanted to know how he was adjusting to plantation life. Beard Junior grabbed his sister Brenda and spoke:

"It is good to see you little, Sis." Brenda looked at Beard Junior with a big sister look.

"Excuse me, little brother. I do recall helping Mama change your diapers when she first brought you from that hospital. Correct me if I am wrong!" Beard Junior looked at Brenda with a silly grin and spoke:

"Beats me, I don't recall you doing that. I just can't say." Brenda grabs one of her brother's arms and makes a comment.

"You must be working out!" Beard Junior answers his sister:

"Right, I am working out alright, out on the Pridgen Plantation. Of course, you are now a big city girl; you would not know about that anymore!"

"Oh, I have not forgotten. When I lived here, I worked alongside you guys and could hold my own with all three of you until you and Gregg got into your twenties. I believe that I can still earn my keep around here if I have to!" Beard Junior looks at his sister and speaks:

"Yes, you were always the tough one!" After the breakfast, everyone went to the porch, except for Lilly, Lillian, and Brenda. The dishes and everything had to be cleaned and put up. After a couple of hours of socializing, John Wesley suggested that he and his brothers carry David and his children on a ride around the lake. Brenda finishes up in the kitchen and walks onto the porch and hears talk about going to the fishing lake. The children are all excited about the prospect of going to the lake and are jumping around. David speaks:

"Well, let's go. I would love to go to the lake! Brenda, are you coming along with us?"

"Yes, I have not been out there in years; it is beautiful!" Several voices were heard asking the question:

"Who wants to ride with me?" Everyone piled into two pickup trucks and our characters make a mad dash to the lake. Brenda speaks to Beard Junior:

"Slow down, Beard, you are going too fast, let them see the horses and the gristmill." Half a mile on the right the beautiful Black River flowed. The road went downhill for about half a mile until they reached the huge red barns, horse stables, and the twelve one hundred foot tall silos, which are painted white. The silos are very impressive because Zeb Pridgen hired an artist years ago to paint huge murals of Black River on each of them. The sight is so impressive that it has been featured in several magazines and once on a news program. The silos are equipped with photosensitive lights that automatically turn on at night. Near the silos were parked several large trucks used to haul grain from the fields to the silos. A heavy white wooden fence encloses the nearly two thousand acre pasture where over a thousand horses of many colors and sizes roam around. Horses are free to go to the stables to get out of the weather or feed when fed. David speaks to Gregg the next to the oldest brother:

"Very impressive, how many horses are in the area?"

"We have a little over twelve hundred now. We only use a little over four hundred of them for work on a regular basis. The rest are at stud, too young to work, or used to rotate the workload."

"I see that you guys do use modern equipment on this plantation. I was under the impression that everything around here was horse and buggy." Gregg laughs and speaks:

"Well, almost, we do use heavy trucks to haul in the corn and other heavy grains and for most of the planting. We still use horses to haul the hay bales to the storage cribs. Heavy horses are still used to do most of our plowing around here."

"Who works on the trucks and tractors around here?"

"My brothers and I do it sometimes, but we usually depend on a company in Burgaw to do our routine maintenance for us. The mechanics come every other week. They do a good job and keep us informed if there is something we need to know about. David, I am sure that you can see for yourself. The barnyard is separated from the pasture. The yard and all of the stables have cement floors. The stables are cleaned every day or so and the animal waste is carried to the compost pile where it will eventually be spread by machines to our crops and orchards. Pa might have told you that Mr. Preston's son is in charge of that now."

"Yes, he told me something about that. I understand that Preston runs the plantation like a general."

"Yes, he does not put up with a lazy butt. He is fair, but he wants everyone to do their jobs and to take interest in the overall operation around here."

"I guess that means he is your boss too?" David grins:

"Well, I don't know about that." Brenda smiles and speaks:

"Come on, Gregg, Preston cracks the whip around here. I had to listen to him when I was here!"

"OK, he is the boss, but he knows that we will one day own the plantation. That is when Pa turns it over to us." David speaks:

"I was told that your Grandparents are still the legal owners of the plantation."

"Who told you that?"

"Your big sister, I believe." Gregg speaks:

"I did hear Grandpa get on to Pa one time some years back." He told him to tighten up on security around here." David makes a comment:

"So you have security around here?"

"We have no uniformed guards. We do it a little differently around here. People are assigned odd jobs all over that require little physical effort or mental attention to speak of. I am sure that you saw the young black teenagers fishing on that bridge when you all first arrived. The oldest young man is eighteen years old. He actually was being paid to fish. The other young people were fishing strictly for pleasure and the opportunity to take a mess of fish to their parents' homes. The security guy or watchman was carrying a two way radio on his person. He would call Mr. Preston if he saw trouble. If Preston did not answer, he would call one of us or even the county." Gregg looks over at Brenda:

"Brenda, did you tell David about the helicopters and the small planes?"

"No, Gregg, to be honest with you, I have not thought about our sky patrol in years. Do you want me to tell David about the sky patrol or do you want to do it, Gregg?" Gregg speaks:

"I will tell him, Brenda. David, we have an airport with a hanger. Someone is always there. Charles Sidbury manages the airport. Gus Norman is the head mechanic." David questions Gregg:

"I know that I am probably asking a silly question, but why would you need a manager at a small airport in the woods?"

"You should go over there one day and see. Someone needs to be there to see to it that the runways are clear and level at all times. The airport covers about four hundred acres. Mr. Sidbury does not do the work personally, but sees to it that the ground crew people do their jobs. We own a large road grader that is used to keep the place safe and looking nice. We have a tractor that is there to plant special grass seed, mow, and fertilize the grass."

"So the airport is not paved?"

"Oh, no, it is a lot easier on the tires of the planes. Most of the planes are small planes used by people for pleasure or business trips. Having our own private airport does have its benefits because one pilot reported a fire on plantation property about fifteen miles away some years back. The airport is similar to a marina where boats are parked, stored, and maintained. There are usually about forty small planes in the hanger or on the runways at any one moment in time. Owners of the planes must keep their planes in top repair so that they can legally fly. Mr. Sidbury sees to it that everyone is in compliance with the Government. The airport has only one large hanger, but when you park on the paved parking lot and walk into the lobby; you will be impressed. The building is two hundred feet long and about a hundred feet wide all steel structure on the outside. The front office and lobby are paneled with real knotted pine.

There is a snack bar in the large lobby that serves hot dogs, hamburgers, various snacks, and soft drinks. A large hundred inch television is in the lobby that features only the weather channel and a travel channel. As you know, all pilots, even in small planes, are required to file flight plans. Pilots can file their plans via several computers in the lobby." David speaks:

"I would have never dreamed such a place existed around here. I am very impressed!" Brenda looks at Gregg a little funny and speaks:

"Gregg, I am sure that David appreciated you telling him about all of the amenities the airport possesses, but you forgot to tell him about the air patrol!" Gregg's face froze for a split second as he realized his error.

"Sorry, I guess I just got carried away a bit. We hire several pilots to fly over the entire property day and night. We own two four seated planes and two small helicopters. The choppers are used mainly to fly people from one place to another around the plantation. Last week we had a problem with a large tractor we use to cut down and process trees with. A small part needed to be replaced, so we flew the chopper to Fayetteville to pick up the part. The choppers go about a hundred and eighty miles an hour. The pilot was able to get the part three times faster than a truck could deliver it to the logging camp. No traffic, just a straight shot there and back again."

Dan and Betty are in the pickup truck that John Wesley Pridgen is driving. When the children saw the big horses walking around back of the stables, and barns, grazing in the two thousand acre pasture, they get very excited! Dan speaks:

"Uncle, John, can I ride a horse, can I?"

"Dan, most of the horses out there are too big to ride; they are good for pulling plow and heavy wagons. One day, I will carry you to the riding stables and put you on a pony."

"What about me?"

"Betty, I am afraid you are still too small for riding a horse. Don't worry, the time will come when you can ride also. We have small carriages that we hook up to fast horses. One day, one of us will take you on the ride of your life." Dan speaks:

"Why do you keep carriages here?"

"They are a lot of fun to ride. Sometimes we get on the carriages and have a carriage ride around the plantation. Grandpa used to carry the carriages to Wilmington every year so he could ride in the Azalea Festival. I was about your age then. It was a lot of fun to wave at all of the people looking at us riding by on a carriage."

"Can we do that?"

"I can't say that we can. Your Grandpa has never used the carriages in a parade. He likes to get one once in awhile and ride around here to check on what is going on. He seldom goes over twenty miles a day. He always uses a truck for long trips." Betty understood most of what her uncle was telling her. The kids were amazed at the scores of huge horses walking around. Their uncle John stopped the truck and patiently allowed the children time to look at the animals. Betty comments:

"Oh, they are so beautiful! Can I touch one of them?"

"We can't today, Betty, because we have several other places to go. I promise you that you will get lots of opportunities to rub the horses. I give my horse an apple and other treats when I visit him. I will let you give him an apple." Dan speaks with amazement when he sees the twelve one hundred foot silos.

"Wow, what are those big things?"

"They are called silos. We store, beans, corn, and all kinds of things in them for the animals." David and Brenda are in the lead truck and the truck Dan and Betty are in is following. John Wesley Pridgen is driving the rear truck. Gregg is in the backseat of the cab with his nephew Dan. On the left about two hundred feet from the wooden bridge that crosses Possum Creek is a large two story grist mill with huge wheels on each side of the building. Several hundred feet back of the mill is a large holding pond where the water is dammed up. The water rushes through a large wooden trough that is about eight feet wide and about three feet deep. A hundred feet before the water gets to the wheels it is diverted into two separate troughs that dump water into the catch basins of the turning wheels. The water is then released to immediately plunge back into Possum Creek where it will eventually join up with Black River, which is about half a mile away."

A wide covered porch surrounds the entire mill. Hundreds of bags of grain of various kinds are stacked on the porch while men are loading wagons with the bags. Horses are patiently waiting while the wagons they pull are filled to their capacity. Huge electrical fans are hanging from the porch to help disturb the tranquility of annoying insects flying around and to give a measure of comfort to the people loading the grain. Huge blood sucking flies commonly called Horseflies are flying around the horses hoping for an opportunity to land on a horse. The truck Beard Junior is driving has come to a full stop and David and Brenda take full assessment of the scene before them. A huge fly lands on a horse and the horse swats it with its tail. David noticed that the horses could control their muscles so that it appeared that they were having muscle spasms. The muscles of the horses would jerk so violently that a fly would be thrown off the horse into the ground or forced to fly away. David is amazed when all of a sudden a large plump insect that had strips all over it grabs a horsefly and makes off with it.

"Wow, did you see that? That is amazing; I have never seen one of those things!" Beard Junior is amazed at David's ignorance or at least ignorance in a sort of queer way.

"We call them guards around here, David. They guard our horses for us by capturing and eating blood sucking flies." On the porch an older black man with a workman's apron on is busy sweeping or rather pushing corn and other unusable grain off the porch with a push broom. This was done so that people would not lose their footing and to keep the place looking nice. Everyone gets out of the trucks they are riding in and David and the children walk on one side of the porch to get a better view of one of the huge turning wheels that reminded David of a Mississippi paddle boat's paddles except these wheels were designed with huge catch basins. It was amazing to hear the rush of the clean creek water as it roared down onto the wheel. One could hear a little creaking and groaning as the giant wheels turned around on their shafts. David and the children stood mesmerized by the power of the great wheels.

The operator of the mill walked out on the porch and was surprised with joy to realize that the very striking figure of a young lady whom he had known about even before she was born was standing on the porch. He realized with amazement that the two children and the young man who stood next to her and the children had to be her husband whom he had heard about for years, but had not met. Uncle Preston speaks out loud to Brenda while holding his arms out toward her.

"Well hallelujah, what a blessed day this has turned out to be! Miss Brenda, don't tell me they done ran you out of Boston! Oh child it is so good to see you again! It has been such a short time ago it seems to me that you were just a little red headed girl coming all the way from your mama's big house to visit Uncle Preston!" For a moment the children did not realize Preston was referring to their mother, but Preston grabbed Brenda and was preparing to give the excited but humbled Brenda a big hug. Preston paused just long enough to get permission from David to give his wife a big country hug. Tears formed in Brenda's eyes and Preston's eyes as they embraced each other. Preston let Brenda go and introduced himself as the general manager of the Pridgen Plantation, but to call him Preston that he was just one of the many people who were privileged to work and live on the Pridgen Plantation. David shook hands with Preston and introduced his children to him. The children were so impressed by the warm feeling of such true love Mr. Preston had for them that they walked over to him and put their arms around him as he looked down and smiled.

"You sure do have some mighty fine looking youngings, Brenda! Your little girl reminds me of you once upon a time. Oh, they were good days back then! Me and a lot of the folks around here have truly missed you, Brenda! You know we all have been a witness and very privileged to watch you grow up from a sweet little girl to a talented and beautiful young lady all of us plantation folks are mighty proud to know!" Brenda felt humbled as this most gracious older black man whom she had always known as Uncle Preston expresses his feelings. Mr. Preston paused a moment in time and again spoke to Brenda:

"Come on into my shop, Brenda. Things are about the same. We did lose our mama cat last year. You know she was about your age. Here come our new cat Miss Mavis with her little kittens. She loves to show them off to folk." Out of a dark corner of the rather large mill comes Miss Mavis walking like the Queen of Sheba followed by six darling little kittens that looked like toys. Their little undeveloped eyes looked like two black beads glued to the front of each little ball of fur. Brenda speaks to her children:

"Children, be careful, remember they are just little babies. Don't pick them up. Just rub them and let them get to know you." Mavis looks up at Mr. Preston's face while she rubs against his legs. Mavis seems to be on the very thresh hold of human speech as she tries to express her feelings about the situation. The children are on their knees petting the little cats that are convinced that there is no danger. Betty exclaims:

"Oh, Mother, they are so beautiful! They are so sweet." David makes a comment to Preston:

"I bet she eats a lot of rats around this mill!" Mr. Preston comments:

"Oh, I have not seen her try to tackle a grown rat before, but I see her with their young or a mouse every day or so. I suspect that this is the reason why we don't have a lot of rodents around here." Dan asked a question:

"Mr. Preston, do you feed Miss Mavis?"

"Oh, you bet you! I give her and her kittens a little milk and some moist cat food almost every day. If I feed her all the time, she will lose interest in the varmints. I had rather have her around than to have to put out rat poison. I bet there are two or three hundred cats on this here plantation. They help us keep the place varmint free and we lend them a helping hand. We have what is called a no work no eat policy around here." Dan could not understand all that Mr. Preston said, but he would remember what he was told until the day he would be old enough to profit from Mr. Preston's statement. Up above hanging from the ceiling were six large fans on medium speed. On the other side of the building David and his children could see what appeared to be an office with one very large glass window. Dan looks over near the office and notices several black looking ropes or something hanging from the ceiling. When he went over to them to get a closer look, the hair stood up on the back of his neck. He called out to his sister to take a look. Betty speaks:

"How gross! What are they, Dan?" Dan stands and stares amazed. Stuck to the strips of paper hanging from the ceiling were thousands of flies and other insects. David their father asked Brenda why such a primitive method for capturing insects was set up. Brenda smiles and speaks:

"Preston does not want to spray poisons around for the flies."

"Then why does he not buy an electrical bug zapper? I believe it would be a lot more sanitary."

"I don't know, David. I guess that the fly strips are a tradition around here, who knows?" It had been many years since Brenda had smelled the rich healthy earthly aroma of the fresh ground corn, barley, oat, and rye. Against one end of the building were hundreds of cloth bags on pallets filled with animal feed. In another area she noticed large blocks of salt for the cows and horses to lick. David notices a hall and two bathrooms. Near the entrance to the hall are two drink machines and a snack machine. Several men were sitting at tables talking and laughing. One of the tables had a checkers game painted on its top. The playing pieces were in a wooden box on the tabletop. The wall back of the tables was decorated with a huge mounted catfish.

"Brenda, would you take a look at that!" Moments later David and Brenda stood before the mounted fish. A plate below the monster said that the fish, when caught, was one hundred and seventy five pounds and that the operator of the gristmill had caught the fish a year ago. Preston walked up beside David and Brenda and smiled.

"Yea, I caught Old Thorn Face last summer. I swore when I was sixteen years old that I would catch him one day after I lost my two month old puppy to him." David's curiosity is stimulated:

"I don't understand. How on earth did that happen and how do you know it was this particular fish?"

"That oversized catfish had a state tag on it the day the Fish and Game people offered it to Mr. Zeb. It weighted about eighty pounds then. They brought the thing in a special tank on the back of a large truck. The fish is from South America. I understand they can grow large enough to swallow small people." David comments:

"Why did they bring the fish here?"

"The state had originally planned to stock some of the rivers around here with them until it was realized that it would be a bad thing to do. Most of the fish were displayed at the State Fair that year. I have no knowledge where they went after that except for this one. I went fishing with my two month old puppy named Hunter. The puppy saw something in the water and jumped into the pond. I saw the fish coming for him and tried my best to get my puppy before that fish did. That thing came to the surface and I hit at it with my paddles, but it dived under the dog and grabbed a leg and pulled him under. I jumped into the pond with my hunting knife, but there was no use. The pond is over eight hundred acres and deep. Now that dog was not one of my kin, but I was mighty attached to him. I confess I did a little cursing, praying, and swearing. I swore that I'd catch that devil one day and avenge the lost of my puppy." David speaks:

"I am sorry to hear that story; catfish this big need to remain in the Amazon and its tributaries." Gregg and Beard Junior walk in and want to know if they are ready to go see the catfish pond and the fishing lake. Gregg speaks:

"It is going to take awhile to see everything; are you guys ready?" Mr. Preston speaks:

"Oh, don't let me hold you folks. Stop by anytime now you hear! It sho is mighty nice meeting you, Mr. David! I believe that Miss Brenda has a mighty nice young husband!" While Brenda, David, and the children get ready to go back to the pickup trucks, they notice the activity around them and outside on the loading dock. Trucks and even some horse pulled carts were constantly being loaded. Some of the trucks had logos on their sides informing the public that the owners of the trucks owned horse farms. Several children were inside buying some peanut candy from one of Uncle Preston's sons. A large sign above the office door said:

"Honey for Sale." A life size drawing of a young lady holding a jar of honey in her hand that sported the picture of a bee was featured on the office's outside wall. Strawberries were stacked on the floor next to the main entrance door. The smell of the strawberries filled the air around the door. David saw the berries and spoke:

"Brenda, those strawberries look delicious and smell wonderful! Where did they come from?"

"They are most likely the first berries picked this year on the plantation. Don't worry; Mama will be serving us strawberries almost every day until the season is old. I can't wait until Grandmother starts to bake those strawberry cakes; they are mouth watering!"

"Brenda, have you ever tried strawberry pie and rhubarb mixed together?"

"Yes, your mother served me some. It is OK, but the rhubarb was a little tart. I enjoyed the pie." Minutes later everyone was once again in the pickup trucks riding on the main business road through the plantation. Up ahead of them, David and the children see what they believe to be a huge lake. John Wesley speaks:

"David, this up ahead on our left is the famous catfish pond. Looks like the boys are already catching fish." Near the pond is a large fish house. A hundred foot T shaped dock stands offshore in front of the fish house. Several large flat bottomed boats about ten feet wide and thirty feet long full of catfish were docked to unload their catch. Brenda speaks:

"David, the boats go out three times a month. The fishermen spend all day collecting the fish. Most of the fish are less than ten pounds. We sort them by size."

"Brenda, I understand that much larger fish are in the pond."

"Yes, I told you sometime back that there are fish in there fifty pounds or more." Beard Junior speaks:

"David, we basically have three sizes of fish we sell to the public. We have to sell uniformed sized fish to fish markets. Most of the fish are in the five pound category; however, we also sell ten pounders. Larger fish are caught per request. Folks have cookouts and want more fish for their money." David speaks:

"How many tones of fish are caught in this huge pond a month?" Beard Junior speaks:

"We catch about ten tons of the ten pounders and about fifteen tones of the smaller five pounders. A lot of fish of different sizes are never caught. They are there to have babies. We have estimated that there are about three thousand tons of fish in this here eight hundred acre pond. Preston feeds them about five hundred tons of grain every month. Of course, they find the rest of their food on the bottom of the lake."

"How does Preston put out that much corn and other grain into the pond?"

"Let's get out and I will show you, David." Everyone got out of the trucks and walked onto the dock. Brenda and the children watched as the fish were unloaded by the workers. Each boat contained a ton or more of fish. The fish were in large fish traps stacked on the boats. David and Beard Junior walked a few hundred feet beyond the dock via a sidewalk toward a cement ramp that went out into the pond. David sees a small barge about ninety feet long and about twenty five feet wide. He speaks with excitement.

"So this is how the grain is dumped into the pond!" Beard Junior speaks:

"Not dumped, David, more like broadcasted. You see the barge is filled from large trucks that park near it. The trucks are high so they can go into six feet of water. The grain is removed from the trucks via this large portable auger. It takes about one hour to fill the barge. This is no ordinary barge as you can see. The auger which is in the center of the barge, and lowest spot on the bottom of the barge, draws up the grain into the housing up there that looks like a small tower with long arms sticking thirty feet out of its sides. As the auger draws up the corn or whatever, it goes to the top of the tower which rotates at high speed propelling the grain evenly as far away as five hundred and fifty feet from the barge. It all depends on how hard the wind is blowing. It takes almost all day to empty five barge loads. The little barge carries around a hundred tons at a time." David speaks:

"So that means that about seventy tones of grain per hundred acres of pond."

"You have got it, brother!"

"Beard, how are the fish sorted by size?" Beard Junior answers David.

"Well, David, we could do it the stupid way and catch just any size fish and keep the ones we can sell, but that would cost us too much time and it probably would not be good for the fish. What we do is bait fish traps with dead fish, fermented corn, or anything they will eat. The cages have holes in them that allow only a certain size fish inside. The cages have a float or red ball that surfaces when a cage is dropped into the pond. We have eight boats that do the fishing. If you are in a boat that is suppose to pick up five pound fish, the red ball that floats on the surface of the pond will have a black number five on it. The traps are twelve feet long and are four feet wide. These traps collapse for storage purposes. A power boom on each boat stacks the traps and larger booms unload the traps onto trailers at the dock. Each trailer can carry one boatload. The traps are empted, pressure washed, and stacked into the warehouse side of the fish house." David speaks:

"So all of the processing of the fish takes place in the fish house."

"Exactly, David, they are skinned, gutted, and put on ice. From the fish house, our customers show up and purchase the fish."

"Beard, I have only seen a small fraction of this plantation. It reminds me of a multifunctional corporation there are so many things taking place. I never realized that a plantation could be so diversified."

"We try to keep things simple around here, David. I know that it appears complicated around here. I grant you that there are a lot of individual trades and skills worked on this plantation. Few people know all of them, but remember that we have been in business for about two hundred and seventy-five years. Now we only fish this pond eight months out of a year. Every once in awhile we skip a month if we see that the catch for a particular size fish is low. Our objective is to not over populate the pond with too many fish because that is not a healthy way to raise fish for public consumption like a lot of fishpond owners are guilty of. We have the water tested for harmful bacteria generally caused by the presence of too much fish fesses. We could produce several times more fish if we stocked this huge pond to its full capacity, but our family puts public health above profit."

"Beard, let's go back to where Brenda and the children are." The children, Brenda, and their other uncles, John Wesley, and Gregg are watching traps full of smelly catfish being unloaded from the large flat bottomed boats and loaded onto the dock into the awaiting power carts. As soon as a cart is stacked with fish cages, they are driven down the dock into the fish house where workers are waiting to process the fish. David and the children are amazed at the size of the pond at over eight hundred acres. The smell of the water arouses the fishing instincts in David. It had been six months since his last fishing trip. David has been very busy with making arrangements between the University of Boston and the University of North Carolina at Wilmington. Dan is all excited and questions his Uncle Gregg.

"Uncle Gregg, can I go catfish fishing?"

"Dan, there are catfish in this pond that are as big as you are. I believe you would be better off fishing the lake for perch or bass or trout. A catfish can put a hurting on you with their thorns. Don't worry, Dan, you will get a chance to fish. I can't promise you who will take you." Beard Junior speaks to his sister:

"We had better go on to the lake because it is nearly ten o'clock. We want time to allow David and the children the opportunity to enjoy the lake Brenda." Ten minutes elapsed and everyone was in a pickup truck headed for the huge lake that is over twelve and a half miles wide. After fifteen minutes of driving on the dirt road, the lake is sighted partially hidden by a multitude of trees. Beautiful blue and reddish colored Grape Myrtle grew near the road. Behind them closer to the lake, thousands of oak trees stood. Beyond the oak trees guarding the shore of the lake and waist deep into the water itself stood majestic cypress trees. There were millions of wild flowers growing everywhere. Rows of beautiful weeping willows, pine, water oak, popular, gum, and ash are only a sampling of the variety of trees that grow around the lake. The trucks came to a stop and everyone quickly exited them. Dan speaks:

"Wow, it is huge, it is almost like an ocean." Waves over two and a half feet high crashed into the shoreline. No one had to invite David and the children to walk onto the dock that ran for over two hundred and fifty feet out into the lake. At the end of the twenty foot wide walk is a hundred and forty by eighty foot wide double decked pavilion. David and the children can't believe the natural beauty and the craftsmanship of the building. David takes careful notice.

"This place is one of the best examples of highly skilled craftsman-ship I have ever seen! Where did all of this beautiful cedar come from to build this place, Beard?"

"Most of it was cut right here on the plantation, David. We normally do not cut our cedar and never sell it. This place was a grand exception. The pylons are, of course, made out of treated cypress and the decking is made out of oak wood because of its strength and its tendency not to run or split." Everyone walked onto the porch of the first floor and looked across the lake. Dan notices the ornate decor on the railings and speaks out:

"Look, father, look at the beautiful fish carvings on these..."

"They are called railings, son. The railings are attached to the banister. They represent the many kinds of fish that live in this lake." David stares out across the large lake and notices something.

"Brenda, am I seeing things? It looks like an island out there."

"Yes, it is the most beautiful little island you will ever see. It rivals any spot on Earth. We don't have time to go there today, but you will want to visit and carry scuba diving gear when you get to go over to that island. We call the island Paradise."

"So you are saying that it is like a paradise?"

"My folks named it Paradise about a hundred years ago."

"How large is the island, Brenda?"

"Daddy told me that it is about twenty four hundred acres." David exclaims:

"Wow, talking about water front property! To think the island is in the middle of a privately owned lake that is on a privately owned plantation." The smell of the lake and the pavilion's cedar wood excited everyone in the party. The children ran inside the building's first floor to get a look at the beautiful structure. The ceiling has beams that are over a foot thick and about twenty four inches wide. The beams are not machine planed, but were hand planed. David noticed the many beautiful long tables and chairs in the main room.

"Brenda, this place is beautiful!

"David, we use this place for our family gatherings. This is more or less a private area for our people. Several times in the summer and fall, we all come here early of a morning and get in our fishing boats and fish for an hour or two. There have been times we would catch all we could use in much less than an hour. We bring the fish back to the pavilion and clean them to cook. Mama and Grandmother bring along vegetables like cabbage, onions, and carrots for making slaw. We keep most of the other supplies in the kitchen all of the time. Come let's go to the kitchen."

"This is an unbelievable place! What huge pine cabinets! I see you have a large gas range in here, a commercial barbeque pit, and a large skylight that must run thirty feet over the kitchen area." David continued to look around. He noticed the extra large sink with four basins and the extra large counter top covered with granite steel. The refrigerator is a commercial size stainless steel unit.

"Brenda, I want to be here the next time our family meets here!"

"Don't worry, we will all be here. Sometimes we cook catfish here. When we do, we usually do not fish in the lake. We fix the catfish several different ways. I try all of it."

"How many different ways can you cook catfish?"

"We strip the small fish into pieces about six inches long and about an inch wide. We dip the strips into an egg and milk batter. We next have a mixture of fresh cornmeal and flour. The strips are placed into the flour and cornmeal seafood mix and rolled about six or seven times in a hand turned machine for a thick patter."

"What kind of seasoning do you use in the mix?"

"Most of the time we put black pepper, garlic, and salt. I have seen Mother try something different like soul food seasoning or fine ground up lemon peelings in the egg and milk mix. The lemon gives the fish a bit of a zesty flavor. Now my grandfather likes to cook the catfish stew. He takes a fifteen pound catfish and puts it on the gas stove in a large iron pot. He adds several quarts of water, whole onions, carrots, garlic quarters, black pepper, and salt. If Mama or Grandmother have left over homemade biscuits at the house, he will bring them along and put them on top of the stew after it is cooked. The biscuits are allowed to get hot and moist before the stew is served. Brother Gregg is always experimenting with his cooking and he will get a fifteen pound catfish and put it in a large iron pot. I have seen him put a mixture of juices, spices, and vegetables all over the fish before he places it into the oven. On top all over the fish he places chopped ripe tomatoes, green tomatoes, green onion tops and bottoms, whole garlic, black pepper, red pepper, celery seed and a little parsley. He also places a few lemon halves and uses some Cajun seasoning salt.

"Now we do not always eat fish. I remember several times Mama and my grandmother killing and getting chickens ready to bring here the day before our got together. We have regular fried chicken and barbecued chicken. I have seen family members cook deer and barbeque pigs here. Grand Daddy used to hash a raccoon and cook it. It is delicious!" David smiles and speaks:

"What about Opossum?"

"No, David, I can't recall us cooking any, but I am sure that one of my brothers could accommodate you if you are hungry for baked Opossum. I understand that they are good with apples or sweet potatoes. Now, I know that you are joking, but just realize that a lot of the people on our plantation eat Opossum. In fact, they might invite you to a meal you just can't turn down. You would not want to offend them. Daddy and Grand Daddy tell me that it is good if prepared correctly. Uncle Preston who we met at the mill keeps Opossums in cribs. He feeds them good food for several months before he slays them. A lot of the folks raise snapping turtles for the same reason. Now that stuff is good! It tastes like beef, chicken, pork, and other meat flavors. Grand Daddy used to raise them, but he has cut back since he has reached his eighties. Some of the folks on the plantation give him turtles already ready to cook once in awhile. He has been mighty good to them and they are just saying thank you." David remembers that the children and their uncles are on the second floor.

"Brenda, let's go upstairs. I would like to see it. This place is huge!" David sees the children over near the games. On one side of the seventy by forty foot room are games that require no electricity or batteries. A large chess game is marked on the floor. The figures or playing pieces are two feet high and are made out of hollow wood. They are only about twenty pounds each. The game is not a sit down game. The players must work a little to position their playing pieces. Occasionally the older adults will play the game and the young people will push the wheeled figures around to the desired positions. A large checker game occupies one table. The *Game of Life and Monopoly* are on two tables next to the windows.

David walks past several games and sees up on the wall two very impressive dart games. One game has heavy duty darts that require a good bit of skill. The other dart game has a huge seven foot diameter board. Instead of darts, the business ends of the darts are magnetic.

The windows on the front side of the building facing the lake can be opened up by turning hand cranks to allow fresh air into the building. Beautiful leather couches face the lake for people to sit down, relax, and talk.

"David, come over here and look at my family photos." Several hundred large photos hang on the opposite wall David is standing near. The framed photos are historically arranged and include black and white photos of Zeb's parents and even grandparents on fishing trips.

"Brenda, that little girl proudly holding up that Big Mouth Bass looks like you! That is precious! I have seen so few pictures of your childhood. How many pounds did that fish weight?"

"It has been a long time since I caught that fish, but I believe that it was about nine pounds."

"Here is another one of you standing beside a catfish about as big as you were."

"That thing nearly pulled me into the pond! I was holding onto a post at the ramp for dear life crying for help. Daddy came the moment he heard my cry for help. That catfish weighed over thirty-five pounds; a big fish for a little girl in the fifth grade!"

"Here you are with a black lab. What a beautiful dog!"

"Uncle Roy Henry gave that lab to my parents the day I was born. Her name was Miss Blackie. She lived until I was fifteen years old. I will never forget her love and friendship. Miss Blackie shadowed my brothers and me everywhere we went. She would go down to the swimming hole with us and swim. She once killed a Rattlesnake that was in the area. Daddy had a nice place for her to sleep and stay warm on the porch. When she got older, her eyes were not very good and her legs were a little stiffer, but when we kids would get up from the breakfast table and head out to play in the yard, we would always be greeted by Miss Blackie. When she passed away, I thought that we would never get over it. She was a family member whose love was as pure as the gold on the streets of Heaven!"

"Where was she buried, Brenda?"

"Daddy buried her in a special pet cemetery next to our family's cemetery. Daddy told us all that she deserved the honor, that Miss Blackie was bound to meet us one day in Heaven because Heaven wouldn't be perfect without her." Brenda could not help, but to feel emotionally sad at the loss of Miss Blackie even though it had been about twenty years ago."

"Brenda, I had a Boston Terrier. He followed me everywhere I went. We had a nice neighborhood and old Pop Eye played with my friends and me and once defended us kids from a man who stalked children. Pop Eye bit his hand and when the man turned and ran, he took off after him and bit the bottom of his pants ripping off a nice piece. A policeman recognized Pop Eye and us boys. He questioned the man and eventually arrested him. My parents and my friends' parents were called by the police and were informed about the man. He was not supposed to be around young children. He got into some more trouble and we did not see him again." Brenda speaks:

"Isn't it amazing that Pop Eye sensed that you kids were in danger!"

"Yes, because when the police later questioned us children. We told them that the man did not hurt Pop Eye or one of us. He only offered us a big bag of candy and asked us to go to his house where he promised to serve us some ice cream." Brenda listened amazed at this story that David had never shared with her. David once again spoke:

"I have a picture of Pop Eye and all seven of my friends from a large *Boston Tribune* clipping. A reporter came by and took our picture with Pop Eye. He was considered a dog hero. When he was eighteen years old, my parents were advised to put him to sleep by our family's veterinarian. Old Pop Eye was blind and in a lot of pain from arthritis to diabetes. We invited my friends over and their parents for the funeral."

"Don't tell me you had a real funeral for your pet?"

"We really did and Pop Eye was buried at a famous pet cemetery not far from our home. He has a small headstone with his picture on it and a beautiful poem on it. The footstone has a write up about the way he rescued us kids many years ago. An animal minister actually preached a twenty minute sermon." Brenda is amused, but saddened because the dog was precious to David's family.

"David, what did the preacher say?"

"He told us about the importance of family pets. He said that good pets were more than just something to play with, but close friends that teach children responsibility and love. He said that pets are the source of precious childhood memories when we grow up and assume the responsibilities of adulthood. He told us that love is from God and our dear pets are manifestations of God's love for us. He finished the sermon by praising Pop Eye for rescuing us kids from a child stalker." Brenda reflects on what David shared with her.

"Yes, David, our pets are truly a big part of our lives. I believe especially when we are children. I have heard stories about how family pets have saved entire families by waking them up when their houses were on fire."

"Yes, Brenda, there are many books of true accounts about pets saving people's lives. Often they lose their own lives in their efforts to save their human friends." David looks at the other photos on the wall. He is amazed to see his wife's grandfather when he was a young boy and man.

"Brenda, I see that Mr. Zeb was born in 1944. That would make him young enough to be a baby boomer, how about that!"

"Yes, David, and his father who is our kid's great-great-grandfather, served during World War II. His father before him would be old enough to be our kid's great-great-great grandfather, served in World War 1."

Six

Brenda's Childhood Friends Visit the Plantation

John Wesley walks up to David and Brenda and speaks:

"Brenda, Ma called and let me know that a bunch of our old friends are at the house to see you." Brenda speaks:

"I have not seen most of those guys in over ten years! It is hard to believe. I guess they have changed a lot. David let's get the children and go visit them!" Thirty minutes later Brenda and her Boston family rode into the yard. Brenda's childhood friends were all outside waiting for her. Except for being a little taller and heavier, Brenda saw no earthshaking changes in her friends. The first person to grab Brenda was Tommy Cobb. He was amazed at how beautiful and polished Brenda looked.

"Brenda, you look like the Queen of Sheba! It is mighty good to see you again! I feel like more of a brother to you than a friend. How long has it been since we laid eyes on each other?"

"Tommy, it has been ten years. I saw all of you guys in Atkinson walking together."

"Oh, that is right. We were going to the new restaurant. All of us try to keep in touch. Actually all of us live around here, but we have to make an effort to get together. Brenda, here is my wife Joann and my son Tommy Junior. He will be ten years old next month." Brenda and Joann speak to each other. Brenda tells Tommy Junior that Dan is also ten years old.

"Remember me, Brenda?"

"Betty Baker Edwards! I could never forget you!" Betty and Brenda hug.

"Brenda, where did all the years go? I can't believe it; it is scary! It seems like only yesterday we were upstairs in that big house playing with your dolls or swimming at the swimming hole." Dan hears the words swimming hole and turns to Tommy and speaks.

"Mr. Tommy, did you ever find your pants at the swimming hole?"

"Brenda, you have been talking about me!" Brenda's face turns a little red before she speaks.

"Dan, you should not have asked that question!"

"It's, OK, sure I found those old cut off jeans. I didn't have a proper swimming suit back in those days so I cut off a pair of jeans that were a little too large for me." Brenda speaks:

"Allow me to introduce my husband, David, my daughter, Betty, and Dan my son." Everyone acknowledged David and the children. Johnny Wallace speaks up:

"I believe, I read something a year ago about you, David. You are supposed to be the assistant department head at UNCW's science department."

"Yes, that is correct, Johnny. I will start my main duties next January."

"Wonderful, we will all have time to get to know each other! Brenda, we could all reenact the good old days and take a swim at the swimming hole. It sure would bring back a lot of memories!"

"I don't know if it is safe now. It may be completely grown up. Our constant visits there years ago in the summer months kept the snakes away and the path free of undergrowth."

"Don't worry, it has not changed, we still use it all summer."

"You didn't tell me that, Gregg!"

"I didn't think it mattered. Even Ma and Pa use it." Brenda speaks:

"Well, Johnny, as soon as it gets nice and hot, I believe we should all take a hike down to that swimming hole! Is the rope still on that limb?" John Wesley speaks:

"There is a rope there, but not the one we used as children. This one is much heavier." Brenda speaks:

"Thank you for that information, John. If it were not for my family, I could wish that I could go back in time and start all over again. We had so much fun back in those days. How blessed we are!" Mattie walks down the steps and approaches Brenda with a message. Brenda turns toward Mattie realizing someone sent her.

"Miss Lillian says she has some cake and ice cream for everyone."

"Thank you, Mattie, I guess everyone has heard." A few minutes later, Brenda, David, their two children, five friends, three brothers and the parents and grandparents are sitting at the table. Mattie and Lillian pick up two huge strawberry cakes and place them on the table. The smell of the moist cakes with freshly picked strawberries is almost breath taking. While Lilly and her daughter-in-law Lillian pass out plates, napkins, and utensils, Mattie goes out into the porch and takes two gallons of homemade pecan ice cream from the refrigerator and brings it to the table. Brenda looks across the table and sees her dear friends and feels almost like a child again. It had been too long since she had sat down at the table with them! Life is not fair in many ways! Lillian speaks:

"Now you young people eat all you want because there is plenty more where this came from." Zeb speaks to Lilly and Lillian after he puts a folk full of new strawberries into his mouth.

"I believe that you gals are getting better every year! This stuff is wonderful! I can enjoy this natural pleasure as much as ever!" Lillian speaks:

"Well, thank you, Zeb. They sure beat those store bought berries!"

"When have you eaten store bought strawberries, Lillian?"

Well, sir, I have not eaten all of my meals here on the plantation. I have eaten strawberries at school and restaurants."

"That is true, Lillian. We had better enjoy them while they last!" Lillian speaks once again to her Father-in-law Zeb.

"We could have a few rows in the greenhouse."

"I don't know, Lillian. You can grow what you want in there, but I believe they are worth waiting for. Things seem to taste better when they are in season." Brenda's childhood friends stayed all day with her and promised to return for a dip in the swimming hole in the summer months and to see each other as occasion permitted.

A month passed by quickly. One day after breakfast Mr. Zeb asked David to go with him to the Herb Garden to gather herbs for medicine. David was informed that Lillian and Lilly were getting ready to fix up some medicine.

"David, I thought that you might want to help me with the medical herbs and you can help Lilly and Lillian later or do as you please."

"I believe that will be just great, Mr. Zeb. Brenda told me about the medical herbs and compounds. I was hoping for a chance to see this." Fifteen minutes later, David and Mr. Zeb were inside the herb garden standing in the drying house.

"David, I make sure that I name and date all of the roots and leaves I dry. As you can see, I put all of the cures in these large jars."

"Where did these hundreds of beautiful jars come from, Mr. Zeb?"

"I believe that most of them were ordered by my great grandmother. These are real medicine jars."

"Mr. Zeb, this place reminds me of the shops I saw in China some years ago. I took a tour with Brenda and some friends from Boston. The physician is the druggist in most cases. Patients tell the physician what they want and he pulls out a drawer and gets out leaves or maybe roots. I saw them also sell natural minerals that are used to prepare compounds with. The doctor carefully weights out the cures and writes the instructions on the bag he puts the prescriptions into. Sometimes a patient goes for an examination, but I believe most of the old school doctors do house calls."

"I am not a doctor, David. Oh, I recon I could put together a thing or two for most common ailments, but I let Lilly and Lillian take care of that department. We have been doing it this way for centuries. Years ago people in general knew more about their bodies and how to take care of themselves. For decades in our country and what I call the West, folks lost that knowledge and probably started depending too much on professional doctors for every little problem. Now don't get me wrong, doctors are very important. I am sure we possess more knowledge around here than average folks. Just like any trade, we make mistakes, but we learn from them. Lilly and Lillian read all kinds of books about natural cures. We have Medical Board doctors to stop by once in awhile that tell Lilly and Lillian that they are really doctors and should be recognized as such. Lilly and Lillian have no interest in any kind of recognition. They just want to keep us all healthy. Lilly tells me that she probably could be considered a student of the Eclectic School of Medicine."

"I am not aware of such a school, Mr. Zeb."

"I understand. Mostly everything Lilly and Lillian use for their cures are derived from the vegetable kingdom. They do not use manmade chemicals of any kind. Now that is not to say that we do not use some natural minerals in our cures. We use sulfur, silver nitrate as antiseptics for example. Of course, there are some plants that can serve as antiseptics. We use something as simple as baking soda or apple vinegar for dozens of common problems. The trick in any cure is to first of all be able to identify what is wrong with the patient. You can go to all kinds of medical schools for twenty years and know all of the fancy names and still not be necessarily exceptionally good at identifying your patient's problem. A fine young doctor in Burgaw has asked Lilly or Lillian several times for assistance. I have a lot of respect for him. Lilly and Lillian don't mind asking him either. Just as long as both sides are reasonably humble and keep their eyes and ears open for what is best for their patients. Another thing is, of course, what herbs to administer and the dosage; too much or too little can cause a lot of trouble. Our herbs are dated. We get rid of herbs that lose their medical value.

"In these jars are what we call Linctures. We use only in season fresh green herbs that are bruised well and put into a jar like this. We cover the herbs with a good strong whiskey we purchase at an ABC store. Sometimes we use one part water to three parts alcohol. We cork the jar and let it stand about two weeks."

"Do you always use alcohol, Mr. Zeb?"

"No, sir, we also use water. We use about half an ounce, of whatever, leaves, bark, and roots to one pint of water. We boil the ingredients in water and cork the jars." David looked and saw hundreds of marked and dated jars. These jars were subdivided into classes of medicines.

"David, I know that I can't teach you everything about making medicine today. I need to soon get the herbs Lilly and Lillian need. They cook up their medicine or use alcohol as I explained. They then bring the medicine out here for storage. We do keep some medicines inside. The Alternatives are the herbs we usually keep in the house under lock. I think of them as our tone up herbs. They also help keep the body regulated. Those herbs often have more than one purpose. One herb can serve as a tonic, laxative, stimulant or diuretic. Notice some of the names of the plants: Mandrake, Poke, Yellow Dock, and the Black Cohosh. Back of each medicine jar is a color photo of the herbs in the jar. The information describes the plants and their medical use. Look over here. Here we have what we call Anodyners. These are painkillers."

"Yes, sir, I see a jar of Hyoscyamus or what is known as Hen bone. I see Poison Hemlock, Belladonna, Camphor, and Hops; how about this!"

"What are you looking at, fellow?"

"I am looking at Anthetmintics. I have never heard the terminology. It says on the picture that the word means 'against a worm,' the herbs are used to kill worms in the human body. Santonin is used to get rid of pin worms when it is combined with Podophyllin."

"What is Podophyllin, Mr. Zeb?"

"That stuff comes from the root stock of the Mandrake. The Santonin comes from wormwood. I get dried flower heads of Santonic and extract the wormwood that serves as a vermifuge or agent that expels worms and trouble makers in the body." David continued to look at jar after jar of herbs in various forms. Drugs like Yellow Jessamine, Yellow Lady Slipper, Logwood, Witch Hazel and Stone Root to name but a few.

"David, here are the herbs Lilly and Lillian need, would you mind delivering them? I sure would appreciate the effort!"

"Not at all, I am truly amazed at the medical knowledge you folks have, Mr. Zeb." David helped Lilly and Lillian for several hours preparing home cures that were getting depleted. Lillian speaks to David:

"David, we are going to have a party of a sort at about seven tomorrow night. I have told Brenda already. I have invited friends and family to be with us. We are a little late this month in having a crawdad party."

"Mrs. Lillian, I have tried crawdads before and I can tell you that they have as much flavor as Maine Lobster. The only problem I have with them is they are very small."

"Well, ours are a lot bigger than most. We have been raising them in the fishing lake's ditches for centuries. Anyway, Roy Henry and about eight young men are going to set hundreds of traps this afternoon. Roy wants to know if you would like to go with them."

"I would love to go with them!"

"I will tell Brenda where you will be at. I will fix you a lunch and a nice cooler of fresh homemade lemonade." Thirty minutes later what sounded like horses and wagons was heard outside of the kitchen area.

"David, I would suspect that Roy and the boys have just arrived. Here is the lunch Lillian fixed for you."

"Thank you, Mrs. Lilly. I believe that Lillian said that the work will take about three hours." David walked onto the porch and saw, five, four wheeled, open carriages, commonly called buckboards. All five drivers pulled on the reins and yelled out whoa to their mules. Roy Henry's buckboard was in the lead. All of the wagons had collapsible crayfish traps in the back and long poles with hooks at their ends. When David walked beside Henry's buckboard, Uncle Henry took his pipe out of his mouth and spoke to David.

"I believe that you are the young gentleman who married Brenda. My name is Roy Henry. Most of the younger folk around here just call me Uncle Henry. You look like one of the younger folks. Climb on board and let's take a ride to the fishing lake." David grabbed the side of the buckboard and climbed on board.

"Thank you for stopping, Uncle Henry. My name is David Smith."

"Yes, sir, Mr. Smith, or should I call you, Doctor Smith?"

"Oh, no, David will be just fine. I expect folks to use that title when I am at school."

"I understand. You have got to get your respect!"

"Well, I guess you might say that, Uncle Henry. It just lets people know who is supposed to be grading the papers. My classrooms are like a ship. When someone walks on board, I am the captain." David smiles at Uncle Henry. Uncle Henry smiles back.

"Well, today, you are on my buckboard and those boys on those other buckboards work for me. So I am Uncle Henry right now."

"I understand, sir. I have been looking forward to meeting you. Brenda told us about you and a lot of the other people living on this plantation."

"We think mightily highly of Miss Brenda. She is all of us folks little girl. I watched her grow up. It sho has been different around here since she left for the big city of Boston. When she left, it seemed like the flowers were taken out of the vase. That gal knows how to do most anything around here! She even took over my job catching crawdads one time when I got down in bed. Yes, sir, that gal knows how to pop the whip. The boys minded her just like they mind old Uncle Henry here. She has helped set the catfish traps and knows how to clean them for market. Her brothers tell me she can operate all of the heavy logging equipment."

"What, I didn't realize that!"

"Yes, sir, Mr. David, I spects she does not want to brag about it. Her Grandfather Zeb said that Brenda reminded him of himself, except, Brenda is a lot prettier. I have seen her make horseshoes, shoe the horses, and even run the feed store many a time when Preston was too busy to manage it."

"Uncle Henry, how does Preston manage to run this huge plantation and the grist mill at the same time?"

"He has got help now. His three boys take care of a lot of the work on the plantation. The office not only is for the gristmill, but for the entire plantation. Mr. Beard spends about half his time in the office also. Don't discount him. He can do it all. He probably spends the other half of his time in Atkinson and Burgaw overseeing the hardware stores."

"Uncle Henry, I am told that he wants to open up four or five hardware stores in the Wilmington area. How is he going to manage that?"

"I am not sure. His boys are about too busy to help him. The boys manage the logging camp and most of the farming."

"How many acres of farm land do they manage, Mr. Henry?"

"I believe I heard Beard Junior say about eight thousand acres. They grow several kinds of grains like, corn, rye, and oaks. They grow hay, cotton, and beans. Preston's sons manage the orchards and such things as peanuts and sweet potatoes."

"Uncle Henry, beside the crayfish ditches what do you manage around here?"

"I do a little of this and that. I take care of the honeybees. I keeps up the hand tools. You come by my shop one day and you will see that old Uncle Henry is plenty busy. I make handles for axes and all kinds of tools. I make thousands of handles every year for Beard's hardware stores. When Miss Lilly or Miss Lillian need their knives sharpens, they send Mattie over with a wheel barrel full of big butcher knives and vegetable choppers. I grow the sugar cane and make about a thousand barrels of molasses. I have to make the barrels also. Once in awhile Beard lucks up and finds a truck load of barrels for me so I won't have to make them."

"What kind of wood are the barrels made out of?"

"Usually they are made from White Oak Wood. Now why don't you come by Uncle Henry's shop? I will show you what is cooking." David laughs and is pleased at how Henry expresses himself.

"I am going to do just that, Uncle Henry! Yes, sir, I believe I could learn a thing or two if I hang out around that shop of yours."

"Well, I don't know how much of it you can carry to school with you, but around here we survive by the knowledge us plain simple folks possesses." A little noise or disturbance is heard back of David and Henry's wagon.

"You boys cut the foolishness out. We ain't here to play. You fellows should have played enough at home when you were younger. We need to get there and back. Mr. Zeb is counting on us catching enough crawdads for tomorrow." David looks back and sees one of the young men getting up out of the back of the buckboard floor he is riding in. Another young man from the wagon back of his tosses him his hat. He looks at David and smiles as innocently as an angel. It required about an hour to ride the wagons to the backside of the fishing lake. The backside of the lake is over fourteen miles away, and it takes time to get there. If it had been a cloudy day it would have probably been impossible to see it from a mile away behind a forest of trees, but the bright sun overhead made the lake look like a mirror sending rays of sunshine in all directions. David had heard about the crayfish ditches, but he was not prepared for the size of them. The ditches were cut from the lake. Each of the twenty-five ditches is fifteen feet wide at their bottom and has about two and a half feet of water in them. Waterweeds grow in the ditches and provide habitat for the crayfish and whatever small creatures live in the fishing lake. There is a ramp on the end of each ditch so that boats can be lowered into them with ease.

"David, all of these flat crawdad traps are already baited with chicken parts and whatever we could find. We put the meat into cheesecloth bags so it will not make a mess or get spilled on the way here. The crawdads smell the chicken in the bags inside of the traps and go through the trap doors. Tomorrow when we come back here we will use the poles with the hooks on them to grab the traps. We will have special gloves on when we sort out the crawdads. We throw away all of them except the ones that are six inches or longer. We will bring along a large ice cooler tomorrow. We can put about seven hundred pounds of these critters in it. The ice will not touch them. It will calm them down until we get back to the barn where the party will be held. We have set up large butane gas burners in the barn. Large stainless steel pots with water and seasoning will be set to boil when folks start coming in for the party."

"So all of the crayfish are boiled like shrimp?"

"Most of them are. Gregg likes to put about forty pounds of them in the oven after the outside shells are removed. He puts them in a large metal pan and puts a mix all over them. They are a little spicy, but people like them. Most of the folks like them dipped in a butter sauce. Mrs. Lillian likes to chop them up and put them in Cajun style rice. That stuff is real good, Mr. David!"

An hour later the boats were in the ditches. Each boat had a crew of two people. David and Uncle Henry walked while the boat crews placed the traps into the ditches. The traps were strung out for nearly half a mile in each ditch. There were so many crayfish in the water swimming or walking around that David wondered why they were bothering with traps. He felt that nets with handles on them would be just as effective.

"David, we have tried several ways to catch these little critters, but the traps seem to work out the best for us. At night during mating season, these crayfish or crawdads as us country folks calls them visit each other. Thousands, maybe millions of them, leave the ditches and crawl from one ditch to another. There are twenty-five ditches running side of each other on this side of the lake. Each ditch is half a mile long. That makes room for a lot of courting! We used to grab them up while they crawled around on the ground, but we decided they needed to make babies more than we needed to eat them." One more hour passed by and all of the boats were back at the ramps where they would be tied to post until they would be used once again to retrieve the traps full of crawdads the next day.

"David, it is past time to eat. The boys and I brought our dinner. We would be glad to share ours with you."

"No, sir, Mr. Henry, Mrs. Lillian prepared dinner for me. I believe she put fried chicken, potato salad, slaw, and a piece of pie in my basket."

"Sounds good! I don't know what everyone brought along. Two of the young men working today are my sons. My wife fixed us catfish stew with cornbread and strawberry cake. I usually bring a gallon or two of sweet tea along. Now we will be back out here with my crew about two tomorrow. I will have help tomorrow to take the traps out of the water and sort the crawdads for size. You are welcomed to come along tomorrow."

"I appreciate the offer, but I believe that I would like to see some of the plantation tomorrow. I am not sure what kind of transportation is available for me around here. My SUV is too large for that." David and Uncle Henry and his helpers go back to the plantation's mansion to drop

David off. After supper that night, David asks about a small truck or something so that he could ride around and see the plantation and the neighborhood. Zeb gives David permission to use one of his small trucks. Brenda, Mattie, and the children decide to go fishing on the lake in a rather large fishing boat while David drives around the plantation the next day.

Brenda walks into the kitchen area where her mother is working and speaks:

"Mother, I am thinking about carrying the kids on a fishing trip at the fishing lake tomorrow. Do you know if my old fishing poles are still at the pavilion?"

"As far as I know there should be several cane poles already with hooks on their lines. We still raise earthworms around here. If you want to, you can use them."

"I believe I will use artificial worms because of the children."

"Why don't you take Mattie along with you? She could help you watch out for Betty."

"I will ask her if she would like to go with us. Does she have a cane pole, mother?"

"Sure, Mattie never gives out of cane poles. If she needs one, she will visit Roy Henry's farm and get one from Roy. Zeb has showed her how to spray the poles with a waterproof lacquer so that the poles will last more than one year."

"Mother, I will need transportation. The SUV is not practical and probably should not be used for a fishing trip."

"You take my truck then. There are two large coolers in the pantry at the pavilion. We put in an ice making machine last year. I don't know if you saw it or not, Brenda?"

"No, I did not go into the pantry, but I did go to the kitchen." Lillian and Brenda heard a noise on the porch and Mattie walks into the dining area with Betty and Dan following her giggling.

"Those bad children of yours are playing tricks on me. I am going to have to cut switches." Mattie was shaking her head and trying to suppress a smile. Brenda speaks up:

"What are you guys up to?" Dan speaks:

"Nothing, Mother, we were just having a little fun that is all."

"What did you guys do to have fun?"

"We just knocked on Mattie's door and ran and hid ourselves." Mattie was laughing and coughing and pointing a finger at Dan and Betty and spoke:

"I knowed it was you two; I just knowed you guys were trying to trick me." Brenda and Lillian could not help but to laugh a little. Brenda questions Mattie:

"Mattie, how did you realize that Dan and Betty were knocking on your door?"

"I opened the doe and I heard them in the dog house on the porch so I went back of it and hit it hard on the top with a broom handle and Betty started screaming. I told them that I knowed that they were trying to trick old Mattie." Mattie started laughing and pointing at Brenda. "You used to like to trick old Mattie too! Yes, I remember that time you and your brother Beard Junior knocked on my doe and when I opened it, Lau I thought that I was going to have a heart attack. Mattie looks at Brenda's children and continues. "Your mother put a huge spider wed across my doe with a spider on it. I opened that doe and I saw that huge spider as big as my hands and I got a broom and I hit that thing something furiously!" Brenda bowed her head a little while shaking it and smiling as if she had been caught at something bad! Lillian speaks up:

"Why, Mattie, you didn't tell me that Brenda and Beard Junior did that!"

"Yes, ma'am, I thought I was going to die. I broke the handle I was hitting so hard!" Lillian shakes her head while smiling and looking at Brenda.

"So now I know what happened to that broom handle!" Mattie did not say anything, but moved her head in a nervous twitch, as was her custom. Her eyes were shining brightly with pleasure as she recalled something that happened when Brenda and Beard Junior were children. Betty looked at her grandmother with a serious look and speaks:

"Grandmother, does that mean that you have to spank Mother for being bad?"

"Well, it is a little late for that. I believe that the statutory legal limit has run out for that crime." Betty looks puzzled as she looks up at her grandmother. "No, dear, I don't spank your mother, she is now a big girl." Brenda chuckled a little and spoke:

"I had almost forgotten about putting that plastic web and spider across Mattie's door! Mattie you beat that thing like it was a rattlesnake! You do understand that it was a toy?"

"Yes, Miss Brenda, but I didn't know then cause it looked for real!" Lillian speaks up:

"Well, there is nothing wrong with a little fun and teasing just as long as no one gets hurt. All of us have done it a time or two in our childhood. Shucks, Zeb still likes to play tricks on me once in awhile.

Why I bet it was not over six months ago I walked on the porch at night to sit in a rocking chair and all of a sudden the thing started rocking on its own. Now I didn't know what to make of it because the wind was dead as could be. If a cat or some varmint had been on it and jumped when it saw me, the rocker would probably have rocked for a second or two at the most, but that chair just kept on rocking. I was beginning to think that I had just stepped into the Twilight Zone or that one of Beard's kin decided to come back from the grave and pay me a visit. A minute or so later, Zeb could not suppress his delight and started laughing ever so low. I realized who it was and called out to him. I said:

"Now, Zeb Pridgen, you stop that foolishness, you hear! I know that it is you." He walks out of the dark corner on the bottom front porch just a laughing. He had tied a very thin black line on the rocker so I would not be able to see it." Brenda looked surprised.

"I did not know Grandfather played tricks on you, Mother!"

"Yes, he used to play then on Lilly, but he told me that he did not want to scare her too bad that she did not have as many years to spare as I have." Brenda speaks:

Do you kids want to go fishing tomorrow in the fishing lake?" Both of the kids started jumping up and down all excited at the invitation.

"Well, I guess the answer is yes. Mattie, would you like to go with us?" Mattie looked at Mrs. Lillian for an answer and Lillian speaks to Mattie.

"Go ahead, Mattie, you can help look after the children. Are you going to use a boat, Brenda?"

"Yes, I thought that we would have a better chance and would get to see more of the lake in a boat."

"Well, then, there are life preservers and whatever you guys need already in the boat. Carry a telephone with you so that you can call someone if there is trouble. That lake is big and it can get rough as you know out there if a storm suddenly appears." That night while everyone was in their bedrooms, David and Brenda talked.

"Brenda, I enjoyed riding with Uncle Roy Henry to the ditches. I believe I will take a little tour of the plantation tomorrow for five or six hours. There are a lot of things I would like to see. I asked your father for a truck."

"David, I am going to take the kids fishing tomorrow on the lake. Mattie is going to go with me; she can help watch out for the children."

"Are you going to fish off the pier?"

"No, I want to use one of the fishing boats. It will afford us a better chance to catch fish and all of us to enjoy the lake. Mother tells me that life jackets, bait, tackle, and ice are at the pavilion. I will carry some ice along, but I am going to use the boat that has a well. We will be able to keep the fish alive." David speaks:

"Who is going to gut and scale them?"

"I am not worried about that. If I have to, I can handle that. I feel sure that Mother and Mattie will help. Now we will not eat the fish until tomorrow at dinner. Remember that tomorrow we will have the crayfish party at seven." David speaks:

"Brenda, are you guys going to come back here for dinner?"

"No, we will start our fishing adventure somewhere between nine thirty and ten tomorrow morning. I don't want to get up too early with the children. We will stay about three or four hours."

"Are you guys going on the island?"

"No, David, we will probably pass by it, but there will be no time for a tour."

Seven

Brenda takes the Children Fishing. David Visits Uncle Roy Henry's Shop.

The next morning came with high hopes and great expectations for Brenda, the children, and Mattie. Mattie was all excited and she had a straw hat on. Mattie had already placed her two cane poles into the back of the double cab pickup truck Brenda was to drive. Before David could leave the house, he received a phone call from Boston University informing him that the exploration submarine had been released by the University of Boston and that he would be needed to sign some legal documents and handle the shipment of the submarine nick named *the Sea Explorer* to UNCW's marine science department's holding pen. David learns that he needs to be at the University of Boston in seven days. He calls Doctor Fletcher at UNCW's science department to let him know about the news. When David gets through with the second conversation, he walks down the stairs and realizes that Brenda, Mattie, and his children are gone. David gets into the pickup Mr. Beard loaned him and prepares to enjoy a self guided tour of part of the plantation.

David is impressed with the beauty of the great magnolia trees that surround the great house. These trees were the giant form of magnolia with over sized green leaves and over sized flowers. Thousands of birds evidently used the trees for their favorite place because their voices charmed David's ears. It sounded like a bird sanctuary. Farther out from the giant magnolia trees are huge live oak trees David estimated to be nearly eight hundred years old. He felt fortunate to have the rare privilege to enjoy these great trees that were old when the first people crossed the Atlantic to settle in this vast new country. David decided to follow the main road that links up with several heavy duty wooden bridges. The third bridge he crossed is the first bridge one crosses when driving toward the mansion. The bridge is the first bridge he and his family first saw the teenager black boys on that were fishing.

When he nears the bridge, David notices that only one young boy is fishing. He appears to be about fourteen or fifteen years old. He has a rather large straw hat on and blue jeans that are rolled up half way between his ankles and his knees. Leaning against the railing of the bridge are two spare poles. There is a tackle box on the rail and a knife that is standing up with its head buried into the wooden railing. David stops the truck and lowers the passenger window with the power window control so that he can speak.

"Having any luck?"

"Yes, sir, I have already caught seven perch. Ma will be glad because she has been wanting a mess of fish. She has been too busy to go fishing here lately. She has been freezing vegetables for two weeks now. Ma told me that I could help her by catching supper for her." David speaks:

"Well, I am glad you are having good luck. I am going to try and fish one of these days before I forget how!"

"You are welcomed to use one of my poles. I have plenty of worms mister."

"I am tempted guy, but I promised myself that I was going to see some more of this plantation."

"You must be Miss Brenda's husband!"

"You are right!"

"Yes, sir, everyone has been talking about Brenda coming back from Boston with her family. It sure is good to meet you, sir! My name is John Henry. My father is Roy Henry."

"Yes, I met your father yesterday. I went with him and two of your brothers and some other young men to watch them lay crayfish traps. In fact, your father invited me to go by his shop."

"Well, you are not far from it. Turn left on the next road. His shop is about two thousand feet from where we stand."

"Is he there?"

"Yes, sir, he will not work there as long as usual. He and his crew are supposed to go back to the ditches on the other side of the fishing lake and bring in the traps so they can sort the crawdads by size. He will leave at about two this afternoon and be back at the barn where they are going to have the party at about six o'clock."

"How many pounds of crawdads do they usually catch, John?"

"I believe about seven hundred pounds. They fill the big cooler up and the rest go into smaller coolers Pa brings along in case they need them. The party is for the Pridgens, but our family will get enough crawdads to last for a week or more."

"I will see you later, John." David turned left and went down a dirt road for nearly half a mile and saw an old country dwelling at the end of the road. The woods on both sides of the road are thin and most of the trees are small oaks, hickory, and a few small pine trees. David could see huge old charred stumps here and there in the woods that represented the remains of a forest that had been cut down a generation or two in time.

The house was a plain, but a sturdy unpainted structure that was probably a century old. The clapboards on the side of the dwelling appeared to be constructed from cypress wood. A few azalea bushes are on both sides of the house in full bloom. A large short live oak tree stands about a hundred feet from the house. A swing hangs from an unusually large limb that is almost parallel to the ground. Still farther back are several dozen tall poles that looked like old light or power poles. Attached to the poles are scores of Martin Bird houses that are made from large gourds. An old oversized outhouse stands two minutes walking distance from the house. A chicken wire fence surrounds the outhouse. Back of the outhouse are red clustered Cannas Lilies that average five feet tall. David had noticed that every old abandoned outhouse he had observed in the South had Cannas Lilies growing around them. It could be a tradition. Fifty feet from the outhouse he noticed a large brown mule hitched to a two wheeled cart that was tied to a tree.

Roy Henry's two oldest sons saw David and recognized him as the guy who had gone with them the day before to the ditches to set the traps for the crawdads. Tolson the next to the oldest spoke first:

"Morning, sir, I hope you are having a blessed day!"

"I can't complain, I guess you fellows are going back to the ditches today to get the crawdads?"

"Yes, sir, Pa will be leaving about one o'clock this afternoon. Are you going to go, Mr. David?"

"Not today, I have been wanting to drive around the plantation. It is totally new to me."

"It is a big place alright. If you get lost just follow the signs. All of the roads eventually lead to the main road this side of Highway 117."

"I don't plan to go that far. I just want to see the part on this side of Black River today. How do I get to your father's workshop?"

"Turn around and go back to the big tree with the swing tied to a limb and turn left again. You can't miss the shop on the left side of the road."

"Thanks, I will see you later." While David is having one of the best times of his life exploring a real functional Southern Plantation that is over flowing with a living past, Brenda has just stopped the pickup her and her companions are riding in. The children are borderline controllable they are so excited about the prospect of actually getting into a boat and going out on a big crystal clear lake with their mother and Mattie who is so much fun to be around. The truck is parked and everyone goes into the pavilion to get the fishing poles that are stored in a closet and other supplies.

"Mother, what boat are we going to use?"

"We are going to use the one made out of stainless steel because it is wide and has a flat bottom. Be careful, Betty, I want you to sit here in front of me. Dan, you sit on the other side of Mattie. Remember fishing hooks are dangerous. Fish only on your side and watch your poles; we don't need someone getting hurt today." The children acknowledged their mother's warning.

"Mattie, I believe that Dan will be OK. He has fished lots of times, but watch out and don't let him hit you with his pole."

"I will look out fer him just like I used to look out fer you, Brenda. I remember that time you caught that big old fish and didn't know how to get it off the hook!" Brenda frowned and then smiled when she recalled what Mattie was talking about.

"Mattie, you are so precious! I honestly forgot about that! Yes, I remember now. I was so small in those days. I looked at that big fish and I was afraid to touch it. I remember you taking the hook out of its mouth for me." Betty speaks:

"Mother, why didn't you bring worms like Mattie?"

"Honey, when you get a few years older, you can fish with live worms and crickets. It is a lot easier for both of us if we fish with these artificial worms; they look and feel like the real ones so we should be able to fool the fish."

"Mother, why are these worms so slimy. They are a little hard to handle." Brenda answers:

"I believe they are really made from a bean protein. The bag says here that the liquid they are in attracts fish. They may actually be better than real worms; we will find out in a few minutes." Brenda started the motor and the seventy five horse powered Johnson outboard roared as she shifted into first gear. Dan looks around impressed with the boat.

"Mother, this is really a nice fishing boat, how big is it?"

"I believe that your great grandfather Zeb told me that it is twenty six feet long and eight feet wide. It makes a good boat to carry family out in because of the double bottom and the nice hand rails."

"What is that large box in the middle of the boat?"

"Son, that is a fish well. Be careful and walk over to it and open up the lid."

"There is water in it and holes in its bottom. We are going to sink!" Brenda could not help but to laugh.

"No, Dan, that is a fish well. It is suppose to have water in it. When we catch fish, we drop them into the well. That away the fish will be alive when we get back to the shore. When we get back, we will take the fish into the pavilion and clean them for dinner tomorrow."

"Why can't we have fish today?"

"Because we will have crayfish tonight; remember we are going to have a party at one of the barns."

"What do crayfish taste like?"

"Dan, you have eaten Lobster before, right?"

"Yes, ma'am, lots of times."

"Well, they are like Lobster. They are smaller, but have more flavor than the Lobster you are used to. Tonight crayfish or crawdads as a lot of people around here call them will be fixed several ways. We will have strawberry cake and homemade ice cream for dessert."

"Mother, I am glad we moved. I miss Grandfather and Grandmother Smith, but I feel like I am living in a fairy tale book on this plantation!"

"Look, look, little fish! There are thousands of them, look, Mother." Little Betty is very excited by the little four inch fish under them bunched into a large swarm for their protection. Dan speaks:

"Mother, what kind of little fish are they?"

"Son, I am not positive, but I believe they are juvenile trout." Brenda starts the engine again and decides that the little fish will not help their chances of catching fish with artificial worms."

"Mother, where are we going now?"

"Dan, we need to get away from the baby fish. We need to go where the larger fish are finding it harder to find food. I am going to take us into deeper water." All of a sudden little Betty screams out and almost loses her cane pole. Mattie helps her gain control of the pole and coaches Betty as she works on the task of landing a large fish.

In the main time back with David's adventure, we learn that he drives down the dirt road and a large panel truck stops several hundred feet in front of David to allow him the opportunity to drive around. There is not enough room for two way traffic. As soon as David gets back on the road, a female dog with seven puppies that David estimates to be about six weeks old crosses his path going toward the shop. Apparently mama dog and the puppies have visited the creek that is about a thousand feet away. When David drives up to the so called shop, he realized that there was more than one building. There was a loading platform that also had a large cement ramp. Near the ramp was a truck bay designed to serve medium and large size commercial trucks. The yard surrounding the buildings is covered with crushed rock. David gets out of the truck and walks into a large open shed that appeared to be about three hundred feet long. Inside, David noticed about forty men, mostly black men, whom he guessed lived on the plantation. David recognized Roy Henry the moment he entered the work shed.

"Well, look a hear, look who has come by to see old Roy Henry. It sho is good to see you! How are you doing, sir?"

"I am just riding around looking. Please don't let me interfere by slowing you down, Mr. Henry."

"Oh, no, don't you worry about that none! I am just sharpening a few knives and saws. Now, I don't control everything that goes on in these buildings. The timber from the logging camp is brought out on the other side."

"Is the lumber sold here?"

"In a way it is. The Pridgens do not sell lumber. They can make a lot more money by cutting less trees and turning them into furniture and other useful products."

"Do you make furniture?"

"Noosa, I am not in that department. I sharpens the knives, saws, or anything that is dull. I sharpens household knives, and heavy duty commercial saws, and blades. I also make thousands of handles for hammers, axes, mallets, and anything that needs a handle. Of course, I don't do it by myself. We are caught up for this week. Come over here and I will show you some of the handles I made and the knives and saws I sharpens." David speaks:

"You use foot powered sharpening stones! I have only seen these in books or at a museum. I didn't realize that people still used them." Up on a wall were hundreds of saws of all kinds held up and held in place by wooden pegs. David saw crosscut, keyhole, coping saws, circular saws and bucksaws displayed. A sound was heard and David turned his head to the right and was somewhat surprised and delighted to see the female dog or bitch hurrying up the ramp with her seven puppies.

"Is that your dog, Uncle Henry?" Henry looks at the dog while smiling and shaking his head a little. Uncle Henry speaks:

"I guess that Miss Clover is getting ready to feed her puppies."

"What breed of dog is she, Mr. Roy?"

"You call it and she will acknowledge it. I specks that Miss Clover has a little of everything in her, but she is a good old girl. I have even carried her coon hunting half a dozen times."

"So, she is your dog?"

"Nassa, I can't say that; she belongs to no one in particular. Miss Clover is like a cat. She chooses her own human family. Clover has been over half this here plantation. She takes up with a family and lives with them a season or so and moves on. Half of those places she has dropped off a litter of half grown puppies. Everyone seems to like her and her puppies are highly valued as watchdogs and coon dogs. I don't believe she or her kin would be what you would look fer; say fer a deer dog. Most people want a big bloodhound fer that job description. Go on over there, she is friendly and so are her puppies!"

David went to the large wooden box Miss Clover was in and she started waging her tail and got up to greet him. The puppies took the hint and they acted liked excited human children. They were wagging their little tails and jumping on David's legs for his attention. David looked around and noticed various odd looking tools by the scores in Uncle Henry's shop. Some were obviously not completed while others were ready for use.

"What are these clubs used for?"

"Oh, these are not clubs. I recon they are kinda like a club of a sort. These are called mallets and the larger ones are called mauls."

"What are these tools used for?"

"I don't use them that much, but the builders use them in their building. We, I say, we build log cabins with most of the lumber. Actually the carpenters cut all the wood according to seven patterns or cabin styles. People want the cabin wood or lumber worked the old fashioned way. It requires more work, but the carpenters have been doing this kind of work around here for about eighty years. We have log cabins in the woods that are there to show folks what their cabins will look like."

"So the customers pick out the cabin they like and the plantation cuts the lumber to specifications?"

"Yes, but most times the lumber is already cut and in storage around here. It is all marked by letters and numbers."

"Who assembles the cabins?"

"Sometimes the people who purchase the cabins; a lot of folks have no problem putting together their house in a few months. The instructions are easy to understand. Anyone can rent a forklift or a truck with a lift boom to set the logs in place. There is a couple, a man and his wife, that puts together these cabins for a fee. These folks make good money at it!"

"So they work for the plantation?"

"Nosa, they work for themselves. We have an advertisement or two in each cabin about these people. Zeb or Beard do not make a red penny off it, but it sure encourages timid folks who would not be able to tackle building a cabin to purchase a log cabin kit." David picks up a mall and looks at it. "Mr. David, we find a small oak tree that has a large knot. The reason being is that the knot is extra hard. Try using even a sharp ax on a cured knot and you will see how hard they are. I have come to the opinion that a knot is an injury or a diseased section the tree tries to grow around." Uncle Henry picks up a section of a white oak sapling from his stockpile and shows David the big hard knot. "Yessa, I cuts just about here a few inches above the knot like this one and then I cuts about three feet of wood from this here knot. I get a pole ax and shapes the handle. Here is a pole ax. I next finds me a nice seat and gets out my knife I use around here and smoothes out that handle like this one." David comments:

"I can understand why people would want these houses. Not only for their beauty, but they, I believe, are a lot sturdier than most houses made out of particle wood or plywood!"

"Yessa, I tend to be agreeable with your thoughts. Yessa, that particleboard gets wet and you have a disaster. The plywood gets wet and it wants to warp on you. Let's walk through the lumber shed and see people notching and jointing logs, making shingles, and drilling holes with augers. One guy does nothing but makes wooden pegs."

"You mean to tell me no nails are used or steel bolts?"

"No, we use pegs. They are probably stronger and can last for centuries." David was amazed at how the logs were split into lumber. No power machinery, just tools like pole axes, go devils, mauls, froes, mallets, and human muscle.

Little Betty Smith is having the time of her life trying to figure out what to do with the large fish that is on her line. Her face is red and it appears that she could lose the pole. Dan speaks:

"Betty, do you want me to help you?"

"No, it is my fish. I can catch it!" Mattie is not sure what to do. She is prepared to remove the hook from the mouth of whatever is on the line. The fish jumps out of the water and Brenda realizes it is a large Bass approximately nine pounds in weight. Betty stands up and leans against the side railing. Mattie holds unto Betty to stabilize her. When the fish came to the surface, Betty had the pole as high up as she could hold it. Mattie grabbed the line and pulled the struggling fish into the boat. Mattie speaks to Betty:

"No, hold the pole up. Hold the line tight so I can get that thing!" Mattie put her foot on the fish to control its movement and pulled the hook out. She grabs the fish by the mouth and speaks to Betty.

"Hurry, Betty, open that lid on the well." Betty strains a little to lift the fish well's door and Mattie drops the fish into the well.

"Mother, what kind of fish did I catch?"

"Honey, that fish is a Bass. I should have brought along a camera. There should be one in the pavilion. I will take your picture several times and we can put one of them up on the wall just like my picture after I caught a fish when I was a little girl." Brenda, Mattie, and the children continued to fish until everyone was happy about the fish caught. Brenda speaks:

"We have plenty of time to go around Paradise Island. Now when we get back to the pavilion we can clean the fish and put them on ice before going back to the house." When the boat came within a hundred yards of Paradise Island, Betty screams out in total excitement.

"Look, horses, they are so beautiful; I have never seen horses that beautiful before!" Dan's eyes are wide open. He stands up without saying a word over come at the magnificent majesty of a white stallion running with its tail held high and his nostrils flared in full gallop with dozens of mares and colts back of him trying to keep up. The scene was breath taking, raw, and wild. Dan composes himself and speaks:

"Mother, where are those beautiful horses going so fast?"

"I am not positive, son, but probably Pridgen's Mountain."

"Where is Pridgen's Mountain, Mother?"

"It is on the other side of the island. It is a four hundred foot hill that stops at the beach on the island."

"You mean there is a mountain on this island?"

"It is not a real mountain, but it is very impressive. The horses love to go up there to graze. My brothers sow grass and clover on the hill. In the cold months the horses have winter grass growing on the hill for them."

"Where do the horses go in the cold winter time for protection?"

"Son, they have caves to go into if the weather gets rough. The caves are manmade. Your great-great-grandfather had the caves dug into the sides of the great hill. They are lined with reinforced concrete. The horses can go about eight hundred feet into the caves where the temperature is a constant seventy degrees Fahrenheit year round." Dan speaks:

"Mother, does anyone feed them?"

"Honey, Uncle Preston feeds them. They are almost wild and no one rides them." Dan once again questioned his mother:

"Mother, do the horses stay on the island all of the time?"

"I have never seen them off the island. All of their needs are met by staying on the island. I do believe that Grandfather Zeb once told me that the very first horses were seen swimming the lake, but decided it was not worth leaving and turned back." Dan speaks:

"Mother, where did they come from?"

"I understand that the original two horses came to America from overseas. Children, I am going to take us on the other side of the island and try to get there before the horses get there. I want you guys to see them when they look down at us from four hundred feet up." Fifteen minutes later, Brenda stops the engine and waits for the horses to come running up the slope of the huge hill. The children hear the thunder created by the hoofs of the horses as they galloped up the hill. Looking down from four hundred feet the magnificent horses stood gazing across the lake. The kids scream and wave their hands at the horses trying to get their attention. While Brenda and her children look on, the lead stallion raises himself off the ground, rears back on his hind legs, and sticks out his front legs kicking almost like he is boxing. He paws the ground, snorts, and turns around to race back down the hill followed by the mares and the colts.

"Children, I am going to take us on the other shore of the island and show you a natural wonder of this lake." Thirty minutes later Dan speaks:

"Mother, this is scary. How deep is that cave down there?"

"It is nearly two hundred feet down there."

"Have you ever been inside of that huge thing?"

"No, Dan, I am not qualified to do that. Your father might be; he is an oceanographer. He takes deep dives in the ocean as you know." Dan notices something special about the huge hole or cave at the bottom of the lake.

"Mother, what causes the water to look blue down there?"

"Son, I am not an expert on the subject, but I do know that the huge cave down there is an underground river that has been exposed by the lake."

"What does exposed mean?"

"Uncovered, son, something that you would not normally be able to see is revealed. The river down there is like a garden hose and the water is running through it. We will pretend that someone buried the hose and you can't see it. The person who buried the hose later decides to dig a pond in his backyard. The hose he forgot about is seen on the bottom of the small pond and the water is coming out of it."

"I understand, Mother."

"Now I believe, son, that the water is blue because of how light is absorbed. All of the various colors of light are captured by the deep hole except the blue rays which are reflected back into our eyes. This is what happens when light goes into a deep hole like this one. The water inside the cave's mouth appears blue to us."

"Where does this underground river come from?"

"I would imagine the mountains from snow melting." Dan speaks:

"There is very little snow to melt in North Carolina, Mother?"

"Who knows; I will let your father explore the underground river. Maybe he can answer our questions." Dan questions his mother while looking back toward the island:

"Mother, where did these beautiful horses come from?"

"Your great-great-grandfather received the Lipizzaner horses from Vienna, Austria, shortly after World War Two. Two horses, a stallion and a mare were brought here for their protection. They came close to being destroyed by the German Government during the war. A gentleman from Austria of high government standing met your great-great-grandfather during the war. He was aware of our family's plantation and the island surrounded by the lake we are in. He wrote your great-great-grandfather George Pridgen and asked him permission to keep the two horses on the island just in case another war or something would come along that would endanger the beautiful Lipizzaner horses again. Grandfather George was delighted and honored at the request. We keep only a few dozen or so of these horses on the island. When there are too many horses, Grandfather Zeb writes the Austrian Government officials in charge of the preservation of their famous horses and tells them to come to the island and capture young horses to have them shipped back to Austria. We do not claim to own the horses. We just provide some of them a safe place to live." Brenda, Mattie, and the children go back to the pavilion to prepare the fish so that they could be cooked for dinner the next day.

David and Uncle Roy Henry move to the back of the large building they are in to the area where logs are prepared in size and shape for log cabins.

"Mr. David, as I said, we prepare kits for seven styles of log cabins. An over sized pattern of each cabin style is over here as you can see on the wall. Every two weeks mostly everyone is rotated to a different spot so that folks will not become bored and so that everyone will know all of the work we do here." Roy stops to speak to about forty young men who are making shingles for the cabins.

"Hey, how is everything fellows? Hope you boys are doing well. Look ah here, I want you fellows to meet Miss Brenda's husband." Roy turns toward David and speaks to him with a low voice. "Do you want me to say, Doctor Smith, David?"

"No, no, just David will do. Remember I am not in class."

"OK, may I present Miss Brenda's very fine young husband, David Smith, from the big city of Boston." All of the guys either spoke to David or nodded their heads to recognize his presence.

"David, as you can see, we are splitting oak to make it into shingles. Just watch Jeremiah there and you will see the first process. The stump is first cut in half using the go devil and a steel wedge. Hit makes it a lot easier to do it this way. Here, you now try. Just use common sense and divide this half into four equal parts as near as you can. If you want to, you can mark them. We fellows who have done it a million times don't need to do that. We kind of guess, but I guarantee we will be right on the money. Don't worry about messing up anything." David hits the go devil with a maul and the wood splits all the way through. David speaks:

"I can't believe how easy that was! The wood practically splits itself." Roy speaks:

"That's the ticket, one more time and you will have this side. Now take this here stick and use it to mark off the center of the log's face. That away, each shingle will be the same length." All of the young men clap their hands delighted that David finished his first half of a log. David goes over the process.

"So you split the log into half. Next you divide each half into four equal slices. The last thing is to cut the center out so the pieces will all be the same length." David was next showed how to remove the outer layer of wood on each piece of wood or bolt as they are commonly called. Next the bolts were farther split using a froe. From there David sits before a shaving horse and picks up a drawing knife to smooth out the singles so that they can be used.

"Mr. Roy, I appreciate you and the fellows showing me how to do this! I don't have time today, but I would like to learn how to do all of this work. I don't plan to do it for my living. I have put too many years into my own profession to do that, but I love to learn how to do things this practical. Mr. Roy, if you don't mind, I believe I will come back tomorrow and remain here and see how many shingles I can make. How many shingles does it take to cover a nice sized log cabin now days?"

"Of course, it depends on the style you want, but I would say about six thousand for a nice sized house."

"How long does it take to make that many shingles, sir?"

"I believe that these fellows can make that many in about two hours. Sometimes the wood is not as agreeable to work with, but I believe I am right. Now, I don't build cabins anymore; I retired from that line of work about twenty years ago. I have my hands full running my shop as I call it on the other side of this building. My brother Troy is in charge of this here cabin building right now. He works hard keeping up with all of the orders coming in. Alice his wife helps him with the office work."

"How many cabins are sold here a week?"

"We sell about five a day. Now, we have a couple that puts together log cabins for our customers. I believe I have already spoke of them."

"Yes, sir, you said that they were both school teachers before going full time into putting together the cabins. I guess they take care of putting together most of your cabins."

"Nosa, not on your life! Nosa, they can only put together about two a week. They have several men to help them. Those folks even deliver the cabin kits to where they are going to assemble the houses. The Pridgens sell the cabins all over the country. Sometimes they have dozens of them on one train going out West or high country in the mountains of North Carolina or Tennessee. Yessa if you want to learn the trade, there is almost unlimited work available for a fellow who wanted to assemble these here cabins."

"I have no doubts about that, Mr. Henry. I am sure there is money and a lot of personal satisfaction setting up these beautiful cabins for folks all over the country. A man must make a choice as to where he will spend the bulk of his time and energy. I struggled for years as a teenager as to what I wanted to do once I finished school. I will admit that I don't have to work for a living. I could spend all of my time investing and playing the stock market. My father is a medical doctor. He has always been of an opinion that a man has to have something that so inspires him that he is compelled to devote his life to it. My father still works long hours and he continues to put his best effort into his work because he is helping people.

"I am a scientist. I love my work; it has been very rewarding and practical. I have actually been able to save lives not by my medical knowledge, but by understanding the great forces that move the surface of our Earth about."

"How did you save lives, Mr. David? I don't understand."

"I was able to more than once forecast earthquakes, when, and where they would occur." Roy looks perplexed and takes off his cap and messages the back of his head a little before putting the cap back on again.

"Mr. David, I am not sure about what you are talking about, predicting the future." I know that there was an old woman who once lived on this here plantation when my father was a boy who claimed she could predict all kinds of misery to come. Grandpa used to call her a female prophet. She used Tarot cards and gazed into a crystal ball that she claimed to see into tomorrow." David chuckled and shook his head.

"No, Uncle Henry, I am not a prophet. I don't use magic or some religious powers to predict earthquakes. I use pure science. I depend on very sophisticated and delicate instruments and complicated computer programs I have invented to help me make accurate forecast about earthquakes." Uncle Henry smiles and speaks:

"I understand, you are kind of like the weather man on television. He sometimes explains how he gets his information!"

"Yes, sir, I guess I am similar. I have never compared myself to the weatherman, but your illustration or draw of comparison is very clarifying."

"So, who did you save if I may ask, sir?" David smiled before he spoke:

"I see that you are not going to let me go on my statement. Well, sir, I was fortunate enough to have predicted several major earthquakes near Asian cities. One coastal city in the country of India was evacuated when I expressed my concerns to the mayor of that city. I even met with the president of India and presented my case to him. He accepted what I believed to be an imminent disaster and had several million people evacuated. A huge earthquake took place four days later and destroyed that city." Henry stood in almost shock.

"Mr. David, I am glad you are so caught up in your kind of work because I specks you saved more people in that one incident than your father has in all of his years doctoring!"

"Well, sir, I have never thought about it that away, but I am thankful I was able to put my education to practical use." David laughed and spoke again: "I know this is just vanity, but they did put up a large statue of me when the city was rebuilt in the main public square beside city hall. I was actually invited over for a ceremony to show their appreciation for saving their lives." Henry speaks:

"Oh, I know that you were proud! I can't imagine such. The closest to fame I came to was several years ago when I saw a house on fire in Atkinson and managed to get the family out before the place was surrounded by fire. Yes, sir, I saved the newspaper that week. Here I am standing there with those folks and them just full of my praises! Those folks even invited me several times to that new restaurant they built in Atkinson."

"Uncle Roy, it has been a pleasure touring your shop this afternoon. I hope to have the pleasure to come back here. I am not sure what tomorrow will require of me, but if possible, I would like to drop by and see what I can pick up from you and the fellows that are building these log cabins. I love to work with my hands."

"Now you just drop by anytime, Mr. Smith, and I am sure that we can find a spot for you to work in. I will see you at the get together tonight at around six thirty or so. Me and the boys will need to get to the barn and start the water to boiling about thirty minutes before the party. They usually talk for about an hour before the meal is ready. I supervise the crawdad boiling and Miss Lilly and Lillian handle most of the other fixings. Yes, sir, there will be a mess of crawdads and country cooking brought to that place tonight!" David speaks:

"I do look forward to that party. I understand a lot of old friends and family will come. I look forward to meeting them! I will see you later, sir."

Four o'clock in the afternoon found, Brenda, Mattie, and the kids back at the Mansion. Mrs. Lillian and Lilly Pridgen were in the kitchen finishing up on the food they had plans to carry to the party. On the big table were platters of deviled eggs, a dozen oversized strawberry cakes, and scores of sweet potato pies, cornbread, and several huge twenty gallon commercial sized coolers full of ice cold tea. Over thirty gallons of pecan and strawberry homemade ice cream would also be carried over to the barn at six thirty that evening. Already long tables were being set up with red checkered pattern table cloths covering them. Brenda enters the kitchen holding one handle of a large heavy fish cooler. Mattie had the other handle. The children, Dan, and Betty, followed their mother into the kitchen all bright eyed with excitement written all over their young faces. Mrs. Lilly speaks:

"Lillian look who is back from the fishing lake. Brenda, you guys must have caught a real nice mess of fish for dinner tomorrow." Both children started talking loud at the same time trying to tell their elders about their adventure on the big lake. Their mother speaks:

"Betty, Dan, you guys need to calm down and decide who is going to start talking first or nobody will understand you." Dan catches his breath and speaks to his sister:

"OK, you speak, Betty, you speak first."

"I caught a nine pound big mouth bass and I have a picture to prove it!" Little Betty reaches into a deep pocket in her jeans and pulls out a picture of a very proud little eight year old girl holding a large Bass while her picture was taken. Miss Lilly speaks:

"I hope you brought that fish back with you because I don't believe we will be able to eat that picture." The children giggle.

"Yes, ma'am, Great Grandmother, it is in the cooler with the rest of the fish." Mrs. Lillian Pridgen asks her grandson Dan about his luck at fishing.

"Well, Grandson, I hope that you had luck catching fish!"

"Yes, ma'am, I caught three trout, six perch, and a gold pocket watch!" When Mrs. Lilly Pridgen heard what her great grandson said her face turned a shade white.

"Son, did you say that you caught a gold watch?"

"Yes, ma'am, Great Grandmother, here it is." Dan reaches deep into a pocket and proudly pulls out an old Elgin pocket watch that her husband had told her about nearly sixty five years ago."

"Son, do you mind if I hold that pretty watch."

"No, Great Grandmother, isn't it beautiful? Open it up." Mrs. Lilly cautiously opens up the beautiful old pocket watch that her husband Zeb had told her about long ago.

"Son, this old watch belongs to your great grandfather Zeb." This old watch is now about a hundred and fifty years old. Mrs. Lilly could tell that her great grandson was a little concerned about the watch's ownership and she calms her great grandson's fears."

"Son, I am sure that your great grandfather will let you keep the watch. You know the old saying, finders keepers, losers weepers, but I do feel that your great grandfather has a right to see the watch. You see, the watch was given to him by his great grandfather when he was a lad of about twelve years old. He kept it in a large dresser bureau by his bed. One day when he came back from a fishing adventure, he decided to take the beautiful watch out just to look at his new treasure. To his horror and sorrow he discovered that the watch was missing. He reported his lost to his family and a search was done all over this huge house and folks continued to look and talk about that watch for years afterwards on the plantation's grounds. When we got married, my grandfather gave me a watch identical to the one Zeb once had. We have kept it upstairs in our bedroom for a very long time." After the fish are put into the icebox, Brenda, Mattie, and the children quickly get ready for the party. A few minutes later David arrives after spending a very fulfilling day riding around the plantation. David walks into the kitchen where his mother-in-law and Mrs. Lilly Pridgen are finishing up their work. David walks in with a very satisfied and refreshed look on his face and takes a quick, but thorough glance at all of the food on the huge preparation table. He realizes that the get together this evening is taken very seriously by the Pridgen Clan. David speaks:

"It looks like we are going to have a feast on this here plantation tonight!" Mrs. Lilly answers him:

"That we are and I hope you are on empty and need a fill up. We usually have crawdads six times a year around here. We don't want to eat them too often or they will become too common to our taste buds. I would imagine that Roy and the boys will be driving by here anytime now past the house headed to the old barn we use for entertainment and our family museum." David speaks:

"Did you say museum?"

"That I did. Why don't you and Brenda go over to the barn about an hour early so that she can show you that place? I believe that you will be surprised at what you will see!" David speaks:

"Who is going to help you guys get all of this food and stuff to the barn?" Mrs. Lillian smiles and speaks:

"My three boys will be here in just a few minutes. I will take the children over there with us. Zeb and Beard will also be here in just a few minutes to help. I hope you enjoyed your tour of the plantation!"

"I had a wonderful time! I can't wait until I have opportunity to go back to Uncle Roy Henry's workshop. He carried me to the other end of the building and introduced me to the fellows who were building log cabins. I even had the chance to try my hand at making shingles. I told Roy that I would love to visit him again and learn as much as possible about that trade." Lillian speaks:

"Well, David, I would encourage you to learn all you can around here. A fellow never knows when he might just have to call upon skills that he would never dream he would need in order to make it in this life."

"Well, Mrs. Lillian, I don't expect to discontinue my work as a scientist, but as you say, a fellow cannot always assume that things will remain the same." Brenda walks into the kitchen area with the children. Mrs. Lillian Pridgen speaks to her daughter:

"Brenda, why don't you take David over to the museum part of the barn and show him all of those wonderful old things over there?"

"Who is going to take care of Dan and Betty?" Mrs. Lilly Pridgen speaks:

"Now, don't you worry about that. Your Mother and I are going to bring the children over to the barn when it is time to set the food on the tables. That should be in about thirty minutes. Roy is already over there with his crew. I suspect that the water will be boiling in those huge pots in about twenty minutes or so."

"Mother, is Gregg going to do any cooking this time?"

"He will be going over there in about thirty minutes. He will wait until the crawdads are about half cooked before he can take their outer shells off so that he can put his Cajun sauces all over them for the oven. It will take only a few minutes to get the gas oven hot enough to bake those crawdads he wants."

"Mother, how many pounds is he going to fix up?"

"He usually cooks about forty pounds. I will use about ten pounds of them to chop up and put into the rice. It will take us about five minutes to chop what I need for the rice." Brenda turns toward David and speaks to him.

"Well, I believe that Mother and Grandmother can take care of the children for us. Would you like to go over to our family's museum?"

Eight

A Visit to the Museum and a Crayfish Party

"Yes, I would definitely love to go. I have never heard of a family having its own museum. I have been to the museums of several presidents, but never a family's private museum." Brenda and her excited young husband walk out onto the front of the huge porch that surrounds the mansion's first floor and quickly make their way down the twelve foot high steps adored on each side with a huge male African lion. Brenda is excited because she realizes that her husband is about to get a real surprise. It has been nearly two months since the Smith's moved to the Pridgen Plantation. Everyday has been an adventure since their arrival. There is always something exciting to see or do! Spring flowers are everywhere in full bloom. The smell of the clean fresh air far from any major city and the fragrance of the millions of flowers, blooming trees, and fresh green grass, reminds David of his early years in Sunday School. One of his teachers was an old scientist who had worked and experimented with beautiful flowers and exotic plants for over fifty years. That man loved to mesmerize his young teen class by describing in detail, as only a scientist in his field could, the famous Garden of Eden as detailed in the Book of Genesis and other ancient literary sources. When David was a boy, he dreamed of one day taking a faraway trip with a team of explorers and finding the most famous garden in human history.

David calculated that there was about two and a half hours of good daylight left. There was a still calm in the air. About half a mile away Brenda and David could catch glimpses of the boundaries of the scenic Black River. If they had been looking out from a third floor window in the mansion they could actually see the water. Once every week or so someone walking around on the third floor of the great house reports seeing the Henrietta 1V, a two hundred and fifty foot long sternwheeler as it passed in view. In fact, the Henrietta 1V is about to go past the Pridgen mansion even as David and Brenda prepare to visit the museum. People on the upper decks of the Henrietta 1V could also catch glimpses of the great Pridgen mansion high up on a bluff. The great Southern Queen has guarded the banks of the river for nearly three centuries. The sight was breath taking! People were stunned not only by the magnificent size and rich beauty of this old Southern Monument, but by the unrivaled size and beauty of the huge live oak trees that were nearly five hundred years old when the mansion was built by Zeb Pridgen's ninth great grandfather and his wife, a great lady from France. The ship's captain was quick to point out that the mansion and the plantation were not part of a tourist attraction, but a real functioning Southern Plantation that did not welcome curiosity seekers. The top deck of the largest sternwheeler ever to glide down the Black River was crowded with tourists who were amazed at the raw untouched wilderness that the river passed through. Huge cypress trees stood proud and tall along the Black. Many of the giants were well above a millennia old. Red Headed Woodpeckers hammered away at the trunks of the trees. The intense primitive hollow noise the woodpeckers created, vibrated for miles around the swamp. Once in awhile a bird would disappear into a hole created by perhaps another bird or formed naturally in the trunks of the trees due to a limb rotten out leaving a hole.

As the Henrietta 1V glided along, passengers were amazed at the old logs floating huddled together where and when the river would curve around a bend causing the waters of the River to slow down a bit. On these old rustic looking logs covered with green algae, mushrooms, and snails, people were delighted to see rows of snapping turtles basking, taking advantage of the warmth of the sun. One group of people on the top deck are delighted and very excited to see a mama black bear and two cubs quickly getting out of the water as the big boat approaches. Up ahead a familiar sight by old timers is a flock of huge Turkey Buzzards circling overhead looking for a meal or sunning their feathers cleaning them of dangerous bacteria. Squirrels delight the passengers of the Henrietta 1V by chasing each other from tree to tree as they chatter away. One young man spots a flock of wild hen turkeys following an old gobbler who was displaying his magnificent multicolored feathers. A mama Opossum and family is taking an unwanted ride on a large old log scrambling from one end to the other trying to find a way off, hoping for solid ground. Apparently the Opossum walked onto the log when it was resting against the river bank to eat something she saw. When the sternwheeler started coming by, it formed a wake as it pushed itself through the water. The water surge forced the log off the riverbank into the deep channel.

People were amazed to see all manner of wildlife as they continued to witness a wilderness that most of them had never had the privilege to experience before. While the excited tourist continued to behold the beauty of creation, the tour guide shared with the people the history of the region. He pointed out the location of several lost and abandoned towns along the banks of the river. Passengers were amazed as the story teller spoke of the early people who first settled on the banks of the Black. Even the names of these people and their occupations were not forgotten. How times had changed! The early settlers along the Black River could have never even dreamed of how our world would change. Up miles above the stern wheeler, the Henrietta 1V, the familiar roar of a large commercial jet was heard and seen as it quickly distanced itself to parts unknown to the passengers of the riverboat.

Nothing stood in the way of change or what some consider progress; that is almost everything else had changed. The passengers were amazed and some a bit frightened as a very rough river man sporting a long unkempt beard rushed out at the sternwheeler as it passed by him as he stood on a mud bank. The man was catching fish with a cane pole and did not appreciate the presence of the sternwheeler full of tourist north of the Mason Dixon Line. In addition, the man had a large tub full of freshly caught fish that were almost washed away as the wave of water from the passing sternwheeler washed over the mud bank he was standing on. It was an intrusion into what he considered his world. The wild eyed muscular man was a frightful sight to behold! He expressed his opinion of the situation and rushed toward the stern wheeler like a charging male gorilla as far as his little island or mud bank jutted out into the main river channel. He picked up large sticks and anything he could lay his big weathered hands on and threw them at the passing tourist while managing to hit the side of the boat. Several people took film and photos of the man thinking that he was a paid professional actor. The story teller made a comment to lighten the moment suggesting that the incident was staged. In reality, he was glad that they were now hundreds of yards away from this man of mystery. He had once been told by an old timer that the man was old man Zeb Pridgen's younger brother, the owner of the famous Pridgen Plantation.

Hundreds of happy birds were making a big fuss high up in the branches of the scores of ancient magnolia trees that surrounded the house. David was amazed at the size and beauty of one of the trees as he and Brenda walked under its branches as they continued to make their way toward the enormous red barn in the distance. David stops and reaches down to pick up a fallen magnolia leaf. He speaks to his wife:

"Honey, I can't believe the size of these leaves. They have to be over twice as large as any magnolia leaves I have seen before. It must be because of the age of these trees."

"No, David, I believe that it is the species of Magnolia, not the age that determines the size of the leaves. There are some trees around here that are centuries old that produce regular sized leaves."

"Brenda, what is that lovely little building used for?"

"We make soap in it."

"Why would you need a place to make soap?" Brenda answers her husband:

"It beats making it in the house." David pauses and appears slightly confused.

"I suppose you are right, but why doesn't your family buy its soap at a store?" Brenda smiles and answers David:"David, there are a lot of things I suppose we really don't have to do or make around here. We could hire people to do almost everything around here. Mama could hire a couple of cooks and a troop of maids to keep the mansion clean. We could give up the herb garden and buy all or most of our medicine and popery in Burgaw or Wilmington. The list could go on and on. You see, we enjoy our lifestyle. If the stock market crashes and all hell was to break out, we would not have to worry about getting something to eat, or having to buy shoes, belts, hats, or cloths around here. No one has ever died of over working around here and I don't believe any of my kin have died in their youth. Grandfather Pridgen tells me that he feels as good as he did when he was in his early sixties. To tell you the truth, I am very proud and feel privileged to be part of this family. Not many young women my age now days can make her own cloths and participate in all of the activities around here with confidence. I know how to build a log cabin from the ground up and I can even work alongside my brothers logging huge trees. I have learned to take care of animals, bring them back to health or help birth them. I can make horse shoes or work mostly anything going on around here. Daddy once told me that he thought about going modern around here, but if we do, it will not be long before we would live like everyone else. We don't have to worry about restless nights around here and having to take sleeping pills. No one has ever complained of nightmares or has needed a shrink to help him or her manage their thought life. I believe that our biggest secret around here is diversity. No one burns out on a job. We constantly rotate most of our jobs except for key management positions.

" Even our plantation youth help around here. A person around here may find himself or herself fishing at a creek, the fishing lake, or the catfish pond. The guys or gals who do that are really keeping an eye on the property, and they get to keep the fish they catch. We even have a small riverboat that is used to patrol up and down the Black River just to watch over the plantation which goes for miles on both sides of the river. We make quilts around here once a year in the big barn we will be visiting. Mother and my grandmother invite our respected black friends who live around here to quilting parties. The quilts are very beautiful and almost all of the girls and young ladies want to learn how." David speaks:

"Brenda, who else helps with the quilts?"

"About ten white ladies from and around Atkinson also come over or they did when I lived here years ago. I believe most of grandmother's friends are giving up their quilting days, but Mother told me yesterday that the ladies still come over to help teach the girls how and to do a little socializing. Of course, the older ladies like to show off their cooking and bring cakes, pies, and good food like fried chicken, potato salad, or whatever." David speaks:

"Maybe, I should attend one of those quilting bees!" Brenda frowns a little and then smiles while gently shaking her head no.

"No, David, I feel that you should confine your curiosity to log cabin building or making tools or something the guys have traditionally done. You understand, of course. You would probably be a little out of place around here. It is a girl thing." David smiles and speaks:

"I was just teasing. I am sure that I would not want to challenge an old custom." Brenda and David walk into the soap house. David looks around and sees bars of all different shapes and colors in fancy rope baskets hanging from a wooden beam. A large picture on a wall shows an old woman washing the face and ears of a young freckled faced boy, about ten years old, who is crying out in protest apparently afraid that the large woman is going to scrub him to death with the washcloth. Below the woman and the boy are posted the familiar old words, "cleanliness is next to Godliness." On a large shelf David sees several containers of Red Devil Lye. On the floor are two large stainless steel pots or cauldrons sitting on gas burners. Back on a wall hanging by large hooks, he sees large wooden paddles used for stirring the mixture that turns into soap.

"Brenda, this place smells wonderful!" I never realized homemade soap could be so eye and nose appealing!"

"David, most people who make their own soap don't go to this extreme, but we love our soap!" David picks up an oval shaped bar of soap out of a hanging basket and smells it.

"Brenda, the soap in this basket smells like lavender. The soap in this basket smells like oranges and these bars smell like peppermint." David frowns a little and speaks: "This bar smells like tar and this one like camphor or something. I don't believe I would like to wash with them!"

"No, David, and neither would I. They are for cleaning cuts and abrasions on the animals. I don't believe they would hurt us either. We use this antiseptic soap to wash the area gently before applying a salve or something to the wound. We even make our own dish washing soap which remains a liquid. I don't have time to tell all, but I will quickly say that we make many different kinds of soap according to our needs. Some soaps are made to help cure a rash, or a dandruff problem. Still other soap is to be used as a body wash, some for shampoos or regular hand soap. We make heavy duty soap for washing floors. Some of the soap is for hands that are covered with extra heavy ground in dirt or a special heavy duty grease remover. Well enough about soap. Let's get over to the barn so that I can show you our family's museum. If you want to actually make soap, I am sure that you can help us one day make some."

"Brenda, I have never seen such a beautiful barn before! It is as large as the mansion!"

"David, this barn was actually built before the house. It served as a temporary residence for my ancestors. Their wagons and coaches were stored there. I understand that it took about twenty five years to complete the mansion and the grounds." David noticed that the mega barn and first residence of the Pridgens has a small forest of huge red bricked chimneys sticking out from the roof and the sides of what he believed the old living quarters. A very nice porch was on part of the first floor. Fancy chairs and tables were arranged out on the porch for people to enjoy. Beautiful ornate windows imported from France centuries ago adored the living quarters of the so called barn that Captain John Henry Pridgen and his beautiful young wife Madam de Lafayette Pridgen from, Paris, France, dwelled in. Captain Pridgen's Father-in-law and his Mother-in-law from Paris also dwelled in the structure along with twelve house servants that came over with them from France. Captain Pridgen protested saying that the house servants were unnecessary, but he was over ruled by his wife's family. Just because they were moving to America didn't mean that they were going to give up their privilege life style. These servants were highly trained and skilled at a host of trades. Many were master carpenters, bricklayers, gardeners, cooks, musicians, and skilled at all manner of art, and metal work. Two of the servants were highly educated, cunning and experienced business people capable of helping Captain Pridgen and his new family manage their business empire. Of course, all of these people came with a price. They were paid for their services and the servants in turn recognized that they had to perform their jobs well or they would be dismissed just like people today from a job or as some prefer to refer to them as careers.

Before founding the Pridgen Plantation, Captain Pridgen lived in a medium size stone mansion not far from the Cape Fear River in a very modest settlement originally called New Liverpool. More people were moving into the area because of the growing naval stores business up and down the Black River and Cape Fear. New Liverpool (Wilmington) was also physically safer from storms and attacks from ships than the earlier settlement called Old Brunswick. Captain Pridgen earned his fortune by buying shiploads of merchandise and sailing up and down the East Coast. Most of his business was confined to what would later become the United States of America. Many a load of tobacco, rice, naval goods, lumber, and cotton were shipped from Charleston, South Carolina, and Wilmington, North Carolina, to Boston or the growing town of New York.

Occasionally Captain Pridgen would load up a fleet of ships and sail to Great Britain or even to France, where his trade was greatly valued. It was in Paris, France, while doing business with a certain man of great wealth named M Colbert that he met his future wife Madame de Lafayette. Captain Pridgen remained in France for over a year while getting aquatinted with the movers and shakers of the city and signing numerous business contracts with these people that would reward him with vast revenue. Pridgen made a reputation for himself in Paris as an outstanding young Yankee who knew how to handle himself with great dignify and tact with the leading citizens of the country. Months after their marriage, Captain John Henry Pridgen convinced his lovely wife to move to America. In order to get her to agree to leave her motherland, Captain John Henry Pridgen had to agree to bring his wife's parents along and their household. These People were fabulously wealthy and expected to live in America befitting people of their social standing. Pridgen agreed to accommodate them and promised his wife's parents a large plot of land on a vast tract of land he had recently purchased up and down for miles on the shores of the Black River. Many years later this area would be part of Bladen, Sampson and Pender County, named so in honor of General Dorsey Pender a famous Confederate General during the American Civil War.

Our couple walks to the front of the great three story structure and David is delighted to see two large statues of Captain John Henry Pridgen and his lovely wife Madame de Lafayette Pridgen standing together holding hands. The life size statues were carved from a single block of granite. The statues not only included the lifelike images of the couple, but they stood on a large granite platform that was the size of a large living room in a nice house. The platform was carved by expert stonemasons that came over from France. The beautiful work was an extraordinary picture of the life of Captain Pridgen and his lovely wife in stone. Captain Pridgen and his wife Madame de Lafayette Pridgen were depicted standing on the steps in front of the current Mansion on the Pridgen Plantation. The Mansion was carved out of several huge blocks of granite that towered twenty five feet over David and Brenda. Even one of the giant oak trees was part of this scenery. A very beautiful heavy duty black iron fence surrounded the entire platform. The fence was actually embedded into the solid granite being part of the scenery. The statues of Madame de Lafayette Pridgen's parents were standing on an identical construction except the mansion in their scene was different. David speaks:

"I can't believe that such stone carvings are here. They are huge! The statues of your ancestors are magnificent! They are so lifelike. It is as if they are saying to us in a very big way that we were once here. Don't forget about us; we were here first and very much alive." Brenda speaks:

"Yes, I am sure that they did their best to remind later generations of our family that the rest of us would not be here if it had not been for them. I, of course, don't know what our future great-great grandchildren will think of us. I am sure that they will not be looking at works of art on this grandiose scale of us, while reflecting on our legacy." David speaks:

"I just hope that twelve generations from now there will be a country left. Nearly three hundred years from now the way things are going our country will probably be a state within a weak much larger and diluted empire. I believe politicians will follow the lead of big international corporations to liquidate establish borders. The people will either rise up and get control of things by force of arms or will be so dumb by then that they will not have a sense of who they are, where they originally came from, or our founding principles or forefathers."

"I have never heard you speak like this before, David!"

"The reason I have not is because I have never thought of such until I moved down here from Boston." Brenda speaks:

"What does that have to do with moving from Boston?"

"Well, Brenda, I guess it has to do with cultural invasion. You have opened my understanding of keeping one's identity and family values intact. In a sense, a nation is like a family. Look at almost any country in the world and a local identity of that particular peoples beliefs, values, and traditions can easily be cataloged. For example, people in Mexico eat very different than the people of China. They dress differently. They have very different opinions about a multitude of things. The majority of people in most countries represent a particular race of mankind. In fact, most countries don't even allow just anyone into their country. This country is now over run with people who do not share our beliefs or values. They are here strictly for the Greenback. I don't believe they would sacrifice their lives or fortunes in defense of this land. They have no true roots here. They have shed no blood in defense of what we have had here." David looks up at the large building before him. He is impressed with the porch and the beautiful banister surrounding the porch. The carvings were exquisite. The entire front of the structure was high class and represented the taste of French Nobility. Every six feet of the banister was provided with a rich carving of a male peacock showing off his beautiful feathers. The post that held the roof of the porch up were pregnant with rich carvings of beautiful flowers and humanlike shapes. Some of them looked like beautiful young maidens, of horses, lions, dragons, and mythical creatures as often part of European public works like palaces and fountains. The roof was covered in a bluish colored slate.

The building above the roof of the porch did not disappoint David. The entire face or facade of the building was made of polished granite. From the third floor huge lead lined windows with little porches extending from them gave the structure an old European look. Huge shinny clay pots with flowers and birds and house cats hand drawn on them sat out on several of the black iron porches. Two of the porches had small fancy tables on them. Above the tables attached to the side of the building and over shadowing them were large beautifully decorated parasols or sunshades to protect the rich planter and his extended family from the unpleasant rays of the sun. Apparently the original people who lived here would occasionally have their meals brought out on the small porches by house servants so that they could enjoy themselves at the end of a pleasant and rewarding hot summer day, and to feel the cool breeze before the age of fans and air conditioning units coming from the forest of giant oak trees. Carved into the solid granite face of the building are the family coats of arms for both the Pridgen clan and the Lafayette clan. David speaks:

"I feel like I am standing in front of a museum. The carvings around here are as good as any I have ever seen in Europe!"

"This is one of the reasons my family has started calling this place our family's museum." David and his wife Brenda walk onto the porch and stand ready to open one of the two twelve foot high doors. The front of each mega sized oak door was carved with a picture of a Roman Arch. The doors were carved with the arch at Orange, France. The huge structure in France was built at the Roman colony of Arausio, which is on the banks of the River Rhone. Today we call the colony, Paris, France. The great structure was erected in commemoration of the victory the

Roman armies had over the Gauls, a huge barbaric tribe. The arch is crowned with the emperor of Rome in his war chariot being pulled by four magnificent horses. On each corner of the arch at the top stands a Roman soldier with two decorated shields extended out. The story of the victory is depicted all over the arch to glorify this mighty and successful triumph over this dangerous and powerful enemy. David stands and studies the face of the door and shakes his head in amazement. David speaks:

"Unbelievable, what can I say?" Brenda pulls hard and proudly opens up the huge door to let her excited husband inside the building and once living quarters of her ancestors. "Oh, Brenda, this place is magnificent! It looks almost like a French palace in here! The ceiling and the rich wood carvings are unbelievably fancy! Where is the furniture, Brenda?" Brenda speaks:

"David, I understand that the furniture was carried to the Chateau a very long time ago. I am sure that my ancestors did not want to leave such expensive handmade pieces of furniture in this temporary dwelling. I would imagine that a lot of the furniture was passed down by French nobility centuries ago. David, I am sure that you realize that the front of the structure is basically French. The living quarters are divided into two condos. In between the two condos is the living quarters for the house servants. Now some of these servants did not do a lot of work inside this building, but were very useful in building this building and creating the statues, all kinds of ornate structures, formal gardens, wind and watermills, and providing the leadership and expertise for a host of trades around here to get the plantation fully functional. They were also in charge of building the huge French Chateau on the partial of land given to the parents of my eleventh great grandmother the former Madame de Lafayette of Paris, France. The carving outside is identical to the Chateau just like the carving of the Pridgen Mansion looks identical to the house my family currently lives in." David speaks:

"You mean to tell me that a Chateau was built around here? Surely not! Surely it would not be around now days, but burned or torn down a very long time ago!" Brenda smiles and speaks:

"You have a reasonable theory, but not a factual one. Yes, there is a huge two hundred and seventy five year old Chateau on a twenty four hundred acre land tract that was given to Madame de Lafayette's parents. You see both couples lived in this structure that served as both living quarters and a place for their wagons, coaches, farm equipment, workshop, animal feed, and you name it."

"How did they keep the place from being overrun by rats and other creatures that would visit by the thousands to eat the grain and the family's own personal food that they would store away after the gardens and fields were harvested? I don't understand."

"I was told that there were a lot of cats around here in those days. In fact, the cats that live around here now are descendants from that line of cats. All of these cats were originally derived from two cats that my ancestor John Henry Pridgen had on one of his frigates. I understand that they were very big cats averaging about twenty pounds each. The cats had free access to and from any room in this building. All of the doors to this day have cat doors. I understand that one of the gentlemen who was a house servant was good at tinkering and he invented traps to catch unwanted varmints until enough cats were born around to manage the rats and other troublesome pests. I also understand that the guy was a good scientist. He knew a lot about herbs and gardening." David speaks:

"So I suppose that he was the guy who taught your people about medicine and herb gardens?" Brenda speaks:

"I am sure that he taught them a lot, however, my people already knew a lot about the use of Herbs and farming in general. One of the reasons this man's work is valuable is that he wrote a book about all of the things he had learned from his formal schooling and what he learned from my people and the local Indians that once lived around here." David speaks:

"I suppose that all of the Indians were ran off the land once it became legally your ancestors' property."

"No, David, I understand that Grandfather John Henry Pridgen allowed them to remain on his vast land holdings. The Indians did not destroy the land, but respected it. They lived off the fat of the land and loved to bring my people deer and other animals they harvested so that my people could benefit from their land when they first settled on the property. These Indians were a source of great delight for my people. They were all good friends and the Indians never forgot who their benefactor was. These people shared their stories and skills with my people. One old medicine man was credited for saving the life of one of my great grandfather John Henry's daughters. When my great grandfather John Henry Pridgen died, the Indians brought my people gifts and camped out next to the mansion to hold ceremonies to remember and celebrate the life of a great and noble friend in their estimation. The gifts they gave my great grandmother, Madame de Lafayette Pridgen, are still kept in this building." David speaks:

"I am truly impressed! I would have never imagined your people have so much going for them." Brenda speaks:

"David, there is a hidden bell in this room that was rung before a house servant entered the French quarters. It alerted my ancestors that someone was about to walk into their private quarters. I would imagine that most of the visits were scheduled and were expected. If a servant was needed at unscheduled moments, a rope was pulled that is attached to a bell in the servant quarters. I understand that it was proposed that a different rope and bell be rung according to the particular servant asked for, but my ancestor, John Henry Pridgen, devised a code whereby the master of the French quarters or his wife could get the person he or she desired." David looks around with curiosity written all over his face and he speaks:

"Honey, I don't see the ropes or the two bells. Have they been removed?"

"No, dear, open up this chamber and you will see the rope used by my great grandfather John Henry's in-laws." David saw a type of built in cabinet that stood out from the wall of the eighteen foot ceiling. The chamber is actually part of the wall and ran to the top of the ceiling. On the front of the chamber at head level is a rich carving of a large bell. There is also a fancy handle made out of silver below the carving. David as directed by his wife pulls on the handle and opens it up exposing the beautiful pull rope that was made out of hemp. The blue rope which was half the diameter of a human arm was decorated with a golden ring every eight inches and tassels extending from its bottom knot. David pulls the rope and the bell tolls out a pleasant rich sound. David speaks to his wife:

"So the bell is at the top near the ceiling hidden from view behind that fancy lattice work! How would one of your ancestors alert a particular house servant that his or her services were needed?" Brenda points to a beautiful chart with bells arranged in different patterns.

"David, all that was necessary was for the ringer to pay attention to this chart. For example, the person who took care of my people's medical needs was summoned by three rings of the bell, wait five seconds and repeat three rings again. Go ahead you do it." David speaks after pulling the rope.

"I would imagine that all the house servants were awakened when one of them was summoned in the middle of the night!"

"No, I don't think so. You see three or four of the servants took turns to sleep in a chamber closed out from the servants' quarters inside the large hall that separates the servants' quarters from the master's living quarters."

"You mean to tell me that all those servants did was to listen for the bell to go off and then go get the servant that was needed without waking all of the rest of the servants up?"

"Yes, sir, that is the way it worked. Of course, as I have explained, this duty was not assigned to just one gofer, but several of the house servants were assigned to the, shall I say, the communication room. Now on the other side of this heavy duty wall is a hall. In the hall about thirty feet from the so called communication chamber is a bell installed just like this one. To make it easy to understand, when one of my French ancestors rang the bell according to the code to summon a particular person, the ringing of the bell would be heard by the servant who was assigned to be in the communication chamber. That servant would immediately go to the door of the person my ancestors needed and knock on the door and make sure the person got up and was on his or her way to the French quarters. Just before the summoned servant entered the French quarters he or she would go to the panel or cabinet on their side and pull the rope attached to the bell. This bell sounds different than the bell you just rang. The servant would ring a code acknowledging that he was about to enter the master's living quarters." David smiles and shakes his head a bit as he looks down toward the floor.

"Brenda, I have not heard this much talk about ringing bells since I listen to an historical program about the Liberty Bell or perhaps that year when I helped ring one of the musical bells at the Christmas Cantata at church." Brenda smiles and speaks:

"And that is not all of the story. During the day when everyone in the master's living quarters is awake, a trusted servant remains nearby. When he or she hears the ringing of a hand bell by one of my ancestors, he or she immediately goes to that person for their orders. That servant was usually the person who rang the bell on the master's side. Only at night when all the servants were asleep was it necessary for one of my people to ring a bell. I am sure it seldom happened. Are you ready to visit the servants' quarters, Master Smith?"

"Why not, maybe I could get a job working in the communication chamber or something. I, of course, am joking with you, Brenda, but I can't imagine being surrounded by servants ready to run errands or wait on me hand and foot at the ringing of a bell. Not even the wealthiest people on earth now days get that kind of treatment."

"That is true, except for certain areas in Africa where thousands of people are captured and forced into slavery every year. Our country is working to stop the practice, but it is not a small task."

"Yes, I am aware of that, but the servants who once served your French ancestors were well paid for their, shall we say, their services?" Brenda and the amazed David walk to a large double door that has raised life size heads of French noblemen carved as the center attraction in the middle point of each door. Brenda opened it for her husband. They walk into a foyer or chamber room between the French Quarters and the servants' rooms. A very large beautiful oil lamp sits on a fancy granite top table that was no doubt imported from France. A rather large richly framed painting of Eighteenth Century Paris, France, hangs on the wall. Above, hanging from the ceiling, is a large crystal chandelier. Twenty four extra large white candles rest in their holders in the chandelier. David was amazed at two beautiful cushioned oak chairs covered with red velvet in the foyer. The chairs were adored with legs that were fashioned into the shape of eagle's feet at their bottoms near the floor. The claws were positioned on top of and wrapped around the glass balls. David remembered seeing a very old piano that had a fancy swivel chair that sported such unique legs. A very large golden framed wall mirror stood against one wall in between two wall mounted oil lamps. The mirror was placed there for servants to see themselves before they entered their employer's living quarters. Servants were bound to strict dress codes in those days. A button unbuttoned, or perhaps a collier that was not in its place because it was not properly starched would bring an untidy servant a swift reprimand in those days of extreme protocol. David speaks:

"Brenda, I am amazed at how different your family lives today compared to your ancestors that originally settled down here! That was a day when the rich and powerful had royal titles and were high born to rule over the rest of God's creatures. The man who was born a servant usually died a servant. The thing of it is, folks back in those days accepted their estate as being from Providence. A fact they dared not question." Brenda speaks:

"I do believe that the Church was as responsible for that line of thought as much as the Kings and Nobles were, but revolution was just around the bend and Kings lost territory and some lost their heads later on in the Eighteenth Century."

"That is all true, Brenda. The Americans revolted against Great Britain and the French learned that they could live without a king." Brenda opens the door that leads into the great hall between the servants' apartments and the French quarters. The hall David walked into was huge, about twenty feet wide with a ceiling that was eighteen feet above their heads. David turned his head to the right and noticed the stairwell that led all the way to the third floor of the servants' quarters. A huge window decorated with gold leaf worthy of a palace went from the first to the third floor allowing in the hallways an abundance of sunlight when the sun was up. Directly in front of David across the hall encased into the wall of the building was a small library of about five hundred books that were very old, but in mint condition. These were the books that the house staff had to read to increase their general knowledge and to delight them. David looks at the old beautifully bounded books, most with real gold on the outside covers and speaks again. "Brenda, they sure don't make books like these now days! They are magnificent works of art in their own right!" Brenda makes a comment:

"I don't believe it is practical to print books that are works of art on this level now days. Most people could not afford to read if they were still printing like this. The servants who lived here were privileged to be able to enjoy such." David speaks:

"I guess it was a fringe benefit for folks working as educated house servants for the rich and powerful back in the Eighteenth Century. People centuries ago did not have televisions, radios, or computers, to learn about their world. A rich man's books in a way reflected his level of learning. They really took the time and spent their energy learning from books. The knowledge was put to practical use and application. Today you walk into an office and see scores of beautiful expensive books in a fancy bookshelf behind an impressive desk and chances are that the owner of the fine display of knowledge has done no more than a cursory glance at the pages of his or her library. It is just a show." Brenda smiles and is impressed with her husband's sarcastic opinion. The great hall ran for over two hundred and fifty feet. Encased or sunk into the same wall the bookshelf was encased in, David saw the bust of twelve men and women skillfully carved out of granite embroidered with delicate crafted frames like picture frames. The design of the frames were art pieces in their own right. Each bust was extensive enough so that an onlooker acquainted with Eighteenth Century France would be able to know at a glance who these busts represented based on the attire of the persons, which reveals the individuals' positions or duties.

"Brenda, if I am not mistaken, these magnificent busts encased in the wall represent the twelve house servants you spoke of earlier. I am amazed and truly touched! Your ancestors must have thought a great deal of their house staff to have their images preserved for future generations of your family to see and ponder about." Brenda looks at her watch and speaks:

"David, we will need to be at the party in about ten minutes. I will show you a few more things before we leave the servant quarters." David pulls a very old book from the bookshelf and looks at the inside cover.

"How about this, Brenda, I read these old tales when I was in the eighth grade." Brenda looks at the open book held in David's hand and speaks.

"Selected Fables by Jean de la Fontaine. I have read the cover of this old book while passing through here, but have never taken time to read any of it."

"Brenda, these are little short stories that have a punch line to them. I understand that many of Jean de la Fontaine's fables were garnished from other people's writings, both Greek and Roman. I do remember that he did borrow stories from a 6th Century Greek named Aesop." Brenda nods her head a little and speaks:

"Now, I do remember that name from a class in Western Literary Sources I had to take. Perhaps I need to take time to really go through these old books. I may be surprised at what I might learn. If I saw something worthy of my time, I would see if I could order a paperback copy of the book. I would not feel comfortable handling these old books; they are far too old and valuable to use for my personal enjoyment. Now this small room in this oversized hall is, of course, the so called communication room. The person who had to remain in here during the night had more responsibility than just listening to bells and getting people up out of bed." Brenda opens the door and allowed David to look inside the room. There was an enormous writing desk inside with people's names below their mailbox in the desk. The person in the communication room was responsible for keeping up with what was going on around the house and writing the orders or wishes of their employer down on note paper. All house servants were required to get their mail or orders every day. Mail even from Europe was sent and received via the communication room. A ship would go to and from Great Britain and France about once a month. Most of the mail was not idle gossip, but were business transactions involving large sums of money." Brenda and her husband continue to explore the building. Brenda pushes open a door and allows David to take a quick look.

"David, this large room is where the house servants met for their staff meetings. It is also where they had their parties and entertained their friends."

"Brenda, this huge room is really nice. It kind of reminds me of the modern motor inns or hotels we have in our country now days. I love the huge fireplace! I see they had nice tables, chairs, and couches. I believe that it was a real pleasure to have worked for your folks a long time ago!"

"Thank you, David! I am sure that they were well taken care of. Mostly all of them were off on Sundays, and when the sun went down they usually did not have to work. Most of them could call it a day and grab a nice book and read it or play the games you see in here with their friends. Now we will not have time to see my grandfather Captain John Henry's living quarters this time. We need to go to the party. One day you and I will come back here and I will show you the rest of this huge place. I feel that you will enjoy the experience."

"Brenda, where on the plantation is the French Chateau?"

"That huge house or medium sized palace is about twelve miles from here. My grandfather Zeb's brother owns that property. It was given to him by his parents."

"I would love to go visit that house and meet your great uncle!" Brenda hesitated a moment before she spoke:

"I am not so sure we should go by that place."

"You surprise me, Brenda. What is wrong with visiting your great uncle's house? Surely he would be delighted to see you. I do find it strange that neither you nor anyone else has ever mentioned a word that your grandfather Zeb has a brother on this huge plantation."

"David, I am not sure how to respond to your inquiry. I am sure that you have heard the old saying that ignorance is bliss."

"Yes, I have heard that saying. I never would have guessed that your family, which is so open, laid back, and friendly, would have some deep dark secret hidden away somewhere! Did your grandfather Zeb and his brother have a falling out a long time ago?" Brenda paused and looked up at David's face with a look somewhere between dread and caution. "David, if you are determined to pursue this mystery farther, I would suggest that we do it together. Do not discuss it with anyone else." David looks at his wife's pretty face with a puzzled expression and says nothing more about this strange conversation.

"David, we will now enter the shed room on this side of the barn." Brenda pulls at the huge door and David helps her open it. David is immediately surprised that they had just walked out onto a large stage used by performers entertaining people. Six feet below them out beyond the rows of huge tables dressed with red poker dot table cloths, David sees Uncle Roy Henry and about eight young black guys. He recognizes two of them as being two of Uncle Roy's three sons. The instant Roy sees Brenda and David he waves his hand and smiles while he stoops down to adjust the heat of one of the gas burners. The smell of hundreds of pounds of crayfish is in the air notwithstanding the smell of scores of large platters of delicious food sitting on the tables. Gregg, Brenda's next to her oldest brother has already placed his forty pounds of shelled crayfish into a large gas oven. Gregg has his special brand of Cajun Sauce all over the crayfish. They are already over half cooked and will be soon ready to be served. Many people have already arrived for the big occasion. David recognizes several of Brenda's old friends. Brenda and David quickly descend the steps to greet their excited friends. It was not long before David realized that nearly two hundred people were inside the huge barn laughing, talking, and having one of the greatest moments in their lives. Zeb Pridgen, the Patriarch of the Pridgen clan, and his dear wife Lilly Pridgen walked up on the stage. Everyone respectfully stopped their talking and looked up toward the stage. Zeb Pridgen with a very proud and pleased look on his face slowly turns his head scanning the crowd and speaks.

"Well, here we are again. I consider myself the luckiest man in the world to have such fine friends and neighbors I have known all of my life. I went to school with a lot of you folks." Mr. Zeb makes eye contact with several of his old school buddies and instantly remembers many of the pranks and tricks he and his friends played on teachers and students alike. "I don't know how many years we will have left on this Earth to enjoy each other's company, but as long as I am able, we will continue this get together. I believe that after my wife and I are up there on our plot, my son Beard will continue this fine tradition for many years to come." Zeb stops talking and looks toward his wife to allow her to talk.

"I know that a few of you have met my granddaughter's husband Doctor David Smith. He will be teaching at the University in Wilmington next January. Most of you may have heard talk about him, but have not met him. David, would you come up here with Brenda so that I can show you off to our friends. Lillian if you or Beard want to come up here you are, of course, free to do so, after all, he is your son-in-law." Lillian speaks:

"No, you go right ahead and introduce David. I am sure that he will not mind." David and Brenda walk up onto the stage and Brenda grabs David by the right hand and speaks with a very excited voice.

"I am sure that all of you are aware of David. I also know him well enough to let all of you know without asking him to call him David, not Doctor Smith, unless you are at school or a formal public function." One very old lady in the crowd speaks out all excited and pleased to see David for the first time.

"Brenda, dear, I believe that you have married a very fine, and may I say, an exceptionally good looking young fellow. David, I can speak for all of us since I am about the oldest thing around these here woods, that you are standing amongst friends. I look forward to talking to you tonight before I depart!" While everyone was looking up at the stage, a local Gospel Group called The Halleluiah Choir got up on stage and started singing the old songs of the faith such as, *I Will Fly Away, I Will Meet You In the Morning, When The Day Is Done, I Have A Mansion Just Over The Hillside*, and *Never Grow Old*, to name a few of the selections. That night David met a lot of very exceptional people. It was good to experience the love and respect David sensed from the friends and extended family of the Pridgen Clan. That night he heard a lot of old hunting and fishing stories, and of school days long passed into history before David was born from the old timers. Of course, all of the ladies had to hug David. Some of the older ladies, while teasing, David, told him that they could easily wish that they were forty or so years younger.

Later on that night, after the party and everyone was in bed, David and Brenda lie in bed and have conversation before falling into a very restful night's sleep. The next morning while David and Brenda get dressed to go down to the breakfast table, they reflect on the night before.

"Brenda, I never realized that your family has so many friends and cousins. I met the Corbetts, the Pridgens, the Marshalls, the Andersons, the Woodcocks, the Bakers, the Wallaces, the Cobbs, the Browns, the Lees, the DeVanns, the Eakins, and many other people. These people treat me like they have known me all of their lives. I am not used to such openness. People are usually not this friendly where I come from."

"David, I would suspect there are good reasons behind that attitude up North."

"What do you mean, Brenda?"

"There are a lot more people up where you come from. People are moving in and out all the time. Down here where I was born, we know people. Most of us are actually akin to each other if you started tracing family trees. Not everyone was invited last night. The bad ones, which are not many, are known by all. Most of the folks around here have attended the same churches together for centuries. Our ancestors have stood beside each other in war and peace. When the first people settled around here, their biggest enemy was an occasional hard winter, or the smallpox or something. Folks had to depend on each other if they were going to make it."

"Brenda, I will need to go to Boston to sign papers and get the submarine delivered to UNCW's marine science facility."

"Do you want the children and me to go with you?"

"No, we will not have time to go for a visit. I will be at my parents' house in less than two days. Mother is aware that I will be coming to Boston. I miss Boston. I have a lot of friends there. I miss the University also, but I believe that I have made the right decision to give up my job there as the head of the science department. I am sure that Doctor Dennis Miller has not lost too much sleep over my departure. He is now the head of the science department." Brenda smiles and speaks:

"I believe that Doctor Miller is a good guy. He has eaten many a meal at our table." David speaks:

"Yes, I am sure he also misses me. I as you know, hired him and gave him his position as my assistant. I could not give him his current position, that was up to the president of the university."

"You were asked for your opinion."

"That is true. I recommended him as the new department head, but the university had the responsibility to choose the most qualified person it could recruit."

"David, the kids want to see their grandparents. When do you believe that we can all go back for a serious visit?"

"I believe that we should be able to visit my parents in about two weeks. It will take about a week to get the submarine to UNCW's holding pen. I will need to test the submarine out once it is delivered. I don't expect trouble, but I am not going to take a chance. I will do no serious work with it. I will simply make sure that everything is functional."

After breakfast the next morning, everyone goes to his favorite task or to an appointment. The fog has not completely cleared, but it appears that it is going to be a lovely late spring day. Great Grandfather Zeb Pridgen is in his favorite seat on the first floor porch looking at the rising sun and the variety of birds either flying around catching insects or hopping around the yard in front of the mansion. Beautiful flowers surround the mansion for acres and delight the nose and the eyes of anyone who enjoys nature. Zeb is pleased to see hundreds of honey bees flying here and there gathering pollen from the multitudes of flowering plants. He realizes that there will be plenty of high quality honey not only for his plantation, but to sell to the public. He reflects on the crawdad party they had the night before. My how had the years gone by! He was concerned and alarmed at the looks of several of his old school buddies. He feared that they would not be around too many more years. It was probably too late, but he just wished that he and his friends had compiled a sort of history of their adventures and the changes they had witnessed throughout the many years they had shared their lives together. It really did not seem that long ago when he was first sparking that Moore girl from Canetuck Township. While Zeb was deep in thought, his great grandson walks up to him. Inside the mansion Zeb hears the huge grandfather's clock announcing by its seven deep tolls that it is seven o'clock.

"Well, look who is here! I hope you got enough to eat for breakfast."

"Yes, sir, Great Grandfather, I believe that I ate too much!"

"Well, I am sure you will run it all off before you go to bed tonight. Great Grandfather Zeb realizes that something is up because his great grandson is usually outside playing this time of the morning with his sister or upstairs playing with the huge train set."

"Well, what is on your mind young fellow?"

"Great Grandfather, I heard that you lost a very special gold watch long years ago." Zeb was surprised and wondered why his young great grandson would bring up such an old subject.

"True enough, I did have one taken long years ago even before your grandfather was born. My grandfather gave it to me. He told me that his grandfather traded a man a large mule for the gold watch. I guess that work animals were scarce in those days not long after the war between the states. The old boy he traded with was a farmer without an animal to pull his plows with. Anyway, I was very proud as you can imagine too receive that beautiful gold watch with over thirty nine jewels in it. I did not dare to carry the valuable watch around with me lest I lose it. I always kept it in a dresser drawer in my bedroom. One night before I went to bed, I decided to look at my watch. To my horror the watch was not where I always kept it. I looked for an hour or more for the watch and could not imagine what had happened to it. My mother knocked on my door and wanted to know what was going on in my room that time of the night. I opened the door with my eyes filled with tears. I told her what had taken place. She told me that I had probably misplaced it, but I insisted that I always kept it in the second drawer of my dresser. My mother spent about thirty minutes looking with me for the watch. The next day everyone knew about the missing pocket watch. A full scale search was made for the watch, but no watch turned up. I bet we all talked about that watch for five years. One of my sisters saw something shinning one day under the house and went under there all excited thinking she had solved the great mystery of the missing watch. Unfortunately, all she was looking at was a wad of gold colored wrapping foil."

"Great Grandfather, who do you think took your beautiful Elgin watch?" Zeb was surprised that the boy was aware that the watch was an Elgin. Mr. Zeb did not answer the question:

"Great Grandfather, I am sorry that beautiful watch was stolen from you. When we went fishing the other day, I caught more than fish on my hook." The boy had the old man's full attention. "Great Grandfather, look at what else I caught on my hook." The boy reaches deep into a pocket and pulls out a beautiful gold watch. Zeb does not believe what he sees in the boy's out stretched hand. He almost loses control of his voice. Before he manages to speak again the boy tells him to go ahead and take the watch. Zeb reaches out with both hands slightly trembling and gently clasps both hands around his very valuable watch, taken from him seventy four years ago."

"Oh my word, son, I gave up all hope of ever seeing this watch even before your grandfather was born."

"Great Grandfather, I want you to keep it. You deserve it."

"Now, Great Grandson, that would not be right. You found it."

"I know that I did, but keep it as long as you like. If you want to, you can give it back to me one day." Mr. Zeb got up from his porch chair and gave the boy a long hug. The child runs off to find his sister who by permission from her mother, was going to walk around the beautiful yard that surrounded the house. Mr. Zeb sits back down in his favorite porch chair still holding the beautiful watch in his hand. He carefully opens it up and tears fall from his eyes as he vividly remembers the young boy who once desperately looked for his beautiful watch so long ago. He shakes his head in unbelief. He whispered out very low to his God so that no one else could hear the sound of his voice. "Lord, I have always been told that you always answer prayer and that your answer is always, yes, no, or wait a spell. Well, I have the answer to that prayer in my hands today, but did you have to wait so long? I can't complain, they tell me that there are streets of gold where you live and I am sure that it will not be another seventy four years before I will be walking down those streets."

Nine

James Henry Invites Brenda and David to a Party

Several days passed and one morning after breakfast was only a fond memory, before everyone had departed to their favorite task, a black man driving a John Deer tractor rode up to the mansion. The man had an old brown leather hat with a black band around it on his head and a dark brown leather coat on; he held a pipe between his lips. David and his wife Brenda were upstairs in their bedroom making plans about next week. David walks to a large window and looks down out into the big yard and sees his father-in-law Beard Pridgen talking with the man. David speaks:

"Brenda, do you know that man?"

"Oh, that is James Henry the Third. We call him James most of the time. Daddy thinks a lot of him. James is full of interesting stories of yesterday and tales of, shall I say, of strange encounters of unexplainable phenomena. His grandfather used to work a lot with my great grandfather Zeb's father. Daddy told me that James Henry's grandfather was not a very big man, but he was a giant when it came to his ability to pick things up."

"What did he do, lift weights or something, Brenda?"

"Not to my knowledge. I feel sure that he had no time for weights. Hard work and hard times I understand turned him into a man of steel. Grandfather Zeb told me that when he was a boy of about fifteen, he was taking a walk through the black neighborhood on our plantation just for the pleasure of enjoying a nice hot summer afternoon. In those days there were little roads around here, mostly trails surrounded by thick trees. No one heard or saw grandfather Zeb as he stood behind a large gum tree watching Mr. Henry work on a John Deer tractor. Grandfather told me that the tractor had a front flat tire and poor Mr. Henry did not own a jack to jack up that heavy tractor."

"So what did he do?"

"I am almost afraid to say because you will not believe what happened. Henry had a large stump positioned near the tractor that he had plans to set the tractor on so that he could take the tire off and repair it.

149

The man lowers his left shoulder below the belly of the tractor and at the front of the tractor and lifts the tractor stump high. He reaches out with his free hand and grabs the stump and pulls it under the tractor." David speaks:

"Brenda, that story sounds like a tall tale, but I realize that your grandfather would not make up something. That man should have been in the Olympics! Did Mr. Henry see your grandfather Zeb behind that tree?"

"No, I don't believe so, or at least Mr. Henry did not seem to notice." Mattie comes to the door and knocks getting David and Brenda's attention. David opens up the door wondering what Mattie wanted."

"Mattie, what brings you to our door this time of the morning?" Mattie is all excited and her head is shaking a little as was her habit or as some would say part of her affliction.

"David, Mr. Henry wants to see you and Brenda." David turns his head with a look of curiosity toward his wife and speaks.

"I wonder what that man wants to see us for, dear?"

"He probably wants to meet you and see me. I have not seen him in years."

"Where has he been?"

"Oh, I am sure here on the plantation. There are a lot of folks I have not seen as of yet. People stay busy. Henry and his four sons run one of our Blacksmith shops for us. He likes to fix farm machinery. A lot of our farm machinery cannot be purchased and parts have to be manufactured here on the plantation. The patents have long expired. Henry is also a good mechanic on modern cars, trucks, farm machinery, or whatever needs fixing around here. My brothers and I learned how to work on machinery helping Mr. Henry. David let's not hold him." David and Brenda quickly make their way outside and walk down one of the huge twelve foot tall steps out onto the yard and then step over to Mr. Henry who is still talking to Beard Pridgen. Mr. Beard realizes that Brenda and David are near and turns his head in their direction.

"James, here they are." James Henry gets off the tractor and Brenda hugs him and introduces her husband David. The sweet smell of Prince Albert pipe tobacco fills the air and has taken residence in James' leather jacket. James next holds out his hand and David shakes James' powerful right hand. James momentarily takes his pipe out of his mouth and speaks.

"Miss Brenda, it sho is good to have you back! I calculate that it has been four years the last time I laid eyes on you. How have you been doing?"

"Mr. James, I have been working and raising a family."

"What line of work are we talking about?"

"I taught at a local university. David is a marine scientist and a rock expert." James speaks:

"Well, I have never taught at a fancy university, but I hope that I was able to teach you and your brothers a thing or two?"

"Yes, sir, you are a good teacher." James takes off his old brown leather hat and scratches his head a little and speaks:

"Brenda, me and some of the folks are planning on a get together like the ones you know us folks hold around here. It has been a long time since you have joined us. I believe that was years ago before you started going to that university in Wilmington. Now, Mr. David, you are most welcomed to come along too. We are just simple country folk around here. We will not be drinking hard liquor or doing anything we shouldn't, but we will be staying up until one o'clock the next morning. Brenda, you just explain everything to your fine young husband if and before he comes; I would not want to put him in any embarrassing situation; you know the routine." Mr. Henry gives David and Brenda a courtesy nod while holding the front of his hat between his thumb and index finger. He gets back on the tractor and drives off with his John Deer tractor. David does not know what to make of the situation and speaks.

"Brenda, what sort of party is he talking about?"

"David, it will be an experience I am sure you will not forget nor have the luxury to turn down."

"What do you mean by that?"

"We would not want to offend them. I am sure that you will have a very interesting and fun time. The folks around here hold parties like they did over a hundred and fifty years ago. You will learn what is meant by soul food. When all of the eating is done, we will sip a little homemade wine and we will sit and listen to ghost stories that will alarm you and are guaranteed to keep your interest." David looks pleased and speaks:

"Why, not, I enjoy faraway travel and now we can have a cultural experience right here without having to pack our bags!" Brenda smiles and speaks:

"You mean that it is you that can experience something different. Remember, I was raised around here. Just know that I have always eaten anything offered to me."

"Come on, surely it is not that bad, Brenda."

"No, David, I didn't say anything offered was bad, just that most of it is different than what you are accustomed to."

"Brenda, I look forward to the party. I will have something more to tell my parents and friends about when I get back to Boston." Our story skips a day and finds the Pridgen Clan at the breakfast table. Everyone is aware of the get together that Brenda and David are invited to. Mrs. Lilly Pridgen smiles and looks toward David while speaking.

"David, the get together at James Henry's place tonight is their way of welcoming you as an official member of the Pridgen Clan. When I first married Zeb here, Henry's grandfather invited us over for a party. Of course, we have now been to dozens of them. Now we will look out for the children and you two can go over there and come back when you feel like it. Lillian and I will save a nice breakfast for you when you guys decide to wake up. I would imagine it will be one or two in the morning before you can break loose from Henry's house." That evening at around six thirty, David and Brenda get into one of Mr. Beard's small pickup trucks and drive to the black community located on the massive Pridgen Plantation. David drives to the first bridge that he and his family first saw the black youths on who were fishing when the Smiths moved from Boston to the plantation. He turns left beyond the heavy duty wooden bridge and goes about two thousand feet and turns right on the road that goes side of Uncle Roy Henry's house.

Both David and his wife Brenda look left and notice that some small children are having a great time on the swing that hangs on a large limb under the oak tree that is a hundred feet from Henry's house. David notices that Roy's aged mother is on the porch with a large pan apparently shelling peas or beans; he is not sure. Henry and his family, except for the older matriarch of the Henry family, are probably already at the James Henry house. Great Grandma Henry will stay at home and watch the small kids. Our young couple passes the workshop Roy Henry works in and the huge building where the lumber is prepared and stored for the log cabins. Only two young men are walking around the premises. Brenda told David that they were there to protect the place. Miss Clover the dog is standing near the road with her seven puppies. She apparently recognizes David and is waging her tail. David slows down and speaks to her to let her know that he recognizes her presence. Brenda speaks:

"Aren't those puppies cute!"

"Yes, they are Brenda. Uncle Roy told me that the mother is called Miss Clover. I met her and her puppies the day I came this way to visit Uncle Roy at his workshop. He tells me that Miss Clover will remain at one house or wherever for no more than a year. She drops off litters of half grown puppies every where she chooses to stay."

"Who owns her, David?"

"I was told that no one owns her, but that everyone takes care of her and her puppies when she chooses to live at their house." David notices that a buckboard carrying a black man and woman has just entered the road they travel. The couple had arrived from a side road.

"I see that we are being followed, Brenda." Brenda looks back and realizes that the people in the buckboard being pulled by two large brown mules are the Corbetts.

"Oh, they are the Corbetts. I have known those folks all of my life."

"I guess that they also live here on the Pridgen Plantation?"

"Actually they don't. These people live on Highway 210 about nine miles from here. I understand that Mr. Corbett is a very good farmer. He is well respected by both black and white neighbors." David continues to drive down the narrow white sandy road. Brenda points the way because there are few road signs. On both sides of the road David takes mental note of the houses and the way these people live. He sees that most of these people love to decorate their yards with large seashells. He wonders where all of the shells came from. Some of them are unusually large and appear to be very old. Tires surround many of the smaller shrubs and trees as a form of decoration and a way to keep mulch around the young plants. Dogs and cats were everywhere for the children to play with. Occasionally he would see a goat or two in a yard. One group of children had two large male goats hitched to a small cart and they were having the time of their lives riding around the yard and on the road when there was no traffic. David speaks:

"Brenda, these people live like people much over a hundred years ago in many ways. I can say that they appear to be happier than any group of people I have seen before. Why don't they paint their houses around here?"

"I am not sure. I can tell you that they seem to last forever. Father told me that most of these houses are over a hundred years old. He told me that the houses are rot resistant because they were constructed from mature heart lumber. Lumber companies today seldom find such trees to cut. Around here we protect our virgin trees. I know, the houses are not beautiful by today's standards, but will probably be still standing after the particle board mansions have long rotten down. I am sure that you have noticed that all of them have plenty of chimneys for fireplaces. Folks around here are always stocked up on plenty of free wood. Every family always has a big garden three times a year around here, spring, summer, and fall." David speaks:

"Yes, I have figured that out. These people worry about little. I am just concerned about those who would like to live differently. I would believe that if you are born here on the plantation you are stuck here."

"No, not always; I have heard little complaints. We do have a few who have so called escaped the plantation and have gone up North to big cities like New York, but they often return."

"Why is that?"

"Well, some leave for the wrong reasons and as Father says and the older black folks around here say; they return back dressed in wooden overcoats." David looked perplexed for a moment and catches on to what his wife is saying."

"In other words, they get into the wrong crowd of people and find themselves at the business end of a gun or a knife?"

"Something like that, David." A few do make it and we are always proud to hear about their success. Several young Corbett and Barnhill girls are now respected nurses in big cities. We have had a few to become popular musicians. I do remember that one guy became a high school principle, but he remained in North Carolina. Once in awhile some of these folks will drop by our house and say hello. It is always such a delight to hear them talk about their new life. Grandfather Zeb tells all of them that they are always welcomed back before or after retirement."

"Do any of them actually take him up on his offer?"

"No, not very often, but once in awhile, a person will come back to the plantation because he or she simply could not make it. Often the culture shock in unbearable. They miss family and friends, and the good food. These people are not used to living off of pizza, pasta, hamburgers, and canned food." David and Brenda at last see the James Henry house. Already a crowd of laughing, loud talking people have arrived. People's mules are being unhitched from buckboards and are being led to the barn where the animals will be fed and watered before being led out into the small pasture where they can relax or do what they do naturally. Practically everyone is carrying platters and pots full of food to long tables situated between a grove of large live oak trees that are naturally decorated with hanging strands of curly gray moss. Benches for the people are nailed and bolted secure in between trees for people to sit on. The benches are actually made of a couple of eight by two inch boards running side of each other. Three large swings hang from tree limbs. Several black ladies are in them swinging slowly and are using hand fans to cool down and discourage unwanted insects. Two large yard dogs are on patrol in the yard apparently feeling the need to look like they are on to something. David notices several half grown kittens under the house looking and wondering what all the commotion is about.

About forty feet from the house stands an old outdoor well. Apparently it is no longer in service because the top is covered with plywood and it has been bricked all around. On top of the well are several decorated porcelain flower pots showing off the beautiful jonquils growing inside them. Running along a split rail fence that is in front of the house are hundreds of Iris reticulate. The yard is also decorated here and there with white ceramic animal forms like ducks, hens, rabbits, and one laid back bullfrog wearing sunglasses while holding an umbrella over its head.

"Brenda, I believe that we are the only people driving; everyone else appears to be coming here on wagons. I feel out of place!" Brenda speaks:

"The next time we are together around here we need to ride some horses. I believe that we will have a wonderful time!" David parks the truck and the couple gets out. About two hundred feet away David notices a rather large barn with an old John Deer tractor parked side of it. A tin can sits on top of the tractor's old exhaust pipe and a large washtub covers the seat or what is left of the original seat. David learns that the tractor once belonged to James Henry's grandfather. The tractor had been temporarily removed from the barn so that one of the sheds built on the side of the barn could be used in case it rained. David notices animal shapes or something hanging on the side of the shed that arouses his curiosity. He walks toward the barn to get a better look. When he got closer to the shed, he realized that he is looking at a history of Uncle James Henry's or somebody else's hunting trips. David speaks:

"Brenda, take a look at all of these animal skins, skulls, and horns will you! Mr. James must be part caveman!"

"People around here like to display their hunting skills! David there was one white man near Canetuck that had over thirty black bear heads mounted in his den."

"I hope for the bear's sake that his kin are not also trying to kill all of the bears they can kill legally!"

"No, I don't believe that any of his grandchildren have followed his practice. I think he over did it, but it was not unlawful and I am sure that he never considered the fact that there were only five or six thousand wild bears in the entire state back in those days."

"Brenda, how would you know that?"

"I heard Grandfather Zeb talking about it. Grandfather Zeb does not allow bear or big cat hunting on his plantation. He tells me that the Good Lord did not intend us to shoot up everything just for sport." David speaks:

"Are there any black bears around here now days?"

"I only know about one around our neck of the woods. Grandfather Zeb calls him Old Scar Face. Who knows, he might just pay us a visit when we are walking in the woods around here?"

"That does not sound very safe, Brenda?"

"I would not worry about it too much. He has never bothered anyone. I believe that he kind of likes human company." David speaks again:

"It looks like a couple of Old Scar Face's kin are up on the side of this here barn!" Take a look at the size of that skull! I bet that bear weighed over eight hundred pounds!"

"I was told by James that his grandfather shot the bear because he was caught in the pig pen trying to kill a young sow with her pigs. James Henry Senior tried to scare off the bear by firing his shotgun up in the air, but he was forced to shoot it." David counted a hundred deer antlers nailed to the side of the barn. One skull once belonged to a horse. David was not sure why the skull was not buried along with the rest of the animal.

"Brenda, do you mind if we walk under the main building?"

"No, and I am sure Mr. Henry does not mind." David noticed a large wooden water trough in front of the garage part of the building. Inside there were several tractors and one truck being repaired. Thousands of tools, and shop machines were under the garage. David noticed that the shop did not have a heavy lift like most modern garages, but a cemented bay with steps running down both its ends. Cars, trucks, or whatever that needed to be worked on were driven over the bay and the mechanic would walk down the steps into the bay to get beneath the machinery to work on it.

"Now that is neat, Brenda. I have never seen a setup like this one. No lift ramp, but this bay works just as good." Brenda speaks:

"Actually it works better than a modern hydraulic lift because this one works when there is no electricity, and you don't have to worry about it having a mechanical failure and it collapsing on you while holding a heavy truck or tractor."

"Brenda, where is the blacksmith shop?"

"It is behind those garage doors. Henry also does a lot of welding around here. David, we need to get out of here and join the rest of the people." James Henry sees David and Brenda and welcomes them to the get together.

"Well, I be dog, looks like Miss Brenda and her fine young Mister has seen fit to drop by. It sho is good to see you all! It has been a bunch of water that has done went under that bridge since I last laid my eyes on you here at one of our little get togethers, Miss Brenda. How is big city life now days?"

"It is a lot different, for sure, than the way I was reared, Mr. James, but it is like everything else a body is not accustomed to. I adjusted myself to big city life so that I could survive the experience." James speaks:

"Well, I have not had the notion to travel much. I did go to South Carolina once to buy some fire crackers so that we could have a good time on the fourth of July, years ago, when I was a young man. A white law dog stopped us and tries his best to find us at fault on some law, but while he was walking around our old truck and kicking at the bumper and the fender, a hot rod flew by him going about ninety miles an hour in a fancy red Camaro that caught his attention. I could tell that he really had his heart set on staying with us poor country folks so that he could write us a passel of tickets, but he knew that he had to try and stop that white boy before he got his fool self killed and half of Horry County." James pauses and gives David a serious inquiring look.

"Mr. David, I hope that you have found our ways to your liking since you settled in?"

"I have loved every minute of it, Mr. James. It is true that big city life is a lot different than the life you are accustomed to. Boston is a big city, but it is not New York City. We do not have the crime and the many gangs that some large cities are infamous for. The neighborhood I was raised in is a very old neighborhood. It is actually older than the plantation here. People in my old neighborhood still have old fashioned values and work hard to preserve their heritage. My father is a physician that works not because he has to work, but because he enjoys helping people."

"He must be blessed with a lot of this world's goods to not need to work. I can't imagine such!" David chuckles and speaks:

"Our family has lived in Boston for about three hundred years. My tenth grandfather back centuries ago moved to Boston from England. He was a merchant whose wise business practices and sound decisions have benefited his heirs for centuries. He invested in land and all kinds of enterprise in New York City. Mr. James, I am like my father. I believe that a man is called to work. A man who does nothing but lays or wallow around in his wealth is no better than an animal. He has no good reason to be a man." James is surprised to hear Brenda's young husband speak with such conviction. James looks around at the people arriving and turns back toward Brenda and David and speaks:

"Well, I don't believe that me or any of the folks around here will ever be accused of not fulfilling our work destiny in our lifetimes, but even the animals have the good sense to know when to have a little fun once in awhile! Come on and let me introduce you to some of the folks David." David and Brenda look around and realize that they have recently seen some of the people around them. Mr. Preston sees David and Brenda and goes over to them and speaks:

"Well, look ah here. It is sho good to see you, and I see that you have brought your other half to join us tonight! It is good to have you! David. This is, Mr. Jackson Corbett, he is one of the finest men I have ever known, black, white, or yellow!" David holds out his hand to shake Jackson's hand. Jackson grabs Brenda and gives her a hug and gives her an unusual belt. Jackson speaks:

"I was told that you would be here, Miss Brenda. I want you to have this Rattlesnake belt." Brenda holds the belt out so that David could see it. David speaks:

"I have never seen one of these belts except on television. Mr. Jackson. Do you make these belts?"

"Yessa, I do, but mostly I just send the skins off to a company that makes belts, head bands, hat bands, neck ties, and pouches out of them. There are people who drop by my place that simply want the skins so that they can put them in a picture frame behind glass. One time a fellow from a museum came by and wanted an unusually large skin so that he could have it mounted like the snake was alive. You come by one day and I will show you the snake business and all the other things I do to make it in this life. I never find a dull moment." Brenda thanks Mr. Jackson and tells David that they would pay Mr. Jackson and other people on the plantation a visit one day. James sees Ivey Bell Corbett and motions her over.

"Ivey Bell, this here is, Mr. David, Brenda's husband. He come all the way from Boston to live down here." Ivey Bell walks over to David and extends her hand to him.

"David, it is so good to meet you! I bet you have never been to a party like this before. Brenda let me give you a big hug. I believe the last time I saw you, you were getting ready to go to Boston. I helped you with your things."

"Yes, Ma'am, I remember it well!" Ivey Bell speaks:

"It seems like only just a few years to me, but I imagine it seems a lot longer for a young lady. It seems like every year goes by quicker than the next. I scramble to get ready for Christmas and it is not long before it seems I am having to plan the next." Brenda speaks:

"Yes, Mother has told me that it seems like the clocks are running over time. I do know that when I was a little girl in grammar school, it seemed like my summers would last forever. We all had so much fun and never gave out of something to do!" James holds his hands high to get everyone's attention and speaks:

"Neighbors, I am mighty honored to have you all again. As you can see Miss Brenda has come to gather around the tables with us. David, her fine young husband has come along with her. Be sure to speak to him before we depart to our separate ways when our little get together is part of our history. Let's get started. Mr. Roy Henry, you are a praying man: I know. Why don't you say grace for us before we eat our vittles?" Roy says grace and everyone around David and Brenda says amen.

"Brenda, you and David just grab a plate and get what you want." David speaks:

"It looks very good to me, Mr. James." Brenda speaks to David:

"Now, Honey, on this side of the table we have food that you are accustomed to. When you have eaten you fill, we will have a little homemade wine and sit around on chairs and benches and talk. About ten o'clock or so tonight, we will have enough room for the other kind of food."

"You are talking about soul food, right?"

"Something like that. Some of it is on ice to preserve it and to hold it together. Brenda looks around and smiles before speaking to David:

"Well, David, your chance has arrived. Why don't you just bring your large plate down here and help yourself to Uncle Preston's Opossum. Remember, I told you that he captures them and holds them in pens and feeds them for a couple of months until he feels they are safe to eat."

"Yes, I do remember you telling me about the Opossums." David stands near the two large Opossums that are on large cookers surrounded by sweet potatoes and sweet onions. Even their heads have not been removed. While David considers the possibility of having to eat Opossum, Uncle Preston walks up to him and very excitedly offers David a big slice of Opossum and a nice sweet potato. David cannot refuse the offer. More familiar foods are also on the table. David and Brenda put pork into their plates that is still over a slow cooker. The taste is unbelievable good! The shoulder had been in slow cooking very early that day with careful attention to the special barbeque sauces applied to it. Collards, potato salad, cornbread, and fresh roasted corn delighted the guest. David covered the Opossum over with the other food hoping to get by from eating it, but Uncle Preston's watchful eye caught the cover up. Later on that night after David ate the Opossum on his plate, Uncle Preston told Brenda that he made sure David was properly initiated. All true plantation folks needed to learn to eat Opossum. It was a tradition as old as the plantation itself.

"Well, David, how was the opossum, dear?"

"It was not bad. I do believe that it is a little greasy, but other than that, I guess that I will live." I can say that barbeque is probably the best I have ever eaten. Brenda, what other kinds of foods do we have to eat before we leave tonight?"

"Honey, I believe that you should wait a few hours before you learn all. Don't worry, no one has ever died from this food. You like to experience cultural differences. I guarantee you that you will not be disappointed!" Brenda looks directly into David's eyes and cannot help but to laugh a bit. Eleven o'clock finds the good neighbors of James Henry having the time of their lives. James has already filled everyone's glass several times with the rich homemade grape wine. No one is drunk, but everyone has forgotten their troubles if they had any in the first place. James and several of the men have lit yard candles to discourage biting insects and to provide a little light outside. Mrs. Henry has just stepped from the house with two other black ladies with large salted trays of parched peanuts and roasted pecans. Everyone is encouraged with little effort to indulge; the nuts are wonderful! James lights his pipe and the rich smell of Prince Albert pipe tobacco fills the night air. Mrs. Jackson Corbett brings over a nice size plate of soul food for David and Brenda. When she hands the platter to David, he looks down at the platter wondering what he would have to eat next. He remembers his wife's words well. He must not offend anyone. David looks up at Mrs. Corbett and thanks her.

"Mrs. Corbett, thank you for getting this for us. Please don't feel that you need to wait on us; I have two strong legs."

"Brenda, what have we here. I am sure I have no clue."

"David, I will tell you, but I will not break it down and explain the details or at least I will wait until tomorrow. Don't worry. I am not afraid to eat whatever is offered and you should not be concerned. The stuff in the middle of the platter is called hog head cheese, that over there is called souse meat, that is called C loaf, and this is called chit lings. Now I would suggest that you pour a little of this hot pepper vinegar over this food. It helps to bring out the flavor. Take some of this hot moist cornbread to help swallow it."

The Moon was in full bloom and looked absolutely magnificent as it rose above the Pridgen Plantation. There were enough dust particles miles up in the atmosphere to give the Moon a bloody red shade. A nice red and blue colored ring surrounded the Moon. One could just imagine seeing a wicked looking old hag on a homemade broomstick dressed in black with a pointed hood on her head crossing the Moon high in the sky. The sounds of male bullfrogs could be heard from a distance. A large flock of birds fly by apparently having been spooked from their sleep. Bats are seen everywhere circling and swooping down catching insects that are enjoying the light of the full Moon. In the distance, just beyond the edge of the forest, a strange plasma like light moves about. David was told that it was fox fire. Occasionally the hoot of a large owl was heard. No doubt the great bird was on the move going from tree to tree hunting for small rodents. A heavy blanket of fog was silently rolling in on the party making the scene more mysterious and enchanting. James lit a fire and everyone pulled up their seats around the natural psychological comfort it provided. Several people start telling old hunting stories and ghost stories. Uncle Preston, the general manager of the Pridgen Plantation, who was respected by one and all, raised his hand to get everyone's attention.

"Now let's do it right. I want Mr. David here to hear our stories, but if everyone is talking at the same time, no one will get much out of what is being said. Now, James, why don't you tell us that old story your grandfather James Henry Senior used to tell us boys long years ago. I know that no one will ever tell it like Mr. James Senior, but I still believe it worth repeating." James Henry the third clears his throat and takes his pipe out of his mouth and empties it of the used tobacco and puts it into one of the front pockets of his overalls. He reaches up to his face and massages his chin between his thumb and his index finger. James always did this when he was thinking deeply.

"Well, it has been a long time since I have shared this story told by my grandfather James Henry. The story I relate happened way back in the mid nineteen sixties. I understand that Grandpa James was tending the field back of the old Carrie Lamb estate. Now I know where the house was located, but it had long passed into history before I came along. I understand that old lady Lamb had long left this earthly pilgrimage, but that the old home place was still standing. Grandpa told us boys that the roof was about to cave in. Now Miss Carrie's shrubs were still around the house marking off the boundaries of the yard from the field. Grandpa knew the old white school teacher and he had worked for her doing odd jobs in her yard when he was a boy. Things like working in her garden, planting shrubbery, flower bulbs, or raking her yard. Now I understand that the old lady was mighty good to her neighbors, but was very particular when it came to her yard, and she didn't mind getting you straight if you crossed her, shall I say, customs.

"Grandpa told me that back when he was a boy, people's property was respected. You didn't even walk on a road in the woods in the middle of nowhere unless you asked the owner permission. Now that respect extended long after the owner had passed his or her earthly journey down here. To this day, I still do not walk on top of folk's gravesites and mess up the mound where flowers have been planted by the living in honor of the departed. Grandpa James told me in those days folks minded their own business. They did not go out of their way to tend to other people's business living or the dead. I can remember one time when me and my brother were just starting to school good that we were with Grandpa James one day while our folks went to Burgaw. I believe to take care of some legal business. Grandpa used his old John Deer tractor to get around. He hitched a wagon to the tractor and us young-ins rode in the back on the trailer. He was babysitting and entertained us by driving us around the neighborhood. I remember that we went by an old Corbett house that had been abandoned before we came into this life. The owners had long passed into history.

Now Grandpa liked to smoke a pipe just like I do. I spects, I probably picked up the habit from him. Anyway he stopped that old tractor and got out his pipe and was getting ready to fill it with fresh tobacco. Us young-ins jumped off that trailer and ran to the old house and got on the porch and started peeping into the windows. Our grandpa saw what we were doing and had a fit and almost fell in it, to be sure. He made us get off that porch and scramble back to the trailer as fast as our little legs would carry us! I thought that we had just committed an unpardonable sin the way he acted. He told us to mind our own business that we did not want to stir up the wrath of those who were living mostly in the next world. I thought that he had lost his mind. Later on that day he told us children that he learned his lesson when he was working the Miss Carrie Lamb place. Grandpa had finished his work in the field and decided to disk up the shrubbery near the side of the house in the old yard. He felt that it didn't matter. He was in charge of the farming and Miss Carrie had been dead for many years.

He did recognize that some of the shrubby was some that Miss Carrie had a particular affection for. As the disk cut into the shrubs, Grandpa James saw an old lady dressed just like Miss Carrie behind a shrub. Before he could draw another breath, the old lady appeared somewhere else as fast as lightning. Grandpa told us children that it didn't take a rocket scientist to know that had to be Miss Carrie Lamb that no mortal could move that fast. She was no doubt very upset at him plowing up her shrubbery. Now Grandpa was very careful not to attract too much attention from Miss Carrie, so he gently raised the disk the tractor was pulling and without changing his speed or direction slipped out of there."
Ivy Bell spoke:

"James, that story gives me the creepers every time I hear it. I don't know if I could have been as gentle as your Grandpa leaving that place. I believe that I would have torn all of that shrubbery up getting out of there!" James speaks:

"Grandpa told us that he calculated that would be a big mistake. He was already aware that the tractor or even if he was in a fast car, it could not have moved faster than a spirit. He decided to respectfully correct his actions and not arouse the old lady's wrath. He knew how angry she could be in life and he sure was not going to test her temperament out now that she was not restrained by the limits of her mortal frame." James looks at Jackson and speaks:

"Brother Corbett, now this would be a good time to share with our folks here that story you told us one time about the graveyard."

Jackson hesitated and spoke:

"Well, I guess that I could share the old story with our new guest, Mr. David. The rest of the folks have heard it several times. It is not exactly a story about spirits, but it is a good starter story to get us in the mood for some more real ghost stories tonight. My father told his children this story long years ago when we were sitting on the front porch after supper one hot summer night. He said that the old story had been repeated a million times by folks all over our part of the country. I understand that a young man was late getting back home after a hard long workday. He did not have a mule or any transportation like we are blessed with, but had to walk everywhere he went. The sun was about set and he did not have a flashlight. It was in the day when most folks did not have such fancy aids to see in the dark with. Anyway he needed to get home and decided to use a short cut. Now he would not have minded using the short cut in broad daylight, but he did not fancy having to walk through an old huge graveyard after the sun was set. He got up his courage and decided to go ahead and chance it and go through the bone yard. The trip, if successful, would save him a mile of walking and stumbling around in the darkness trying to get home. He started walking and was doing a little praying to comfort his mind, when all of a sudden, to his horror, he fell into a deep pit. Now the experience nearly froze him with fear. It was all he could do to move about, but he realized that he had to get out of that fresh hole that had only been there a day or two.

"It was common knowledge that a neighbor had passed and the funeral would be held sometime the next day. A great dread fell upon him. He did his very best to get out of that six foot deep hole. The harder he tried, the bigger the hole got. He could not get a foot hold because the entire graveyard was a sand hill. In fact, he soon discovered that he had dug into the side of a metal box. He realized that the metal was from a coffin. He stopped digging fearing that he would cause the coffin to slip or fall over into the hole he stood in. He decided to stick it out and prayed that the night would pass quickly so that someone would happen along and hear his cry for help and get him out of the grave. He fell asleep and was awaken by a scream and a thud. He realized that someone else shared his fate and had also fallen into the grave. He watched the fellow on the other side of the hole desperately trying to get out. He heard the young man pray for help and ask for the strength to get out of the deep hole. Having compassion on his fellow man, he speaks to him and tells him that there was no use trying to get out of the hole that he had been trying all night himself without success. Now I am sure that second young man did not expect help to arrive so soon, especially just a voice from the grave, but his prayers were gloriously answered and the second young man instantly received the strength he prayed for to get out of the deep sandy grave.

The instant he heard those words of comfort from the first young man, he jumped straight into the air like a pair of rockets were attached to his legs. He had absolutely no problem exiting that grave and took off running for his house like no Olympic runner would even dream to keep up with." David and many of the other listeners laughed until the tears fell from their eyes." David and Brenda listened with anticipation to story after story. David wished that he had a disk recorder so that he could save these wonderful stories for others to hear and enjoy; they were spell binding! Several people had to leave around one o'clock and David and Brenda thanked Uncle James Henry for a wonderful time. Brenda and David were given a nice platter of food to take with them before they left for the mansion. Our couple gets into the truck and start back toward the mansion. The fog was thick and there were few road signs to guide them around the maze of trails to get back to the house where they had plans to get into a soft bed and sleep the night away. Brenda speaks:

"Well, David, how did you like the party?"

"I am truly impressed. I have been to a lot of fancy balls and corporate functions sponsored by the upper crust of Boston and have experience the glamour and the limelight of the movers and shakers of society, but I can truly say without reserve that I don't remember ever having so much fun since I have been an adult! I will never forget the food and the down to earth entertainment these so call simple folks have shared with us."

The next morning, at nine thirty, David and Brenda get up feeling rested and very peaceful. They hear their children outside having a great time playing with the two yard dogs. David looks down and sees his mother-in-law and Mrs. Lilly Pridgen walking down the steps holding baskets in their arms. Mr. Zeb is probably either on the first floor porch or is somewhere nearby on the grounds. Beard has already gone to Atkinson where he will stay about four hours at his hardware store. Mattie is probably taking care of some chore.

"David, I am hungry, let's go down and have some breakfast. Mother told me that there would be plenty for us when we decided to get up and eat." During breakfast David tells Brenda that he will be leaving for Boston the next day.

"I will miss you, David. I wish we could all go with you, but there will be no time to visit. I am sure you will have your hands full making arrangements for the exploration submarine to be delivered to Wilmington."

"Yes, I will get to be with my parents only about one day. I have never been away from home this long before. I miss my parents, my old neighborhood, and the school I worked at for seventeen years. When we go back there in about two weeks, I want us to stay at least two weeks. Our children need to really get a chance to see their old neighborhood again. They are very young and I do not want them to forget the city of their birth. I want us to go as a family to all of the important historical buildings, monuments, and museums we can. I want our children to appreciate the importance of Boston to our country. What happened there changed the course of history."

"I totally agree with you, David. I too want to visit the places you are talking about. I wish every American had the chance to visit Boston. It is one of the most historically significant places in our country. I do believe religiously that people need to understand who they are and why they are here."

Ten

David Goes Back to Boston to Take Care of Official School Business

Two days later David was in Boston. It has been over three months since David moved to the Pridgen Plantation located a few miles outside of a small town called Atkinson, N.C. He felt almost like a stranger or tourist in the city of his nativity. The Pridgen Plantation was old, but it was only middle aged compared to the history Boston could boast of. David missed the old historical sites that filled the world of his childhood. David's parents and his ancestors all the way back for hundreds of years called the Boston area their home. David went to a special private magnet school that was geared to the task of training exceptionally bright young people who were able to demonstrate an IQ of at least a hundred and eighty. Only a hand full of the most gifted of people on earth had the aptitude to be privileged to be in the program. In fact, by the time David finished high school at seventeen, he had also taken enough college courses to enter into Boston University as a graduate student taking a double major. By the time of his graduation at the age of twenty three, he had earned a doctorate in both geology and oceanography. Nearly ten years later he was dean of the department of science and had already taken his place as a heavy weight in both fields or disciplines.

The early Puritans, who founded the city in 1620, were big believers in education. They would have been very proud of this native son. In fact, Boston is considered the Athens of America. It is also the Cradle of Liberty, because this is the city that produced the spark that initiated our struggle for independence from Great Britain. Every informed American is aware of the Boston Massacre, the Boston Tea Party, and the several battles that took place in and around Boston to win our independence. How many American cities can boast of places of such historical significance as Faneuil Hall, Paul Revere's house, or Bunker Hill, or boast that it has our country's oldest University, Harvard University, founded in 1636, in its metro area of Cambridge? In fact, Cambridge Common is where General George Washington himself first took over the Continental Army.

David's earliest ancestors lived in Charlestown and later moved to Back Bay near the Charles River. Back Bay was once about three thousand acres of useless swampy land on the banks of the Charles River. The City of Boston decided in the 1850's to drain this part of the swamp so that the city would have room for expansion. This area of Boston near the Charles River is famous for its old very beautiful townhouses. High class restaurants and costly shops line Boylston and Newbury streets in this part of town. Things have changed since the famous townhouses were first erected. Today most of Boston's wealthiest families have moved from Back Bay and college students and many unmarried young educated people have taken their places. Records reveal that affluent families started leaving Back Bay Community around the nineteen twenties. Today the wealthy live mostly in northern and western communities. David's great grandfather moved his people back to Charlestown in 1930. Charlestown was founded by English colonists in 1630. Later many of these people moved to what we call Boston and helped found Boston. Charlestown was annexed by Boston in 1873. Anyone who reads about American history is aware of the U.S.S. Constitution, also known as *Old Ironsides.*" The *U.S.S. Constitution* is docked at the Charlestown Naval Yard. While a young boy, David had spend many days walking the decks of the famous ship and had come familiar with many of the people responsible for the upkeep of the vessel. Not far away is the monument that was erected to commemorate the famous battle of Bunker Hill in 1775.

David turned into the drive way of his parents' house. He looked back of himself through his rear view mirror and saw his old home. The house had been once owned by a Jefferson family. Mr. Jefferson had been a prominent merchant when David was growing up. He remembered the Jefferson's two children, Billy Jefferson and his sister Debbie Jefferson. Billy went to Africa after graduating from Bible College to become a missionary. Debbie married an engineer and the last time David had heard about them, Debbie and her family had moved to Florida and her husband was working for NASA. Both of the Jefferson kids were finishing up high school when David was in the eighth grade in a private school. David just sits awhile and looks at his parents' home and scans the neighborhood. A hard lump forms in David's throat. He truly misses the old neighborhood where he and his dear friends grew up together. Some of his old buddies were still living in the neighborhood. They shared good times together that will not be forgotten! David had visited many places in the United

States in his childhood. His parents carried him once to London, England, and then on to the continent to visit Paris, France, but David had not been away from home for over a few weeks at a time. He grew up in Boston, went to school in Boston, and had taught in a local university for over seventeen years.

David's parents' house was once the house of David's great grandparents. The house was over a hundred and forty years old. David was told that the three story red bricked mansion had been built by a gentleman who was considered a ship baron. Captain Horn Blower owned a fleet of ships that he sailed back and forth from Boston to Great Britain. This was over two decades after the American Civil War. Business was booming in those days in Boston and Captain Horn Blower was one of the locals who was riding the crest of the wave of prosperity. A very beautiful heavy duty black iron fence surrounded the front of the mansion and its sides. In the back, a heavy wall made out of ballast stones stood guard. The house stood on a five acre plot. David's mother had a nice greenhouse in the back and a sort of mini-park that even included a pond that had a stone bottom. The pond was filled with several dozen over sized goldfish that were familiar friends. A walk made of flagstone surrounded the pond along with ornate stone picnic tables and benches. A cement walk provided the Smith's and their occasional guest a comfortable walk around the huge yard all the way to the back gate. Tall ornate black lamp post provided light and beauty to the walk. Great care was given to the yard, which was really a biotical wonder of mostly small trees, shrubs, flowers beds, and beautiful statues. The garden even has a large gazebo made of white brick that is large enough to seat twenty people on a nice afternoon for a tea or perhaps light lunch.

David's father, Doctor Smith Senior, was not home, but David's mother was in the house preparing a seafood meal for her family. Mrs. Patsy Smith was almost finished cooking her meal. She was preparing Seafood Gumbo, Asparagus Casserole, Squash Casserole, Sweet Pickled Beets, Crab Cakes, Lemon Cake, and Banana Nut Cake. David walks onto the huge porch of the mansion and almost wished he had not moved to North Carolina, but he was thankful that his wife's parents were very special people who lived like most could only read or dream about. David rang the door bell and waited for his mother to come to the door. David's mother was aware that he was coming for a visit. When the door was opened, David and his mother just stood and looked at each other for a second. The warmth of love generated between them could have melted an iceberg! Mrs. Patsy Smith spoke first:

"David, I feel like you have been gone for over a year. Let me hug you! I hope you are hungry because we are going to have Seafood Gumbo." Mother and son embrace and kiss each other.

"Your father will be here in about twenty or thirty minutes. He had an unexpected medical emergency to drop by just before he was preparing to come home."

"What kind of emergency, Mother?"

"The police brought old man Captain Turntable by his office. They found him outside his home half out of his mind. He was preaching to people passing by on the sidewalk. Now normally the police would not be too concerned unless he was harming someone or doing himself some harm, but they know that the old salt is no religious man. The police said that he would preach to people walking by on the public sidewalk in front of his house, and then start cursing them out if they did not give him their full attention."

"What is going to happen to him, Mother?"

"I am sure that his family will have to put him into an institution where he will be taken care of." David smiles a little and shakes his head.

"Mother, I can't imagine that old man preaching to anyone! He hates preaching and preachers. I would imagine that the police had their hands full trying to handle that huge old guy!" Mrs. Patsy speaks:

"Yes, I understand it was quite a scuffle to control him. He knocked out three of our best officers and broke one of our officer's arms. When he was a young man, they say he could do the work of six good men. Come on in David. I am almost finished cooking." David is directed to go to his old third story room that has not changed since he was a child. David puts his coat and suitcase in the closet. It was good to be home again! David was thankful that his mother had kept his room just like it had always been. On one wall was a huge picture of the *U. S. S. Constitution*, or as some call it *Old Ironsides*. A beautiful fireplace was the center attraction of the very large and stately bedroom. Over the mantle was a beautiful hand carving of a three foot long Atlantic Cod Fish. Over beside one of the windows stood one of David's favorite childhood toys, a twelve inch reflecting telescope Santa brought him one Christmas. David would spend several hours each week looking at the stars, the Moon, and the myriads of celestial wonders from the widow's watch above the third floor. He could also look at the ships and pleasure boats that were in the Charlestown River. Over on a fancy table stood the huge microscope his father gave him after his father purchased an electron microscope for his practice. David's father is a prominent doctor in Boston. In a museum style display cabinet, behind glass, and in front of mirrors of very large and fancy shelves, laid David's rock collection of beautiful and rare gems and minerals. Special lights like infra red lights were attached to the inside of the shelf to bring out the beauty and hidden properties of the collection. Even the hundred and fifty gallon aquarium filled with small saltwater fish, beautiful coral, plants, and a miniature model of an old wooden sailing ship were kept just like it was when David was a boy. His mother hired a man to come over once a week and see to it that the beautiful aquarium and its inhabitants were kept healthy. While David and his mother were talking in the front hall, the door bell rang. His mother speaks:

"I can't imagine who it could be. David, would you mind seeing who it is?" David turns and walks down the long hallway into the foyer that leads to the double entrance door while his mother walks to the kitchen to finish her cooking. David opens a door and his father is standing facing him with a smile on his face.

"Father, you never ring the bell. I am sure that you have not forgotten your house keys!"

"Well, it could be only one other explanation as to why I rang the door bell." David's father smiles and prepares to hug David. "Son, it is good to have you back! I just wished that plantation was about eight hundred miles closer so I could visit you every week. I miss seeing you and the kids and Brenda across the street coming and going to work and play."

"I understand that you had a last minute patient this afternoon, Father."

"Your mother told you. Yes, that was exciting, I will assure you! I gave him a shot to make him manageable and called his son and advised that he meet the police at the mental facility when they carried him over there. The old man is a terror for sure, but he should not be put in jail because he really is no criminal. I am sure the inmates at the jail will appreciate my looking out for their mutual interest because that old man could hurt somebody." David smiles and speaks:

"Yes, sir, I have seen him in action a few times. I once saw him scatter a crowd of dock workers when one of them made a smart remark about his fishing boat."

"David, let's wash up; I would imagine your mother wants us to go to the small dining room and eat." Doctor Smith said grace as was his custom and the Smiths indulged.

"Mother, the Seafood Gumbo is wonderful! I have been eating a lot of Catfish and other freshwater fish, but I have not eaten seafood but once since moving to the plantation." After the meal is over with and the dishes are put into the dishwasher, David and his parents go to the beautiful den in his parents' home. This room also has a magnificent fireplace! It is much larger than the bedroom fireplaces. The huge fireplace is nearly fourteen feet wide and is made of specially designed fireplace bricks that are several times larger than ordinary brick normally used for fireplaces. Wood is stored in a large insert in the wall that holds three cords of wood at a time. The outside of the fireplace is made of beautiful red sandstone. The mantle is a magnificent work of cherry wood. Rich carvings of the heads of two Polar Bears are on each end of the mantle. A twelve by seven foot oil painting of a clipper ship in full sail in a light gale is above the mantle. The painting was created by David's great grandmother on his mother's side of the family. A huge chandelier hangs from the ceiling of the great den. On one side of the room is a magnificent grandfather clock that was imported from England over a hundred and forty years ago. The clock stands over nine feet tall. The room is decorated with wall paper imported from China back in the nineteenth century. One could spend a life time casually looking at this beautiful and extensive work depicting rural life in China and continue with delight to discover its secrets. The room is filled with antique furniture that has been handed down throughout the centuries. David's father is a doctor, but he loves to smoke a pipe in the evening after his work is over. The rich smell of the expensive tobacco fills the room where David and his mother sit. David's mother catches him up with the local news and she next briefs him on the whereabouts of his old buddies. David's father speaks:

"Well, son, how is plantation life now days?" David grins and speaks:

"Good, no one has escaped." David's mother speaks:

"I hope they are not forcing anyone to stay there!"

"No, mother, I was just kidding. I was told that once in awhile someone might decide to leave the plantation, but I have also been told that most folks find their way back." Doctor Smith speaks:

"David, I would love to get a chance to visit that place. I have read about plantation life, but I have never visited one. I understand that there are not many of them left in the South."

"Yes, sir, I have read a few books about some of the remaining Southern Plantations. The houses are usually very large and beautiful and the original owners owned a lot of property that had all kinds of activity going on." Mrs. Smith speaks:

"When I think about Southern Plantations, I think about the huge fields of cotton and sternwheeler boats parked alongside docks being loaded, but I guess those days are now just a part of history."

"Actually, mother, the Pridgen Plantation still grows cotton. I understand that they have about two thousand acres of the crop." Doctor Smith speaks:

"David, what person is responsible for the planting and harvesting the crops on that plantation?"

"A fine gentleman the folks call Uncle Preston manages the plantation. He has a big responsibility because that place has a lot of business going on that keeps a lot of people busy."

"What kind of wages do people earn on that plantation?"

"None that I am aware of; except, for the money given to the younger folks to give them some spending money." David's mother speaks:

"What, I can't believe that the employees or field help work for nothing! That is against the law, unless the laws are different down there!" David chuckles and speaks:

"I have heard no complaints. Everyone is as happy as I have ever witnessed." David's father, Doctor Smith, speaks:

"Maybe, I need to send some of my old buddies that are in the mental health profession down to that plantation to discover the secret to all of that peace and happiness." David speaks:

"Well, I understand that you guys are going to visit us one day. I hope that you will change your minds and visit us before we find a place near Wrightsville Beach. I want you to visit the Pridgens and stay a few weeks. They are very special people. I am very impressed with their lifestyle. I wish that someone would write a book about this most unusual family and their wonderful friends. They are a very private family, but they do have a lot of friends in and around the town of Atkinson. I do believe that plantation must be a little part of Heaven itself." David's mother speaks:

"Well, son, I guess that your father and I will just have to plan a trip there and visit those folks. I don't believe I have ever heard you speak like this about people before." David continued to tell his parents about the many wonderful things that he had experienced while living on the plantation. His father has already decided that he wants to go fishing in the lake and see the many unusual activities taking place on this wonderland David described to his parents. David's mother can't wait to see the beautiful mansion and learn about herbs and see the huge trees and the many flower gardens on the two hundred acre yard.

The next morning after breakfast, David tells his parents goodbye. David gets into his SUV and heads toward the University of Boston where he is expected at the Marine Science Building to get up with the department head, Doctor Dennis Miller. It was good to be back. Goose bumps ran down David's back and neck. He imagined that he felt like a ship captain going back for a visit to his old command. He had put his heart into his work and was able to obtain a lot of government funding and free money from private endowments during his tenure as the department head. The school of science was only about two decades old for the University, but David worked during his seven years as the department head to see to it that it was on a solid foundation that would insure its permanent success. When David was within eye sight of the huge central forum where all the halls on the first floor led from, he noticed a lot of changes that he was not aware of. He was surprised because Doctor Miller usually would call him and give him updates on any new thing going on in the department.

David continued to walk toward the forum and the closer he got he once again felt goose bumps on his back and neck. He saw a large statue of himself standing on an impressive platform in the middle of the forum. A beautiful silver plaque bolted onto a solid block of granite had David's full name and the years he served as the department head. Over on the circular walls of the forum are large lighted panels depicting David's achievements both in words and scores of beautiful greatly enlarged photographs. A wall size computer generated aquarium of sea life delights the mind and the eyes of the beholder. A button could be pushed that would light up the history as presented by voice in chronological order. The computer controlled scene not only had narration, but hours of video clips of new scientific discoveries, the new research ship the university obtained, and impressive deep dives by the science department in special research submarines to photograph and document the wonders of the ocean. The massive work David did to create computer software and delicate cutting edge instruments designed to accurately forecast earthquakes was proudly presented. The school was especially proud of this breakthrough in earthquake prediction because the scientific effort had already been responsible for saving millions of lives.

David just stood before the statue and smiled and shook his head from side to side thinking that this was just too much. He actually was embarrassed. A hand touched his left shoulder and the familiar voice of Doctor Dennis Miller spoke to him.

"It is so good to have you back! I hope that you like our new decorations around here!"

"David turned around all excited and grabbed both of Doctor Miller's hands. He fakes a frown and speaks:

"What is all this about? I come back to my old school for a simple visit and you have already captured me in stone! I do believe that you miss me a little, Dennis!" Doctor Miller also tries to fake a facial expression. He smiles, but behind the smile he has the look of a young man who has lost his best friend.

"Well, David, I suppose we could have all of this removed as soon as possible, if you don't approve." David smiles and takes on a more serious facial expression as he looks about.

"No, I would not want more money spent on this project. Don't believe that it would look good for you if you suddenly decide to have all of this removed. I realize that I will now have to do good at UNCW because I can't imagine coming back here to teach and have to look at my statue every time I leave my office or go to a classroom! I just hope that you have left enough room for yourself if someone decides to put a copy of you in this public place." David smiles and Doctor Miller speaks to David:

"Come on into my office wing. All of the papers are ready waiting for you to sign for the delivery of the submarine to UNCW. The Sea Wise from UNCW will be delivered by a sea going submersible barge in a few weeks."

"Yes, I am aware of that Dennis. I call Doctor Fletcher once or twice a week on his project. He told me that he did not trust a conventional barge to deliver the Sea Wise to Boston University because it would have to be hoisted on the deck of the barge. This is the reason he contracted Barns Shipping Company to use a self powered submersible barge." Doctor Miller speaks:

"His decision will cost over two hundred and seventy five thousand dollars more than a regular barge."

"Yes, I am aware of the cost factor. I am also aware that both institutions will have to bear the burden of the cost. I agree with him because the underwater scientific living quarters is very long and the slightest damage could jeopardize the entire project and put people's lives in danger if the Sea Wise is put in water over a hundred feet deep. The submarine is only about fifty five feet long and lifting it on the back of a barge should not prove to be a problem." Doctor Miller speaks:

"I can't complain because you are saving us a lot of money by having the submarine put on a large barge that was scheduled to arrive in the Port city of Wilmington anyway."

"Yes, I figured that there was no point in paying for a barge to deliver the submarine when I could catch one already scheduled to deliver thousands of tons of expensive equipment to local factories in the Wilmington area. There was plenty of room left on the barge to accommodate our exploration submarine. When it arrives at the State

Ports in Wilmington, a large specially equipped truck will deliver UNCW's new submarine, or at least it will be new to UNCW." Doctor Miller hands David a fancy pen and he is asked to sign several papers to release the submarine.

"You know the routine, David, just sign your John Hancock here and on the last page at the bottom and we can get into our vehicles and drive to the docks where the barge is docked." Thirty minutes later David and Doctor Miller stand near the Barns Tug Boat. David's SUV is being loaded onto the barge because he is going to take the trip with the exploration submarine to the State Port in Wilmington, N.C. where a specially designed truck will deliver the submarine to UNCW's holding facility. "It has been a real joy to get to be with you again, David. I just hope that we will get the pleasure of a soon future visit to our humble facility." David's friend Doctor Dennis Miller holds his right hand out for David to shake. He has a firm, but somewhat sad look on his face. David speaks to his once assistant in the science department.

"I should be back for a visit in about two weeks or so. My kids miss their grandparents so we are going to come back here and stay for about two weeks. I don't want the kids to lose the closeness they have with my parents. I am sure Brenda also wants to see my parents, they are very close. You do realize that I will still be working for Boston University? I will be traveling back and forth from Wilmington to Boston about six times a year. I told my children that we would take advantage of these trips to visit their grandparents. My parents told me that they would in turn try to visit us several times each year. I just hope they will come on down and visit Brenda's parents before we find a home near Wrightsville Beach." Dennis speaks:

Yes, I would imagine that your parents would want to visit that plantation. I didn't realize such a place was still functioning. I was under the impression that the Civil War put them all out of business."

"You are mostly correct, Dennis. Most of the plantations owners had to sell their land off just to eat. There are a few left, but they are usually state owned or serve as motor inns or bed and breakfast inns. People pay to stay in a bedroom a night or so. I saw one some years ago on television that not only serves the traditional meals, but have tour guides." Dennis speaks:

"Yes, I believe that the history and some of the so called haunting attract most of the people interested in staying a few days in one of those big plantation houses." David smiles and speaks:

"I have heard no information about the house I am staying in being haunted." The horn of the tugboat sounds off and both men look in the direction of the tug. David walks up and boards the tugboat and is greeted by the first mate, Doug Browning.

"I suppose that you are the owner of that fine looking little submarine on our lead barge?" David extends his hand out to the man, smiles a little, and speaks.

"No, sir, I can't say that I own it, but I am responsible for its safe arrival to the City of Wilmington, N. C." Doug Browning speaks again to David.

"Well come on and I will show you your luxury suite that I am sure you expected."

"As long as I have a decent place to sleep and take a shower, I believe my expectations will be met." The first mate speaks:

"Well, sir, I believe then that you have come to the right place. We are a virtual floating hotel with all the amenities money can afford. I also have a nice piece of land I would like to sell you in the middle of a lake in Canada if you believe me so far." David realized that the first mate was a fellow who loved to talk and tease. David speaks:

"I suppose that the only problem with that fine piece of property you no doubt want to sell me at an unheard of bargain price is that it is unfortunately underwater and not on an island in the middle of that lake?" Doug Browning smiles and realizes that David will be a lot of fun. First Mate Doug Browning walks with David to the crew's quarters. The large tug has three complete stories and a smaller wheel house comprising the fourth level. Our subjects climb the stairs to the third floor where the crew sleeps and lounges out. David is impressed with the size of the thirteen by thirteen foot bedrooms where there is plenty of room for a small bed, cloths closet, and a small desk and chair. The lounge is larger than the den of most average houses. There is a nice fifty four inch plasma television mounted on one wall. Couches, tables, and chairs are available for crew members to enjoy. Several tables have games on top such as *The Game of Life and Monopoly*. On one wall are photos of several past captains and their crews. A large very impressive model of the tugboat is on a table against a wall. David speaks:

"I see that you guys really have it rough on board." The First Mate answers:

"I would imagine that we are like firemen. There are periods of time when our days could not be better. We get a chance to relax a bit and enjoy each other's company and call our families, but a storm can come up that can make our existence practically a living hell! We do have all of the modern equipment on board and we are aware of storms coming our way, but that can't stop us unless it is a major hurricane. Doctor Smith, most of our work is done in the Intracoastal Waterway that goes all the way to Florida. Once in a blue Moon we are contracted or asked to assist an ocean vessel that has run into some kind of trouble. I remember us several times going on search and rescue missions when large fishing trawlers were lost or in distress due to engine failures or a storm that overwhelmed the vessels. This ship was originally designed to work on the ocean because of its size and horsepower. It was sold to the company I work for about fourteen years ago. We carried the tug to Newport News Ship Yard and had it refitted so that it could push barges. Today we are pushing three barges at fifteen thousand tones each. Most river tugs and Intracoastal Water Way barges will not handle this much weight." David smiles and speaks:

"That is a lot of tonnage! No wonder this tugboat is called the River Ox! How long is this vessel?"

"It is a little over two hundred and fifty feet long and has two massive diesel engines with nearly fifteen thousand horsepower each. Most of the time we don't need all that power, but it can be a life saver in a storm when we are bringing in a ship that has foundered in high seas! Let's go up to the wheelhouse and meet some of the boys and our captain if you care to."

"I would be delighted, sir, just lead the way." David and Doug Browning walk to the fourth level where the captain and two of the crewmembers are stationed. The door is opened and everyone looks at David. The captain speaks:

"You must be, Doctor David Smith, unless I have a crewmember on board that I am not aware of." Captain Johnny Black looked like a movie character of a rugged and massively built sea captain. He stands at over six feet ten inches tall, and David judges that he must weigh considerably better than four hundred pounds of mostly muscle! Captain Black sported a medium length thick black beard. The hair on his head was also black and somewhat curly complimented with some white showing around his ears. On his huge head was a very impressive captain's hat. "Welcome aboard, I hope that my fine mate here was able to assist you in finding your quarters?"

"Yes, sir, I am very pleased. You have a very nice tugboat here. How long have you been her captain?"

"I have worked with the company for about eight years. Before that I served in the U.S. Navy as a captain."

"Were you the captain of an armed ship?"

"No, sir, my ship carried mostly tanks, troop carriers, and what the Navy wanted it to haul. The ship also can carry hundreds of combat ready

Marines with all their gear and vehicles. That is a nice submarine you are bringing along. How many meters will it go down, Doctor Smith?"

"It will go about 4500 meters down. It does not have the ability to go down to the very bottom of the ocean abysmal, of course, but life down near 4000 meters is a lot different than what we normally see on the surface. It was originally designed to investigate valuable mineral deposits on the bottom. It was replaced by a larger submarine. The Sea Explorer is a DSV or commonly called a deep submersible vehicle. For years there were only about fifty of these vehicles in the world. Governments were the first institutions interested in the development of these small submarines. Much of the desire to design and pay for DSVs came about as a result of the so called Cold War between the former Soviet Union and the United States. For years ROVs or unoccupied tethered vehicles have been the vehicle of choice for most large companies or governments. Why have human occupants with all of the risk involved, when you can use a ROV to inspect cable lines or pipe below offshore oil rigs?" Captain Johnny Black speaks:

"I believe the Navy uses what they call AUVs to do most of their utility work. They are amazing. They are almost like your DSV except no one is on board. They just go about their business on their own. I was told that all the information for the entire mission is on their computer." David speaks:

"That is mostly true. We have tried radio waves to communicate with the computers on board AUVs, but radio waves do not travel very successful underwater. Some more advanced systems on AUVs are now equipped to receive acoustic information." The captain speaks:

"That is amazing. Whales and some other animals have been sending and receiving acoustic information for tens of millions of years and we humans are just learning how! It makes you wonder about our intelligence sometimes." David smiles and speaks:

"I do believe that a lot of the abilities animals possess are like those AUVs you were talking about. The information was programmed in the system. The old folks commonly referred to it as natural instincts or abilities."

Four days later David looked at the clock on the instrument panel of his SUV and confirmed his belief that it was around five o'clock in the afternoon. When he parked the SUV, he got out his suitcase and started walking toward the mansion. He heard the children's high pitched screams of joy. He walks up the twelve foot high steps and walks onto the front porch and realizes that his two children are on a swing their mother is pushing rather hard to excite and thrill them. David walks up facing the swing and sets his suitcase down onto the porch and his wife immediately stops pushing the swing. The kids scream out with joy the moment they jump off the swing running toward their father's outstretched arms. After the children felt that they had been sufficiently hugged, Brenda walks into David's awaiting arms and speaks.

"Well do I get a hug and kiss also?"

"I believe that I have one of each left just for you, Brenda. Did you miss me while I was gone?" Brenda smiles and speaks:

"Don't I always? How was the trip?" David had not called his wife as was his custom except to let her know that he had arrived in Boston and the moment of his departure when the tugboat, the *River Ox,* started moving down the Intracoastal Water Way. He also called Brenda and told her that he was in Wilmington getting ready to follow the big truck that was hauling the DSV to the Masonboro Sound Facility.

"The trip could not have been better! It was so good to see my parents, but I didn't have time to visit any of my old friends in the neighborhood. I did have a wonderful supper and breakfast with my parents and I slept in my old room. Now that brought back the memories! I felt almost like a boy again!" Brenda speaks:

"That is understandable; your mother keeps your old room just like it has always been." David continues his conversation:

"My parents naturally wanted to know about the plantation and if everything was going well around here."

"And what did you tell them, dear?"

"I told them that everything was OK and that no one had escaped!" Brenda looks a little surprised and speaks:

"Come on now, you didn't say that did you?"

"I am afraid I did, but I told them that few had a desire to leave this wonderful place. I believe that I have gotten them all excited about this place and they will visit us here one day and hopefully will stay here a few weeks so that they can really get to see the place and have the opportunity to know your grandparents." Brenda pauses and then speaks with a somewhat sober tone.

"Yes, it would be nice if they got the opportunity to get to know my grandparents before they pass on. I wish that they could be with us for many decades to come, but like their parents and grandparents before them, they will be only fond memories one future day." David speaks:

"I believe that they are much more than that. They all live through each of you. Not only do you guys look very much like them, but you no doubt have similar opinions, habits, customs, and certainly live on the same plantation they are privileged to live on. You all are literally their living legacy. Like a living tree, limbs may die and fall off, but the tree is still alive." Brenda laughs and speaks:

"Yes, David, I suppose this is the reason we call our ancestors and extended family our family tree." David smiles and speaks:

"Oh no doubt what you are saying is true." David smells the air and speaks: "Do I smell something wonderful cooking? I am starving!"

"They didn't feed you while you were on that tugboat?"

"Yes, but the guys took turns cooking and some of them lack the culinary skills I have come accustomed to. Besides, I have not eaten since early this morning when we docked at the State Ports. I ate a pack of nabs and had a coke, but that didn't go very far."

"Why didn't you go somewhere and eat?"

"We were far too busy delivering the DSV to the Masonboro Facility." The so called dinner bell rang and David and Brenda washed their hands and walked into the smaller dining room that is really part of the kitchen. Except for Brenda's brothers, everyone else was sitting at the table waiting for Brenda and David to come in and sit down to eat. Brenda's three brothers were at the logging camp miles from the house. Beard said the grace and the meal of freshly caught fish, cornbread, slaw, apple salad, which was made with raisins, celery bits, cut up walnuts, fresh pineapple, parmesan cheese, sweet vinegar, and salad dressing was eagerly eaten. For desert they ate chocolate cake with pecans on the top, sweet potato pie, and homemade ice cream.

Eleven

Dan Goes Fishing While David, His Father, Visits the Neighborhood

The next morning, Mattie, Brenda, her mother, and Great Grandmother Lilly Pridgen left with Betty, Brenda's eight year old daughter to Burgaw to do a little shopping and to look around a bit. Great Grandfather Zeb Pridgen was going to spend his day working with his herb garden. Ten year old Dan was invited to go fishing at the bridge near the large creek that runs near Uncle Roy Henry's house and the shop he works in. Two young black boys show up at the mansion and call for Dan Smith. David helps Dan get his two cane poles and his tackle box. The boys are a few years older than Dan and they have promised to take care of young Dan and see to it that he gets back home no later than two o'clock in the afternoon. Dan excitedly grabs his gear including enough lunch for all three boys and follows his new friends to the creek. The day is so beautiful! The temperature is in the mid eighties and a slight breeze is blowing. Young Dan Smith takes in a big breath of the fresh country air filled with the fragrances of a multitude of flowering plants. He especially likes the smell of the huge magnolia flowers. In fact, he and another boy reach down and pick up a blossom each just to smell them. The background noise that surrounds our young friends is typical of a Southern Plantation or many farms out in the country. A flock of crows perched on the limbs of a dead pine tree are heard making their strange noises. To Dan it sounded like the crows were laughing at them. The cows at the cow barn were heard mooing apparently pleased that they had been milked and were free to walk around in their large pasture to graze and gaze. The boys continued to walk until they got to the huge barn that was also the first living quarters of the Pridgen family. One of the black boys stopped and looked at the beautiful statues of Captain John Henry Pridgen, and his wife, the beautiful Madam de Lafayette Pridgen and her parents. The young black teen just stared at the impressive statues and shook his head in unbelief.

"I have looked at these statues all my life and I still can't figure out exactly who these people are!" He looked at Dan Pridgen and the other black boy for answers. Jack the great grandson of Jackson Corbett looked at Dan with a questioning look and spoke.

"Hey, aren't they some of your kin people?" Dan looks perplexed and speaks:

"Yea, I think so. Mother said something about these people when she was talking to my grandmother one day when we first started living here." Ivey Bell's great grandson speaks:

"Sure, I know who these people were. These people were the first owners of the Pridgen Plantation. I believe that man is Captain Pridgen. Come on, we need to go on down to the bridge and see about catching a big mess of fish. The water is nice and warm today. We should be able to catch a whole tub of them!" The boys all put red earthworms on their hooks and dropped their fishing lines into the coffee colored water of the creek. The sun was just beginning to seriously warm up the railings of the heavy wooden bridge. Dan sees something moving in the water and points with a finger while he cries out to the other boys for attention.

"Look what is that thing coming over here?" It became obvious that the dark brown oval shaped creature about the size of a large platter was a snapping turtle. The head of the turtle almost looked like a snake head it was sticking out of the water so tall. One of the black boys threw a few small rocks and sticks at the turtle because the turtle could either eat their bait or frighten the fish off. A noise was heard and the boys look up from looking down at the creek and are delighted to see Miss Clover with her puppies. The little dogs line up along the bank of the creek and start lapping the clean cool refreshing water into their mouths with their little red tongues. Dan calls out to them and Miss Clover wags her tail and walks onto the bridge to greet the boys. The puppies soon follow Miss Clover all excited having the time of their young lives. Dan speaks:

"Does anyone own these dogs?" Ivey Bell's great grandson speaks:

"No, not yet, folks around here usually start adopting her puppies about the age of these little fellows." Dan speaks again:

"They sure are cute. Maybe I can adopt one of them. I will have to talk to my parents about it." Jack speaks:

"You may as well adopt at least two of them. Most of the folks around here have about all of the dogs they can afford to feed. I believe your grandpa will have to put up pictures of these puppies in his hardware store in Atkinson to try to get people to take them before they get much older." A huge four winged dragonfly lands on the tip of Dan's fishing pole. He has never seen a dragonfly and surely not one over three inches long. Dan shakes the dragonfly off and it once again lands on the end of his fishing pole. Jack speaks:

"Don't do that. Let it land because my grandpa told me that is a sign of good fishing." Dan looks frustrated and speaks:

"What has a big fly got to do with good fishing? I can't believe that, come on!" The instant Dan got those words out of his mouth a hard pull was felt on his line. He almost lost the pole. The boys were all excited wondering what could possibly be causing all of the commotion on the end of that fishing line. Dan was almost afraid to pull in whatever was on the hook. Both black boys were shouting loudly and very excitedly for Dan to pull the fish or whatever was in the water. Dan struggled and saw a long snake like ell on his fishing line. When he managed to pull the struggling ell onto the bridge, all pandemonium broke loose. Miss Clover and her puppies were going crazy with excitement barking and growling at the ell. Apparently Miss Clover thought that the ell was a snake. Miss Clover and snakes didn't get along! The black ell was about three feet long and had nasty looking teeth in its mouth that demanded respect. Dan was not sure what to do with the imposing creature. Jack helped him get the eel off the hook and threw the fourteen pound eel into the large fish cooler he and his friend had brought along. Dan speaks:

"What are we going to do with that thing? We can't eat it, can we?" Ivey Bell's great grandson speaks:

"Pa catches these all the time. They are very delicious if fixed right. I am just afraid of those nasty looking teeth. Pa tells me that they are just a type of fish. It is your ell, Dan. Do you want it?"

"No, I will give it to you guys. I was hoping to catch some blue gills, a trout, or maybe a bass." Jack speaks:

"I have never heard of anyone catching a bass in this creek, but who knows, you might just break the record."

David Smith decided to relax and enjoy himself by riding around the plantation and the Black River Community for about half a day. He borrows a small truck and rides out of Atkinson and crosses the bridge on Highway 53 going toward Kelly. He turns left and follows Highway 11 for a few miles and comes to the junction of Highway 11 and Highway 210. There were two stores on opposite sides of Highway 210. He noticed a crowd of country folks, mostly men in their twenties and thirties, laughing and clapping their hands about something going on inside the small unpainted grocery store. It was not long before he realized what was going on. A young man of average size ran out the door followed by a very large powerfully built woman People gave her and the man plenty of space to do their thing. David was not sure what had started the ruckus, but he knew that the man was in trouble. The woman pushed him down and she grabbed his legs and started spinning him around faster and faster, his head barely missing the posts that held the porch up. No one seemed concerned about the guy. At last, the woman let him go and he fell on the dirt floor beneath the porch. He heard one person laughing and telling the man on the ground that he hoped that he had learned his lesson. A few moments later all of them, including the man who had been slung around, followed the huge woman back into the country store. David wanted a drink and a pack of nabs or something because it was about twelve thirty in the afternoon. He thought about it and mustered the courage up to go inside the store and buy what he wanted. The huge woman was back of the counter and was as friendly as any person he had ever met.

While David looked around the store that looked like something he had seen in an old magazine about rural life in the early part of the Twentieth Century, he was intrigued by the many stories he heard these fine folks share with each other. One young man about nineteen years old sat on the many cloth bags of animal food piled against one wall. David believed that one of the men called him MP Ward, but he was not sure. David noticed a large round of hoop cheese and decided to get a quarter of a pound of the stuff, a pack of nabs, a soft drink, and find a high back chair and take time to hear some of what these country folks were talking about. Within a minute an obviously well respected member of the community walked into the store to join the excitement and the intriguing conversations. He had an open newspaper with him and he was reading an article about a local farmer that all of them apparently knew named Bayard Corbett. Corbett's last hunting trip down Black River became news that the county's paper, *The Pender Chronicle*, thought was news worthy.

Apparently Mr. Corbett found himself surrounded by bears as he made his way through the thick forest on the banks of the Black River. He heard a noise and a Black Bear started climbing a tall tree very close to Corbett faster than the average man could run on good flat ground. Startled, and a little shaken, our mighty hunter takes aim with a steady hand and fires his shotgun. The moment the bear hits the forest floor Corbett hears a terrible racket of a very large fast moving body headed his way. Mr. Bayard quickly loads his gun for the encounter and no sooner had he positioned himself to face his enemy, a large angry Black Bear charged him. Corbett instantly fires off his double barreled shotgun and the bear makes a terrible noise and turns around and runs as hard as she could away from Corbett. The paper accused Mr. Corbett of also turning around and doing better than a mile in five minutes putting distance between himself and that bear.

Several more stories were told by some of the old timers who were standing or sitting around in the store. He heard about steamboats that once plied the waters of the Black and the Cape Fear Rivers. He learned that nearly two hundred and seventy five years ago before ferry boats and bridges crossed the rivers, that runners were contracted to quickly make their way back and forth between Wilmington, once named (New Town) and the land or region between the Black and the Cape Fear Rivers. These runners were responsible to bring back much needed medicine, mail, and anything of great value that could be transported across the rivers and down the trails through the thick virgin forest of the region. David had never heard such tales as these before and felt almost like he was a foreigner, but he enjoyed the stories and the people were friendly. Before David left all eyes were turned in his direction. One older gentleman wanted to know who David was, probably not expecting such a distinguished and accomplished guest as the non assuming young white fellow who had slipped in to just listen to their tales.

"Young fellow, I don't believe that we have seen you around our neck of the woods before. Do you mind if I ask you who you are and your whereabouts?"

"No, sir, I don't mind at all telling you who I am. I am Doctor David Smith from Boston, Mass. I have been living on the Pridgen Plantation for nearly four months now." David saw several of the country men whisper something very low into each other's ears. The old heavy set man speaks again.

"What kind of doctor are you, sir?"

"I am a teacher. I will be teaching in the science department at UNCW next January." MP Ward's curiosity is stimulated and he speaks.

"Exactly what kind of science courses do you teach, sir?"

"I teach Oceanography and Geology." MP Ward continues his conversation with David.

"I read something in the paper about six or seven months ago that had nearly a page devoted to some world famous scientist from Boston who was going to be the second in command at the UNCW's science department. The paper went on to praise and credit this scientist for his work in predicting earthquakes. I understand that he once saved the lives of millions of people in just one incident, could that be you, sir?" David smiled and spoke:

"It's me, I if I can still be one of the boys around here." Several of the people started laughing pleased at David's laid back non assuming personality. The older man, Mr. Jack Burns, spoke again while laughing and holding out his hands for David to shake.

"Sir, my name is Jack Burns and my wife Myra is at the counter.

We are just plain country folks around here, nothing fancy, but I believe that most of us are good hard working people that if I might say so, earn respectable livings despite our lack of formal education. I am mighty proud to have such a fine young educated gentleman like yourself to sit down and chew the fat with us country folks!" Another man wearing a cap that had a logo on its top front that read "Bell and Williams," spoke up:

"Sir, are you just visiting the Pridgen Plantation or do you have kinship ties with the Pridgens?"

"I married Beard Pridgen's daughter Brenda about thirteen years ago. We moved from Boston about four months ago." The same man spoke again:

"I bet life is a lot different on that plantation than what you are accustomed to!" David smiles and answered:

"Yes, very different, but I have loved every minute of it! I will not be able to live there permanently, but will remain there until Brenda and I find a house and settle near Wrightsville Beach." Another gentleman asks a question:

"What is wrong with remaining on that plantation?"

"It is not because of lack of room, sir. It would be impractical for my family and me to live on the plantation when I will be working at the university and spending a lot of time on or under the ocean. I am a hands on research scientist as much as I am an instructor. I will be teaching at the department of science in both geology and oceanography. I will also be doing research off our shores and training future scientist to operate exploration or research submarines. We refer to them as DSV's or Deep Submersible Vehicles." David gets up from the seat and prepares to leave, but speaks to everyone. "Gentlemen, and you too ma'am," David looks over to Mrs. Burns: "It has been a joy fellowshipping with you nice people, but I promised myself that I would take the next few days off and ride around the area and see and meet as many people as possible. I will see you all around good day!" David gets into the truck and drives toward the Black River Bridge on Highway 210. He is not very far from the bridge when he sees a sight that causes him to slow down and pull over onto the side of the road. Two teen boys are shouting and waving their hands high in the air trying to frighten a rather large male hog down the hill from the house toward a very large powerfully built man who stands and waits for the hog. David can't figure out what is taking place because the man has no weapon in his hand nor is there a fence or cage for the beast to be led to. The hog makes a sharp turn and runs by the man who kicks the hog with a mighty blow in its side with his oversized shoe. David estimated the hog to weigh better than five hundred pounds. The hog falls over onto its side just a panting trying to get its breath and before the animal can recover and get up and run away, the man does an elbow drop like a professional wrestler and disables the hog. One of the boys tries to grab one of the legs of the hog so that the man could tie its legs together with ropes, but does not have the strength to hold onto the jerking leg. The man grabs both back legs in one huge hand and expertly hog ties the beast. He does the front legs the same way. From a distance, David sees a woman pulling a very heavy wooden drag by hand with little effort on her part. The drag was too large and heavy for most men to pull it with a rope through the soft white sand in the yard he was looking at. David could not believe his eyes when he saw the man snatch the hog several feet off the ground like he was testing its weight. Directly, he speaks:

"Boys, if my back wasn't out today, I would just throw this hog on it and walk up the hill and put it back into the fence." The man next places the subdued animal on the back of the heavy drag, and he and his wife effortlessly pull the drag up to the fence and release the hog inside its prison. David was dumbfounded, these people were beyond belief! No one would believe him in Boston if he told them what he observed. They would have to see to believe!

Late that night after David gets back from his tour of the plantation and everyone was in bed, David and his wife Brenda talk before settling down to a restful night's sleep. Brenda speaks:

"Honey, how long will we stay in Boston when we go back for a visit?"

"We will stay long enough for me to get the new program underway. I will work almost independently of both Doctor Fletcher and Doctor Dennis Miller. Both men can advise me and help me keep the mission coordinated or recommend my dismissal. I will be concerned about the actual work of being a research scientist out in the field for both institutions rather than being a paper jockey all of the time." Brenda speaks:

"David, I do believe that you are like a pioneer because no one has coordinated such a working relationship between two universities in two different parts of the country before." David speaks:

"I may be considered a type of pioneer, but I could not have done it without the cooperation of a lot of people. People working as adjunct professors or as visiting professors are not new under the sun. Most institutions years ago could not afford people with specialized training or experience. Some of the first ones were well known politicians who were not running for office again or were members of powerful organizations and offices in our country. Lots of military leaders or big business people have been hired to teach classes for specific periods of time. I guess that what is different about what we are doing is that two schools are legally joined together at the hips so to speak in a limited way. It all depends on federal and state cooperation, the approval of school boards, and school officials." Brenda speaks:

"David, suppose it does not work out, what then?"

"I don't expect trouble because both institutions will profit by the venture. If it does not work out, I could possibly work as a special assistant to both universities on a contractual basis."

"David, have you ever thought about going on your own?"

"No, I would not want to drum up the money to get into anything worthy of my background. Some people have quit teaching and have gone commercial. Who is better qualified to go into exploring the oceans for lost ships full of treasures, or maybe even something such as the field of crypto zoology?"

"David, I believe that the word refers to hidden animals. I once saw a program on animals scientists once considered extinct that are now known to exist."

"Yes, that is true. Every once in awhile someone catches some creature from a body of water that was thought to have died out millions of years ago. There are recent reports of giant sharks seen by fishermen or animals in earth's last remaining rainforest reported by the indigenous people of those remote areas. If I were single, I would seriously consider pursuing such a profession." Brenda and David stop talking and embrace in each other's arms for a couple of minutes.

"David, I am not worried about you going into the business of hunting down lost animals or going on some other venture because it would take you away from your friends and associates at school."

"No, Brenda; that would not be the main reason that would prevent me in pursuing such careers. I would not want to spend most of my time away on some fantastic adventure and leave you and the kids on this plantation."

"Don't forget about your parents, David!"

"I haven't. An explorer's life may be exciting and it has the potential to put the explorer in the headlines, but it is not for the married with kids crowd!" Brenda frowns a little and speaks:

"You could bring your family along."

"No, dear, I do not want us to turn into a band of gypsies on the go all of the time. Sure we would all get to see and experience a lot, but I want us and our children lives to be more stable and orientated around our own country. I believe we would all become more international than national. People need roots."

"David, let's borrow some horses tomorrow and ride around a bit. We might even have time to see the chateau my great uncle owns."

"Brenda, have you ever visited the place before?"

"I have ridden by it and could see glimpses of the mega house, but it is a separate piece of property given to my great uncle by his parents. I understand that the tract of land the chateau sits on is about twenty four hundred acres of the finest land around these parts." David comments:

"Not the size of your average yard!" David's face wrinkles slightly as he ponders his next question. "Brenda, who is going to inherit the property after your great uncle passes? I ask the question assuming you don't have aunts or uncles I am not aware of. Have you heard your grandparents say anything about the place?"

"I once heard my grandparents talking about the sorry state the place was in and that my great uncle was a queer one that was a great mystery. When my grandparents realized that I might be hearing their conversation, they started talking about something else."

The next morning at the breakfast table, everyone seemed to be in high gear. Great Grandfather Zeb and his wife Lilly talked about their plans that morning to go and visit some of Lilly's kinfolks in the Canetuck Township. The old home place still stood and the land was tended by one of Lilly's nephews, Robert Moore the third. It was not nearly as large as the Pridgen plantation, but Lilly loved the old place she grew up on. She tried to visit two or three times a year. The farmhouse was a nice white seven bedroom two story wooden structure surrounded by a fancy white wooded fence. Lilly loved to bring flowers and place them on the graves of her parents and grandparents. Back of the house, which stood on a sizeable hill, was a bottom or lowland not much above legal flood stage. A fast moving creek ran through this part of the homestead on its way to a huge swamp. The creek was particularly valuable long years ago before modern water pumps and plumbing in people's houses. A beautiful covered red bridge crossed the creek. The cover provided the bridge protection from the elements and provided shelter for anyone caught fishing in the rain from the bridge or a person who is stranded in a rainstorm unable to get to the house or a shed fast enough. Nearly half a mile from the house, was a large swamp full of large cypress trees and all kinds of living critters. Beard agreed to take ten year old Dan with him to Atkinson and let him spend the day with him. Little Betty was going to be dropped off at the Blizzard's house where she would have the opportunity to play with her new found friends, Becky and Susie Blizzard. Brenda and David catch a ride to the horse stables on the Pridgen plantation where they saddle up two horses. It had been about two years since David and Brenda had ridden horses.

"Brenda, it has been awhile since we have ridden horses!"

"Yes, David, the last time we went horseback riding was when we went with your friend William Bean to Arizona to stay on that ranch for three weeks. Have you called your friend lately?"

"No, Brenda, but I should. Lewis as I call him, has been a good friend most of my life. He, as you know, was my best fishing partner."

"Just maybe you should give the guy a call. He is a lot of fun and it is hard to find such a loyal lifetime friend. I believe that I heard one of his songs played on television not long ago." While Brenda and David are on their way to Colly Mills so that David can see the beautiful site the old basket mill once stood, he gets a phone call that surprises him. Beard calls him.

"David."

"Yes, sir, Beard?"

"I forgot to ask you if you would like to go down Black River with me. I need to check on the property anyway. I thought that you might like to be entertained."

"I would love to, but I would need to ask Brenda about it. How long would a trip last?"

"It will take three or four days. We can do some fishing and I will take you through a walk in history."

"You are talking about your people?"

"Well, maybe some of them. There is a lot of history about the region that most people know little about. There are folks who have lived here all their lives that have only a sketchy understanding of our history. I can guarantee you that we will carry along plenty of supplies for our trip."

"Your plans sound great, Beard! Are we going in a small fishing boat?"

"No, we could, but I am old enough to appreciate our riverboat that we use to patrol our Black River territory. It is a seventy-five foot craft that my father and I built over forty years ago. It has several nice bedrooms, a kitchen, a dining room, a bathroom, and a nice sitting room. The roof was designed to put heavy duty outdoor chairs, tables, and couches on so that folks can relax and enjoy the scenery. If you want to, you can bring along a camera and film the trip while I do a little narration.

This way, the information and the beautiful scenery will be recorded for whoever wants to see it in the future."

"Yes, sir, I will ask Brenda. I will see you!"

"What was that all about, David?"

"Brenda, your father wants to check on the plantation land that borders Black River. He said that the trip would take three or four days. Do you mind if I go?"

"David, you have just gotten back from Boston and now you are wanting to go on another trip?"

"OK, if you do not want me to go, I will call your father and tell him." Brenda smiles and speaks:

"No, David, I am sure that you will enjoy the trip. It will give you a chance to get to know my father by being alone with him on a trip. I am impressed that he wants you to go. That means that he has a good opinion of my husband." David frowns a little and speaks:

"Are you saying that he had a different opinion of me before?" Brenda thought a moment before she spoke:

"David, I had better be careful as to what I say. I might be misunderstood. My father up to the time you have lived on the plantation has not had a real chance to know you. He probably believed that you are a very smart city slicker who is the husband of his daughter and the father of his grandkids." David speaks:

"Say, no more, I get the point. I guess that I am fortunate he has had a change of mind."

"No, not really, David, he would have always treated you with respect, now he realizes that you may be from the big city, but that you are also a man who likes to work with your hands and that you get things done on a big scale. He is actually very proud of you!"

Twelve

Doctor Hardin Teaches a Class at UNCW While Brenda and David Visit Colly Swamp and Moores Creek Battle Ground

Our story now takes a leap in distance and continues in room 129 in the science department at UNCW. Doctor Hardin, the man who covets David Smith's place as second in command at the science department is temporarily filling another teacher's classroom time because his fellow instructor was out due to health related issues. Our good professor humbled himself to teach a freshman level class, Oceanography 101. The great man did not grieve too much because it gave him the opportunity to make disciples. He was a master at influencing young minds to his advantage. There was no question that our good professor was very good at his trade and he sparked the imagination of many bright young minds to follow his or her calling in life; the call of the Sea and all of the wonders it stores in its treasure vaults hidden just beneath the waves. If our professor had left it at that, he would be a man worthy to follow or emulate. Unfortunately, he was usually up to something. He loved to prove other instructors to be inferior to his genius. He seldom openly ridiculed or called a name, but he was a master at, shall we say, allowing the brightest students to sense the direction or drift our good professor invited them to.

What Doctor Hardin is practicing is nothing new under the sun. It happens not only in science classes, but mostly any discipline taught, including history, theology, philosophy classes, and you name it. To illustrate, many a professor who is of the Calvinistic persuasion has and still teaches in Bible schools founded by evangelist who were believers in free will. That is, these founders firmly believed that everyone can be saved and go to Heaven. It is a matter of the individual repenting of his or her sins and accepting Jesus Christ as Lord and Savior to become a born again believer. Within these free will colleges and universities are those who are called Hyper Calvinist or those fully persuaded that mankind couldn't make a real decision about its eternal destiny. Now the individual is fully convinced he or she is a sinner and stands convicted of sin and guilt before God in his or her own mind, but the Calvinist say in reality that individual was selected, ordained, chosen, or picked out from the billions of humans who will be born. In the field of philosophy, or the love of knowledge, there are people who firmly believe and teach certain schools of thought. It may be that an individual looks for truth through metaphysical philosophy, but realizes that the founders of the school he or she teaches believes in, let's say, Practical Philosophy, and considers those who believe in Metaphysical Philosophy impractical and a little touched in the head. Despite being aware of the opinions of the founder of a said school, the good philosopher feels compelled to dress in sheep's wool and manages to not get fired. Doctor Hardin, a mortal man of clay, simply allows his lower nature and his unbridled ambition for position and praise to get in the way of his true potential. A student raises his hand and Doctor Hardin recognizes him as class begins.

"Doctor Hardin, when does the new man from Boston start his work around here?"

"I understand that he will start sometime next January." Another student, a young lady, questions the instructor.

"Sir, why didn't the school simply choose someone already teaching here to fill that position?" Hardin was not overly pleased with the question, but manages to hide most of his concerns about the affair by quickly stating that the decision was made without a vote.

"Students the names and terms listed on these handouts I have passed out should be taken seriously. This is a university not a trade school. College students need to have a general understanding of the founders of the majors or disciplines they are going into. Now, I don't expect you to be history majors, but trust me, it is to your advantage to learn something about individuals such as Charles Darwin, Edward Forbes, and Charles Wyville Thompson. Does anyone among the bright young faces I look upon in this class have a clue as to who Charles Wyville Thompson was?" After waiting a minute, Doctor Hardin speaks. "I hope that all of you now realize why this class is called Oceanography 101. When you build a house, you first of all have to lay a solid foundation before anything else can be done. In any field, no matter what it is, a in the beginning must occur. Before one can read, he or she must know the alphabet, or in music, he or she must know what the notes represent on paper or in practice. If you look up the name, Charles Wyville Thompson, for example, you will discover that he is considered the father of modern oceanography. There is a list of famous research ships such as the Beagle and the Challenger. I expect you all to take an interest in learning about these ships. I am a little old fashioned and I expect students to actually learn about geography and how to plot a course from one point to another as if you were preparing an ocean voyage without all of the fancy computers, satellites, and GPS equipment available now days. Who knows, the Chinese could shoot all of the satellites down and the man or woman who is not dependent on fancy equipment to take the place of human thinking could actually be in demand!" Students laugh at Doctor Hardin's statement.

"I love to lecture on the oceans. Some people teach that there is but one ocean, but I have found it practical and scientifically wise to distinguish different areas of the planet's ocean as individual oceans. I will go into some detail why this is a better approach to understanding what is going on. I will illustrate. I have but one family, but that family is made up of very different people. The oceans such as the Pacific, Arctic, Antarctic, or the Atlantic are different in so many ways. We will study the great currents that run below the world's oceans. The study of them and how they affect life on our planet is amazing! We will study waves and get into a little math to help you understand their speed, direction, height, and how they cause erosion or even great destruction. If you are lucky, we might even take a field trip or two before my several weeks as a fill-in instructor have expired." Doctor Hardin continues to talk about plants and animals in the oceans from phytoplankton to the great whales. He promises the class that if they will study hard, they will all be assured of a solid foundation and a workable knowledge of the field they are entering.

"Brenda, where are we going to ride today?"

"I thought that we would go by Colly Swamp and look at the mill pond. From there we can go to an old church I have attended a few times. Some of my kin people are buried there. From there we can go by the old Corbett house on Highway 210 and visit the folks there. We can go back through Colly Swamp on Highway 53 and I will show you a huge ditch one of our kin dug about two hundred years ago."

"It must be a sight for you to want us to go by and look at it!"

"Yes, it is, but I will not tell all, but will wait until I show it to you before I share what I know about the project."

"Brenda, how long will it take us to get to Colly Mills?"

"It will take about three hours."

"That will be bad on the horses!" Brenda speaks:

"No, not really, we have plenty of provisions for them and us. The kids will be taken care of by my parents, so let's make two days of it and enjoy ourselves." There is nothing like a ride on a beautiful horse. A person can go to places and see things off of the so called regular trails." The morning air was fresh and clean and a few beautiful white clouds decorated the sky a mile or two above Brenda and David. One of them reminded David of a steamboat. Another one looked very much like a cat. The sun had already climbed several hours into the sky on its daily circuit. A nice breeze was blowing from the direction of the Black River. The smell of the clean wide stream was very refreshing! The sound of a large river craft was heard in the distance coming toward our couple on the river. The roar of several light motor boats was heard as they passed the slower moving large craft.

David and Brenda rode their horses to the last bridge leaving the plantation. The sound of the horses prancing across the heavy wooden bridge was enchanting and very pleasant to the ears of both our subjects. Over head a large bird of prey flies by with business on its mind. Apparently the great bird had seen an animal swimming on the surface of the river or saw fish near the surface of the river. The moment David and Brenda crossed the bridge they heard voices to their left. A left turn across the bridge goes down the dirt road that leads to Uncle Roy Henry's shop. Six black teenagers with fishing poles, buckets, and coolers threw up their hands and called out to Brenda and David. David and Brenda momentarily stop the horses they are riding to allow time to say hello to the young people and give them the opportunity to touch the horses. Brenda tells them goodbye and our happy young couple continue their two day tour. The road David and Brenda rode on was now only about three hundred feet from the river. In the middle of the stream glided the magnificent Henrietta 1V. David speaks:

"That is truly a nice little ship! It is so authentic looking and its colors are outstanding."

"Yes, David, it is a nice way for people to get a realistic view of our past history." David speaks:

"Did they have riverboats in the Black River years ago?"

"Sure, there were a lot of steamers on the Black River. Grandfather Zeb has a lot of the accounts of river boat traffic. I have read some of the accounts. I remember Grandfather talking about the Lisbon. I understand that the boat was owned by a gentleman named Luther Sherman of Point Caswell. I remember the names of many of the small ships and flats that went up and down the Black, but I will let you learn more about this fantastic history from my father when you go with him to check on our plantation." David smiles and speaks:

"Those boats must have been very large and impressive for people to still be talking about them after all of these years!"

"No, David, I don't believe they would be very impressive for most traveled people now days, but for folks back in those days in these remote parts, I am sure that a huffing puffing steamboat with a whistle was very exciting and a fun way to go to Wilmington." David speaks:

"Yes, I can certainly understand where you are coming from. I believe I would be impressed myself! In fact, why don't we try to get a ride on the Henrietta 1V one of these days. I am sure we would enjoy the experience!" Brenda speaks:

"Yes, I believe that our children would also love to go along with us." And hour later Brenda and David walked their horses through the small town of Atkinson. In the year 2030 few horses were used for riding; except, inside fences, at horse shows, or horse ranches where the public paid for a chance to learn how to ride a horse. People stared at the beautiful horses as they pranced down the broad street in the middle of Atkinson. A few people stopped their talking and acknowledged the couple on the horses by waving their hands high with big smiles on their faces. Our couple passes the little town of Atkinson and find themselves several miles outside of the town surrounded by woods. David and Brenda stop the horses and dismount. The horses are watered and David and Brenda drink from their thermoses. A nice cool breeze is causing the tops of the hundred foot tall trees to wave gently back and forth. David especially notices the smell of the pine trees and the millions of wild flowers all along the road and extending for hundreds of feet into the forest on both sides of the road. Honey bees and other flying insects are gorging themselves on the nectar provided by the flowers. A flock of crows swiftly fly by making their strange sounds. In the distance the couple spots several frisky cat squirrels playing around a rather large oak tree. Brenda looks around and takes in a deep breath of unspoiled air and speaks.

"David, can't you just imagine how it was around here two hundred or more years ago?"

"Brenda, I am not completely sure that I could do that era justice. I have, of course, seen lots of old movies that were about life two hundred or more years ago. I could not imagine the peace people must have had that many years ago. No paved roads, no airplanes, no telephones; about the only mechanical marvel beyond a water wheel or maybe a windmill to pump up water would be a steam engine that could power a sawmill or perhaps a small ship." Brenda speaks:

"Steam engines are still very interesting to watch, especially the few steam locomotives that still operate around the country just too impress tourist." David speaks:

"Don't tell me that they operate steam trains around here?"

"David, I am sure that you are joking, but there is actually a full scale steam locomotive near the Cape Fear River in Wilmington." David speaks:

"I would imagine it would be far too slow to be used on modern tracts." Brenda speaks:

"The museum says that the old train is fully operational, but it is not licensed to be used on the tracks around here, but to answer your statement. I understand that the old passenger train would have no problem keeping up with modern diesel engines and pound for pound steam engines are a lot more powerful." David speaks:

"I would like to visit that railroad museum and see the train!"

"Yes, David, I wouldn't mind seeing it again myself. The museum has a very nice model train set. Dan would love to see it. It is computer controlled like the one my brother John owns. It is very large and there are many trains on the tracts." Our couple rides the horses at a slow trot to Murphy's Cross Roads and turn left and go all the way to Highway 210. David sees several large signs near a bridge that informs the public that a famous Revolutionary Battle took place nearby. David speaks with excitement to Brenda:

"I did not realize that we were going to be near a Revolutionary Battle Ground! Why didn't you tell me?"

"I honestly forgot about it. We can visit tomorrow before we leave and go back to the plantation. I have known about this place all of my life and forgot that you probably would not be aware of it. We can walk around the battle ground tomorrow and go to the visitor's center. It is a nice park. We can also get something to eat and enjoy ourselves at one of the many covered picnic tables just across the road from the main part of the park. David, we need to turn right here and continue along side of Highway 210 until we get to Colly Swamp."

"Brenda, did you bring any mosquito spray? The bugs are biting me and the horses!"

"Sure, I brought along several cans of Cutter Repellant. It is cheaper than so called major brands, but it will keep most of them off. I feel sorry for the horses. Their skin is thicker than ours, but the larger insects can still trouble them." David speaks:

"What is wrong with us spraying some of this stuff on the horses?"

"David, I have never heard of anyone spraying insect repellent on horses. We could possibly very lightly spray some of this stuff on them, but I believe that bug spray will stop up their pores and they might over heat." David speaks:

"That looks like a very old church! I bet a lot of history is associated with this old building!"

"Yes, this is the old church I was telling you about. Bethlehem Baptist Church is over two hundred years old."

"You mean to tell me this building is two hundred years old?"

"Yes, I am sure it is about that old. Now the membership for this building is two hundred and thirty years old. It was established in the year 1800 and it is, of course, now the year 2030. I believe that I heard someone say that this is not the only place the membership has met. It could be that the original building was burned down. You would have to ask my father or grandparents to get an accurate answer. I have actually attended this old church a few times. I have some cousins who are members here?"

"You have Pridgen kin going to this church, Brenda?"

"Yes, and a lot of Corbett kin. Now I am sure a lot of families around here claim blood ties. Some of my Corbett kin go back before the American Revolutionary War. A lot of them before the Civil War are buried here. One of them was a locally well known soldier."

"That sounds interesting, Brenda! Yes, I would like to read some of the memorial headstones and learn about these people." David and Brenda continue down Highway 210 and turn right down unto a road in the woods. David realizes that the road is more than just a road, but a dam blocking the water of a creek in the middle of a swamp.

"Brenda, how long has this dam been here?"

"David, I am not sure, but I believe about a hundred and thirty or forty years." David speaks:

"I know, I will have to ask your folks for more details." Brenda smiles and speaks:

"That is right, David. I was a child the last time I heard anything about this place. Since then, I have gone to school and have earned three degrees. I have taught school and have started raising a family." David smiles and speaks:

"Don't forget that I also got married sometime in that brief period of accomplishments."

"David, I realize that you also got married sometime in that brief period of major accomplishments. David, I knew that we would be here today, so I asked my grandfather about Colly Mills. He told me that the mills were in operation before his time, but that his father remembered seeing the large building that stood over there where the stream is falling." Brenda points in the direction of where the old basket mill stood across the stream. Grandfather told me if we walk the area where the old building stood, we might possibly see some of the old flooring." David questions Brenda:

"Brenda, what did the mill produce?"

"I understand that the last company to own the mill was called Colly Veneer Works Company. The plant made cypress baskets by the tens of thousands."

"What is so important about baskets made out of cypress trees other than their beauty?"

"The baskets were more important than they are today. As you know, baskets are now once again a hot item, but when the mill was opened, the baskets took the place of plastic and paper bags. A woman would walk into a store with a large basket and get what she wanted and then go to the counter to buy the items in the basket."

"Yes, I do remember old movies about life over a hundred years ago when people would use large fancy baskets to put their groceries into. I would imagine there was no other practical way to carry things."

"Yes, I am sure a wooden box would be too heavy to shop with for the average person." David looks around and considers the huge human effort in hauling the thousands of tons of dirt to block the stream in order to form a dam that could backup a large holding pond in the middle of the swamp. It took a large amount of water to turn the huge machinery in the buildings of the veneer company.

"Brenda, how do you suppose they built this road dam we are standing on?"

"I could imagine Mack trucks, but Mack trucks did not exist when all of this dirt was hauled into this swamp. David, I can only guess that they hauled it here with the use of animal power. I don't know what kind of animals. I would imagine mules or possibly oxen."

"Brenda, how far does this pond go?"

"David, I have been told that it went past the Bladen County line. There were three or four other mills such as sawmills located along this swamp basin. I am not sure how the mills were situated. They were probably in the middle of Colly Swamp just like the old basket mill. I do believe this mill was the last to operate and the one closest to Black River." David looks around carefully taking in the great beauty of his surroundings. Huge Cypress trees dominated the area. From deep in the swamp, David and Brenda heard primitive sounds of the local wildlife. To their collective amazement, a great Bald Eagle swooped over the mill pond and snatched up a large struggling black fish in its deadly talons.

"Oh, Brenda, will you take a look at that! I feel like I am in the middle of a rain forest!" Directly the great bird takes its prize up high in the top of the largest cypress tree David had ever looked at. David estimated that the great tree must be over seventeen hundred years old. A huge bird nest straddled several branches at the top of the aging tree. Brenda runs to her horse and brought out powerful field binoculars to get a close up of the great birds. Brenda estimated that the tree the birds were in was nearly three hundred feet away across the pond. Brenda lifts the binoculars to her face and it lights up with pleasure.

"David, I can see the heads of the baby eagles in their nest! Take a look." David is raptured with excitement.

"Brenda, I see four chicks. They are already larger than average domesticated chickens." Brenda speaks:

"Their parents could not have chosen a better place to raise their family!"

"Brenda, I am very surprised that some redneck has not already shot those birds out of their nest!"

"David, I have a feeling that people feel a lot different about such wildlife around here than they did a generation or two ago. Most of these great birds are tagged and are under Federal protection. No doubt fish and game officials guard these eagles almost like their own children." While David and Brenda continue to talk and enjoy the beauty of the swamp, they notice something that looked like two eyes crossing the pond. In moments of time, they realize that a large alligator swam only a hundred and fifty feet in front of them.

"David, that thing is huge! Look at it with these binoculars to get a good look at it." David followed the great amphibian with his eyes looking through the powerful binoculars.

"Brenda, that thing must be nearly fourteen feet long!" The alligator crawled up on the bank toward what appeared to be a nest. Brenda frowns a bit and speaks:

"Grandfather Zeb tells me that when he was a boy, a person almost never saw one of these creatures around here. Folks could swim safely without a thought about such dangerous animals, but not anymore!" David speaks:

"Brenda, the Federal Government in all of its wisdom put them on the endangered list and now that act is a mixed blessing. Of course, they naturally help control the deer population, but we are also somewhat in danger. The people who love alligators are thrilled. What do you think about the situation, Brenda?"

"Well, I like you, have little to say about it one way or the other. In general, I am not overly concerned about the alligators. We are not their natural prey. I also realize that they have been here longer that we have.

They do have a right to life like everything else that lives unless we humans know that we are their main food source. People build houses in wilderness areas so that they can enjoy nature and the first thing that seems to happen is that they have an unpleasant encounter with a bear or maybe a moose and they get together with their neighbors and demand the removal or destruction of the animals. Look, David, fish are jumping over there! I guess that they are after insects flying by." David speaks:

"They could also be moving away from something that is after them." The shrill cry of a hawk is heard as it passes over head. The heads of several snapping turtles are seen raising their heads out of the water inspecting their environment. David speaks:

"Brenda, let's go over to where the basket factory once stood. I would like to look and see if there is any of the old mill's floor still left on the bottom of the creek. The space where the mill stood looks to be at least a hundred and eighty feet long. Didn't you bring along our rubber booths?"

"Yes, I did; David, I suggest we put them on or we will have wet shoes and socks all day long. I forgot just how high this dam is above the creek." After our couple put their rubber boots on, they walk where the water picked up speed and where it goes over a little hump.

"Brenda, I do not see a floor, but I can tell that there was one here a long time ago. Oh, here is a single old board. It is definitely part of the old floor. It appears to be tongue and grove."

"David, I understand from my grandfather Zeb, that there was once a large stone wheel lying over there just below the roadbed."

"That would have been interesting to see!" Brenda speaks:

"Yes, I was told that it had been lying around here for about one hundred years before it disappeared. Let's go visit the old church we passed by earlier." Our couple walks the horses down the Colly Mill dirt dam and turn left on Highway 210 and go to Bethlehem Baptist Church. A heavy duty black iron fence runs across the cemetery and sits back of the little white wood frame church. David and Brenda walk up to the double gates and push one of them open to enter the graveyard. David speaks:

"Brenda, this church building is very small. I am used to church buildings that hold thousands of people, but there is great beauty in this simple little church out here in front of this swamp!"

"David, this church, as I have shared with you earlier when we passed this way, is about two hundred years old. There is little difference in its original size. This tells us that the population of this region has remained about the same for a very long period of time in our country's history."

"Brenda, you say that some of the people buried here are akin to your family?"

"Yes, I am akin to the Corbett family and those they joined themselves in marriage to. David, look at this monument. I understand that these people are distance cousins to the Pridgen side of my family, George W. Corbett and his wife Ellen M. Corbett." David speaks:

"I suppose that this one must be one of their children since it is included in the same monument."

"Yes, that was their daughter Mary E. Corbett." David speaks:

"I see that George was born in 1837 and died in 1914. The guy never got to see an airplane."

"That is true, David, but he was in the American Civil War, and he got to see a lot of things the average citizen back in those days would probably never see."

"Like what, Brenda?"

"Well, I would imagine that he got to see a lot of federal balloons over the battlefields as observation post to help direct the Union Army's cannons."

"That is true." Brenda speaks:

"He also was in the age of seeing steam machines and the steam train." David speaks:

"I see that this gentleman was one of the so called, *the Immortal Six Hundred*. I am not an expert on the Civil War, Brenda, perhaps you can tell me who *the Immortal Six Hundred* were."

"David, I am also not an expert either. It has been a long time since the American Civil War. I believe he was one of about six hundred regulars and officers who were held for about a year by the Union Forces. I understand that the South was being punished because fifty union officers were held prisoner in Charleston, S.C. and placed in a location where Union shells were being fired into the city. The Southern general believed that he could help save the city or try to reduce the damage done to it if Union Soldiers were put into harm's way. David there is more to this man than told on his monument."

"Oh; yea?"

"Yes, he was the officer who gave the orders to fire when General Stonewall Jackson was shot. I understand that he was a lieutenant at that time." David speaks:

"I can imagine that this once young lieutenant was devastated when he later learned that the soldiers they were firing at were Confederates!"

"Yes, I understand that he never got over it. He truly felt bad about the incident, but I am sure that he was never blamed for any wrong doing.

He was simply following orders. Everyone thought that the men on horses coming their way were Union soldiers preparing to attack them. Grandfather Zeb has an old newspaper article about the incident. I understand that the article was written by one of George W. Corbett's great grandsons."

"That is very interesting, Brenda. I might have to take a look at the old newspaper and read the entire story!" David and Brenda continue to walk around the graveyard looking at monuments. David speaks:

"I see that there are a lot of Corbetts buried in this cemetery. I would assume that they are all members of the same clan."

"Yes, I am sure that you are right. Look at this one here; Zebulon V. Corbett, born in 1876 and died in 1952 and his wife Sattie Pridgen Corbett, born in 1882 and died in 1954." David speaks:

"That has been a long time ago, nearly eighty years ago when Sattie Corbett died."

"David, Mr. Zeb Corbett was one of the sons of George W. Corbett."

"Amazing, I suppose that these other people are also his sons and daughters and great grandchildren." Brenda speaks:

"Yes, you are right. This one here, Katie Corbett Hilburn, was one of his daughters. His other daughter here is Lorena Corbett Rawls." David and Brenda continue to look at the many headstones. Brenda speaks:

"David, let's go to the national park you saw earlier."

"Yes, ma'am, I do believe that I would like to see the place!" Brenda and her husband David trot the horses to the Moores Creek Battleground A few cars honk as they pass our couple. The day is very mature and Brenda and David asked one of the park rangers for permission to tie up the horses for awhile while they take a quick tour of the park.

"Brenda, how many acres is this park?"

"I believe about ninety acres. David let's go back into the visitor's center and watch the documentary about the battle that took place here. That away, you will not be asking me a lot of questions I am not an expert on." David speaks:

"Brenda, I believe that I would like to continue this another day. Why don't we go back to the plantation and get a good night's rest and continue our adventure tomorrow? I believe that I would like to visit the old Corbett place and that canal you told me about another day."

"Sounds great, we can visit the fishing lake and Paradise Island tomorrow." After a good night's rest at the plantation, David and Brenda prepare to go visit the lake and Paradise Island, an island nearly in the middle of the great fishing lake. This beautiful little island of over twenty four hundred acres is where Pridgen's Mountain is located and the beautiful Lipizzaner horses from Austria.

The next morning after a good night's rest, everyone at the Pridgen Plantation is up and around the breakfast table all bright eyed and as hungry as wolves around a fresh kill. The sun's rays are dancing through the several large windows that are in the dining area where the family sits. Excitement is in the air. Everyone is eager to get on with it and enjoy the wonderful country meal and grab the day by the horns and enjoy life to its fullest. There is always plenty to do and a million places to go to and lose one's self on this huge plantation that is bursting with activity and beaming with life and beauty. Nature itself seems to sense that this land the Pridgens call home is a noble reflection of how things used to be before men in their greed started robbing and disfiguring the jewel of the universe, planet Earth, a colony of Heaven itself. Dan and his sister were excited because their grandmother was going to take them fishing with Mattie. They were going to fish off a fishing pier at Wrightsville Beach. This was a rare opportunity because the Pridgens seldom went saltwater fishing. Mrs. Lillian Pridgen heard that a mixed variety of fish were biting and she decided that it would be a good time to fish in the ocean.

Mr. Beard and his father were going on a tour of the plantation. Beard seldom had the opportunity to get out with his father and go to the homes of the folks that lived on the plantation. Mr. Zeb usually tried to touch bases with the people who lived on the plantation about three times a year. In the past, he would get a horse and carriage and travel by himself, but Mr. Zeb was getting up in age and he realized that he would not be around forever. He wanted people to see him with his son who would one day become the owner of the Pridgen Plantation. Beard was not a boy by any means at sixty two years old, but the Pridgens left their property to their children after their journey was completed on this side of eternity. Beard was not concerned that his aged father was still the legal owner of the plantation. The fact that his father was still the legal owner gave him something to live for. He was proud to travel around with his father and be seen together with him because once he became the legal owner of the plantation, folks would remember the association he had with his father. People would realize that the torch of leadership and respect had passed down to the next leader of the band. He, like Elisha, would wear the mantle Elijah once wore. II Kings 2:13. David and Brenda prepare to go to the huge fishing lake and visit the island. Brenda wants to show her husband, who is an expert oceanographer, the great blue hole not far from the island.

"Brenda, are we going to ride the horses again?"

"No, David, I don't want to have to carry them over to the island."

"How would we carry them over to that island?"

"We have a small barge that is used to transport horses back and forth. When the Lipizzaner herd gets too large for the island to support, the Austrian officials are contacted by my grandfather. He tells them that it is time to have a round up. When they arrive, they use the barge to transport the horses they capture back to the mainland where they are loaded on special trucks. These horses are shipped back to their mother country."

Thirteen

Brenda and David Visit the Fishing Lake and Paradise Island

David and Brenda get into a pickup truck and drive toward the fishing lake. When they cross Possum Creek, they see Uncle Preston on the porch of the mill waving good morning or perhaps hello. Several heavy trucks are already being loaded with grain. Our couple notices that cows are making their way to the pasture to graze and do what cows like to do. Apparently the milking operation for that morning is about to finish. The Pridgens do not have fancy computerized machines to milk their cows, but several dozen young men and women who take care of that operation every morning bright and early. The milk is rich and pure with enzymes and protein like the Good Lord intended it to be. The Pridgens like whole milk that has not been robbed of vital nutrition. They like the rich taste of natural milk. Our excited young couple continue to travel down the main road through this side of the plantation. Activity is everywhere as people are going about their early morning preparations to be in a position to do their work. David and Brenda pass several teams of huge draft horses that are being led to the massive fields where crops are tended. The Pridgens make sure that weeds and grass do not thrive in their fields! After a couple of miles of travel, Brenda and David see the catfish pond that is over eight hundred acres in size. Two commercial fish trucks are parked near the fish house where they are being loaded with fish. Several large flat bottomed fishing boats are seen on the water with their crews loading them with traps filled with catfish. A few miles more and David and Brenda realize that they are near the lake. They can actually smell the fresh clean water. The first thing that one sees when approaching the lake is the beautiful flowers and the massive cypress trees that stand like soldiers knee deep in the water. David speaks:

"I don't know what it is about these trees that attract my attention so much. They are not the most beautiful tree by any means. The cypress trees are not going to win a beauty contest for their beautiful flowers or their delicious fruit, but they are so primitive looking. Most trees would drown in water that deep, but these trees thrive in water." Brenda speaks:

"They may not be the beauty queen of the tree world, but they are one of the longest living and they continue to grow in size as long as they live. I would suspect that the distant cousins of these magnificent trees were around in swamps with dinosaurs. They have a way of making you believe that you have somehow traveled back in time or there is more to see out there in that lake than we are able to see right now. Perhaps something huge and dangerous is hiding out there waiting to pounce on a careless individual who does not respect what nature can throw at him or her." David parks the truck they are riding in and they get out at the lake that is miles wide. The waves are washing against the shore and they almost remind David of the ocean. At over six miles away, Paradise Island can be seen. It is a place of mystery, especially for David who has not had the privilege to visit the place. The smell coming from the cedar pavilion fills the nostrils of our couple. This is the building that stands out in the lake where the Pridgens have their private get-togethers. This beautiful place with its rich carvings that testify of the handy work of master craftsmen is a sight to behold! David speaks:

"Brenda, when are we going to have a cookout here? I can't wait to get up one morning and go fishing in this beautiful lake and later bring back the fish here to cook!"

"I don't know, David. I have heard no one talk about a cookout. It seems that we are so busy all of the time. Our plate is about as full as it can get. I will mention it to my mother and see what she thinks about a grand get together."

"Who will be invited?"

"Only our immediate family. We do not use this place for friends and extended family. We like to have a place just for us. Some of my fondest moments are associated with this place. David, we will not take time to visit this pavilion today because the island will be adventure enough." David speaks:

"I love water! If I were not married and did not have the drive to accomplish a lot of things, I would buy a huge houseboat and live on a beautiful body of water somewhere. I never get my fill of the adventure water offers."

"I love water also, David, but probably not as much as you do. I love to fish and swim. I enjoy looking at programs on television and looking at science books about the water world. Water is necessary for life, but it is responsible for taking life."

"Which one of these boats are we going to use, Brenda?"

"I thought that we could use this one. It is a good stable boat that is large enough to walk in. It also has a double bottom and I like the nice handrails. This is the same boat I used when I carried Mattie and the kids fishing several months ago. I asked Dan to open up the fish well and he saw the holes in it and he thought that we were going to sink. I could not help but to laugh a bit. I am sure that he will remember the incident when he is our age with humor. I know that a lot of things happened to me around this lake that I will never forget." Brenda cranks the engine and the boat starts to swiftly move toward the island. A fog hovers slightly above the water surrounding the island and it almost has a surreal appearance. The closer our couple gets to the island the larger Pridgen Mountain towers above everything. The five hundred acre hill appears even larger than it really is from the viewpoint of the passengers in the twenty six foot fishing boat.

"Brenda, that looks almost like a mountain! I am surprised that such a large hill is located in this part of the country! The earth must have folded here creating this magnificent hill. Do you know how many feet it rises above us?"

"I have been told that it is four hundred feet at the shore where it stops. A lot of this huge hill was put in place by enormous earth moving tractors and shovels."

"When did all of this take place?"

"I understand that our family has been working on this hill for a hundred and fifty years. I understand that the area has always had a natural lake and that most of the hill is natural. There is another hill outside of Atkinson called Moores Hill. It may be that these elevated areas have something in common. When we complete our visit on the island, I would like to show you a large hole that is at the bottom of this lake." Brenda drives the boat to the west side of the island and David is delighted and surprised that there is a large manmade canal nearly a hundred and fifty feet wide. Brenda drives the boat for about a thousand feet before entering a manmade harbor that is large enough for small yachts of seventy five feet long. There are slips for docking small fishing boats and larger watercraft. On a hill stands a magnificent small lighthouse that David estimated to be about forty feet high not counting the twenty foot hill it stands on. The lighthouse looks just like the one near Nags head N.C. David had not personally seen the old lighthouse, but owned a travel guide book that has beautiful pictures of all of the lighthouses along the Atlantic Seaboard. A large very old looking wall surrounds most of the harbor. David instantly recognized the wall, the buildings and the streets of the city as a miniature of Casablanca. David looked stunned as he gazed upon this miniature of the city in North Africa. It looked exactly like the city as seen in the old movie entitled *Casablanca.*

"Brenda, I am simply overwhelmed with this miniature of this ancient city in Morocco! Who among the Pridgens came up with this stunning place on this island?"

"My great grandfather George Pridgen was there for about a year during World War Two. He did a lot of traveling during the war and was impressed by the old city. When he came home after the war, he decided to build the place. I am sure that he had help, but he was the one who had the vision so to speak. The canal and the harbor were already here. It was created because it is a lot easier to park boats in a harbor than to try to drag them up a shore. When we have storms, the lake can generate waves over seven feet high. It looks like the ocean during a hurricane. We have pictures of the lake during major storms. You would be surprised at how rough it can get." David and Brenda tie up the boat and walk onto the dock and step into the streets of the miniature of Casablanca in Morocco.

"David, let's go down to the beach. We need to follow this little path to get there." Our couple eventually make it to a beautiful beach that is covered in white sand. The sun is directly back of them sending its warm rays onto their shoulders. The trees back of them are gently moving their branches due to the updraft of the wind that is stirring the lake area. Sea birds are seen diving at the water catching fish. This is not the ocean, but sea birds will catch fish anywhere they have opportunity. David is surprised at the thousands of palm trees that grow near the shore. He feels almost like he is standing on a far away island out in the middle of an ocean. The trees were put there to thrive over a century before our story to add to the beauty of the island and to give it a tropical paradise appearance. The island is rich in orchards of fruits trees and ancient grape vines that delight the eye and please the taste buds. It would be easy for a stowaway to survive on the island if he had to do so. Nearly half a mile away, David and Brenda are delighted to see horses on the beach coming toward them. The lead horse seems to be full of caution and his form is bursting with wild energy.

"Brenda, have you ever been near the Lipizzaner horses?"

"I have had them to cautiously walk a hundred or so feet from me out of curiosity, but they do not hang around hoping I will give them a carrot or perhaps a pat on the neck like the horses we ride. Let's not alarm them and we will see how close they will walk toward us." Ten minutes later, the herd of forty-five horses is only about a thousand feet from our couple. They are not in a hurry, but seem to be enjoying themselves just like people taking a nice walk on the beach just for the joy of it. A young mare moves slightly ahead of the herd urged on by curiosity. The stallion not to be outdone runs ahead of her and turns slightly sideways to let the young mare know that he would decide how far the herd would advance toward the humans. David and Brenda do not move a muscle; they are filled with delight and wonder as these beautiful creatures gaze upon them for the first time. The horses are whiter than the sand beneath their hoofs. These were not your ordinary run of the mill type of horses. They were bred for their beauty, speed, coordination, and intelligence. They were the jewels of the horse world. No wonder the Austrian officials made special arrangements with Great Grandfather George Pridgen to put these magnificent creatures on Paradise Island. David and Brenda continue to not move a muscle hoping that the Lipizzaner horses will move just a little closer. Moments later, the natural instincts of the leader of the herd, the lead stallion, cancelled further advances. The great horse snorted and turned around with great speed and coordination, raised his tail and ran off at a full gallop with the rest of his little kingdom in hot pursuit. David and Brenda continued to remain in a frozen like state for a second after the horses distanced themselves. David speaks:

"I have seen movies about these magnificent horses, but I have never seen these beautiful animals in person. They are unbelievable!"

"Yes, David, I think so. I am thankful for our sakes and the horses that my great grandparents were willing to provide this safe sanctuary for these horses! We have pictures of all of the horses that have been born on this island. We even keep up a family tree for the Austrian officials." David speaks:

"Who takes care of that task?"

"My grandfather has been doing it for decades. I believe that Daddy has been helping him with the project for many years. Both of them know the horses as well as yard dogs. I have not spent enough time with the horses to know individuals except to recognize the lead stallion and if a horse is a male or female. My brothers sow winter grass on Pridgen Mountain every year and are getting familiar with the individual horses. Uncle Preston feeds them every week and is very familiar with the individual animals. He tells me that they will come within a few yards of him without fear. He feeds them corn, oaks, and brings over a few salt blocks for them every six months or so. If a horse gets sick, we capture it and nurse it back to health. If we feel that the situation is very serious, we contact the Austrian officials and they will help us decide on a course of action. We have had only a few horses that have come down with anything.

"David, let's get off of the beach and walk down one of the trails." David and his lovely wife Brenda walk off the beach and travel up a winding path that is decorated on both sides of the road with beautiful flowers and trees. Every once in awhile they come to a little garden spot that has a lovely little gazebo to sit under to rest and enjoy the beauty of the island. A water fountain freely flows from each spot to provide refreshing cool water that is almost unrivaled in taste. Along the path are statues of oriental gods and figures that are there to please the eye. Many of the figurines have been in place for well over two hundred years. Off the trail barely within eyesight David and Brenda smell the apple trees that are heavy with the delicious fruit. The ground around the trees is marked with horse hoof prints where the horses have reached up and plucked the delicious fruit with their mouths. Grapevines over two centuries old are ripening with their heavy bounty. Bees and birds are everywhere taking advantage of the nutritional wealth. David and Brenda grab a huge bundle of grapes and go back to one of the gazeboes and partake of the ripe fruit.

David has never seen such huge grapevines before. The vines and the trees are no doubt a gift from Heaven itself! No grass or weeds are allowed to grow around the trees or the grapevines to rob the soil of its natural nutrition. Uncle Preston makes sure that the island's garden of fruit trees, grapes, ornate shrubs, and flowers are well fertilized with natural compost. Minutes later, our couple comes to a beautiful stone bridge that reminds David of some ancient bridges he saw in China. The bridge is humped backed, not flat, to add to its beauty and structural integrity. The bridge has a cover over it that is overlaid with red tile. The rails on each side of the bridge are a sight to behold because there are so many beautiful carvings in them of Chinese gods, dragons, famous Chinese warriors, philosophers, emperors, and palaces. The deep banked stream over a hundred feet below the bridge is moving rather swiftly and there are large boulders in the stream that are very beautiful to look at. The boulders were placed there to give the stream a mystical appearance. Rocks of all different colors and sizes were put in place to give a realistic look of a fast moving mountain stream somewhere in Ancient China. Along the banks of the stream are trees, bushes, and plants one would expect in some remote mountainous area in China. David is compelled to speak:

"Brenda, this place is as beautiful as any spot I have ever been to! I am amazed at the realistic layout here. A lot of careful planning was required to bring ancient China to this island! Who thought of this beautiful Chinese theme for this part of the island?"

"David, I understand that the third generation of Pridgens to own the plantation traveled and did a lot of business in China. In fact, the bridge we have just crossed was not made in this country, but was actually taken apart and shipped to this country and reassembled where it remains to this day. It was a massive undertaking in those days because the bridge probably weights around thirty thousand tons. It took many shiploads back in those days to bring the entire structure to this country. Chinese engineers and laborers were hired to reassemble the bridge over the creek." David speaks:

"I suppose that the rocks, trees, flowers and the entire panorama of decor were also shipped from China?"

"Yes, because I am sure that you recognized, for example, that the bonsai trees, and the chinaberry trees are not native. Even the bamboo along the steep banks were brought from somewhere in China. The rocks and boulders that decorate the stream and its banks came from the mountains of China. They are obviously not local rocks and rock formations. David it is going to take us about one hour of walking, but I would like for you to go with me to Pridgens Mountain and look down at the lake and see the landscape from that high hill. If it were a few hundred feet higher, I believe that it would be almost considered a mountain." David and Brenda continue to climb. The great hill itself covers five hundred acres of the island. David cannot believe his eyes when he realizes that a huge cemetery sits just below the summit of the great hill. The cemetery cannot be seen from the lake. David speaks:

"Oh, my word, I didn't realize that a cemetery was located on this island!"

"Yes, David, this is our family's private cemetery. It is not huge, being only fifteen acres in size, but it is one of the most expensive cemeteries in North America." David and Brenda continue up the hill until they reach the cemetery. A huge black iron fence twelve feet high surrounds the final resting place for the Pridgen family. On both sides of the double gate stands an angel carved out of white granite. Their huge hands are held out in front of their bodies as if they are holding something. David speaks:

"Brenda, these angles are unbelievable. I can't believe their size and the skill of the people who carved these creatures out of stone! How tall are they?"

"I believe that I was told that they are eighteen feet tall."

"Look at their faces, Brenda, they are so realistic that I am almost struck with fear."

"Yes, David, I am sure that they were carved this way to inspire a sort of dread or at least to provoke people to understand the seriousness of death and the responsibility each of us has to savor life and to use it wisely while it is ours on this side of eternity. Every generation of my family has been abundantly reminded by this place that it's time will come to an end to allow another generation to assume its earthly duties."

"What you say almost frightens me, Brenda! I realize that we will not be here forever, but I am too young to live with such a philosophy dominating my thoughts right now. When we get older, I will probably appreciate such an outlook on life." Large ornate headstones stand upright near each angel. Carved into their faces are words of wisdom to remind the living of the brevity of life and the certainty of eternity. David reads aloud the words taken from the ancient book of Job that are carved into a large headstone that stands in front of one of the angles.

Man that is born of a woman is of few days, and full of trouble. He cometh forth like a flower, and is cut down: he fleeth also as a shadow, and continueth not....Seeing his days are determined, the number of his months are with thee, thou has appointed his bounds that he cannot pass; Turn from him, that he may rest, till he shall accomplish, as an hireling, his day. For there is hope of a tree, if it is cut down, that it will sprout again, that the tender branch thereof will not cease though the root thereof wax old in the earth, and the stock thereof die in the ground; Yet though the scent of water it will bud, and bring forth boughs like a plant, But man dieth, and wasteth away; yea, man giveth up the ghost, and where is he? As the waters fail from the sea, and the flood decayeth and drieth up: So man lieth down, and riseth not; till the heavens be no more, they shall not awake, nor be raised out of their sleep.

"Brenda, these words are not very comforting!"

"They are not supposed to be, David, but the story does not end here." Our couple pulls hard on one of the doors of the huge iron gates and walk under a large arch made out of stone that leads into a huge foyer that is about sixty feet high. The foyer's ceiling looks like the magnificent work of master craftsmen and artist equal to the best cathedrals and palaces on earth. David is stunned that such a structure stands in this cemetery. Above our couple is an almost unequaled painting of the sad story of the fall of mankind in the famous Garden of Eden. Adam and Eve are being expelled out of the garden by a being of light and great power. In one of its hands is a great sword that glows with supernatural light. In the shadows hidden behind the flora is a serpent that is fast losing its legs and wings. The serpent looks in the direction of the couple with cruel eyes. The round structure is supported with columns that are part of the wall itself. The floor of the beautiful chapel is made out of a rare blue granite imported from France. Twenty feet above the floor of the chapel David sees a dozen carvings that are as large as full sized humans boxed into the wall of the structure. One carving is about the story of the crucifixion of Jesus Christ. The artist used stone instead of a paint brush to tell the story of the crucifixion. The cross Jesus hung on stood between two other crosses occupied by two thieves. The three crosses and their occupants hang on a ghastly looking hill made up of mostly solid rock. The face of the hill looks very much like a human skull. Surrounding the crosses are scores of people dressed in First Century attire. Roman soldiers in full battle dress stand nearby with swords drawn and spears to keep order and to see to it that the ones on the crosses die from this horrible slow form of execution possibly invented by the Persians. Standing afar off from Jesus out of respect are Mary Magdalene, and Mary the mother of James the less, and Joses and Salome. Near the cross stands Mary the mother of Jesus and Jesus' disciple John. Jesus is looking down toward his mother and John. Representing the Sanhedrin, the religious leaders of the day, stands a band of the self righteous organization with faces that are glowing with contempt, mockery, and hypocrisy. Another carving shows the trial of Jesus before the religious leaders of his day. Jesus is standing in front of the high priest who is seated on a chair that looks almost like a king's throne. Near Jesus stands a small wicked looking man whose face epitomizes the face of evil. The man is slapping Jesus on the face while looking toward the high priest for approval.

"Brenda, I can't believe that I am in such a place on a plantation in the middle of the woods. This chapel rivals the most famous buildings in the world in beauty! How many people know about this place?"

"I don't know, David. I am sure that it is not featured or discussed in any book or magazine. My family realizes that it must not reveal all of its treasures. The more the public knows, the more difficult it will be to keep our way of life and our property. Look at the other plantations around these several counties. They are only a mere shadow of their working days. Most of their land is sold off and the original families have left the area or have passed into history. As the old saying goes, if you let the camel get its nose into the door, it will not be long before all of the camel is inside the room. David, this chapel is only the entrance to the cemetery; let's get out of here and walk into the mausoleum where my people are at rest." David does not believe his eyes because he and Brenda walk into a beautiful courtyard that ends at the entrance to a huge gray mausoleum made out of granite. The building stands about five stories high. The top includes a large dome. David sees a porch or ledge that surrounds the dome. The porch is surrounded with a heavy duty black iron fence. There is a large cross standing on top of the dome. The mausoleum has several windows carved into its outside walls, but they are there for beauty because the windows are carved into the solid rock. These windows are about fifteen feet high each and are beautified by the presence of an angel that is also carved near the false ledge of each false window. David estimates that the huge front doors of the building are about twelve feet high. Before one can open a door, a gate must be opened first. Beside each door stands two beautiful angels that are about seven feet tall each. The angels stand sideways extending one hand out toward the entrance inviting the traveler weary of his or her earthly journey into this place of eternal rest. On each side of the building enclosure that surrounds the entrance are large gas lanterns in their holders. Brenda grabs one of the large lanterns and lights it with a lighter designed to light grills or fireplaces. David is almost fearful as he and Brenda are about to enter the entrance chamber. The first thing that David's eyes see by the light of the lantern is a huge horse drawn hearse or funeral coach. The horses are, of course, not included, but six stone horses made out of granite are displayed pulling the coach. The horses were carved with such detail and care that they appear to be real.

"David, this is the funeral coach that was used to bring my people to their final resting place for generations. The horses and the funeral coach were transported by barge to the island. Today we use an old hearse to transport our love ones to this mausoleum."

"Brenda, I just can't believe what I am looking at! The president of the United States will not be buried in a place this expensive or grand. This place is very spooky, but very formal and beautiful at the same time. I hope that lantern will not give out of gas. I don't want to get lost in this place!" Brenda could not help but to laugh a bit.

"No, David, I am sure that there is plenty of gas in this huge lantern. In fact, why don't you take it, it is a little heavy for me. Now these stone steps lead down to the crypt where everyone is buried. The caskets are not carried down these stairs because it could be dangerous. Instead a ramp goes all the way down to the third level below ground. It is hidden behind a movable part of the wall. That lever over there is pulled and a portion of the wall swings open. It is balanced somehow because the wall is very heavy and would require the strength of heavy equipment to move otherwise." David and Brenda walk below ground level into the chambers where Brenda's ancestors are interned." David looks upon dozens of vaults that have beautiful carvings all over them. The names of the people in each stone box is displayed on the wall. A history of the dead individual is included.

"David, this is the final resting place for the original owners of this plantation, Captain John Henry Pridgen and his once talented and lovely wife Madame de Lafayette Pridgen." Beautiful lifelike statues of the couple stand near their vault inviting onlookers to read their history. The plaque is four feet wide and seven feet tall to allow for a complete history of this once dynamic couple. The words were written jointly by Captain Pridgen and his wife decades before their deaths. They wanted to speak to their children and their children's children across the barriers of time. Captain Pridgen and his wife wanted to leave something more than just earthly wealth, but wealth that moth, rust, and thieves could not touch. Here is part of the message that David and Brenda read from the brass plaque that is mounted on the wall in front of the vault.

My wife and I realize that when these words are read, we will not be around to share life with you. We have had our turn at this glorious gift from God called life. We drank deep from its goblet and we cherished every moment that we were privileged and blessed to live on this beautiful plantation. We, of course, don't know what will happen in the future generations from now, but we believe like Abraham in the Bible that parents can bless their children so that they will be blessed and will be a blessing for many generations to come. We do not know the many changes that will take place. We have even heard rumors that one day we will no longer be part of the British Empire. We find that hard to accept, but one day a great new nation may rise up out of this wilderness. If it does, we ask God Almighty to bless this new nation that it may be a land where the Bible is still respected as the final word in all of life's issues. David discontinues his reading and speaks:

"Brenda, I am humbled at these great words! Captain Pridgen and his wife were truly great people. I can't believe that they were not mentioned in history books."

"I don't believe that they were in the right place at the right time. They both died some years before the American Revolution. I am sure that if they had settled up North when they were young, they would have been in our history books. However, the fact that they are not well known, except, by locals, has been a blessing because our family has been able to keep its life private and intact. We are not interested in becoming a museum. David, let's go back up on ground level and walk into the exit chapel and end our tour of this land of the dead." Brenda and her husband David walk up the three flights of stairs and walk under a beautiful covered walk made of stone. The walk takes them through a beautiful enclosed garden of statues and fountains. Flowers of great beauty are everywhere enclosed in large ornate flower planters some standing as high as five or six feet tall. Our couple walks into a chapel that is identical to the entrance chapel except for the painting on the dome above and the enclosed boxed in illustrations made out of marble that were created to inspire and teach the Bible.

"Brenda, the painting that covers the ceiling up above us is magnificent! What a sight! Who painted this place? I believe they are equal to anything in Europe?"

"I believe that they were painted by several artists that my ancestors hired. I understand that they were from France. One of the individuals was a full time servant of my people. In fact, he drew many beautiful paintings that are in the mansion. He painted and experimented with all kinds of medium. He was also the main artist and designer of the chateau. I have been told that he was offered a full time residence by the king of France, but he turned down the offer when my people moved from France and made the colonies their permanent home. I have never been inside the chateau, but I understand that he filled the great house with scores of paintings that are worthy of any palace in the world. I understand that he also painted the main ceilings of the house if it should be referred to as a house. It really is a small palace of about a two hundred and forty thousand square feet." David speaks:

"My parents' house is large at twenty thousand square feet of living space. I don't believe that your people have had a problem not having enough living space! I believe that their mansion is about eighty-four thousand feet. At least the space is not wasted. I notice that your parents and grandparents never brag about their enormous house."

"No, I don't believe that they need to. The house and property speak for themselves. My people appreciate what they have and take care of it, but they don't worship their property. We have all learned to use it wisely and to realize it was all given to us to enjoy and pass down to our children. Along with the physical property, we pass down our culture or lifestyle and our Christian Heritage." David looks up and feasts his mind on the domed ceiling above him. The painting shows the ascension of Jesus Christ from the Mount of Olives near Jerusalem. Hundreds of people in beautiful First Century robes are standing almost in a circle as they look up toward the sky as Jesus is taken up in a cloud. Near and below Jesus are angels who speak to the faithful comforting words of his return to Earth one glorious day. David allows Brenda to read the words out loud to him.

And when he had spoken these things, while they beheld, he was taken up: and a cloud received him out of their sight. And while they looked steadfastly toward heaven as he went up, behold, two men stood by them in white apparel; which also said, Ye men of Galilee, why stand ye gazing up into heaven? This same Jesus, which is taken up from you into heaven, shall so come in like manner as ye have seen him go into heaven.

"Brenda, I could stay in this huge room for hours and look at this huge painting. It is so beautiful and so detailed! How wide is this chapel?"

"The same as the first one, David. I understand that they are a hundred and twenty feet in diameter and sixty feet tall. About the size of a small planetarium building, I suppose. David you can visit this place at your own leisure another day. I would like to show you the lake and the beautiful little island we have a nice cabin on."

"I don't understand. We are already on the island that is in the middle of a huge lake."

"That is true, but there is a four hundred acre lake on this island. In the middle of this little lake is a thirty-five acre island with a beautiful cabin on it. The lake is stocked with Bass and Trout. Our family uses the cabin as a sort of hide away. My parents used the cabin for their honeymoon. It is the most beautiful cabin I have ever seen. A creek runs from the lake. This is the same creek that we walked across when we walked on the Chinese bridge. Several underground springs of considerable size feed this four hundred acre lake. I assume that the water comes from the same source that feeds the huge fishing lake that the main island sits in."

"You mean to tell me that there is a four hundred acre lake on this twenty four hundred acre island, and that this lake has an island on it that your family has put a large cabin on?" Brenda laughs and speaks:"

"Yes, David, I do believe that you have the picture. I realize that it almost sounds like we are living in a make believe world, but we really do have that lake and island here on this island. If we start walking, we should be there in less than an hour. When we arrive at the lake, we can take a canoe and paddle to the island. There is a dock near the shore where the water has been dredged to six feet deep."

While our excited young couple is exploring the small island that is called Paradise Island, Doctor Hardin is busy sowing seed at UNCW. He is not sowing the kind of seed a farmer would sow to reap a harvest in the fall of the year, but another kind of seed that he hopes will yield a bountiful harvest. Doctor Hardin is sowing the seeds of trouble and doubt that will help him achieve his dream of taking over the coveted chair

Doctor David Smith has been appointed to. Doctor Hardin is no amateur, he has been undermining the careers of people for decades. The Chancellor of the University, Doctor Julia DeVann Corbett, is very suspicious, but Doctor Hardin is very good at hiding his tracks. He is a fox that can bag his chickens and be out of the hen house before the yard dog can get a whiff of his scent. January will be here in a little over five months. It is amazing how large the right kind of seeds can grow in the minds of students and faculty in five months if properly tended. Doctor Hardin is about to teach a class in Geology. Most of the students are in their sophomore year. The class today is about earthquakes. Doctor Hardin looks at his class and asks a question for anyone willing to answer the question.

"Can anyone in this class of aspiring scientist tell me what an earthquake is and what causes earthquakes?" After a few seconds, a young lady rises to the occasion and submits an answer.

"I believe that they are caused by the shifting of the earth's crust. A plate pushes against another plate, slides past it, or goes under another plate. A lot of tension is built up when plates push against each other. This tension is stored energy which when released, shakes the Earth violently."

"Not a bad answer, Miss Andrews! I am confident that all of you could have answered the question as well as Miss Andrews. Miss Andrews; however, has earned one point on her final examine by participating in class. Some of you would not do bad if you followed her example. I believe that most of you people plan to graduate with a degree in science. This will be how you all will most likely earn your living. Now all of you people are not going to get your doctorate and become a professor and that is OK. However, most of you people will either teach in secondary public schools or will become scientist in the field such as mining coal, or other valuable resources from the earth or under the ocean. Get used to people asking you questions. Get used to thinking while standing on your feet without a book in front of you to hide behind. If you are a member of a work team and the boss or owner asks a question, you are going to have to give it your best shot. You will not have the luxury to sit and expect someone else to always be first. It may actually benefit your career. You may actually get a promotion or may marry the boss's son if you are a young lady." Several students laugh at the comment. Doctor Hardin continues:

"There are actually many different kinds of earthquakes caused by more than the moving of the plates that float around on the surface of the Earth that struggle against each other. By the way, these plates that float around have names. In your handout you will see a map with these plates.

Be aware of them. They may suddenly appear on an examination. Now before I say more about what causes earthquakes, I want all of you young scientist to look at the list of names on the handout sheets. Notice Alfred Wagener. He was a person who was a key player in our understanding the dynamics of plate movement. He developed a theory about continental drift." A young man raises his hand and speaks:

"Doctor Hardin, I was in church some weeks ago and the minister said that the separation of the continents is recorded in the Bible in the early part of the Book of Genesis. Could it be that someone very early in history noted the drifting of the continents from one giant parent continent we now call Pangaea?"

"I am aware of the passage young man. It is as you have pointed out, in the Book of Genesis. I am not sure that the passage has anything to do with the present discussion. I have read that it may refer to the movements of various peoples as they formed tribes and drifted apart from each other. We do know that all humans originated from Africa from two parents. I am not one of those scientists who will bite off the head of a student that refers to a Bible passage. After all, we were a Bible oriented society at one time. All of the problems and questions people had were once considered answered somewhere in the Bible. Of course, modern professional scientists do not consider the Bible a book of science. I am sure that was not the reason it was written. It is a philosophy book. Now, I usually take little time answering such questions. However; be aware, you atheist or agnostics that sit in this classroom that the Bible, in fact, is very accurate about many scientific questions and observations. This still does not mean that it is a book of science. I am not an agnostic or an atheist. I do not hate or belittle people for their religious beliefs so long as their religious beliefs do not endanger human life or attempt to force by arms their way of life on the rest of us.

"Now back to earthquakes. Look again at the handouts. I see a very important name below Doctor Wegener's name. His name is Arthur Holmes. Now what can cause earthquakes other than plates moving around the earth's surface? A huge herd of large animals can cause earthquakes. We usually think of the earth's plates struggling against each other as the primary cause of the earthquakes. We could go a step farther and say that magma coming from the bowels of the earth is the engine that moves the plates around. Huge volcanoes have caused the Earth to quake. Atom bombs exploded hundreds of feet underground can cause earthquakes. Huge meteorites from outer space have caused tremendous earthquakes. In other words, anything that can violently shake the earth's surface can cause an earthquake. Scientists know where most of our earthquakes will occur and their origin. This does not mean we understand all there is to know. We will probably never know everything there is to know about most things. This does not belittle what we know or the practical applications that take place as a result of what we know. In earthquake prune regions of our country, and other advanced societies, we put our knowledge to practical use by making sure that building codes are up to date so that modern buildings will be able to better survive a quake. We are aware of the risk of tsunamis because scientists know that certain fault lines are at risk for moving violently. These faults are constantly monitored for any significant changes." A young man raises his hand.

"Doctor Hardin, I understand that the new assistant head of the science department has developed software and delicate instruments that have above a ninety percentile of accuracy. I don't understand why there is not more known about this new science!"

"Yes, I have heard of some of these claims myself. I used to listen to a radio program when I was a teenager that often introduced people who claimed that they had seen UFOs in the sky, man like monsters walking around near their campsites, or perhaps claimed to have invented time machines or perpetual motion engines. I was fascinated by these wonderful claims. When I went to college, I could not learn much about these strange and wonderful inventions and sightings in the science department, but I did see them in the science fiction reading section of the university's library." Another young man raises his hand:

"Doctor Hardin, are you suggesting that Doctor Smith is a charlatan or has an out of control imagination?" Everyone became very quite because they realized that the comment could be a challenge, a shot fired broadside at Doctor Smith's credibility. Professors like any other profession are known to challenge or question the opinions of other professors, but usually not in the same institution, especially if the other instructor occupied a higher chair. Doctor Hardin pauses and speaks:

"No, I am not saying that Doctor Smith is a charlatan; his imagination is probably greater than mine. I have not looked at Doctor Smith's inventions or seriously examined his claims. I hope to have that opportunity once he settles down here and starts talking. I have been teaching a long time and I suppose that I have become a little skeptical about a lot of fantastic claims. I have seen dozens of people fall out of the sky like meteors falling from the sky. I am not saying that Doctor Smith is a charlatan. I will not have to. The passage of time will reveal all just like a good x ray machine. I will reserve my opinion until I learn more."

Our story takes us back to Paradise Island when David and Brenda walk up onto the shores of a nice size lake slightly over four hundred acres in size. The lake is about two thirds of a square mile in size and David notices an island in the middle of this beautiful lake that is surrounded by beautiful pine and oak trees that are centuries old. The wind is blowing strong enough to cause waves to develop that are over a foot in height. David notices a building not far from the shores of this lake that has a shed room. Brenda speaks:

"David, we keep supplies in this building and the shed room is used to store our canoes in." Our couple does not enter the main part of the small building, but go directly to the shed room and Brenda grabs a chain and starts pulling on it. The room has a garage door that is manually opened and closed. David is impressed by the beautiful canoes that are stored on racks. In each canoe are paddles, fishing rods, and everything anyone would need to have a successful day fishing.

"David, help me with the canoe. Let's go ahead and put the life vests on before we sit inside of the canoe." Minutes later our couple is paddling the beautiful canoe with Indians and drums painted on its side. The canoe is very easy to paddle and cuts the water creating a nice wake. Brenda and David have used canoes many times together and are very accomplished at the sport. Directly Brenda tells David that she believes that they should bait their hooks and start fishing for Bass or Trout. The very second David throws his hook into the water a large Bass grabs the hook. Brenda speaks:

"At this rate I don't believe that we will have to fish very long before we have plenty of fish for supper and breakfast in the morning." Brenda and David continue to paddle toward the island stopping occasionally to drop their baited hooks into the lake. The lake is teaming with bass and trout! There are no predatory fish to challenge the fish that are only occasionally stocked to keep genetic problems arising from too much inbreeding. The sunlight is dancing off the water stimulating the natural instincts of our young couple. A nice cool breeze swept across the beautiful lake causing the water to stir itself like it was alive. About fifteen hundred feet from our excited young couple, a flock of plump geese land onto the lake to look for small fish darting about here and there. The Moon was barely visible in the sky rising just above the tree line on the other side of the small island situated in the middle of the lake. In the distance, David and Brenda hear the faint rumble of what they believe to be thunder coming from a dark cloud some miles away. David and Brenda are not worried because they have less than half a mile before they reach the shore of the small island.

"David, I believe that we are going to get a nice big rain from that cloud. It looks like it is boiling it is rising so fast!" Directly a flash of lightning streaks across the vicinity of the lake.

"David, I believe that these eight fish will be more than enough food for us. We should go ahead and get to the island and get out of harm's way. That storm could be upon us in thirty minutes or less. The cabin should be fully stocked with everything that we will need to have a good time." Our couple at last reaches the shores of the island and tie up onto the dock. David surveys his surroundings as he walks behind Brenda to the shore. There is a look of excitement and approval all over his face. The cabin is several hundred feet from the shores of the lake up on a flat hill that takes up about ten acres of the thirty five acre island. David and Brenda climb stone steps to the top of the hill. The cabin looks very typical of an early American cabin built in the mountains of Kentucky, Tennessee, or perhaps North Carolina a couple of hundred years ago. The only obvious dissimilarity is, of course, the size of the cabin which is over thirty five hundred square feet of living space. The builders did not use clay to chink or fill in the space or cracks between the logs that make up the walls of the structure, but chose to use a special new material that is a better insulator than the traditional materials used to fill in cracks.

Out in the yard about a hundred and fifty feet from the cabin, David notices a large windmill turning rapidly that pumps up water that supplies not only the cabin with it cold refreshing spring water, but is used to keep the grounds surrounding the cabin well watered for the many beds of flowers and shrubs that beautify the place. A beautiful gazebo sits in the yard surrounded by azaleas. A nice swing hangs from the ceiling of the gazebo that is large enough to allow four people to swing and enjoy the view which includes the beautiful lake that surrounds the island. From a distance a flock of wild ducks swim back and forth near the shore of the island apparently looking for small fish. David points at the limb of a enormous live oak tree that is being used by a mama raccoon to raise her young. There is a large hollow in the limb next to the trunk. A beautiful red headed woodpecker is seen high in a tall cypress tree next to the shore hammering away with not a care in the world it seems. Scores of Black walnut trees and pecan trees are growing several hundred feet from the cabin giving the yard a homestead appearance. Squirrels are running up and down and jumping from tree limb to tree limb in an endless game they play all day. They remind David and Brenda of children playing with not a concern crossing their thoughts. The great thundercloud has now confirmed its domination of the sky up above and will soon produce winds that will move the top limbs of the mightiest tree that stands in the neighborhood. Sharp streaks of lighting cross the sky in ever increasing magnitude. The rumble of the thunder is almost deafening and is getting closer with every breath David and Brenda take as they quickly flee to the comfort and safety of the cabin's huge porch that is surrounded by a specially designed high quality screen to keep the insects at a respectable level and provide a good measure of protection from mostly any rain storm. David and Brenda have their cloths wet with cold drops of nature's water as they run up the steps and unto the porch and close the double glass doors behind them. David is very impressed with the beauty of the cabin and all of the interesting things he sees on the porch to delight the eye and to comfort the soul and body of such a one that is seeking a hide away to regenerate the inter-man or woman. The place has great personality and reflects the creativity and dynamic lifestyle of the Pridgen Clan. The porch is about eighteen feet wide and the floor is made out of heavy four inch thick oak lumber that is fourteen inch wide tongue and groove. A Mack truck could ride across it. This cabin was made to last many years into the future!

The temperature drops almost twenty degrees and the chill in the air causes our couple to shiver. Brenda quickly runs over to the large fireplace in the den of the cabin and places cured starter lighter wood from old pine trees below the firedogs. David thrice runs to the porch and grabs arm full's of small split oak logs stored in the wood box and places the logs on the firedogs above the lighter wood. Brenda strikes a match against the stone face of the fireplace and lights the starter wood. Immediately the cured lighter wood is surrounded by dancing blazing orange red tongues of fire licking the logs as if they were feeling and tasting the wood above them.

"David, we need to get these wet cold cloths off before we catch a cold and hang them up in the utility room and let them dry. There should be something in one of the closets that we can put on, perhaps some house coats until our cloths are dry." To David's and Brenda's surprise, they realized that balls of ice, commonly called hail, were coming down in increasing amounts. The roof was covered with cedar shingles, not tin, but the noise was still very loud. David and Brenda quickly find warm house coats and make their way to a large set of bay windows in the den and look out into the yard and the lake area. The yard was covered with ice balls the size of golf balls. They could see that a few ducks were crippled and that leaves and some limbs were on the ground. A flock of ducks managed to run to safety by going under a large open shed attached to a log crib about one hundred feet from the house. The birds were very excited and were making a fuss loud enough to be heard from inside the cabin's den.

"David, I have never seen hail balls this huge. I don't know what to make of it!"

"Brenda, I am afraid that there might be a tornado in the vicinity." The cloud became darker and the thunder was the worst that Brenda had ever heard. A large limb from an oak tree came crashing onto the ground not fifty feet from the cabin. Brenda grabbed her cell phone to call the house, but there was only a loud crackling noise to be heard.

"David, I can't call with the phone there is too much interference. I hope that everyone is under cover by now!"

"I am sure that they are, Brenda. There are a lot of places to get out of harm's way on the plantation." While our couple continues to look out toward the lake amazed at the storm, the rain, and hail, everything suddenly stopped. This was one time that silence was not golden! It was like being in the eye of the storm. While our couple stood nearby the huge windows in the den, they see a sight that causes them to cringe with fear. It is as if the massive dark cloud above suddenly swoops down from the sky. Brenda screams out with excitement pointing toward the event outside, a thousand feet out on the lake from them. A huge water spout is given birth by the storm above. Our couple cannot believe the size of the spout as it makes its way across the four hundred acre lake. A million tons or more of water is sucked up high into the sky to come crashing back on the surface of the lake and even onto the island. It is as if a mega giant dipped a huge bucket into the lake and throws at least a million tons of water high in the sky.

The cabin is surrounded by a great rush of water that falls from the sky. Brenda and David almost feel like they are sitting in a small car while going through a giant oversized bigger than life car washing station. The sturdy cabin holds its ground, but several trees outside are not so fortunate and are not only on the ground, but have actually been swept to the shore of the lake by the avalanche of water coming from the sky. The great water spout did not have a long life, but suddenly disappeared as quickly as it appeared back into its mother, the huge black boiling cloud that commanded the sky above the lake area. The cell phone that Brenda carried with her rang and she answered with a little quiver noted in her voice. The caller was Brenda's mother, Lillian Pridgen, who was concerned about the safety of her daughter.

"Brenda, are you and David OK?"

"Yes, ma'am, the waterspout has gone back up into the cloud. Was there any damage done around the plantation?"

"I don't know yet because the twister as far as we know did not go anywhere except the lake you and David were visiting. We had some hail and heavy winds for a few minutes. Your father is on his way back from Atkinson to check on the damage and the rest of the folks around these parts will be out and about seeing if anything was damaged or hurt. Your grandfather said that he has never heard of a tornado around these parts before. I understand that a bad one hit the old Corbett home off Highway 210 and near the Town of Riegelwood near the old pulp plant many years ago, but never here on the plantation. I hope that everything survived on the island you and David are visiting."

"Mama, David and I have not had time to go outside and check on things. We do know that some ducks were injured and at least two large pecan trees went down, and I believe they are now near the shore of the lake. The water literally washed them down the hill. I am not sure if the house is alright outside or not. I will call you as soon as we can evaluate the situation. We have only been in the house about twenty minutes. Our clothes are wet and are hanging in the utility room. We have no dry clothes to wear at the moment. I believe that I will get the rack that is in the utility room and dry our cloths in front of the fire that I have going. We will wait about thirty minutes or so because the cloths are nearly half wet. I don't want David or me to catch a cold."

"Brenda, take your time. I don't want you two outside with wet garments on. I am sure that you will call us as soon as you know something. I hope that the canoe you two were using is still tied up out at the dock!"

"Mother, I have not even thought about that! We might be stranded in the middle of this big lake! I don't believe that I will want to swim close to half a mile to get back to the big island."

"Well, don't worry, take your time and find out what is going on. We will get a boat over to you guys if you find out that your canoe is missing or damaged. Just be careful and stay warm." Lillian hangs up the phone just as Beard walks up onto the porch of the mansion all concerned about what happened." Lillian speaks:

"Beard, I have just got off the phone and Brenda and David are OK. She tells me that at least two large trees are down and the torrent of water was so great that it washed them down the hill onto the shore of the lake." Beard speaks:

"If they don't need us immediately, I am going to get Pa and we are going to the fishing lake and check on the property. If any one learns something we don't know about, ask them to call me on the cell phone I carry with me. Call Charles Sidbury and have him to get one of our planes in the air and fly around the area to see if anything needs our immediate attention." Mr. Zeb walks into the kitchen where Beard and his wife are talking and speaks.

"Beard, let's get on with it. I don't want any unexpected surprises. The sooner we get on the trail, the sooner we will be able to prevent further injury or damage if there are any to concern us." Beard and Mr. Zeb get into their truck and speed on toward the huge fishing lake. Beard blows his horn many times along the road to make sure that folks were aware that he was moving faster than usual. Uncle Preston called and informed Mr. Zeb, who had the phone in hand, that he and about three dozen fellows were out and checking on the property. A tree limb on a power line could cause a fire. Perhaps something fell on a person or an animal during the storm. Thirty minutes later Beard drives the truck he and his father are in up to the great fishing lake. In the main time Brenda and David have changed back into their now dry cloths and are getting ready to go outside of the cabin and check on the damage. David and Brenda step out of the cabin with their eyes wide opened expecting anything after such a situation. Several large flood trenches were formed as huge volumes of the lake's water rushed back to the lake after being dumped onto the small thirty five acre island. David turns around and looks up toward the roof of the cabin and notices fish on the roof. All along the grounds outside our couple sees fish here and there. Hundreds of limbs of various sizes have been snatched off the trees that surround the cabin. The ducks are no longer under the barn shed, but are gorging on the bounty of fish that are everywhere. David speaks:

"Well, if I had known ahead of time, I would not have gone fishing. I believe that there are enough fish to feed two or three hundred people all over this lawn!"

"I believe that I had rather eat the ones we caught, David. They are still alive in the fish well under the porch at the cabin. Catching them is half of the pleasure." David speaks:

"True, but who is going to get those fish off the roof of the cabin?"

"Well, I guess that we could ask the birds to fly up there and get them, but since we are here, I will take charge of the situation and I believe that we can manage the fish problem. There is a nice big ladder in the barn that we can use. It will not take us over twenty minutes to sweep them off the roof. We can carry them back to the lake and let Mother Nature handle it from there." Brenda smiles and our couple gets the ladder and two rakes and walk the roof raking and throwing fish off the shingles. They next climb down and get a large wooden wheel barrel and fill it with dead fish which they promptly roll down to the lake where a flock of large ducks are honking and swimming close to the shore excited that David and Brenda are tossing fish in their direction. Unfortunately, most of the fish are larger than a duck can swallow. Larger predators like the raccoons, Opossums, and several eagles in the area will certainly take advantage of the bounty nature provided for them. David walks over to a large pecan tree that is partly in the lake amazed at its size.

"Brenda, what a waste; I would guess that this old tree is around a hundred and fifty years old. There are still bushels of undeveloped pecans on the limbs of this tree. I would imagine that your father will have to cut this monster up into firewood so that it will not go to waste."

"Yes, I believe that Daddy will be coming here tomorrow and start working on the damage around here unless there is something that needs attention somewhere else that is more important. The windmill is still standing, but it does not turn very fast. A lot of its wind catching ability has been lost. We were fortunate that the twister did not destroy the thing. It must be made very sturdy to have withstood a large twister like the one we have just experienced! Uncle Preston and some of the carpenters will no doubt repair the damages unless Daddy and my brothers decide to do the work. It all depends on how much work they are currently involved with. Look at the size of the gullies the water carved down here to the shore. It will take a lot of soil to fill in these huge natural ditches! I would imagine that the dredge barge we keep on the lake will be used to collect the soil out of the lake itself to fill in these huge ditches that the storm made."

"Brenda, we were very fortunate that the cabin did not receive more damage. The huge volume of water coming down so suddenly would have completely destroyed most houses instantly. We would have been history or washed out into the lake in bad shape! Brenda, let's walk around the entire island from the shore and see what happened on the other side as well." David and Brenda walk around the thirty five acre island and back to the spot where the cabin is located. Large trenches have been formed around the entire island, but nothing as large as the ones on the cabin side. No trees were down or anything to be concerned about except the side of the island that faced the twister as it passed about a thousand feet from where the cabin stands on the island. The wind from the twister did not cause the most damage, but the water as it fell back down to earth from a thousand or more feet in the sky above the cabin. Several ducks had been killed, but considering the potential the storm no doubt had, the Pridgen Plantation was very fortunate so far!

Back at the big house, the children are naturally excited and want to get out and see and touch the ice balls that have fallen. Lillian, their grandmother, cautioned them and told them that they could look at the hail near the house, but to go nowhere else. Mrs. Lillian and Lilly her mother-in-law go outside and check on the herb garden and their huge green house that is constructed with steel and heavy duty glass. Mattie goes outside to check on things her own way. Mrs. Lilly speaks:

"I sure hope my garden and the greenhouse have not been damaged! We need to check on the greenhouse first because the plants there are climate controlled. I don't want to lose some of those rare experimental plants the state pays us to grow." Thirty minutes later, Lilly and Lillian have checked on the huge greenhouse. Only a few glass panels are cracked and will be replaced within a week by folks that live on the plantation. Lillian decides to check on the herb garden that her father-in-law tends realizing that he is not available to check on the garden because he is with Beard riding around the large fishing lake checking on the property. Our party quickly walks to the herb garden which is about five hundred feet from the greenhouse. Lillian is the first to enter through the Iron Gate entrance followed by her mother-in-law. Hail balls are seen everywhere on the stone pavement of the herb garden the size of golf balls. About one fourth of the plants have been destroyed or damaged. Fortunately no one thing was completely wiped out. Lilly speaks:

"Oh, my, a certain old man named Zeb Pridgen is not going to be very happy about this! I will offer to help him, but he is usually as territorial about this place as a wolf is with its hunting and breeding grounds. I will suggest that we help him, but I will not repeat my offer. Let's walk over to the little herb drying building and Zeb's seedling house and see if there is any damage. I hope that no medicine jars were broken! It takes time for the herbs to get to full strength before they are strong enough for medicine." Now back to the mansion where the children look with wonder at the huge hail balls.

"Wow look at this one, I bet it is as big as an apple! Betty let's get a big bag and save as many of these hail balls as we can. When people ask us about the hail, we can show them the ice." Dan runs into the kitchen and finds a heavy duty plastic bag and runs back down the steps to help his sister fill the bag with dozens of huge ice balls. While they hurry, Mattie comes back with ice balls as large as soft balls. She is delighted to see that the kids are doing what she was doing, that is saving some of the ice so that people would be able to see firsthand what they were currently experiencing. Zeb gives Brenda a phone call:

"Brenda, what damage has been done around that cabin you and David have been staying in?"

"Grandpa, I see no damage to the cabin so far. David and I got on the roof and removed hundreds of fish that were dropped by the storm. Several large pecan trees are down and were washed down the hill to the lake. I guess that they will be turned into firewood that will last for at least two years to come. The water carved huge troughs as it rushed down the island back to the lake. It is going to take thousands of tons of soil to fill them all. The windmill has been damaged and will need to be repaired. We have seen several ducks that didn't make it, but the rest are all happy and are out and about the yard and the shore of the lake eating fish."

Beard asked his father to call his sons and to find out if they could bring some heavy duty saws and cut up the wood and help repair the windmill. Beard Junior said that he would bring the fellows over the next day at about ten o'clock. Beard Junior will have to stop his work early and get ready for the next day. The island David and Brenda are on is in a large lake of about four hundred acres. This lake is on a larger island; the island that Pridgen Mountain is on. The larger lake would not be crossed by canoes, but by the larger boats that were tied up at a boat ramp. Zeb Pridgen suggested that the barge be brought over so that a medium duty caterpillar tractor can be brought over to the island to push or pull the fallen pecan trees completely on dry land so that they could be cut up into firewood. It was estimated that about eight tons of wood would come out of the giant trees. Most of this wood would be carried back to the woodshed near the mansion. This was a little early to start cutting winter firewood, but it was better than wasting the wood. The mature wood would cure well under the large woodshed. Beard gave his wife Lillian a phone call and told her that the trees would have to be cut up and asked if she and his mother Lilly wanted to come over to the little island and stay a few days in the cabin. Lillian speaks:

"Beard, I would love to come, but your mother does not want to come. She said that she will look after the children, if that is alright with you."

"Why can't the children come?"

"Brenda said that there would be too much sawing and repair work being done for small children to be around. David and Brenda can carry them to the islands another day when it is safer and they can fish and walk the big island and see the horses and all of the beautiful things over there."

"You are right, Lillian. We will all be very busy for a few days. I will see you and whoever wants to come tomorrow. Bring some food over; I am not sure what is available over at the cabin. It has been a spell since anyone of us has been over there to enjoy the place."

"Yes, Beard, I do remember us especially enjoying that place once. I believe that was before our kids were born."

"What do you mean, Lillian? Oh, why shucks, you are talking about our honeymoon! Well at least you have not forgotten about that. It does not seem that long ago. You and I should visit that place again; just you and me one nice weekend when the crops are all gathered and the frost is still on the pumpkins. You know the old saying..." Lillian realized that her mother-in-law, Mrs. Lilly Pridgen, could hear the conversation and she quickly put breaks on Beard's words before she became embarrassed.

"Beard, now watch it, I am not alone." Beard could hear laughter in the background.

"Well, Lillian, I guess that I was just thinking about the old stork, that is all. I will see you sometime tomorrow." For the next three days work is done on the small island repairing and cleaning up the damage done by the storm. Brenda and David promise themselves that they will go back to the cabin and finish their visit and hopefully a storm will not drop by the neighborhood again.

Four days later at the breakfast table the Pridgens are having a wonderful meal and enjoying each other's company and making plans for the day and future days. Beard speaks:

"David, before the weather gets cold I would like to go ahead and check on the property up and down Black River. I usually have already gone, but it seems that something has prevented me from the trip every time I would like to go. When do you believe that you will be free to spend about three or four days at most checking on the property?"

"I believe that I should be able to go in about three or four days. I need to go by the school and take my books and some computers by my office. I will not teach until January of next year, but I believe that I would be wise to finish that job and just walk around and get better acquainted with staff and faculty. It might pay to visit some of the classes and observe some of the classes in action. Most instructors do not like such visits, but I try to make them as painless as possible. I look at it much like a new coach watches his future players on television doing their thing. It alerts me to any improvements that should be made in our teaching methods. I am sure that the instructors at the school are experienced professionals that are always open to suggestions to help them fulfill their goal of creating the best environment in order to train the most qualified workers in the field of marine science and geology as possible."

"Have you ever worked with any of these instructors you will supervise?"

"In a way I have. I stayed with a number of them in an underwater facility for a few weeks studying the marine life near Wrightsville Beach.

We did not discover anything to warrant an article released in a scientific journal, but we did have a good time and I did get to observe the daily routine of these scientist and senior students." Brenda speaks to David:

"David, a bunch of my old friends are coming over for a visit so that we can all go to the swimming hole and enjoy ourselves about two o'clock this afternoon. Would you like to be there with us?"

"I would love to be there! The children and I will get to be with your friends. Are any children coming along with them?"

"I don't know, but I believe that they would also enjoy the experience. Our children would get to play with them and build a lasting relationship with the children of my old friends. I never even dreamed years ago when we were together that such a day would arrive! I will call Tommy Cobb and a few of my friends and ask them to bring over their kids. When their kids get a little older, they can come over and visit our kids like they did when I was a child." Grandmother Lilly speaks up:

"Well, I believe that we can cut up some nice big watermelons outside for your friends." Lillian speaks:

"I also believe that I can add to this by baking a couple of large cakes, and I will check and see if we have enough ice cream in the freezer on the porch for the occasion! Beard, you and I should go out to that swimming hole. I have been so busy this summer that I have almost forgotten how to enjoy the summer months. Life is a little too short." Beard pauses and looks at Lillian without speaking immediately. At last, he speaks:

"Lillian, you are right. I believe that I will call a few of my old standbys and see if they can help run the hardware store today while I am absence. I have seen too many folks in my day work themselves to an early grave trying to make a dollar fooling themselves and their neighbors by saying that they are doing it all for their children's future. I have frequently observed that the children of these people are grown and married and are often in need of nothing." Lilly speaks up:

"Yes, I have heard it said by ministers that people in their last few days in this life usually do not concern themselves with their money or the amount of time spend at work wishing they could have put in more overtime, but the little time they took with their families." Lilly's daughter-in-law Lillian speaks up:

"Yes, I could not agree with you more Mrs. Pridgen. There will always be plenty of work if a fellow wants to spend his entire life obeying its voice. Now I realize that the Good Lord put us to work way back there in that garden to keep our minds and hands occupied so that we would not have unlimited time to corrupt ourselves with evil thoughts and acts of violence. I am sure that we as a race would have destroyed ourselves a long time ago if it were not for our taskmaster we call work, but I do believe firmly that the Good Lord expects us to take out time to enjoy ourselves and reflect on his goodness."

Fourteen

A Visit to the Swimming Hole with Old Friends

Zeb speaks to his wife Lilly Pridgen:

"Well now, put your money where your mouth is old lady. I have not seen you down at the swimming hole in a coon's age. Why shucks, I bet you have just about forgotten which path to take in those woods to get there. I am in agreement with both of you gals about having a little fun and a season of rest once in awhile. It is recorded in the Bible that man and beast need to take one day a week for such." Everyone left the kitchen; except, for Lilly, her daughter-in-law, and Brenda. Mattie shows up to wash the dishes and to put things up after the breakfast is over with. As soon as everything is washed and put in its place, the ladies start to cook cakes for the get together that will take place at two o'clock that afternoon. Time goes by quickly and everyone sits on the porch waiting for their friends to arrive. The first vehicle to arrive is an old F100 1965 Ford pickup truck that Tommy Cobb restored back to mint condition. In the front seat beside him was his wife Janet. His son, Tommy Junior is in the back of the truck with three other boys enjoying a ride in the so called Country Cadillac. The moment Tommy parks his truck, three other vehicles show up and are parked beside the truck Tommy is driving. The doors of the vehicles are opened and the children burst out of their seats followed by the adults. Tommy's son and his friends jump out of the back of the truck. Everyone quickly runs or walks up the huge twelve foot tall steps that are adored by the African lions and greet the Pridgen family on their mega size porch. Excitement is in the air and even Lilly Pridgen has managed to find her old swimming suit and is looking forward to a nice time out at the swimming hole.

The temperature outside is nearly ninety eight degrees out beyond the shade trees, but the white sandy bottomed swimming hole is nice and cool just waiting for the first excited human to take a plunge into its refreshing waters. Great Grandmother Lilly looks over toward her husband Zeb as he walks down the steps into the yard with friends and family headed to the swimming hole which is about a thousand feet from the house in a thick wooded area surrounding the creek.

"Why for an old land frog you still are a fine figure of manhood in a swimming suit!" Zeb appears to be surprised at his wife's statement and looks at her with a challenging look and speaks:

"Well, Lilly, you don't look bad yourself for an old senior citizen. I suspect it is the water at the swimming hole or perhaps the country air and good food you gals are known to cook for our clan on this here plantation." Lilly smiles and answers her husband of over sixty three years:

"Zeb, my theory is that it is all about the genes." Zeb does not catch on to what his wife is saying for a second and them laughs and speaks to her and anyone within ear shot."

"Yes, they told me a long time ago when I was just a yearling man before I started dating you that I needed to start dating gals over beyond our neck of the woods in the Canetuck Township because those Moore girls were mighty high on the hog when it came to their breeding. Yes, they said that they were no doubt the descendents of the nobles of Great Britain herself. Yes, sir, they said find yourself a gal bred from good stock and you will not have to worry about having to marry again in your latter days because they were manufactured just like a fine automobile meant to last for years to come." Lillian frowns a little and looks toward her mother-in-law Lilly who is only a couple of feet away and whispers something into her ears while Lilly looks toward Zeb with a fake hard look. Zeb speaks:

"What are you gals muttering about now? Why I would consider it a privilege to have been married and set up so high on the hen nest by such a nice old barnyard roster that I am!" Lilly turns and speaks to Zeb:

"Zeb, let's just go down to that swimming hole and enjoy ourselves before these young people think that we are getting a little soft in the old noggins!"

Bare feet walk the path that forks and leads to the swimming hole. High up in a sweet gum tree along the path an excited pair of cat squirrels chatter away apparently realizing that today is somehow different than yesterday. The young people, as is their nature, take off running ahead of their elders dashing toward the stream. Mrs. Lillian calls out loud cautioning them to be careful because snakes need the time to make up their minds to leave the area while the humans temporarily take over the area with their activity. Eventually, everyone is standing near the hole just a looking at the soft white sandy bottom of the hole and the unrivaled beauty of raw nature that surrounded the Pridgens and their friends.

Hanging on a large limb that is only about four feet from the ground near the creek, hung about ten tire inner tubes of various sizes. One was the inner tube that once fitted inside an oversized tire of a huge tractor used to pull logs. Several of the kids got together and decided to use this tube to play with. Several of the floats were purchased at stores in Wilmington and were shaped like mattresses with pillows. Zeb grabbed one of these and lays down on it and pushes out into the creek with a very relaxed look on his face like a person who gets into a warm whirlpool tub after a long hard day's work. Brenda and her adult friends go to the rope and use it to swing out as far as possible into the nice refreshing swimming hole. David plunges down and is amazed that the water is so clear partly due to the white bottom. To his amazement several Jack Fish that averaged three feet long, quickly swim away putting distance between themselves and David who startled them when he plunged down to the bottom of the ten foot deep hole. David quickly swims to the surface of the creek.

"There are large fish swimming around here! They look like fresh water Barracuda!" Brenda laughs and speaks:

"Yes, David, we call them around here garfish. A lot of the plantation people get a large cane pole and fish for them." One of the children screams out and points to a large snake like head sticking out of the water looking at them.

"What is that thing?" Beard laughs and answers:

"Oh, don't worry yourself too much. That is Old Hard Head. He is a snapping turtle that has found this area to his liking as long as I can recall. If you don't get too close or challenge him, he will not hurt anyone." David is surprised at the size of the huge turtle and dives below the creature to determine its size and was amazed that the old snapper was around a hundred pounds. David is compelled to speak:

"That turtle is the largest snapper I have ever seen! What a zoo would give to have an old giant snapper as large as Old Hard Head!" Mr. Zeb speaks up:

"Well, I believe that Old Hard Head is a lot better off just where he is, ruling his own territory just like a king. We have not seen any alligators around these parts so I don't believe that Old Hard Head has been challenged for many a year." Lilly looks over at her husband Zeb and smiles before she speaks.

"Zeb, that old amphibian reminds me of someone I know." Zeb looks over at her with as manly a look as an eighty six year old could manage with dignity and speaks:

"I used to be able to do some damage if someone or something crossed my territory, but I have had to mostly turn over that role to my big strong son here who knows how to manage that department. About all I can do is bark and growl and hope I am putting up such a fuss that my reputation will stand up for what the present man used to be able to do. Now I am not dead yet, I can handle most of all the fellows around here that are around my age, but I wouldn't last thirty seconds defending my own against a much younger healthy challenger. I am better at talking myself out of trouble. Not that I have many run-ins with people. People know where I stand around these parts, and I will just have to leave it to that and not worry about what I can't do anything about. At the present moment I am enjoying this relaxing floating cushion. Lilly you and I need to come down here once or twice a week while the weather is agreeable. I believe that it would do all of us a lot of good both for the body and the soul. I bet not many folks have seen such a beautiful unspoiled wilderness as we are blessed to live in."

David looks around taking in full notice of his surroundings. No public park in the South could boast the scenery that this place could boast of! The Pridgens have guarded and kept things as they were since the day Captain John Henry Pridgen purchased the land from a very wealthy gentleman who received the bulk of his land holdings from one of the Kings of England. A gift to him from the King for services rendered. A practice that was very convenient back in those days when gold was scarce and land was plentiful in this once unspoiled wilderness of a continent we call North America. The Pridgen clan, except for the three sons of Beard and Lillian Pridgen, enjoyed themselves in the creek until five. Mrs. Lilly speaks:

"I believe that I am a little hungry. How about us all going up to the house and cutting a cold giant watermelon. When we have had our fill of watermelon, we can start on a cake and see if our cooking is still like it used to be when Brenda would invite her friends down here to the swimming hole about seventeen years ago." Beard looks around at everyone and speaks:

"I believe that Mama has made a suggestion that I am very content with, how about it, should we all get out of this water and enjoy the melon and the cakes?" The children start screaming yes and the adults quickly help them put up the floats and the tire inner tubes. While everyone is quickly walking up the path to the mansion, David speaks to his wife Brenda.

"Brenda, I am going to visit the school tomorrow. I may stay over at a motel. I want to spend about two days observing the classes and talking to the students. I have about a hundred books to carry over to my office also and a lot of software disk and a few pictures I want to try and hang on the walls to make it a friendly looking office." Brenda looks over at David and comments:

"I would suspect that you will display some of your degrees on the walls and probably the huge photo of the citizens of a certain city who are surrounding you during that celebration after you saved the lives of the population from sure destruction from that earthquake."

"Yes, I should put that one up. It is what I work for. I am in the business of using my scientific knowledge in a practical way. I don't feel that I am doing wrong by such a display. I am sure that a furniture salesman feels no shame if he displays his furniture that he wishes to sell to the public. I don't believe that your father is ashamed to show the picture book of his cabins models or styles that are for sale. Of course, I will have a nice photo of my lovely wife and a second photo of our children. People will realize that I am a family guy, and they will hopefully feel more comfortable around me realizing that I am a stable mature adult whose word can be trusted despite my youthful appearance that you lovingly tease me about, dear."

"David, I assume that you will go with my father to check on the property the day after you get back from UNCW."

"Yes, sorry about that. Your father has been very kind and patient with delays and he needs to go ahead and check on the property I am sure. Now after a few days of rest after the experience with your father, we need to pack and prepare to go to Boston as a family. I need to be there. Doctor Fletcher will be transporting the Sea Wise near the end of our visit. I will need to be there at the University of Boston so that the underwater living quarters and lab can be put on the seafloor just off of the Boston Bay Area. I am excited about the project and look forward to working with both school systems in this coordinated effort to increase our scientific studies and opportunities for faculty and senior students alike. Both universities will be able to expand their offerings to their students without having to purchase very expensive equipment to augment the curriculum provided at each institution."

"How much money would it cost if these schools were not working together and had to purchase new equipment, David?"

"I believe that we saved the schools about twelve million dollars each. Research submarines the size of the one I delivered to UNCW from Boston University capable of going down about 4500 hundred meters in the murky depths of the ocean are not cheap. Neither are underwater living quarters that can house ten scientist at a time capable of permanent depths of one hundred feet are not given away everyday by big government nor the private sector."

"I look forward to visiting your parents again. I wish that we could have both worlds. I love your parents like they are my own parents. I miss the old neighborhood and the beautiful homes and markets in the Boston area. I hope that we will have the opportunity to really spent time with your parents. I want to visit the monuments and the famous historical significant places, but what I am most interested in is us having a lot of quality time with your parents just being family. I miss our cookouts in our yards and your mother's wonderful cooking. To tell the truth, I even miss our old house. It is a very beautiful old mansion that I will always have fond memories about. That house is where we initially started our family. I am sure that the kids would like to visit the old home place if the current owners will not object." David speaks:

I don't believe that we will have a problem with the new owners. I don't know them very well since we did not directly sell our house to them, but depended on a realtor to do the work for us. We will see, and if they are a little concerned about our request to visit the place, we can always look at it from my parents' house and yard and reminisce about our roots as a young family."

"David, we promised ourselves and the kids that we would visit the Wrightsville Beach area and look at homes. When are we going to take out time to do that?"

"What do you think, Brenda?"

"Well since you are asking, I believe that we should do that a few days after we get back from Boston."

"I agree. We stay busy all of the time. I would also like to visit some of the historical sites in and around the Wilmington area. You told me about the railroad museum and the steam locomotive near the Cape Fear River. I definitely would like to take a look at that place and also board the Henrietta 1V. I would like to hear what the story teller has to say about the history of Wilmington in the early days. We might even hear your maiden name, Pridgen, among the roster of the honored."

"I don't know about that, but I am sure that we will all enjoy the ride and come out richer with the experience. I would also like to visit Fort Fisher and Eagle Island situated out on Highway 421. My grandparents would take me out there when I was a little girl. Their ice cream is famous all over the area. You should see what I call their pantry. They have hundreds of jars of the most wonderful home style vegetables and other things like pickled eggs, and sausages. They also have a wonderful vegetable stand under their shed. Next to the store is a fish market that our family usually stops by to purchase seafood if we happen to be in the neighborhood. The staff that runs the fish market and the store are some of the nicest laid back country folks I have ever met. Grandfather has carried many a load of collards and other vegetables by to sell to the owners at below wholesale prices."

"Brenda, I am looking forward to the visits, but it will take time to see all. I suspect that we will have long moved into our future home that I hope is near the beach. I don't want to live directly on the beach, but in a nice home with an oversized yard on the other side of the sound and the waterway. It will be safer from storms and we will be able to grow a nice garden a little farther from the beach. We will still be only a few minutes from the ocean by car, and it will not be impossible for us to take a nice walk to the beach just for fun and the exercise." Everyone eventually made it back to the mansion where several tables were set up in the yard with all kinds of wonderful things to eat. There is nothing like a cold home grown watermelon and moist cake and ice cream washed down by a nice glass of ice cold tea with a slice of lemon to give the tea a little zing. Brenda and her dear friends talked a lot about the good old days and the wonderful adventures they had the God given privilege to share together. David and the children along with the other kids present almost felt like they had been there also somehow sharing the adventure and thrills of the years of yesterday. Grandfather Zeb and his wife Lilly almost felt like the hand of Father Time had somehow been turned back just for a little while as they shared by gone memories of those wonderful years with a younger family. Mattie was also very much a part of the equation, especially to the younger folks, as being an integrate part of the family structure, always present to say, and do something funny to make the day a little brighter and the paths each had to take a little easier to walk.

The next morning after breakfast, David prepares to go to UNCW to start the process of stocking his new office with books, a computer, and a few personal items like family photos to be put there to remind him that he has a family to support. Not so much financially since he is wealthy enough to skip this duty, but a duty to their good name and a duty of providing himself and them a reason to live beyond their immediate needs. David like his father, a prominent physician, firmly believes that a man should work and be part of the greater human community to serve with his God given talents to inspire and mentor the masses to excellence, and a sense of duty to realize that no man lives on an island by himself to do his own thing unconcerned and devoted to no one, but his own lower nature. David gets into his huge SUV and starts down the dirt road that leads out of the plantation. The day was bright and few clouds were in the sky. David took full notice of the activity taking place around, near, and far as he continued to exit the plantation. From his rear view mirror, he could catch glimpses of horses being led out of the stables to work the fields. Mr. Zeb and his wife Lilly had the kids with them walking around the plantation grounds. Great Grandfather Zeb has promised the kids that they could get in a light carriage and do a little riding around the plantation. This would be a ride that the kids would no doubt remember the rest of their days. A carriage ride around a huge fully functioning Southern Plantation. The old man realized that he would not be able to repeat this experience with his great grandkids for many years to come. Old age would eventually stop such activity. This does not mean that Zeb was not planning on taking up as much time as possible with the kids, but common sense was his guide.

The kids ran to Zeb's old pickup truck he loved to drive around the place and eagerly waited for their elder to start the engine to commence their adventure. Mrs. Lilly would help Zeb manage the children. After hitching the carriage to two of the horses, Zeb and his wife Lilly are on their way with the children almost as excited as the children are. Beard has already left for the logging camp to carry some supplies to his sons who are hard at work cutting trees down for the log cabins that are sold on the plantation. Mrs. Lillian Pridgen, Beard's wife, is with Mattie on the porch shelling field peas. There are several bushels of them. Mrs. Lillian will cook a nice pot of the wonderful peas with some country ham for supper when everyone is back from their adventure, except, David, who will stay over in Wilmington or Wrightsville Beach at a hotel. Brenda Smith, Mrs. Lillian's daughter, is visiting a friend of hers name Annie Cobb. Annie was one of her dearest friends and went through all twelve grades with Brenda. Annie went off to school after high school to graduate as a nurse.

Brenda almost felt like a kid again as she drives up to Annie's house which is next to her mother's house. It was good to be back in North Carolina! How fortunate Brenda felt. Not many young adults her age had the opportunity to visit their childhood friends in this country now days. Most people are very lucky to see their old friends and flames once or twice at scheduled high school reunions and that is that! Time and distance soon fade the familiar voices, faces, and the adventures shared together; those brief years of growing up that have been often referred to as the wonder years.

Fifteen

David Visits His Office at UNCW
Professor Joyce Brown Warns David of Trouble Festering
in the Science Department

Our story takes a leap in time and location because Doctor David Smith second in command at the science department at UNCW is at his office looking pleased at the way things look. His impressive display of books have been carefully arranged in the beautiful bookshelves that are sunk in the wall behind moldings that look like the carvings typical of the fancy decoration found in display in older mansions of yesterday. Many of these expensive books are authored by Doctor Smith himself. Others are coauthored by him and leading scientist that are his respected friends and colleagues from around the country and the world. His family's pictures are on the walls and he is just about to plug in his computer. On the wall is a very large picture of Sopara, a huge city in India. The wide shot shows David surrounded by thousands of people as they celebrate the gift that David gave their city. That gift was a warning that a major earthquake was about to take place that would destroy the city not only by the buildings falling due to the earth ripping up and pushing all over itself, but the fires that broke out and explosions as gas mains were ruptured. Even after and during all of this dooms day set of events taking place within a minute of time, a great wave from the ocean was to later sweep over the area sucking tens of millions of tons of building debris into the ocean; in some spots leaving nothing but the bare rock void of soil. The city was completely destroyed and anyone who would have refused the warning would have been part of the history of India.

A knock at the door turns Doctor Smith in the direction of the door. David knew Doctor Brown not only because Doctor Fletcher the department head had formally introduced him to her, but also he was aware of her because one of the professors who had worked for him at Boston University had spoken about Doctor Brown with fond affection. David's friend and fellow professor at Boston University had gone to school with Doctor Joyce Brown. David is delighted to see Doctor Joyce Brown standing at the door of his office suite and invites her into his office.

"Come on in, Doctor Brown, it is a pleasure to see you! How have you been doing since I last had the privilege to talk to you?"

"I can't complain for an old girl my age; how are you doing, sir?"

"I can't complain myself. I have been living a very interesting and unusual life now that I am staying at my wife's parents farm. It is truly a once in a life time adventure for me. I have seen and experienced life that few will ever have the privilege to know about experimentally. I hope everyone and everything is OK here at the school. I would assume that Doctor Fletcher would call and let me know if anything was going on that I should be aware of." Doctor Brown wrinkles her face up a bit and answers David:

"Like you said, I am sure that he would inform you of anything that you needed to be cognitive to. However, if he knows nothing about something, I am sure that you understand that he would not be able to share all that may be festering." Doctor Brown looks back at the door with concern which alerts David that an ill wind is blowing on the campus grounds that he needs to be aware of so that he can in nautical terms adjust his sails to better confront the storm that is approaching.

"Doctor Brown, you may shut and lock the door at the entrance to the hall if you feel that others should not be aware of our private conversation."

"I will take you up on your word, Doctor Smith. I am sure that we would be more comfortable and the wiser to talk in private." Doctor Brown walks to the entrance office near the hall where David's secretary will work and shuts and locks the door to the office suite and walks back into David's office and asks permission to be seated.

"Doctor Smith, it has been a long week, do you mind if I use one of your chairs before I talk?"

"Of course not, please be seated. I am sure that your legs are a little tired teaching all of the time and doing your many hours of lab work here at the university. Please tell me what is on your mind. I hope that we will be able to resolve the problem before it gets out of hand!"

"Doctor Smith, I am concerned about the ill feelings that one of our senior fellows has against you. I believe that the rest of the faculty is happy to have you as I am and look forward to working with you. Most of us are in our senior years as instructors, and are comfortable with our positions and our way of life here. We have no ambitions beyond doing an excellent job training future scientist and not having to transfer to another school or getting dismissed by a difficult superior. I have tried to support you amongst our people because I firmly believe that you will be a great access to our school, and from all I know, a very fine person to work for." David is a little shocked by what Doctor Brown says and thinks a few seconds before commenting.

"Doctor Brown, I never realized that my coming here as the assistant department head would cause such a fuss. I do appreciate your comments about me. I am not one to live off of the praises of others, but I believe that you speak from the heart, which means that we will work well together. I have always tried to be fair with everyone. I do not expect people to do anything other than their jobs. I have read the resumes of everyone who will work under me, and I feel that all of you are well qualified for the jobs you are being paid for. I understand that many of you have contributed regularly to scientific reviews and have authored or coauthored books. I am truly impressed and I can't ask for more!"

"Doctor Smith, I do also appreciate your comments. I do believe that our people are academically qualified to fill our assigned post. However, it may be that one of us is not satisfied by this arrangement and wants to conquer more territory very much like the dominate animal in a herd or pride is often challenged by one that feels that he would like to occupy the leader of the pride's position." David speaks:

"I see. Well, I am sorry that there are hard feelings or jealously. I believe that it would be best for you not to reveal who this individual is. I do not want to subconsciously work against this person or have ill will toward the individual. I firmly believe that whoever this individual is, he or she will realize that I am not a threat to their job after I am here a few months. If there is a problem, I would like that individual to reveal himself or herself by word of mouth or by their actions. In this way, I can allow this individual to dig their own exit hole. I don't want to lean on anyone. If things should go sour and I am defeated, I don't want you to lose your job or reputation by being considered by this individual an enemy. Thank you for the warning. Maybe we can all learn to get along. I like to be optimistic. I do not want to start to work here while looking behind my back all of the time worried about being attacked by someone who would like my position. I will speak with everyone individually before I start to work with you people and will also have general meetings where everyone will be present." Doctor Brown gets up and excuses herself. David just sits at his desk considering his course of action if any. David did not like to confront and discipline adults especially people whom he expected to work and act in a professional manner. He had never faced such a situation before because at Boston University he had worked himself to the top with everyone's support and cooperation. David gets up from his chair and walks down the hall to clear his mind a bit and to consider his next move about the news brought to him or to just let it go and hope that the problem will resolve on its own. David goes to an electronic bulletin board and reads the names, times, and rooms instructors would be working. He has a photographic memory and does not have to go to his office for a printout. He decides to go by a classroom Doctor Hardin was suppose to be teaching and walk in and say hello to the man and introduce himself to the students. The class has been in session no more than five minutes when David does a knock at the door just loud enough to be heard, but not over bearing or rude. He opens the door with a smile as Doctor Hardin turns toward the entrance expecting someone lost or perhaps a fellow professor who had no choice, but to share information with him personally or the entire class, an event that did not take place very often. To his surprise, his new boss, Doctor David Smith walks into the room.

"Doctor Hardin, I just wanted to drop by and introduce myself to the class if that is alright with you. I have been putting books and other things into my office so that I will not have to worry about such this coming January." Doctor Hardin does not smile at first revealing an unpleasant side to his personally, but realizes that he needs to be very friendly and puts back on his mask. David sees something in that that surprises him about Doctor Hardin. He cannot help, but recall what Doctor Joyce Brown just shared with him less than twenty minutes ago. David speaks again. "I can come back another time if you are too busy. I certainly would understand."

"No, no, come right on in and introduce yourself! I am sure that everyone is happy to have you here today with us. We were talking about earthquakes. I am sure that you realize that this class is an advanced course in geology and we were discussing earthquakes and how they are predicted." David walks to the front and center and speaks:

"My name is Doctor David Smith. I will be working here next January as the new second in command in our science department. I am from Boston and was the head of the science department there for seven years before I accepted the position here at UNCW." A young man raises his hand."

"Yes, what is your question?"

"Doctor Smith, why did you leave such a prestigious position to take up a lesser position here in Wilmington, North Carolina?" David thinks a second weighing his words carefully.

"I am sure that you realize that I did not move here to UNCW to make more money. I gave up my position at Boston to a man I hired as my second in command. He is also a very good friend of our family. I made my move because I firmly believe that I can make a difference in both science departments. You see, I will actually be working for both institutions. I will spend most of my time here at UNCW because I believe that since I have not taught here and do not know UNCW as well as I do Boston University, that it only fair for UNCW that I have my main office here so that everything will be fair and equal with UNCW. I will teach only about three classes a week. These will be graduate classes for people getting at least a master's in science. The rest of my time will be scheduled between lab time and some administrative duties that I will not be able to refuse I am sure." Many students laugh at the last statement. "I do not want to take up more of the class time. I just wanted to drop by and say hello. I will have information about why I am here posted on the electronic bulletin board, and I will see to it that every student is aware of the changes that will be made around here. I have not even spoken about most of these plans to the faculty and will schedule a meeting with them when the time is right. Thank you for your time, and I hope that all of you will have a nice day." David continues to visit classes that day and felt very comfortable and welcomed in all of them. That night he stayed in a nice hotel on Market Street in Wilmington and got up early the next day and drove back to the science departments at UNCW. The first classes would begin in about thirty five minutes. David walked to his boss's office suite and his secretary was behind her impressive desk. This time she knows who Doctor Smith is.

"Doctor Smith, it is so good to see you! How are you today?"

"I am doing very good. I hope that you can say the same!"

"I can't complain for an old gal my age. I have few complaints and love my job here! I will probably do volunteer work here after I retire just to be around the young people and to be where most of my friends are. I assume that you are here today to visit Doctor Fletcher again. He is in his office and should be preparing for a class in about thirty minutes. I will buzz him for you. Doctor Smith, Doctor Fletcher says that he would love to see you and to please go on into his office without knocking."

"Thank you, Miss Blankenship." Doctor Fletcher was already standing up waiting for David to walk into his office with a smile on his face.

"Come on in, Doctor Smith. It was rumored that you were here yesterday."

"Yes, I have stocked my bookshelves and have put up a few photos and brought over my computer."

"I believe that you also visited a number of classrooms and introduced yourself to the students and one instructor who had not met you before."

"Yes, I did do a little visiting and have enjoyed every minute of it so far! I would also like to meet with the faculty one day and just have a little get together and discuss some of the new changes and opportunities we will have coming next January."

"I see no problem in you having a little get together with the herd. We have a fine group of very professional people here at UNCW. Most of them are not local people, but were born and educated in other parts of the country like you and I were." Why don't you plan to meet the faculty in about a week and just have a nice get to know each other time. I will order the food and we can have the meeting in the cafeteria. We have several rooms over there just for such occasions."

"Sounds great, Doctor Fletcher, I will need to get back to the plantation. I promised my father-in-law that I would go on a trip with him up and down Black River to check on the property."

"How long will this trip take?"

"I understand that it will take three or four days. I assume that it will depend on what is going on. I don't know."

"You mean that it will take three or four days to check on the property!"

"Yes, sir, I understand that the plantation runs for miles along the river. We are going to have to get out and do a lot of walking and Beard my father-in-law is going to tell me about the local history and show me a lot of the sites where old towns and plantations were located on the Black and possibly the Cape Fear River. I have been asked to bring along a camera and record the trip so that future generations will have the opportunity to see things the way they were."

'Your father-in-law must be expecting some big changes in the next coming years."

"Yes, I do get the impression that the local folks are somewhat alarmed at the changes taking place and the destruction of the forest up and down the rivers by folks from up North."

"David, doesn't that make you a little uncomfortable. I realize that you are about as Yankee as a body can be?"

"I have had my moments of feeling a little out of place, but for the most part I have been treated as well as I have ever been treated. The plantation folks and the people in the small town of Atkinson and Currie up and down Highway 210 and Highway 53 are the nicest and the friendliest people I have ever met. You should take a trip there one day and just blend in and get into a conversation with the old timers or just listen and enjoy their lore. They are truly a passing treasure especially if too many people from other parts of the country overwhelm their simple, but elegant way of life."

"Well, Doctor Smith, you just call me and let me know if I should put off the meeting. I would not want to over tax you if you are going to be on a trip checking on all of that property. It sounds like a lot of fun, but I suspect that you will have to do a lot of walking before all is done."

"I will call you, sir, as soon as the trip is over with. Give me a day or two to rest up and I will be prepared to come back here. By the way, if you don't mind telling me, who else wanted my current position around here?" Doctor Fletcher has a reserved look on his face and speaks:

"I usually would not reveal that because I don't want any friction between you two. However, I don't believe that you are the type of person that would use that information against the individual that also applied for the position. His name is Doctor Hardin. He has two doctorates. Actually the same that you and I have. He is very smart and has been teaching for a long time just like I have. I do consider you the right man for the position for a number of reasons. One of them is that you were already the department head of a prominent school. You also gave up your last position for a job that offers less money. I believe that you are more dedicated to your profession than you are to your pocket book, which is very rare now days. I need to go to my class and teach Doctor Smith. You know the routine. I do look forward to seeing you in a week or so. Do have a wonderful day and feel free to visit the classes and talk to the people."

"Thank you, sir, I will do just that. You also have a good day." The morning of the third day in Wilmington, David calls his wife and informs her that he would be back before dinner at twelve PM. Brenda informs her husband that her father has everything ready for the trip down the river that will last for three or four days to check on the property.

"Brenda, does he want to leave tomorrow, or does he want to leave the next day?" Brenda speaks:

"I believe that he would like to leave that to you. He told me that you might want to spend a day with me and the kids before going on the trip."

"Your father is a very kind and thoughtful man to have even considered that! I believe that I will ask him to put the trip off one extra day so that I can be with you guys."

"Did you have a good time at UNCW, Honey?"

"For the most part, I had a wonderful time talking to the instructors and introducing myself to every classroom I could visit. I will be going back there in the near future to have a meeting with the faculty. I am looking forward to the meeting which will be held during a meal in the cafeteria. I will go over the new changes in our course offerings and the new submarine we will be using. I am not sure what kind of experience the faculty has with using deep explorers such as the one we now have housed at our facility on Masonboro Loop Road. I am afraid that most of the people who are teaching at the school have little serious practical experience in these submarines. I am sure that I will have to train the ones who are trainable and try to hire some outsiders that operate these subs on a regular basis. These people will not serve as professors, but will be assistances for the professors and will pilot the submarine. Eventually the school will have enough instructors who know how to operate these submarines. The majority of the folks who will work under me are looking at retirement in ten years or less I am told."

"Well, David, I do believe that you will have your work cut out for you to coin and old expression. You will be walking uphill for a couple of years before enough experienced instructors capable of operating a DSV will join your team."

"That is true, but this is one of the main reasons I am going to be at the school as the so called second in command. I realize that it will be a challenge for the older instructors and I am going to work very slowly and carefully with them. I do not want to discourage them." David drove his SUV inside the twelve vehicle parking garage at the mansion and gets his suitcase in the back compartment. He sees his wife's grandfather Zeb Pridgen and his wife Lilly walking through one of the doors of the large foyer that leads into the small kitchen apparently going in there where the rest of the family was already gathered and waiting. David quickly puts his suitcase up in his bedroom and walks into the small dining room. Everyone is pleased to see him, especially his wife and the children. The children get up and run to their daddy who gives them a big hug. Brenda gets up from the table and receives a hug and a quick kiss as everyone else was looking on. Mrs. Lillian Pridgen looks over to her husband Beard and speaks:

"Beard, you should do a little more kissing like David. That was very sweet!"

"Well, Lillian, if you insist, I will now kiss you to prove that I have not forgotten how!" Beard starts to stand up to go over to Lillian, but Lillian smiles and waves her hand somewhat embarrassed asking her husband Beard to forget it and sit down and eat his breakfast. Everyone laughs as David sits down at the table prepared to eat a wonderful Southern style breakfast that includes homemade sausage, ham with red eye gravy, yellow grits, handmade biscuits made with buttermilk, coffee, and orange juice. The meal, of course, included a nice bowl of fresh scrambled eggs. Just before the meal was over with, everyone got a hot biscuit and buttered it with farm fresh butter and smears their favorite jam or preserves on the hot moist bread. Lilly and Lillian always make sure that homemade strawberry, grape, apple butter, fig and other delicious spreads are on the breakfast table to top off every morning to provide their family the energy to work all day on the plantation. David informs his father-in-law that he would like to wait a full day before he goes with him to check on the property. This means that David will have the current day and the following day to rest and be with his wife and children before the trip. Brenda speaks to David:

"Honey, Mattie and I are going to go to the woods and pick some wild blueberries. We take care of the bushes and they have been providing the most wonderful tasting blueberries for over a hundred years. They are a little smaller than what most farmers want for their businesses, but I guarantee you that they are a lot better tasting because they have not been genetically tampered with."

"Are the kids going along with us?"

"I will ask them, but I believe that they are a little too young to enjoy such activity, let me ask them." Brenda learns that the children want to play and it is not long before several kids from Atkinson show up wanting to play with them. Dan takes his friends to his bedroom so that he can show them the huge train set. Betty takes her friends upstairs also and they play with the huge computer controlled dollhouse. Mattie has already placed a half dozen large baskets into the back of the pickup truck and Brenda asked David to help her with the cooler which contained their dinner. David, Brenda, and Mattie get into the truck together and Brenda does the driving. David has never gone into the woods to pick berries of any kind.

"Brenda, where are we going?"

"We are going about nine miles down the main road that runs through the plantation on this side of the river. We will pass the fishpond and the fishing lake."

"How close will this be to your great uncle's chateau?" Brenda was sorry that David remembered her great uncle's property, but answers her husband."

"It will border that property. The chateau will be about three miles away on the river side of the property."

"I am surprised that the building is not better known about if it is not far from the river!"

"David, there are huge groves of trees between the great house and the river. Near the river are massive thorny hedge bushes like the ones the World War II soldiers encountered when they landed on the beaches of Normandy. You simply can't walk pass the bushes which are about two hundred feet thick. The thorns on these natural wonders are over seven inches long and are very thick. A dinosaur could not get through that mess! I was told that there is also a berm or very tall mound of earth that runs down the property for over two miles. On the other side of this berm on the house side is a two mile long canal that is full of water about fifteen feet deep. On top of the earthworks or berm is a wall that I understand is about ten feet high and very thick. I heard my father say that there are even guard towers along the wall." So you see, the place is very guarded and we know little about it."

"What about your grandfather. It would seem reasonable that he has been there before!"

"I am not sure what he knows about the place. It is as if the place is thousands of miles away in Transylvania or some remote mysterious and forbidden place not meant for humans to visit or worry about. I guess that I have been taught or raised to not concern myself about the place. My childhood was mostly confined to the plantation. The plantation is big enough at much over one hundred thousand acres, to occupy the activity and ambitions of mostly anyone's imagination." Our couple continues to drive down the dusty country road headed to the acres of blueberry bushes. Mattie is a lot of fun to be with. She says nothing and makes no comment about the conversation David and Brenda have about the chateau until David and Brenda finish the subject. Mattie has picked blueberries for several decades in the area. She has seen all. Often Mrs. Lillian or someone else would carry Mattie to the blueberry bushes and just drop her off there so that she could pick the delicious berries for everyone and later that day Lillian or someone else would go back and pick her up. She was not neglected and always had more than enough food and whatever she wanted to drink when she picked berries. Mattie spoke:

"I saw a funeral coach leave the house." Brenda speaks:

"Mattie what are you talking about?"

"I saw a coach leave that yard and it took off as fast as lighting one day long time ago when you were a little girl. Your mama Miss Lillian must have forgot about old Mattie and I was left down there in them woods after dark. I walked past that huge old house and I saw that gate open and out came a huge old funeral coach like the one on Paradise Island in that building. I was so scared I was about out of my mind. Old Mattie didn't go back to that house again, no, sir. I think there must be a haunt that lives in that place. I sho learned my lesson that day! I should have listened to Mister Zeb, but Old Mattie was too hard headed to mind." Brenda and David did not respond to what Mattie said, but listened wondering what all that was about. Our party rides to the woods and gets out of the truck. David notices that there was a small screened-in gazebo in the woods for anyone to rest and get out of the weather. A nice outhouse was also not too far from the gazebo. It actually was a modern bathroom facility with running water. The water was supplied from an artesian well whose water was channeled through pipes and a reservoir or tank. The well had been tested and it was learned years ago that the flow rate was a gallon a second. The runoff water was channeled into a large cement vat that was open for animals to take advantage of the cool refreshing water that was slightly salty. The animals loved the water due to the mineral content. The tracks of all kinds of critters both great and small were always seen by the hundreds around the water. David looks around and realizes that he is in a very ancient forest such as few people had ever seen. Massive trees towered above our subjects and David felt like he had taken a trip back hundreds of years in time. Not since the early settlers had landed on the shores of what would later be called The New Promised Land had human eyes gazed upon such magnificent trees! David speaks:

"Brenda, has this area ever been cut?"

"No, David, what you are looking at is the original forest that was here before the Pilgrims crossed the Atlantic to settle in the new land. Now that does not mean that all of the trees here are that old, but I am sure that a small portion of this area was standing when the people that founded Plymouth Colony first landed upon the shores of the new land. What you are looking at is the type of forest seen all over this vast land on the East Coast of the United States. Almost all of that forest was cut by the year 1900 according to an old article my grandfather has in his possession. It was discovered many years ago that tens of thousands of these huge trees were actually preserved in our local rivers. One company came into being by finding barge loads of these trees buried beneath the mud of the Cape Fear and the Black River. These logs are perfectly preserved in the mud where there is little oxygen to allow bacteria to thrive and create rot. Some of these so called virgin timber logs were cut down when America was a colony of Great Britain."

"What caused these logs to sink before they were turned into lumber and shipped to Britain and Europe?"

"Daddy said that he believes that there were two reasons these huge old logs ended up on the bottom of the rivers to be later covered by centuries of mud. There were so many millions of tree cut down that by the time the loggers and millers could get them out of the rivers, they became water logged and sank. Another theory could be that the logs were naturally very heavy. Virgin mature trees centuries old tend to be much heavier per square inch than young trees under a hundred years old. Most people will never see a truly virgin forest. In fact, most lumber companies and the general public think that a tree that is about a hundred years old is very old. Most trees, if left alone in these ideal conditions on the East Coast live two hundred or more years old. Of course, even if no one would cut the trees, acid rain and all types of pollution will probably cut their chances for a long life time in half or less. Grandfather tells me that he see more tree rot and limbs dying for no apparent reason other than polluted air from airplanes flying up ahead to factories and cars that are as plentiful now days as the great herds of bison that once thundered across our Great Plains three hundred years ago." David continues to look at the huge sweet gum, elm, maple, hickory, oak, and pine, to name but a few that dominate the thick forest on the plantation.

"Brenda, will your family ever consider cutting any of these giant trees?"

"No, we feel that a tree is more than money in our pockets. We have been forced to cut down huge old trees, but it was because of storms that damaged them or lighting that damaged them beyond recovery. Often a very large tree will survive lightning and will eventually repair the damage with a little help. However, we have had the sad task of having to take them down. My family does not sell the lumber to the public, but usually saves it for buildings we will make on the plantation. I remember one of the plantation families losing their house in a fire caused by lightning. The entire house was made from an old giant tree whose lumber we had saved for such emergencies. The house is now about twenty years old. It has not been painted, but made just like the older homes on the plantation with clap boards on the sides. That house should be around for a century or two if nothing else unfortunate should happen again." Brenda drives the pickup truck as far as possible into the woods and stops the truck.

"David, this is where we get out. We do not have far to walk before we start seeing the blueberry bushes. Uncle Preston sees to it that they are kept up. The area around the bushes is kept free of trees and grass. He even fertilizes the blueberry bushes with animal waste from the plantation."

"Nice, real nice, that is a very beautiful gazebo! Who would have ever dreamed that a nice structure like that could be out here in the middle of a forest like this one!"

"We even have a bathroom not too far away, David. Our water supply is an artesian well that yields I understand a gallon of water a second. I love the taste of the water. It is very good for you on a nice hot day like today because we will lose a lot of salt from our bodies." Mattie grabs her baskets and walks away going to her favorite bushes. David and Brenda walk past the bathroom and David drinks from the water fountain. The cold refreshing water coming from a stream of water nearly four hundred feet below is wonderful!

"Brenda, look at all of the animal tracks around this here huge vat filled with the runoff water! The animals around must depend on this water."

"I don't know if they depend on it because the river is only a few thousand feet away, but I am sure that it tastes a lot better than the river water. David, let's go over to the blueberry bushes and start picking. Mama will make blueberry pies, muffins, and cakes out of what we will get today. I believe that Mama and Grandmother are also planning a trip here soon. Grandpapa often helps them for a few days. I have known them to invite some close friends over because there are hundreds of blueberry bushes that are usually heavy with berries every season around these parts." David fills his mouth with the delicious berries and forms a look of pleasure all over his face.

"Brenda, these berries are absolutely wonderful! I believe that this place would rival the famous Garden of Eden, at least with its blueberries!"

"David, I believe that I am going over there a few hundred feet from here for thirty minutes or so and pick berries just to see if there is any difference in size and quality. I will be back and will go to the other side of the bushes you are working." David looks around and just stared in unbelief at the enormous trees and the beautiful wild flowers around him in full summer bloom. Honey bees, butterflies, and other insects David does not have a name for are taking advantage of the flowers. David later learns that about twelve hundred bee hives are in the area placed there by Uncle Roy Henry. There is a breeze blowing through the forest making the area perfect for a nice relaxing summer day picking Blue berries. David continues to pick and has filled up his basket and grabs another one. The bushes are heavy with berries! While David enjoys the beautiful location and the smell of the forest, the enormous Blueberry bush he is picking berries from shakes. He believes that Brenda is on the other side of the huge bush and does not say anything expecting her to come around to where he is in a minute or two. Again the bush shakes and he hears a noise that he is not able to identify. It may be heavy breathing and once he thought that he heard a growl almost like an animal. Of well, he could expect noises in such a large thick forest he told himself. Being somewhat confused, David could no longer hold back his curiosity and calls out to Brenda.

"Brenda, is that you? Are you OK?" No one answered, but he was sure that he heard something, perhaps a dog was on the other side of the large bush that was about seven feet tall and about twelve feet across. David walks on the other side of the bush and to his amazement a huge black bear was eating berries off of the bush. The bear was at least eight hundred pounds and had a scar near his right eye down to his nose. No doubt created by a slap from another bear in Old Scar Face's youth. David yells out at the top of his lungs drops the basket he is working with and starts to run as fast as he could when he was on the track team back in his early college days. He runs past Brenda without seeing her and she screams out to him to stop and tell her what the trouble is.

"David, David, what is wrong with you? David, stop, why are you running so fast? I have never seen you run this fast before?!" David stops long enough to tell Brenda that a huge black bear was back of the bush he was picking berries from.

"Brenda, we need to get out of here! Where is Mattie? I hope that she is alright." Brenda cannot help but to laugh before she speaks.

"David, I am sure that you saw Old Scar Face. He will not hurt you. I would not advise you to go over and pet him, but he has been around here all of his life. He is not near as dangerous as a mean dog. I will go over to the bush with you and we will get your berries and see if the bear is still around. You have probably frightened him off. I have been told that grandfather's brother raised the bear. It is almost like a pet."

"You mean I almost killed myself running from a family pet?"

"Not exactly, he is not a dog substitute, but we do not allow people to harm the bear. I remember his grandma when I was a little girl. We would tease her sometimes, but she must have not been offended by us or she would have left and moved to another part of the plantation." Mattie comes walking up with a big smile on her face pointing at David.

"I knowed that bear was around the way you were running Mr. David. Yes, sir, I saw you running like you were running from a hornet nest that fell on the ground. You sure can run! I saw Old Scar Face running for all he is worth back over yonder somewhere." Mattie points in the direction where she last saw the bear running. Brenda speaks:

"Well, David, I guess that you will have a story to tell your grand children one day. A day long ago when you and grandmother went into the deep woods to pick blueberries and encountered a furious black bear just a picking away at those berries and hoping for a chance to pounce on some innocent greenhorn." Brenda could not help but to laugh a little and eventually David sees the humor and he and Mattie join the merry laugh.

"I have worked in the oceans most of my life and have dived around sharks much larger than the bear, but I am just not accustomed to having to share blueberry bushes with bears. I reckon that if we continue to live on this plantation, I will just have to get used to Old Scar Face and no telling what before it is all over with and done. Brenda, I have picked one full basket, and I believe that you have as many or more than I have. Mattie how many baskets have you picked?" Mattie smiles and lifts up two heavy baskets of blueberries for David and Brenda to see.

"David, we should go ahead and pick enough berries to fill these two remaining baskets and I believe that our trip here today will be greatly appreciated on the table tomorrow when some of them are converted to blueberry pies, and muffins."

The next morning at the breakfast table, David shares the adventure he experienced while picking blueberries with the family. Everyone was almost as excited about the unexpected encounter as David was. The children were amazed at the size of the bear. Betty, David's daughter, questions her father:

"Daddy, were you afraid when you saw that huge bear?"

"Me, afraid, why I just told Mr. Scar Face that he was just a making too much of a fuss on his side of the bush and that I was going to have to cut a switch and use it on him if he did not act like a gentleman or a nice bear." Betty looks at her father and giggles.

"No, you didn't say that to him, did you really?"

"Well, not exactly in those very words, but he understood what I meant, I am sure of that!" Mattie happened to walk by the table with a pot in her hand the moment David made that comment and spoke:

"Yes, sir, you sho got your point across to that old bear. I bet he is half way scared out of his mind!" Mrs. Lillian speaks to Mattie:

"Now, Mattie, mind your manners." David laughed and spoke:

"To tell you guys the truth, I have not run so fast since my sophomore year in college. I understand that the bear; however, ran the other direction even faster and I will leave the subject alone."

Sixteen

David and Beard, His Father-In-Law, Check on Plantation Property Bordering Black River

The next morning at seven in the morning Beard and David left the mansion in a large pickup truck going to the dock on Black River where their big boat was tied up. David was impressed with the homemade yacht Mr. Zeb Pridgen and his father-in-law had made many decades ago.

"Nice boat. You guys actually built this vessel?"

"Yeap, I was just getting out of my teen years when I helped my pa build this vessel. Our older vessel built by my grandfather George Pridgen was in bad shape and we felt it wise to replace it with a newer boat with a diesel engine. The older boat was a little larger, but it was a steamboat. The wood we used to power the old steam engine took up a lot of space and we were constantly having to repair the pipes and the boiler."

"Was it a screw propeller boat or a paddle wheeler, Beard?"

"It had a paddle just like many older river boats. We also had to occasionally replace the paddles because of rot or because of damage done when a paddle board hit a log or something either floating on the surface or perhaps a snag anchored on the bottom of the river."

"What is the size of the diesel engine that powers this vessel?"

"It is a six hundred horse powered Cummins Diesel Engine purchased from a company that went out of business when I was just a lad. I am sure that the engine was purchased to power a workboat designed to carry people and equipment around on the Cape Fear or North East Cape Fear River. The engine was still in the crate when we purchased it at an auction when the old tugboat company went out of business."

"This is a rather large boat for only a six hundred horse powered diesel engine; I would think."

"We geared it down so that it has plenty of pushing power. It can go about eight knots against the current. We are not usually in a big hurry when we are checking on the property. If taken care of, this boat and its engine will last me the rest of my journey on this good Earth and probably tap into a good many years of my sons. If they want to replace the boat or the engine in the future, it will be up to them, of course." After making several trips back and forth from truck to boat, David and his father-in-law are well supplied to commence their trip to check on the property and take out time to enjoy some of the old sites of vanished towns along the riverbanks and to visit the many bridges and enjoy the history of the region. David and Beard climb the outside stairs to the wheelhouse or pilothouse. Inside the twenty foot wide and twelve foot deep wheelhouse is a traditional turning wheel with brass handles. It is very old and fancy! On the back wall are photos of Beard and his father when Beard was a young man. Also there are old photos of Zeb and his father George Pridgen. Beard's three sons, Gregg, Wesley, and Beard Junior are also in several large photographs on the wall. Brenda, David's wife, is shown when she is about nineteen years old at the helm.

Sites of historical note are displayed along the knotted pine wall back of the helm. Some of the pictures are photographs of old prominent houses on the Black River like the Keith house, the old Corbett house near Beatty's Bridge, and the many places where small trading villages now lost only to the history of the region once stood. David is impressed with the old photos of lighter boats and barges piled high with logs and pushed by small gasoline tugboats. On a table in the wheelhouse was a large book filled with pictures of now non existing ship building companies, turpentine distilleries, and famous farms, and plantations up and down the Black, Cape Fear, and the Northeast Cape Fear Rivers. Beard told David that there were many old books about the early history of the region in the boat's library, which was just a large shelf in the sitting room. Beard starts the diesel engine and flips a switch that controls two wenches that pulls up the two anchors. David is surprised that a homemade boat over seventy-five feet long and over forty years old has such luxury.

"I thought that you had forgotten to pull the anchor rope or chain up! I did not expect this vessel to have motor controlled anchors!"

"It has not always been this way. My boys installed the system about four years ago. I don't know why I didn't think about it myself. It sure beats having to winch in the anchors by hand during a rainstorm and you have got a hundred feet or more of chain out! David you are welcomed to look around and explore the vast number of suites and rooms we have on this Black River liner or you can stay in the wheelhouse with me and be my copilot."

"Beard, do you have any kind of captain license to operate this vessel?"

"Oh, yes, I do and so does my father and three sons. Brenda also got her license after she finished high school at seventeen. We have all gone through the program at Cape Fear Community College in Wilmington. I got my license like the rest when I finished high school back in the nineteen eighties. Daddy fussed about having to take the course, but it was better than the alternative." David speaks:

"I would assume that you mean that he would not be able to operate the vessel legally without taking the course and taking the license examination."

"Exactly, but people have had to take examinations even back in the Nineteenth Century. All operators of steam powered vessels were required to take the examination. I reckon that no one complained; because, if you wanted a job operating a vessel of any size you needed to be recognized as a licensed captain. I look at it like a truck driver I suppose. Those fellows have been taking courses to pass their CDL license for a long time now. As much traffic as there is on the roads now days, we need people to be qualified to drive safely on the roads." David speaks:

"Beard, I believe that I will take a little tour of the ship and come back here in about twenty minutes if that is OK with you?"

"Go ahead and knock yourself out. Just don't get lost, I would hate to have to send out a search party." Both men smile and David walks through the door on the second floor that leads to the den. David was thinking to himself what a nice boat! The den was about twenty feet long and about eighteen feet wide. The walls were very formal and elegant made of Teak Wood that appeared to be very old, but in great shape. This kind of wood is very rare and was once the wood of choice on expensive luxury liners, yachts, and many naval vessels. The wood was not just beautiful, but was perfect for decks on large ships. The Navies of the world no longer use this wood for many reasons. The wood is getting to be very difficult to find. The boat David is in is also equipped with a large seven thousand watt marine generator that supplies electricity for fans on the ceilings, lights inside and on the decks, several large spotlights, and the lights required by the law of the land on vessels of this tonnage. Nice leather couches are abundant in the sitting room for the comfort of the passengers. On the wall, David notices a large beautiful chronometer that he estimated to be about a hundred years old. David suspected that it once did duty in a ship where the captain and crew could keep an eye on the weather. A very fancy curio cabinet made of black walnut stood in one corner of the room. The piece of furniture was probably made over two hundred years ago. Displayed behind glass paneled doors were local Indian artifacts. These very old artifacts were marked according to the different locations they were found on the Black and Cape Fear River basin. Many of the items needed no identification because mostly anyone would know what an arrow head is or a Tommy hawk, but there were other interesting collectables that needed to be identified for most ordinary people. Over head, hanging from the ceiling, were three large fans that were turning at medium speed. David notices a large shelf that was nearly as long as the room he stood in. On it were old books and hand written diaries that went back for over two hundred years about life on the Black River. The Pridgens obviously had owned large boats that moved up and down the Black and Cape Fear for a long time because there were volumes of business transactions about delivering thousands of board feet of timber, boat loads of rice, cotton, corn, dog tongue, tobacco, potatoes, and livestock to name some of the main offerings. These precious cargoes were carried down the Black River and into the Cape Fear River to the Brunswick Port near the mouth of the Cape Fear. Later journals indicated that the Brunswick Port was no longer used and the cargos of precious goods were shipped to the Port of Wilmington. David next walks to the kitchen dining room area. The combined room was about twenty feet long and eighteen feet wide.

On board is a nice gas stove and a full sized refrigerator that made ice. The cabinets are very beautiful and David felt that a master craftsman custom built the cabinets and counters. David loved knotted Pine! The counters are made from oak and the counter tops were overlaid with beautiful rare blue colored granite that he had seen on expensive yachts. The double stainless steel sink was extra large and convenient for anyone washing large pots and pans. David next walks onto the porch or second deck. It was not huge only about twenty feet long and eighteen feet wide. Several nice outdoor chairs were on this porch with a large oval shaped table in the middle. A set of stairs was situated on this deck and it led to the top deck of the boat. This deck was actually the roof of the boat. It was seventy-five feet long and twenty feet wide surrounded by a heavy duty guard rail. This deck was made this way to entertain people and for folks that wanted to relax and enjoy the sun and the beauty of the scenic Black River. Many nice tables and expensive outdoor chairs and couches complemented the deck. There was a heavy duty covered grill that David believed could be heated either by charcoal or wood. Someone had even mounted a beautiful Galilean telescope whose tube was made out of polished brass on the deck. The telescope was mounted on a base that allowed it to be turned in a complete circle. David decided that he would walk back down the steps and walk through the dining room and sitting room which eventually carried him to the door that went into the pilot house where his father-in-law Beard Pridgen was standing at the wheel guiding the boat down the stream. Beard recognized David's presence.

"Well, I see that you are back. Did you get lost?"

"No, I was lucky this time."

"We might as well get started with some of my narration if you are ready. Now you just ask any question you need to ask and I will do my best to answer it for you. Pa has been practicing telling the history of the Plantation and the land we call in between the rivers, meaning the Black and the Cape Fear Rivers, for a lot longer than I have. He would be proud to share with you anything that you care to ask him, I am sure. He has been interested in the subject every since he was a lad in the early days of grammar school I understand. Pa has a lot of old records, newspaper clippings, pictures, books, magazines, old letters, maps, many hand drawn pictures and you name it. He has all of this history in a large standing fireproof safe in his bedroom. By the way, did you visit the room in our so called family museum that contains all of the old antiques?"

"We did not have time to see everything that day. I walked through the French quarters and through the foyer that leads into the servants' quarters down the hall out onto the stage where we had the crayfish party. I would like to visit the area that you speak about one day when I have plenty of time to look and take in all of the wonderful history I am sure that is in that place."

"Well, if you have the camera ready I will begin. I will not attempt to talk all day, but will leave plenty of the subjects I will talk about for the next few days we will be together." David got the fancy digital camera out of its case and turned it on and smiled and said action. Beard starts talking. "The Black River comes into existence where the Coharie River and Six Runs Creek in Sampson County join into a single river. The river flows near where the Sampson and Bladen lines meet and continues along the lower part of Pender County where it joins up with the Cape Fear River just about twelve miles Northwest of Wilmington. Its main tributary is the South River which joins the Black River in Sampson County below the Community of Ivanhoe. A study of old maps and documents reveal that the Black River was once called the Stumpy River probably because of all of the tree stumps in the stream. According to the historical records we have, and some old papers compiled by a gentleman name Wilson Angley, a man of wealth from Pennsylvania back in 1731 by the name of Hugh Meredith, a Welshman, explored and wrote about the Black River. He said that there were very good tracts of land up and down the river. Plantations are known to have existed as early as 1738 along the lower boundaries of the Black River. A man name James Wimble published a map that recorded the presence of three plantations on the east bank of the Black. One of these plantations was owned by Mr. Wimble himself.

"According to historians, Governor Gabriel Johnson, who was a colonial governor, wanted the land in the Black River and Cape Fear River area to be stocked with people. He got together with a wealthy merchant from London. The Governor's friend name Henry McCullah received thousands of acres of land. McCullah received the land so that he would attract Scotch Irish and Swiss settlers on the land tracts. Historians say that the Swiss settlers soon departed, but the Scotch Irish remained and were joined by other people such as the Welsh who lived on a large track of land often referred to as the Welsh Track, which was on the Western side of the Northeast Cape Fear River. In 1739, historical records tell us that a group of Highlanders Scots moved to Wilmington and later moved up the lower reaches of the Black to establish their homesteads. This record records that a Presbyterian congregation was formed in 1740 on the Black River near Ivanhoe. During the years between 1750 and 1775, there were significant influxes of people that were Highlanders Scots, Englishmen, and Welshmen.

"The area drained by the Black River was still very thinly populated during Colonial times. Some of the families who were prominent in the area, according to old land records not long before the American Revolution were the Moores in present day Moores Creek area; which is famous for its Moores Creek Revolutionary Battle Ground, the Corbetts, the Lees, the Lewis and DeVanns. Some folks spell their name De Vane. Old records of the period reveal that all of the land that the Black River, and the Cape Fear River drained was part of what was officially known by the Colonial Government as the Port Brunswick District. Records reveal that this port is where tar, pitch, turpentine, lumber, rice, corn and all kinds of produce including livestock was shipped from. This same port was also responsible for receiving the imported goods from ports outside of the area. These imports were cloth, wine, salt, sugar, rum and molasses.

"Let's now talk a little about ferries and a bridge or two and I will bring this subject up later in a little more detail. I will start with a ferry that operated near the mouth of the Black River where it empties its waters into the Cape Fear River System. The closest to the mouth of the river and many miles downstream from us was Dollison's Ferry." David asks a question:

"Beard, how far from Wilmington was Dollinson's Ferry?"

"It was about thirteen miles from the city. Now the most famous of the ferries was upstream from where we are presently on the river. Corbett's Ferry was not far from the little community of Ivanhoe. This little community still exists, but is a shadow of its glory days. I understand that a Captain Thomas Corbett Junior, son of Thomas and Mary DeVane Corbett, was the owner of the ferry. I also am aware that he was a sea captain and was of the line of Corbetts that Captain George W. Corbett of the American Civil War is directly related. Now this same Captain Corbett was son-in-law to Thomas DeVane who owned and operated a ferry on Black River before the American Revolution. The New Hanover County Court made Mr. DeVane the official keeper of the ferry he owned and operated." David speaks:

"How convenient!" Beard speaks:

"That is true, but I am sure that this gentleman took his official position very seriously seeing that he had such a big stake in the operation of this ferry. I am sure that he had that ferry operating come, rain, snow or high water. Mr. DeVane also owned a nice size plantation on the Black River. This means that he probably owned the landing and the land upon which the ferry received its passengers on one side of the river; I believe the east bank. I have read that this ferry remained in operation until the early Nineteenth Century. Mr. DeVane sold his ferry and the plantation to a gentleman by the name of William H. Beatty. In 1792, Mr. Beatty got permission from the New Hanover Court to build a bridge over the Black River. That first bridge was burned down and Mr. Beatty got permission to build another bridge across the river at the same site. A trading village soon developed near the bridge and remained in existence until the early part of the Twentieth Century."

For the next four days David and his father-in-law Beard Pridgen traveled down the banks of the dark coffee colored waters of the mostly untouched wilderness Black River runs through. Often it was necessary to anchor the boat close to the river bank and get in a small lifeboat and paddle to the bank or use the small ten horse powered outboard motor attached to the stern of the boat. From the bank David and Beard would get out of the smaller boat and pull it onto the bank and cover it with bushes or cut off branches of small trees to hide their boat while they walked for several miles inland to see if everything was alright with the property. Once Beard and David came across a campfire that was still burning; they quickly distinguished the fire and caught up with a group of outsiders having a merry time on someone else's property, that is Pridgen property. Mr. Beard made it very clear to the young adults who were illegally hunting on his property and leaving a potential disaster untended that they had best be moving along and the sooner the better. Many small cabins along the river were also visited by David and Beard to check on their condition. These little cabins were situated along the riverbank about a hundred yards back from the stream. They were there to provide shelter for the Pridgens or their plantation employees if they were caught in the woods after dark while hunting, logging, working a huge field nearby or any kind of business that concerned the plantation's interest.

The fourth day found Beard and David back at the mansion. They arrived about suppertime. Excitement was naturally in the air as the children wanted to know about the trip and to beg the opportunity to travel up and down on the river in the big boat. Mr. Beard could not refuse the kids and said that they could go with him one morning after the trip to Boston was over and done with. Dan the Smith's son speaks:

"Grandfather, can I go on that big boat? I have never been in a boat in the river before?" His sister naturally defends her status with river trips after her brother made his plea to his grandfather.

"Grandfather, I have not been either, I want to go too!"

"OK, I don't see a problem with us taking a trip on the big boat, but first of all, you guys will have to clear this trip with your parents, it will be up to them." Both children start talking at the same time asking their parents if they could ride on the big boat. Brenda looks at David and answers for both of them.

"Children, we are going to go back to Boston in a few days. We are going to have to go sooner than your father had originally planned. When we get back and rest up a few days, you guys can go. David, are you planning on going with the children to help my father watch out for them or do you want me to go?" David speaks:

"Beard, how long will the trip last?"

"I believe that two days on the river will be enough of a trip for the children. We will be able to travel faster than our trip this past four days because we will not be making many stops. The children will get to see a lot of water those two days and will get to sleep in the bedrooms and perhaps do a little fishing from the boat." The children get up from the supper table as excited as two puppy dogs with a rag doll between them! They rush over to their grandfather Beard and give him a big hug." Great Grandfather Zeb looks over at his wife Lilly and tells her that he is a little jealous. His wife Lilly speaks:

"Now, Zeb, we have had our turn with four wonderful grand children. I believe that we did a good job of being grandparents and I can now enjoy watching our son and his lovely wife Lillian play grandparent and see if they will do as well as we." Zeb speaks:

"Well, now, I do see your point, but remember great grandkids that we will be here for you children when you need our company." The children run over and hug their great grandparents just to let them know that they would always be very important to them." Beard could have sworn that he saw a few tears in his father's eyes, but he out of respect for him did not say anything about it. Beard was very close to his father and respected him as much as Isaac respected Abraham of old as the head of the house whole even though Zeb was getting up in years, because Zeb made sure that his son was well equipped in every way to replace him when the Good Lord called him to his home above. That night while in bed talking about different things, Brenda wanted to know about the trip David had just experienced with his father-in-law.

"David, how did you like the trip?"

"I thought that it was wonderful! I can't get over the scenery! There are cypress trees growing in the swamps along that river that were old when Columbus was born!" I did not realize that there is a place like this left in North America. About every remote place has been spoiled by people. A lot of the damage was done unfortunately by people who would not agree with what has happened, but when professionals go to these remote places and are followed by a television camera while they show the wildlife and all of the beautiful scenery, realtors soon make plans to sell lots off to the excited public who have been mesmerized by watching television. Most of these people are not prepared to live in these areas and soon start destroying the very things that attracted them in the first place to the area. There are, of course, grand exceptions to this, but most of the time, the wilderness is robbed of its basic function, which is being a wilderness where wild things can still truly be wild and free of the constant presence of mankind."

"David, where did you guys go during your trip on the river?"

"We rode by Beatty's Bridge and rode all the way down to the mouth of the Black River where it joins the Cape Fear River. We got out of the boat several times on our return back up the Black. We passed the old Keith house and later on when we got to the old Corbett house near Beatty's Bridge, we unboarded the big boat and got into the small fishing boat and paddled onto the bank. We visited the Corbetts for about thirty minutes before continuing our trip upstream. A few miles above Beatty's Bridge, we got out and started walking and came upon a large campfire unattended. Your dad was not very happy about the fire and asked me to help him find the campers. We walked about a mile and found a bunch of young men in their early twenties half drunk with beer and shooting at anything that moved. Your father fired his shotgun above their heads and told them to drop their guns and back away from them. You should have seen your father deal with those old boys. He lined them up and was remarkably able to convince them that they had better not step again on

Pridgen property while still in this life. He took their guns and got their names and addresses and promised to send the guns back to them via UPS or some other carrier in a week. Your father would have been a very good Marine drill sergeant because those boys looked like young draftees on their first date with the Marine Corp from home." Brenda laughed and spoke:

"They were lucky that he did not put some salt in their rumps. Grandfather shot a man about twenty years ago that was trying to steal a horse. The man had a large knife and was known to be a bad one. Grandfather fired his gun and put some rock salt in his bottom when the man refused to drop the knife and leave."

"You could get into trouble now days with the liberal laws that often favor law breakers, Brenda!"

"Grandfather was just defending himself at night from a big man who had a bowie knife in his hand making a show of threat with it. When the gun went off, that rascal moved like he was on fire. He dropped his weapon and Grandfather called the sheriff and he sent down several cars loads of officers who helped Grandfather and my Daddy find the man."

"Where was he hiding?"

"We found him in the soap house. He found something to break the lock and went inside so that he could hide. The officers said that we were fortunate that the man was found because he would have most likely attempted to steal another horse or even a truck. The man had escaped from a local prison."

"Why was he in prison?"

"I guess for just about everything. He was a thief. I understand that he stole money from an ATM machine. He had a long rap sheet that included beating up a man with his fist, drag racing for money on a busy street in Wilmington, setting fire to a man's woods just because the man would not lend him some money. I am sure that the man would have never gotten that money back. He was in reform school and you name it most of his young life."

"Brenda, I do believe that your Grandfather did the right thing. Maybe the individual will think several times over again before he plans to walk on someone's land to steal or start a fire or something."

"I hope so, but I am not as optimistic as you. I would suspect that he is no friend of law abiding people. I am sure of that."

"Brenda, your father turned the boat around and carried us down stream on the Black River pass Beatty's Bridge. We got out there and as I said visited the Corbetts near the bridge at their old house on the river. We continued our trip and got into the lifeboat and went a good piece up

Moores Creek and then went on the other side of the stream and looked at Colly Mills Creek. Oh, I forgot to tell you that we went by Red Star Fishing Camp where a small crowd of people were getting ready to launch their boats. We went down stream past the old Keith house on our right. We continued to travel downstream, occasionally stopping to take a little excursion inland for a mile or so before we got back on the big boat. We stopped at Heading Bluff and walked around the area. There were the remains of several old buildings on the bank. I understand that some doctors had a fishing and hunting camp there many years ago." Brenda speaks:

"David, did you guys go by Point Caswell?"

"Sure, we went to a lot of little communities, like Point Caswell and on up to Ivanhoe. I enjoyed the trip immensely and filmed most of it, especially the remains of old ghost towns and significant landings, bridges, and historical locations like Moores Creek where part of the Revolution War was fought. Brenda, I will need to call Doctor Fletcher and set up an appointment. I need to meet the science faculty at UNCW in the cafeteria for a semiformal get together?"

"When do you want to go to UNCW?"

"I believe that I will call Doctor Fletcher and have him to schedule the meeting the day after tomorrow."

"David, when are we going to visit Boston?"

"I believe that we should schedule that trip in about a week. I need to visit Boston University and have a meeting with the instructors at the science department. I understand that two new instructors have been hired since I have been absence. I will need to set up everything for next year when I will be teaching at both schools."

"David, are you sure you want to constantly be driving back and forth between Boston and Wilmington?"

"I will not be in the classrooms as much as a regular instructor. I will teach every other semester at each school. When I teach at Boston, I will naturally have to spend most of my time in Boston. One day I would like to ask for a special assistance that will be in charge of the classrooms. I really would like to do all of my teaching underwater exploring and doing scientific experiments. It will take time to get everything the way I would like it to be. I will presently be content with the progress I have made so far with my objectives. Brenda, I am going to call Doctor Fletcher and ask him to schedule our get together at the school the day after tomorrow. The meeting should not last, but an hour. I will attempt to give a brief outline of the things we will be doing next year."

"David, I am sure that most of the faculty will be excited about the new adventures you will lead them into?"

"Yes, I expect they will look forward to many of the changes, which will be mostly my presence at the school, and the new hours in the classrooms."

"What do you mean by that?"

"They will all be spending more time in the new DSV and a little less time in the classrooms. Students will especially like it because they will get a lot more practical experience that they can take with them. I will ask Doctor Fletcher to hire a few more qualified instructors so that everyone will not be over worked."

"Doctor Fletcher may balk at that request, David."

"I hope not; however, if I really can demonstrate that we will need them, I can hire them according to the new contract that the school has with the new program. The Government will pay most of the instructors' salaries. I made sure that I will have plenty of free grant money that I can use at my own discretion without interference. In other words, my hiring a few new instructors at each school will not take the hide off of anyone. Brenda, what do you want to do tomorrow for entertainment?" Brenda did not say a word at first while she considered the question.

"Well, David, I have not thought about it. I guess that we could borrow a pickup truck and visit my great uncle's chateau." David could not believe what he was hearing!"

"Brenda, you are, of course, joking aren't you?"

"David, you keep bringing up the subject. I do believe that you will continue until your curiosity is satisfied."

"Brenda, I don't know. Who would look after the kids after we told them where we are going?"

"I will try to get my mother to look after them. I don't believe that she has anywhere to go tomorrow or any special projects that need tending to?"

"What are you going to tell her when she asks you where we are going?"

"I will simply tell her the truth. We do not lie to each other around here. Our people will know where to look for us if something should delay our return back here in a timely manner."

"Should we carry a weapon or something? The way you talk about the place, I am not sure if it is safe. We do have to consider the fact that we are raising two young children that may actually need their parents should something strange happen to us." Brenda thinks for a moment."

"We will, of course, need to pack our food and water or whatever we might need. I will carry along several extra large flashlights. I believe that we have a dozen of them in the foyer near the kitchen where we keep them charged all of the time. Weapons, I am not sure what we could carry along with us. I have never visited a house that I have considered the need to pack a weapon. I do own an old twelve gauge double barreled Browning shotgun that I have not used since I was in high school. Let's go downstairs and get everything ready for tomorrow. I will get my old gun and look at it to see if it is in good shape. I put it away in our gun cabinet in the foyer. I cleaned it and oiled it real good before I put it in there. There should be many boxes of twelve gauge shotgun shells. I will put the 00 buckshot shells along with the gun in the truck we have been using. David, let's go down to the kitchen and get this all done so that we will be ready to go immediately after breakfast. It will not take very long."

David and Brenda get a cooler in the pantry of the kitchen and place the food they will eat in it. Water is poured into a large thermos and Brenda gets the shotgun and a box full of twelve gauge 00 buckshot shells and hands the gun and the shells to David to carry down to the truck they will be using. David quickly walks onto the huge porch and notices his wife's grandfather in his favorite easy chair reading from a book under a goose necked lamp. Mr. Zeb does not say anything about what David was doing. David goes to the eight vehicle carport and places the shotgun onto the empty gun rack in the double seated truck. He goes back to the kitchen and helps Brenda with the heavy cooler loaded down with food, water, and ice. David also manages to hold a large rechargeable flashlight in one hand. Minutes later they are walking back up the twelve foot tall steps on the front of the house. The steps that are adored like the other three steps with huge larger than life male African lions. Mr. Zeb is watching his granddaughter with some curiosity because family members do not have traveling plans that the others members are not aware of. Part of this custom was based on common sense and safety purposes in case something unforeseen should occur. It seldom does, but that old custom has saved lives several times on the plantation. Zeb speaks to David and Brenda as they step back onto the porch about seventy five feet from where he is sitting.

"Looks like you two are going somewhere, hope you will wait until the sun shows its face in the morning." Brenda and David are almost startled by Zeb's comment because they were aware that the trip they had in mind was considered taboo. It was probably unthinkable! They also realized that they could not just make up something, and in addition, they also might not be able to get by with not disclosing their plans. A simple yes that they are planning a trip would naturally put them into a position to have to reveal their destination. Brenda answers her grandfather, but inside she is afraid that he will very much disapprove of their plans. If he did so, she would not feel comfortable with defying his wishes to keep away from the chateau.

"Yes, sir, we are putting some things in the truck so that we will be in a position to move immediately after breakfast."

"It must be a long trip, but I am sure that you have already provided babysitters for the children. I hope that you two will have a good time wherever you go. You guys are not slipping off to Wrightsville Beach are you?" David answers:

"No, sir, we will probably do that sometime after we visit Boston. I promised the children to take them there, and we will probably do a little swimming. Later on we will check out some of the real estate in the vicinity."

"I hope you will wait at least until next year before you move to the Wrightsville Beach area because I am pleased and just about as happy as an old man can be with the children and you guys living with us. I have enjoyed every minute of it and wished that I could be around for another twenty years or so, but I realize that Old Man Time will just not see it my, way; I am very sure of that. Well, I do firmly believe that one joyous day sometime in the future, there will be a grand reunion when we will be back together again. I have not told anyone in decades, but I miss my old mother and father, and I was very close to my great grandfather. He lived to be a hundred and one years old and never complained about a thing. I honestly believe that the man never came down with a thing in all of those years. He just went to sleep one morning and I can still remember the smile on his face when I saw him when Grandmother asked me to go check on him on the porch and tell him that dinner was ready. I ran back and told her that he was asleep and that I could not make him wakeup. Grandmother and my mother both went out on the porch to where he was sitting in his favorite rocker and checked on him. He never did make it to that dinner, but has been sleeping now for nearly eighty years. The old preacher told us at the funeral that he was asleep, but I know my great grandfather and I am firmly convinced that he is not wasting away his time or the Good Lord's just a sleeping away. No, I am sure that he is getting a lot of work done up there and is helping the Good Lord with vigor and strength that he never possessed while down here in his mortal frame. Oh, well, I am just a talking too much. I know that you two will need to go on upstairs and get some shut eye, but before you go I must warn you two out of love to be careful tomorrow and pray about the trip. It just may be that you two will be led to find adventure some other way." Brenda and David could not believe what Mr. Zeb said. How could he possibly have figured out what they were up to! I mean that just can't be! Brenda speaks with a little uneasiness noted in her voice.

"Grandfather, I don't understand. We are not even leaving the plantation."

"Well, don't worry, Brenda. I am just a little over concerned. You two can go anywhere you want to go on this here plantation. After all, I will not always be here." David speaks up:

"Grandfather, I am compelled to consider the possibility that you must have powers and abilities that us regular mortals just don't possess. You actually know what we are up to!" Mr. Zeb smiles and speaks:

"I am not sure that I have such powers that you suspect that I may possess, but I have been around a long time and I do have a pretty good sixth sense I believe. My great grandfather was the same way. This was one of the reasons we were so close and the departing was so hard, but I have learned to accept things as they are and not always as they appear to be. Just be careful. I know that both of you are educated and you, David, a scientist of high standing, but everything can't be explained by science nor ever will be. Some things are just on another order or maybe another plane or dimension. I believe that more scientists are accepting what they call parallel universes." David speaks:

"Yes, sir, for a long time professional scientist believed that anyone who believed in another world was not balanced or was just plain ignorant. I know that a lot of work has now been done on the paranormal both by our country, Russia, and most of the major powers. Of course, governments are always looking for anything that might give them the edge over their enemies and their citizens." Zeb smiles:

"David, I am truly impressed with your understanding! I feel that you will be all right going over to the chateau tomorrow for a little visit. I just would not want to be there on the property after the sun closed it eyes so to speak." That night after everyone is in bed and the full Moon had risen out of it prison to dominate the night sky, Brenda and David talk:

"David, I almost feel like a child being allowed to do something that I am not supposed to do. My conscience is saying to me that I should not visit that chateau, but the inquisitive side of my nature drives me on to that forbidden place that has been such a mystery to me."

"Brenda, I also feel that tug to explore this strange place, but like you, I am not sure that I am making the right decision to go over there tomorrow or not. How your grandfather knows what we are up to will always haunt me? Do any other members of your family posses such strange powers?"

"I understand that grandfather's brother is a man of mystery and strange abilities. I was not told directly, but it has certainly been implied."

"Brenda, maybe your family is more special than I thought possible!"

"Special, what do you mean by that?"

"I am not sure, but tomorrow may reveal more than we are prepared to experience. I don't know."

Seventeen

Brenda and David Visit the Forbidden French Chateau Her Great Uncle Owns

The next morning everyone is up and gathered around the breakfast table. The children are all excited because their grandparents are going to carry them to the flea market in Atkinson. Vegetables, jars of honey, hams, butter, a pickup truck full of pecks of raw peanuts, and sweet potatoes, and another truck loaded with delicious apples, plums, pears, and peaches are all to be carried to the market to sell to the people who flock into the small country village looking for fresh tasting wholesome food at flea market prices. Mattie is going with them as usual and will help in any way that she can. Mattie is excited because she gets to talk to her friends and she loves to purchase homemade candy, cookies, and look at all of the wonderful things people make to sell at the market, like wood carvings of animals such as, cats, dogs, ducks, and such things as play castles, lighthouses, and you name it. Beard is getting ready to go over to his store in Atkinson where he will work only a few hours before the store will close for the day because most people will have little interest in his hardware store on Saturday when the flea market is opened. The children are not told where their parents are going and do not seem to care. The less questions the better around the breakfast table where the whole family is gathered; except, for Brenda's brothers, who are at the logging camp about fifteen miles away.

Brenda and David get into the pickup truck they have borrowed and start driving down the main road that runs through the plantation on the mansion's side of the plantation. For awhile no one says a word. It is unusual because they are concerned, but excited about what they may see. Shortly, our young couple realizes that they are nearing the great fishing lake.

"We have plenty of time, David. Do you want to stop here for awhile and just look at the lake?"

"Why, not, it will help to ease my mind a bit. It is very beautiful this morning! Your family is blessed so much to have this huge beautiful lake here on their plantation. What a scene for a classical movie or a television series perhaps about a wealthy dynamic family who must fight to keep their vast land holdings and way of life from hungry outsiders who want to rob them of their beautiful piece of paradise." Brenda grins before she speaks:

"Maybe you have missed your calling; perhaps you should have been a writer or even a movie producer with an imagination like you have!" David realized that Brenda is just teasing and enjoying his company and trying to ease their minds about misgivings about going over to the huge chateau that has always been a place of mystery and suggested evil or danger.

"David, I never did take you to the blue hole in the lake. I am not even sure if I mentioned it to you or not."

"I remember you saying something about it. We did not visit it because we had so many things to do that day. What kind of blue hole are we talking about?"

"There is a huge cave or I suspect that it is a cave at the bottom of the lake on the other side of Paradise Island we did not visit. I carried the children to the site when we went fishing that first time on the lake. I really believe that you should check the place out one day."

"How deep do you suspect it to be, Brenda?"

"I am sure that it is around two hundred feet deep. The cave probably starts at about two hundred feet. I am sure that it is vastly deeper than that if it was measured."

"You say that the water is blue down there?"

"Yes, it looks blue around the entrance of the hole or cave."

"I never realized that this lake would have such an underground system. I am sure that this is why the lake is here in the first place."

"Yes, I understand that the lake has always been here. Our family has enlarged it and most of that soil dredged from its bottom was used to help create Pridgen Island."

"You mean to tell me that huge hill is manmade?"

"No, but I am sure that several million tons of soil have been added to the hill for a hundred and fifty years. The smaller lake on the island was mostly manmade about a hundred years ago. This soil I understand was piped to Pridgen Mountain to add about twenty feet to its height. That hill is about five hundred acres, so that is a lot of earth that was moved and spread out by heavy dozers." David thinks for awhile before he speaks:

"Brenda, I am not prepared to visit that cave now, I will wait until I can get a team of scientist and some special underwater gear before tackling that cave at the bottom of the lake. It could be dangerous. I have known people to get lost in similar caves. I will need to borrow or rent a deep diving submarine that can take us a couple of thousand feet down. Sometimes these caves will go only a few hundred feet down and will run for hundreds of miles below the surface. I will call some contacts of mine and see if I can get the men and equipment to checkout this natural wonder. We will need permission from your family. I know how they feel about outsiders learning too much about the secrets of this plantation. I am sure that they would not want curiosity seekers to be asking permission to visit the lake or reporters interviewing us on our find if we happen to discover anything significant."

"David, could you teach one or two of my brothers to help you operate the small submarine you will need to explore the hole?"

"I do not doubt their abilities, but I am not going to be responsible for the lives of that many members of our family. If something should happen bad, I would never forgive myself nor would your family ever forgive me."

"You know that they would. It would be hard, but they are not that kind of people."

"Brenda, I believe that I know what to do! I will try and talk Doctor Dennis Miller into going with me. He can be trusted with your family's secrets. Your brothers and father could help us launch the small three man sub."

"What an excellent suggestion! When do you think you can do it?"

"When we visit Boston, I will talk to Dennis about it."

"David, have you called Doctor Fletcher about when you want to meet with the faculty at UNCW?"

"Yes, I called two days ago. We are going to meet in the cafeteria in two days." David and Brenda go to the cedar pavilion situated on huge pylons in the fishing lake and sit on the porch enjoying the scenery for about an hour. David and Brenda noticed a fast moving V shaped formation of high flying geese quickly passing over the lake heading in a northerly direction. The almost hypnotic bounding of the waves from the lake bumping into the pylons that held the pavilion up soothed the psychic of our couple as they immersed themselves in the beauty and peacefulness of the lake they blanketed their consciences in. David looked to his left and right and was amazed at the size and primitive beauty of the huge trees that lined the shore of the lake, especially the huge ancient cypress trees that stood knee deep in the lake. A nice breeze was blowing across the lake creating a pleasant atmosphere for anyone who happened to be sitting on the porch that surrounded the pavilion. David and Brenda could tell that two fishing boats were on the water about half a mile out. No doubt some of the plantation folks were taking the day off to enjoy the lake and to take advantage of the bounty of fish the lake was famous for. A large greenish colored fly landed on the porch banister.

"Brenda, look at that oversized blue green fly with black hair all over its head. I am glad that all flies are not that large and ugly. The common housefly is nuisance enough!" Brenda who is in her own world for a few seconds, enjoying and remembering the wonderful times she had as a child on and around the lake looks in the direction of David's fly. Almost immediately a huge dragonfly flies over and grabs the fly faster than a man could say gotcha. David laughs and looks surprised at Brenda.

"Brenda, did you do that!"

"No, David, I claim no special abilities, but if I did, that dragonfly would have been summoned to action. Fortunately, Mother nature has her own bag of tricks she likes to surprise us with. David, are you ready to go over to my great uncle's house?"

"Yes, I believe that I am ready to see and experience the good, the bad, and the ugly. I am sure that everything will be alright, just a bit different." Our couple gets into the truck and drive down the dirt road until Brenda makes a right turn into the road that leads to the chateau that belongs to her grandfather's brother. A man that she had never laid eyes onto. The moment our couple turns into the main road, they see an enormous brown dog with long shaggy fur standing on top of a huge old tree stump that is cut off about four feet high above the ground. It is a mix breed that appears to be close kin to a hound except its ears stood up like a Doberman Pinscher's ears. The dog was snarling and dripping saliva from its mouth. The beast had enormous teeth that were highlighted by its unusually red lips and mouth. The animal's eyes were wild looking with a strange reddish glow to them. It looked directly at David and Brenda, eye to eye, with a challenging stare.

"That beast must have rabies. I have never seen that dog around here before and no one has spoken of it before. I should let my father or someone know that the dog needs to be found and captured before it bites somebody!" David speaks:

"Was that a dog?" Brenda replies:

"I am sure that it is a dog, David, but I have never seen such a ferocious creature in my life and I have been to the zoo off of Carolina Beach Road outside of Wilmington many times and have looked at the lions and the bears. That huge dog makes my skin crawl. I hope he will not try to follow us when we get onto the grounds of the chateau! I am definitely going to take the gun with me!" Minutes later David and Brenda drive up to two enormous lamppost that are made out of granite and brass. They were positioned on both sides of the road that led into the grounds of the great house. The lampposts are about thirty feet high and have a main girth of at least four feet at their bases. David speaks:

"Brenda, what are they, I have never seen such hideous creations before?"

"I will have to believe that they are lamppost, David. I don't understand why my people would have erected such horrible creatures to hold those enormous outdoor road lanterns! They appear to be a mutant form somewhere between a vulture and what I would think that a human vampire depicted in old horror movies looked like." David speaks:

"I see a small very tall ornate building that is made of stone. Wonder what it is there for?" Brenda replies:

"I don't know, let's get out and have a look. Just be on the lookout for that dog! I will not chance it with that animal. I have never shot a dog. I have loved one like a family member, but that creature gives me the creeps!"

"Brenda, this little stone building is as fancy as a palace. Look at all of the beautiful carvings on the outside! I believe that these strange looking devices on the corners of the roof outside that look like demons are called gargoyles. They were put on buildings to scare away evil spirits and to provide gutters outlets for rainwater to leave the roofs and go to the ground down through runoff systems." Brenda speaks:

"I now understand what this little structure is for. I see poles with hooks on them and torches to light the huge outdoor lanterns at the entrance." Brenda and David step outside of the building and notice a hatch below each lantern. The poles were raised and the hooks were used to open the hatches revealing the oversized two foot wide wicks. The individual lighting the lanterns would get a flint and a file and light the lighter torch and hold it up high where the lanterns would be lit. It appeared by the fresh suet on the bottoms of the lanterns and the lighter torches that the lanterns were regularly lit. By whom? No one knew. Perhaps Brenda's great uncle was using this old system to provide light for himself in this very remote and heavily forested area.

"Brenda, should we walk or should we continue to use the pickup truck?"

"I believe that we should use the truck as long as possible. It is possible that we can go all the way to the house with the truck. It will afford us a measure of personal safety if we need to leave the grounds in haste." Brenda and David get back into the truck and slowly make their way up the grand road that would eventually get them to the great house. Along the way David notices dozens of earthen mounds here and there out in the woods. He is compelled to speak:

"Brenda, do you know what those mounds are there for?"

"David, I have been told that Indians buried their dead here. In other words, this area is an old Indian graveyard. I believe that a tribe of so called Cape Fear Indians migrated here and made this part of the plantation their home before our people arrived here." Brenda and David continue driving toward the great house and come up on a massive wall with a huge black iron gate facing them. The wall made of cut stone was about twelve feet high. Every twenty feet an unusual ornament also of stone rested on the battement. It appeared that the ornaments, which were about three feet high each, were distorted human faces of Frenchmen and women looking slightly downward toward the ground. Behind the stonewall on each side of the Iron Gate were guardhouses made from stone and beside of each building stood carvings of French military guards standing at attention. On the patio outside of each guardhouse were twelve cannons in position as if they were ready for action. A very impressive flagpole mounted on a granite base stood near the right guardhouse facing David and Brenda. Brenda and David cautiously rode onto the grounds of the great house.

Huge live oak trees with moss flowing like the beards of ancient men majestically guarded the lawn in front of the mega dwelling. A huge fountain surrounded by a very impressive holding pond rich with carvings, stood on the lawn. Inside the pool filled with water were four magnificent larger than life stallions pulling a Roman Emperor's war chariot. The horses were as large as elephants. Standing inside the chariot was a huge lifelike statue of a very muscular Roman officer with the reins in his hands. Back of him was a man whom David and Brenda suspected represented a Roman emperor dressed in full battle gear. In his upright left hand was a huge sword. The water was gushing out of the fountain heads back of the carving and spraying some forty feet into the air. The horses were so realistic and were possessed with so much eye catching energy that it appeared that they were going to actually rush out of the pool with great fury and trample anything standing in their pathway.

"Brenda, I can't believe that old fountain is still working! That thing is magnificent! I don't believe that I have ever seen such a grand work of art! I just can't figure out where all of that water is coming from; it would take an enormous commercial size pumping station to operate that system!"

"David, I also am absolutely overwhelmed by its size and workmanship!"

"Brenda, I believe that your ancestors must have tapped into the vast underground river that supplies the fishing lake. Otherwise, I see no possible way for such a waterworks as grand as this one to be operating for these centuries without the benefit of so called modern pumps. I am sure it is not operated by electrical or diesel powered pumps, but is powered naturally by the water pressure." In the distance David and Brenda saw what they believed to be a chapel. It was beautiful and it was made out of cut stone. Statues of the saints were standing at various locations near the chapel grounds. Surrounding the saints and on the corners of the roof stood beautiful angles with their hands raised toward heaven. In the distance, in the deep woods surrounding the chateau, came forth the troubling noise of what sounded somewhat like a wolf's howl. It was a very long and painfully lonely haunting sound that seemed to pierce the ear drums of our alarmed and concerned young couple.

"David, that noise was the most horrible sound that I have ever heard. It almost sounded like the howl of a wolf, but it passed through my very soul it seems!"

"Are there any wolves on the plantation, Brenda?"

"I believe that Grandfather Zeb said that he saw wolf tracks near this area when he was a young man. I understand that the state put wolves out into wilderness areas of our state many years ago. They were fairly common many centuries before the white man appeared on the scene and guns." David speaks:

"Yes, I have read about that. I also understand that even the mighty brown bears once roamed this part of the country many centuries ago. Things have sure changed!" David and Brenda turn their attention toward the house. The main structure was three stories in height and was made mostly of granite and marble. The frame was made out of extra heavy timber in the days when huge trees were plentiful and extensively incorporated into the building material large structures were created from. David estimated that each story or floor was about twenty-five feet high judging from the outside. The roof was very tall and added about two more stories of height to the grand structure. Fancy blue tile was used to cover the very complicated ornate roof. Fifty huge bay windows were built into the giant attic to add light and beauty. More than a hundred massive chimneys towered over the structure like towers designed to fortify a castle or a stone fort. The chimneys were capped with copper sheeting. Six massive double doors served the front of the chateau. Carved above each door in stone was the Lafayette Coast of Arms. High up on the terrace of the second story on each corner of the massive house were beautiful chariots, each pulled by four magnificent horses with flowing manes astride of each other. The chariots were each occupied by a driver and a person of noble rank. Behind the horses and the chariots on the terrace balcony was a huge stone banister that occupied the entire front of the main building. Two large towers stood on each side of the house and were part of the main structure. They are about a hundred and fifty feet tall each. The cut stone towers are rounded or curved like the towers of many castles, palaces, or cathedrals. Starting on floor one of the towers, and the ten additional floors, were porches and banisters similar to the leaning Tower in Pizza which is part of a cathedral and university city situated near the Arno river in north central Italy. These structures were decorated with stone columns. The top or capital of each column was carved into beautiful flowers. Human figurines were standing on each porch behind the stone banisters. It appeared that these carvings represented none other than the original owners of the property, the Lafayette family. A large dome of some fifteen thousand square feet near the front center of the chateau added great beauty and mystery to the structure and provided an enormous showroom for the inside of the house. Brenda speaks:

"David, let's check the chapel out and the grounds before we make an attempt to go inside the main building. I believe that we need to act discreetly because I don't want to upset my great uncle. He has never met me and may not realize who we are. If someone approaches us, we will be in a better position of introducing ourselves."

"I agree, Brenda, I don't want to just walk into an enormous place like that without getting to know more about the situation. Do you have the gun loaded, Brenda?"

"Of course, I do. I hate to walk into a chapel with it, but I am not going to take a chance with that dog running free around these parts." Beautiful cedar trees lined the cobble stone road that led to the courtyard that surrounded the chapel. Curved shaped stone tables and chairs with carvings of flowers were stationed on each side of the walk. Up ahead was a magnificent iron gate. On each side of the gate were two huge angels in flowing robes guarding the entrance to the chapel. Inside and beyond the gate our couple is impressed with the well organized and eye catching arrangements of shrubs and flowers that were planted there years ago to beautify the yard. The chapel was not a disappointment. A huge steeple dominated the front and face of the chapel. It started on the ground being part of the main structure of the chapel and reached skyward at a height of about two hundred and twenty five feet.

"David, this building is by far the most beautiful church I have ever looked at!" What Brenda was looking at when she made her comment was the beautiful mega sized three dimensional carvings of the nativity scene carved onto the façade or face of the building and over the main entrance arch that led into the foyer of the church. The carving was a breath taking picture in stone of the Baby Jesus in a manger inside a stable surrounded by his legal father Joseph and his attentive mother Mary. On the straw before the holy child was a band of shepherds with their heads bowed low in an attitude of worship. Several horses, donkeys, and sheep stood in the background looking upon the holy couple and the Christ Child. High up in the steeple works in the make believe night sky was a star of great radiance created from real gold paint and covered with precious stones that was shining down on the holy family and their first guest. In the distance bands of angles were swiftly making their flight back to realms unknown to the lost, blind to the light of Heaven above, far beyond the starry sky.

The manger scene was gigantic, much larger than life, and dominated the entire upper front of the chapel. The entrance was a series of grand arches whose faces were covered with hundreds of carvings of Biblical characters of significance, such as, Abraham, Moses, David, Elijah, and Enoch. The scene was breathtaking and mysterious. Brenda and David felt goose bumps on the back of their neck and on their arms as they looked on. Two huge outdoor lamps stood on stone pedestals before the massive double doors that led into the foyer of the building. When David and Brenda cautiously pulled one of the doors and walked inside, their breath was almost taken away at the magnificence of the sight before them. The foyer which was also the hollow of the steeple was a crowned jewel in stone and beautiful stained glass windows that were placed just above the boxed in part of the entrance above the doors.

On floor level positioned on raised platforms near the walls were the statues of the twelve apostles. Up high in the foyer cunningly illustrated in stone, precious metals, and gemstones, is one of the great events of The Ages, the historical occasion when Jesus will take the book that is the title deed of the universe from God the Father because he is most worthy. Here the glorified Jesus sits on the throne of his glory. Surrounding the throne in white robes are multitudes upon multitudes of both Old Testament and New Testament saints praising and singing to their Lord. Beyond the saints, surrounding the throne, are myriads upon myriads of the Heavenly host worshipping God their creator.

"Brenda, I can't believe that such a magnificent place of worship is out here in the middle of nowhere! Forgotten about; except, by a few members of your family and the plantation families!"

"I know, David, but my family unfortunately must not open its doors to the world. We could lose everything. There is nothing meritorious about our people allowing the public to scan everything we hold dear and sacred. This place is not about people in general, but my family. It was never created to entertain or mystify the public." David speaks.

"Well, let's walk into the main building and see it!" The first thing that catches the wide opened eyes of our young couple, other than seeing the beautiful chandeliers hanging on both sides of the worship room, was a massive story carved out of stone back of the pulpit and back of the choir's sitting area. This was not a frieze carved out of the wall or a flat wall insert, but three-dimensional individuals. The figures were about twelve feet tall if they had been standing. All of the men were not identical in size or height. David and Brenda were stunned when they realized that they were looking at by far the most magnificent depiction of The Lord's Supper in the world. Jesus and his twelve disciples were sitting at a huge ornate stone table with the carvings of lambs in each corner of the table near the tops of each of the four legs of the table. Large wooden dishes were piled high with unleavened bread. Next to the bread were large baked clay serving bowls full of special sauces. In the middle of the table was a roasted lamb with special sauces and spices all over it. The upper post of the door and the two side post of the upper room door are painted with paint that looks like fresh looking almost dripping blood to commemorate the Passover. Jesus is shown turned toward Judas Iscariot while answering the question directed to him about who among the disciples would betray him. He is handing Judas bread dipped in special sauces and speaks these words.

"But, behold, the hand of him that betrayeth me is with me on the table. And truly the Son of man goeth, as it was determined, but woe unto the man whom he is betrayed." These words are displayed back and above the Lord and his disciples by two winged baby angels in the air with an open scroll they hold out for onlookers to read. The words are written in Latin. David speaks:

"Brenda, look at those magnificent arches on each side of the sanctuary. Those free standing angles in each of the six arches on each side of this huge sanctuary room are wonderful!" Most of the angels held a musical instrument in their massive hands. One angle had a beautiful harp and it looked like he was playing it. The metallic harp was plated with real gold for beauty. Another angel had a magnificent trumpet and he appeared to be blowing it with great power. Above the angle, in Latin, was the inscription "the trumpet of the Lord shall sound and all of the dead in Christ shall rise." One angel was dressed in Roman battle dress. This angel was the Arch Angel Michael himself, the general of the armies in Heaven. Still another very powerful angel had a huge chain in his hands and he was binding the arch enemy of God. Lucifer had horns on his head to identify him, and his feet were hoofs. Again a Bible verse was on a fancy plaque above the angel. "And I saw an angel come down from heaven, having a great chain in his hand. And he laid hold on the dragon, that old serpent, which is the Devil, and Satan, and bound him a thousand years. Brenda speaks:

"David, look up at that beautiful ceiling. I believe that it must be around seventy feet high. It is not the biggest I have seen. I have been to Rome and other places to look at huge churches, but I believe that ceiling would rival any on Earth! I am very proud to be part of a family that had such a glorious work of art erected here on this spot about two hundred and seventy five years ago!" While David and Brenda look up at the ceiling, which is an almost unrivaled painting of the ascension of Christ from the Mount of Olives while above five hundred faithful look on accompanied by the disciples, David realizes that it is already five o'clock in the afternoon. He speaks to his wife:

"Brenda, I can't believe that it is five o'clock! What happened to the time all of a sudden?"

"David, I believe that your watch is wrong." Brenda looks at her wrist watch to verify her statement.

"David, you are right! I am unable to account for how time went by so quickly! Let's look at the garden, and if we have time, we can go inside of the great house. I love to look at huge fancy French Gardens, and based on what I have seen so far, I don't believe that I will be disappointed by the experience."

"Are we going inside the house, Brenda?"

"I hope we can, but if not, I am prepared to come back here another day and continue our adventure. I must see all of this place! I just can't believe such a place exists, but we can't denied reality. Let's get out of here as quickly as possible and find the garden. I believe that it is on the other side of the huge wall I saw back of the house. It must cover about a hundred and fifty acres of territory. The yard of my parents' mega mansion covers two hundred acres, but a massive ornate wall does not surround it with carvings all over its face and top." Brenda and David make their way out of the large private chapel and start their journey to a massive ornate wall that is about five hundred feet back of the chateau complex.

"Brenda, aren't these huge oak trees impressive! They have such a character about them. It is as if they are guarding the place. The moss hanging high up in those branches is amazing."

"Yes, David, they are indeed magnificent trees! I would estimate that these huge live oak monsters average fifteen feet in diameter. I would expect such monsters before a palace or a chateau and here they are! I would imagine that they are nearly a thousand years old, but appear to be as healthy as any trees I have ever looked at." David and Brenda turn their heads back toward the mansion when they were nearing the wall enclosure for the garden and were delighted to see that the great house had three porches on the back. These did not look like the Pridgen mansion porches, but were supported with massive stone columns that were decorated at their capitals with carvings of what appeared to David and Brenda as the Roman gods in a massive struggle against the Titans and dragon like monsters from the great abysmal of chaos. Beautiful statues of young lovers embracing each other in miniature fairy tale like gardens, beautiful stone gazebos, and lovely little water fountains were carefully arranged in the back courtyard of the huge house to please the eye and keep the muse on the back of every writers and artist alive with whispers and suggestions of wonderful works of creativity into their attentive ears.

Once again the hideous long lonely howl of a strange and unknown beast is heard in the distance. The very earth beneath their feet seems to resonate to the horrible sound. It sends shivers down the spines of both Brenda and David. There was something mysterious and unnatural about the sound. Brenda checks her old double barrel shotgun just for comforts sake. Assured that the shells were in place and ready should they be needed, our couple continue their tour. The wall was about ten feet high and was thicker and heavier built at the base or foot of the wall. A red stone walk led inside the enclosure. All along the wall as far as they could see were carvings of baby angles holding waterspouts. On the two sides of the entrance gate that led into the enclosure were two statues of the fearsome mythological god of the woods and meadow lands called Pan. A stern warning was etched on the base of one of the statues of the half man half goat god Pan. David is amused at the warning and reads it out loud.

"Beauty is in the eyes of the beholder. If you see me and scorn my beauty, I will turn you into a toad. Enjoy the beauty of my garden, but beware, I might charge you a fee you cannot refuse."

The first thing that really caught the eyes of David and Brenda was a huge enclosed pool. The pool is about three hundred feet long and about a hundred feet wide. It is on a base about six feet above the ground and one can step up to the level of the pond by steps that are actually levels of the foundations of the entire work. Inside of the pond is a massive fountain that is a carving of a huge winged sea dragon with its many humps lined with thick scales and fins. It appeared that the monster is on the move. The dragon's mighty furious looking head is raised out of the deep pool with its huge mouth opened wide full of large teeth and a massive snake like tongue. Out of this mouth gushed out a mighty volume of frothy looking water that represented fire billowing forth from the monster's mouth. The frothy appearance of the water coming from this mythical representation of a dragon is accomplished by the water being forced to gush out under pressure from scores of holes at the bottom of the dragon's mouth. Just like a series of over sized garden hoses with spray nozzles attached to each of them. Of course, the dragon's nozzle and air intake system is very grand and the water comes out with the perfect effect of reminding anyone looking upon this beast in action of fire said to have gushed out of dragon mouths eons ago in a time when our world was very much different and innocence had not been raped of her charm and primitive beauty. The striking splendor of this dragon fountain mesmerized our couple for nearly an hour. They did not just stand in one spot, but walked around the extensive work to view the fountain in action from many locations around the pool.

David tells Brenda that they had better move along if they were going to see anything else that day. Before them was one of the largest and without doubt the most beautiful French Garden in the world. At a hundred and fifty acres in size, our couple had to move quickly to enjoy this magnificent blend of nature's best and man's best attempt to create a paradise with his imagination and sweat. David and Brenda soon realized to their delight that the massive garden was divided into many smaller gardens. Each section has a theme or purpose for its existence. Our couple walks around admiring the first garden, which has a theme centered on fantasy and science fiction, as represented by the huge dragon, and scores of ancient gods, such as the gods of Mount Olympus. The gods are depicted in striking detail in larger than human proportions in their abode on their mountain looking down at mankind from their lofty perch. The mountain is made up of thousands of tons of earth covered by rocks and large boulders that had been put in place by a remarkable amount of ingenuity and human labor. The gods are standing up in all of their glory on the mountain. The chief god, Zeus, is in the center of his domain in full control of the affairs and the lives of us mere mortals whose breath is in our nostrils. David and Brenda stood amazed as they looked up at these strikingly furious looking supernatural giants who were richly clad in long flowing robes carved out of granite.

"David, I just can't get over the huge effort and skill required to put this scene up. Someone sure had a lot of wealth to afford this kind of art work!" David smiled and spoke as he continued to look on with amazement written over his face.

"Brenda, I believe that those people you refer to are your people if I am not mistaken. I do realize that these people had to have the wealth of kings when kings were vastly wealthy to have afforded such splendid and opulent works of art on this vast scale!" No one in this country could afford all of this and I am not sure that anyone in Europe or anywhere else would attempt to create this!" Every garden our couple entered on their way to the great wall on the other side next to the hedge rows that faced Black River was different. One of the favorite gardens that took up much time to explore and to enjoy is the water garden. It is a water world of wondrous things to look at and a place to soak up beauty and rest the soul and mind of the beholder. A large pool is the central theme or climax of this gem. The pool had a blue bottom that David and Brenda believed to be made from cut blue quartz. The entire pool is surrounded by a beautiful granite patio. In the pool live scores of very large goldfish that appeared to be excited the moment David and Brenda show up. The fish were so friendly that both David and Brenda managed to pet them. Brenda spoke:

"David, these beautiful fish must be very old. I can't believe how big they are!"

"Yes, Brenda, I would imagine that the ancestors of these fish were imported from China centuries ago. They are really a type of carp. Pools around royal residences in China were stocked with these beautiful fish. They were often the only pets the families had. The fish are very intelligent and don't mind being touched." In the distance David and Brenda were drawn to the sound and spectacular sight of a multitude of gushing boiling fountains of water originating from far below the surface of the deep waters of a mega sized blue colored pool that represented an ocean of mythical origin that was full of jumping porpoises, mermaids a swimming, giant seahorses, flying fish, swordfish, and giant octopus. Sitting in a huge larger than life Indo-Pacific Murex Sea Shell, called a Ramose Murex is the god of the sea, mighty Neptune. He is depicted as a huge man of massive proportions and a ragged looking mustache and beard. He is extremely powerfully built and has eyes and a face that are commanding and very terrible to look upon. On his head is a crown symbolizing his royal power. In his right hand is a huge three pronged trident.

"David, we had better go on to the wall if we are going to get an opportunity to see it. Do you realize that it is already seven thirty?" Our excited young couple quickly walked to the great brim that the beautiful ten foot stonewall stood on top of for several miles in front of the estate to keep out unwanted guest. After walking up a huge stone staircase, our couple found the steps that led up to the top of the wall. As far as they could see was a beautiful stonewall that was about ten feet high and about eight feet wide. About every four hundred feet they saw a guard tower where people once stood guard over the twenty four hundred acre estate. David looked down and across a gigantic hedge row that was armed with huge thorns by the hundreds of millions.

"Brenda, I can't believe how thick this huge hedge row is! I can't imagine anyone trying to get past this natural wonder!" Brenda speaks:

"Yes, David, I am sure that centuries ago before modern war equipment, this hedge row with its huge thorns and the wall that adds ten more feet of height to the ten foot tall berm, would have been a formidable barrier indeed! I would suspect that the only logical way to get past this thing is to burn a hole in it sufficient for an attacking force to get at the wall. Unfortunately, for anyone attacking, there is a moat full of water to cross and a ten foot berm to climb before the wall is even accessible, and I don't believe that even then, that it would be a cake walk to breach the wall because of its thickness and apparent very solid construction." Out about half a mile from where Brenda and David stood is the beautiful Black River. The forest in front of the two mile wall is very thick and mature, but our couple could still catch glimpses of the beautiful river as they walked hand in hand along the top. Looking back into the garden from the perspective of the height of the berm and the wall, our couple is mesmerized by the symmetry and striking beauty of the layout of the garden. A lot of brain power and strong backs had to have been marshaled in union to have created such a manmade paradise! David looks at his watch and speaks with alarm:

"Brenda, dear, we need to move it or we will find ourselves after dark in this place. I don't believe we could find our way out of here as many mazes as there are in this oversized place!"

"David, let's hurry and try to walk past the front of the carriage house and take a quick survey of the graveyard. I realize that we have used up our time and would probably be wise to leave this estate before the light of day is replaced by the light of the Moon." It did not take our couple over twenty-five minutes to quickly trot through the garden and find themselves running past the huge chateau. Up ahead and on their left about a hundred and fifty feet from the house is the grandest carriage house either one of our characters had ever laid their eyes on! This structure is not a simple garage to keep the carriages out of bad weather, but a complex facility to also house the coachmen and their families on the second story. All of the replacement parts and a repair shop with all of the tools and equipment are included. The front of this building is absolutely magnificent. The carriage house is a two story structure made of cut stone and brick. There is a beautiful multi-arched porch on the outside of the structure on the front and the side that included the shops and the warehouse where wheels, and axels were created. At the top front of the structure on each corner are full sized carvings of fancy passenger coaches being pulled by six magnificent black horses. Included in each scene is a driver and his assistance outside on their covered seat prepared to direct the horses. The doors on one side of each coach is opened and near the doors stand tall well dressed coachmen prepared to assist passengers when they are ready to board the coaches. The yard surrounding the building is paved with heavy duty street brick. Towering over the yard are twenty-four beautiful lamps on tall posts to provide light for passengers either leaving the estate or visiting. Beautiful cement tables and benches had been placed under the multi-arched porch to provide people a place to sit and wait for an outbound or inbound passenger coach. The family's cemetery is located on a large flat hill about a thousand feet back of the carriage house. The base of the hill is surrounded by a heavy duty retainer wall made out of cut stone to prevent erosion.

The retainer wall is decorated with 3D carvings of ghastly distorted human heads every thirty feet. David and Brenda walk past the long arched porch facing the chateau. There are shops of all sorts almost reminding David and Brenda of a strip mall. These shops were put there centuries ago to comfort the weary traveler and house the necessary equipment and tools to provide transportation and aid to the traveler. There is also a blacksmith's shop, a cobbler's shop where horse shoes were made to shoe the horses' hoofs, a leather shop, where harnesses and the metal parts, such as bits that go into the mouths of the horses, curb chains, pole chains, and about twenty other straps and traces along with various pieces of equipment that are used to control the power of horses that are attached to passenger coaches and wagons that were once made. Brenda and David continue to be drawn to the graveyard high up on a hill a thousand feet back of the carriage house complex. David looks at his watch with concern and speaks:

"Brenda, it is past seven thirty, we have only about an hour and a half before it will start to get dark around here. Did you get a flashlight from the truck?"

"Yes, I did, David, it has a million candlepower. We need to hurry as you said if we are going to see anything at all. We will only have opportunity to glance at the place, but no time to go inside the huge mausoleum that dominates yonder cemetery."

"Brenda, I am not sure that I have any desire to go inside of that place. I am not superstitious, but like your grandfather said, some things can't be explained by science and I have no desire to fulfill the moment by challenging the unknown. I have been surrounded by Great White Sharks while in the ocean and have swam near huge squid and even entered deep dark caves thousands of feet below the ocean's surface in small exploration submarines. I realized that I would encounter the known or what could be explained scientifically to my satisfaction, but I am just thinking that this place indeed holds dark unthinkable realities that are probably best left alone!" Brenda and David continue to walk toward the loaming hill as if drawn to it by some strange unexplainable power.

Before they could reach the summit of the hill where the in-laws of Captain John Henry Pridgen are interned, David and Brenda must walk a strange winding ramp all the way to the top. The ramp is as wide as a paved single lane highway and reminded our couple of passage ways shown in fantasy books of long winding roads leading all the way up to some fantastic fairy like castle high up on a mystical mountain. The two sides of the ramp are guarded on either side with heavy duty solid stone sides. Statues of giants with deformed heads, demons, fairies, evil looking elves, and the dead were standing every forty feet on both sides of the ramp to frighten away mostly anyone in such a strange place. Brenda speaks:

"David, it looks like someone went to a lot of trouble a very long time ago to either discourage people in taking a hike up this ramp or to impress people about the world of fantasy and the supernatural. My feet want to turn around and run as fast as I can to the truck and get out of here! I have never felt such a presence of evil or something strange in my life! I just can't explain what is happening." David looks down toward Brenda's shotgun.

"I am sure thankful that you have brought along that twelve gauge shotgun, but I am not sure that it is the type of weapon we need right now." Brenda wrinkles up her face a bit and looks at the gun and back to David's face.

"Honey, I don't have a clue as to what else we could have brought along to protect us or at least comfort us." David speaks:

"Perhaps the story James Henry shared with us about Miss Carrie Lamb is more than just a fairy tale to put children to sleep before the age of television and other forms of entertainment. I have always heard the old saying that ignorance is bliss, but up to now, I have not been a great proponent of this philosophy because I have always been of the opinion that knowledge of itself is not the problem, it is the application of knowledge that causes its revelation to be good or evil." Brenda manages a smile.

"David, I am surprised at you! Surely you do not think we are about to open up Pandora's Box and let out the unthinkable to terrorize the halls of academia and put little children early to bed behind closed doors under the watchful care of good angels, or something?"

"No, Brenda, I am aware that people often stumble across knowledge by accident or design with a lot of perspiration in its pursuit. I also know my history well enough to know that people have come face to face with facts that are hard to swallow and in some cases dangerous in a time when people were burned at the stake for heresy or locked up for lunacy. All of these people were not mad or intent on distorting science or the Good Book. People have reported the strange and the unknown for ages. Look at the early ship logs where even Columbus reported seeing bright disk shaped objects in the sky around his fleet of small ships or disk shaped craft coming up from the dark depths of the ocean he traveled. Sightings of hags on broom sticks crossing a full Moon on a cold winter's night to the reports of fairies, giants, and such tales or reports of Sasquatch, or dinosaurs seen by natives and missionaries in the darkest regions of the Congo."

"David, have you ever read or seen on television the story about the monks that walk the floor in the ancient Winchester Cathedral in England? I understand that actual film has been taken that show the monks in robes walking up to the altar. It has been reported that the monks appear to be very short. A gentleman went to the then current architect of the church and learned that the first floor had been replaced by a second floor that was built several feet above the original floor centuries ago. The ghost monks have been seen several feet down below the current floor walking on the older floor."

"No, I can't say that I have seen the story told on television. Strange, I have no explanation for it. I have confined my studies to my field of oceanography and geology with some modest tribute gained for me."

"Yes, I like your humble spirit, David. I can't imagine living with a guy as smart as you are and the fame you have, who is egoistical, because your humble nature and the genuine pursuit to help your fellowman makes you very special to me indeed!"

"Brenda, you have never expressed yourself like this before! Just don't make a habit of it; I don't need my head to swell up. I like it just the way it is!"

The moment our couple steps on the cemetery's official ground, the temperature seemed to plummet with no explanation postulated by either David or Brenda on how such a queer occurrence was possible. It was summer time and the temperature was around ninety degrees Fahrenheit. A thick white fog was rapidly rolling in covering the grounds. The film industry could have not done it better! It actually rolled upon itself as it advanced and settled as white as cotton. On a hill on top of the main cemetery hill stood the strangest looking tree that David had ever laid eyes upon!

"Brenda, what kind of tree is that? It looks like something from a monster book!" Brenda takes a hard look at the huge tree unable and surprised that she could not identify the type of tree. Brenda was very expert in the types of trees of the region having worked for years helping her father and brothers harvest them for various reasons.

"David, I am not sure. Maybe it was imported from somewhere. It does not look like a native species." David continues to look, totally amazed and somewhat alarmed at the strange appearance of this natural wonder or was this a natural tree? The tree was about a hundred and forty feet tall and had a girth that was so enormous as to make it one of the largest trees on earth. The more our couple looked the more hair raising the thing appeared. There were only a few leaves on the tree. Most of the branches appeared almost dead, but apparently they were not. A huge wound at the base of the tree was a cave large enough for two average sized people to get into to get out of a moderate rain shower. Huge limbs extended out like arms. Many of them parallel to the ground. Brenda noticed that near the top of the trunk itself, which was about sixty feet high, was a face of a sort. Do trees have faces? David speaks as cheerfully as possible:

"I hope that thing is not alive!" Brenda frowns a bit and looks up at David with a questioning look on her face.

"What do you mean if it is alive? I am sure that the tree is not dead. Although it does appear that there might be some dead wood in the branches and the trunk. I can't imagine what caused such a huge scar in the trunk of this monster. Look at the huge roots running on top of the ground a hundred feet in all directions around the tree! I have never seen such a sight before! We would almost have to have a ladder just to reach the trunk to touch it!"

"Brenda, when you were a child, did you ever watch monster movies or fantasy shows of young adults and children getting lost in the deep dark woods of Germany or perhaps somewhere in Russia and discover to their horror that the huge trees that surround them can move and that they grab people up and eat them?" Brenda thinks a moment before she replies.

"I know why you ask such a strange question. It is that tree. It does look like one of those trees. Fortunately such trees are found only in the forest of our imaginations." David continues to stare at the strange monster tree that they can't identify. It is nearly eight o'clock and it is getting a little harder for them to see. Back of them a magnificent red colored full Moon floats above them making the whole experience a dreadful journey. Legs said go, run, get out of this place as fast as possible, but a strange power magnified our couple's natural curiosity over riding the flight instinct. David thinks he sees objects by the scores up high in the branches of the dead like limbs of the giant mystery tree before them.

"Brenda, cut your light on and point it up into the branches of that tree. I am sure I see something up there." Brenda shines the million candle powered spotlight into the branches of the mega tree and almost drops it when she sees scores of huge turkey buzzards looking down at them.

"David, that is not natural! This kind of buzzard is very rare now days. There must be a hundred of them up there! I am under the impression that we should now start heading for the truck! I am afraid that we have crossed over into a very unhealthy realm that is not meant for us to know about as long as we want to remain safe and healthy! I believe that huge dog or whatever it is as you said earlier was a clear warning to turn around and mind our own business!"

"Brenda, calm down now. I believe that there is a logical explanation for this phenomenon. It is getting darker and I am sure that the shadows and the fog are playing tricks with your eyes and emotions. Let's take just a few more minutes before we leave. Brenda, let's go and stand about fifty yards in front of that huge mausoleum. Just point your light at it for a minute and we can go. I will be satisfied then!" Minutes later David and Brenda stand in front of the breath taking building that houses the departed. A huge carving of the Lafayette Coat of Arms dominated the front of the granite structure. David asks Brenda to shine her powerful spotlight on the grounds in front of the mausoleum and they see twelve vaults above the ground. There are two rows at six vaults to a row directly in front of the main entrance to the mausoleum. Next to the vaults, are life size standing statues of their occupants. David speaks:

"Brenda, if I am not mistaken, these statues represent the twelve French house servants that moved from Paris, France, to live here to serve your ancestors: amazing! Now we know where they were all interned! Brenda, we should be leaving this place! I have suddenly become uneasy for an unknown reason."

"Yes, David, I believe that we should obey our natural instincts and get off of this piece of property." Just before our couple turns around to walk down the huge ramp lined on both sides with monsters such as giants, fairies, trolls, elves, goblins and other creatures of darkness, a plasma like light with a faceless head slowly emerges or better yet, wiggles out through the massive solid walls of the mausoleum. Brenda speaks:

"That is strange, it has to be foxfire, but I have never seen it except in a swamp or occasionally in extra heavy wooded areas of the plantation." David does not have an explanation, but agrees with Brenda's somewhat shaky theory to relieve his uneasy feelings he has suddenly developed about the situation. Directly another strange light emerges out of the mausoleum. David looks at Brenda and almost speaks sharp to her.

"Plasma light, I don't think so! Let's get the heck off of this unholy ground!" At that very moment, the strange howl of a wolf or something is heard. It is very long and it had a very unnatural tone to it! Feet are no longer walking, but are running toward the ramp which leads down a winding very steep path to the back of the huge carriage house a thousand feet away. To make things even more alarming, a huge Turkey buzzard flies over not three feet above their heads and lands near one of the statues on the ramp. It does not budge despite the fact that two humans are rapidly running toward it. It is a nasty foul looking creature with a long humped neck that reminded our couple of a goose necked lamp. Its beak was very long and sharp. Dangerous looking huge sharp talons equipped this bird with formidable weapons! A foul odor of something dead for a long time suddenly surrounded Brenda and David as they hastened on down the ramp that is about five hundred feet long.

Quickly they dash down toward the truck. By now scores of huge Turkey buzzards have also flown past the frightened couple and have landed on the thick solid stone railings of the ramp. When David and Brenda get to the bottom of the ramp and look back, they realize that the statues of the giants, fairies, goblins, trolls, and other creatures of mystery and evil were not on the ramp like they were supposed to be; they were swept with a mixture of curiosity and fear. There was no time to do an investigation of this strange occurrence, because the instinct to survive the moment was in the driver's seat to leave behind this place or realm that science cannot explain and will always deny possible. Moments later David is opening the door on the passenger side of the truck ready to get in. Brenda is a little slower and she has not yet opened the driver's door to get in. She grabs the handle and is preparing to open the door when to her horror she realizes that the huge dog or whatever it is, is directly back of her. At first she hears the creature's breathing, but breathing with the lungs of a horse running at full gallop. The creature starts to growl with so much power that the sound actually resonate off of the ground and the side of the truck. She can somehow feel the pressure of the sound waves going through her body! It sends chills through her very soul! Brenda is unable to move a limb frozen in fear! It is as if fear has wrapped its sinister arms around her mind and body like a giant constrictor snake. For a moment, all she can hear is her own heart pounding in her chest and the heavy breathing and ever increasing growl of her enemy back of her.

David pounds on the glass of the door on the driver's side screaming for his wife to turn around and fire the gun. Moments later in time, David opens the door on Brenda's side of the truck. The slight push David gives Brenda as he stands back of her causes her to respond to David's desperate plea for her to turn and fire. She swings around with great speed and perfect timing and fires the twelve gauge gun at the head of the beast. The instant the gun fired with a great noise at the head of the dog or whatever it was, the creature burst into a tremendous explosion of plasma like light with a million streamers of the substance radiating outward in all directions. The brightness of the flash of the light temporarily blinded Brenda and David. A split second later the substance is no more, vanished into the void of the darkness. Strange shadows and forms of the kingdom of darkness were rapidly creeping in to take over the grounds around the chateau where only a few hours earlier the sun in all its glory and majesty held back its influence until its appointed time on its eternal circuit came to a daily closure. David spoke:

"What the heck is going on around here? Let's get out of this place and leave it to the Devil!" The moment David slides back into the passenger side of the truck, Brenda starts to open the truck door with plans to get in and make a most unusual speedy exodus from her great uncle's chateau. A noise was heard in the carriage house and all of the street lamps come on as if by magic. Brenda starts the truck and drives it toward the entrance gatehouse slowly at first, but when she saw one of the garage doors of the huge carriage house open and an enormous ornate passenger coach coming out pulled by six magnificent horses not from this world, she puts the peddle to the floorboard! There was no time for goodbyes, no time to put on the seatbelt, because time was a wasting and fear and a primitive instinct for survival and the over whelming urge to flee commanded her every action! Why had they not heeded the warning of generations of Pridgens who turned away from this unholy ground? The moment the truck sped past the gatehouse where the statues of the French soldiers stood to attention and the cannons were poised to fire, Brenda looked back through the rear view mirror and realizes that the huge passenger coach is fast approaching them. Brenda speaks:

"David, they are coming our way. I hope we can out run them!"

Billows or puffs of cloud like fire, no doubt the breath of Hell itself came out of the nostrils of the six horses. Two coachmen with eyes that glowed like hot coals in a fireplace dressed in Eighteenth Century attire sat outside of the massive coach. One man was the assistance and the other man, if that is a correct description of what he is, drove the six steeds onward with a fancy coach whip that created lightning like showers of fire every time he hit the backs of the animals to drive them on faster and faster.

Standing outside near the door on a fancy platform, was the doorman of the luxury coach. His skin appeared to have a greenish tint to it. His eyes glowed with the light of another world, the realm of the damned, not meant for the living that depend on the sun for their light and healing balm. David warned his wife Brenda with a pleading voice:

"Brenda, watch it when you turn left or you will flip the truck and no telling what will happen to us!" Despite the warning giving to her by her pleading husband, Brenda could not help but to turn the truck sideways along the main road that goes through the plantation. The truck stalls and she desperately tries to get it to start again. The sound of the heavy luxury carriage that was as fancy as a ship of state in the bygone days of floating palaces with its multitude of ornate carvings covered with gold and all manner of precious metals and precious gem stones pulled by the six horses was getting louder as it neared. Our frightened couple looked back and could see puffs of fire coming out of the horses' nostrils. The breathing of these creatures no doubt born in Hell sounded like a huffing puffing steam train. Sparks of fire ran down the backs of the horses and the driver furiously drove them ever onward to visit the world of the living.

The truck responded with a sort of cough, it backfired, and away it sped faster and faster until David was compelled to speak once again out of concern.

"Honey, watch it or we will bounce off of this dirt road and hit one of these enormous trees!" Brenda responds:

"Sweetheart, we have got to get out of here or we will be overtaken by that thing! I am so afraid, how can such a thing as this be possible!" It became obvious that the truck would not be able to outrun this supernatural vehicle. Brenda begins to pray and David was unable to speak or give comfort. If only they had heeded the loving advice of Grandfather Zeb when he warned them to not be on the grounds of the chateau after the sun went down. Of how foolish to challenge the other side of the vale, that thin curtain between the world of the living and the realm of angels, devils, and the departed who were equipped to dwell where mortals are only vaguely able to comprehend.

The next morning both Brenda and David get up at ten o'clock. Breakfast is served on the Pridgen Plantation at six o'clock. Both of our characters are wet with perspiration and are fully clothed in bed. They both get up quickly and take a wild look into each other's eyes. What happened?

"Brenda, did I just have the worst nightmare a human could possibly have or did it really happen?"

"David, I dreamed that we were being chased by a huge passenger coach with horses that were expelling blast of flames from their nostrils. The driver and his assistance were from another century, probably Frenchmen from a long time ago. The doorman's eyes glowed with an unearthly glow that nearly scared the life out of me!" David speaks:

"Brenda, we could not possibly dream the same dream. We are fully dressed! I don't understand what happened! How did we end up here in bed together? I don't recall us out running that troop of monsters!"

Upon the large fancy mantle piece above the huge fireplace in the bedroom beside the old windup clock that had been passed down by many generations of the Pridgen Clan were small figurines that got Brenda and David's attention. David looks at Brenda with a confused look on his face, and he questions his wife.

"Honey, where did those little statues come from? I am sure that they were not up there yesterday!" Brenda takes a hard look and is compelled to rise out of bed and walk to the mantle. She just stood and stared unable to speak for a few seconds. With noted concern and confusion reflected in her voice, she stammers out as best as she could to her husband, David:

"David, please come over here and look at these little statues. Do they remind you of anything?"

David gets out of bed not expecting an earth shaking discovery, but most likely, a situation with a satisfactory explanation. David stands only a couple of feet from the statues that averaged no taller than a foot at most. What he saw made the hair stand up back of his neck and goose bumps developed on his back like he was standing in a cold bathroom after a hot shower. Lined up in perfect order, as they were some hours ago, were the giants, elves, goblins, fairies, hunchbacks, and other creatures seen on the winding ramp that led up or down, depending on your direction to or from the cemetery hill where Captain Pridgen wife's people the Lafayettes were buried in that huge mausoleum. David is absolutely astounded with no explanation and so was Brenda. David quickly grabbed one of the figures with both hands and found out that he could not pick it up!

"Brenda, someone must have glued these statues onto this huge mantle. I can't move it!" Brenda also grabs one of them and could not budge it!

"David, I don't understand why anyone would come up here and glue these figurines to this mantle! I am going to go downstairs as soon as I bath and ask mother or somebody if they have seen these curious carvings on the mantle in our bedroom."

"Brenda, I too will bath and go down to see what we can learn. I am also starving. Do you realize that it is ten o'clock?" I can't believe that our children or someone have not knocked on our door wondering why we did not get up for breakfast!" Brenda speaks:

"David, do you recognize these statues or stone carvings?" David looked a little pale when Brenda asked the question.

"I was hoping you would not ask! Of course, I recognize these figurines as being identical to the ones on the ramp that we walked up and later made that quick exodus. This is very strange indeed that we would see identical copies of those evil looking creatures here in our bedroom. Oh, well, I am sure there in a logical explanation!" As soon as Brenda and David bathed and dressed for the day, they went downstairs to the kitchen. Mattie was the only person in the kitchen when Brenda and David entered it. Brenda speaks:

"Mattie, where is everyone?"

"They are mostly done gone, Miss Brenda. Your grandpa is on the porch and your children and your parents have done gone to Atkinson to stay at the hardware store until about two." I believe your grandma is in the greenhouse. Mr. Zeb said that he would just take a break today and rest a little before he goes out to his herb garden. I spects he is reading right now." Brenda speaks:

"Mattie is there anything to eat around here? David and I got up late."

"Yes, ma'am, Miss Brenda, the breakfast is in the oven. Your ma saved you grits, ham, eggs, and biscuits ready to eat nice and hot!" David looks at Brenda and speaks:

"Honey, I am starving let's eat!" After a wonderful country breakfast, David and his lovely wife Brenda walk almost sheepishly onto the porch where the patriarch of the Pridgen Clan sat in his chair reading a favorite book of his about the history of the Black and Cape Fear River region. Brenda speaks:

"Good morning, Grandfather, how are you doing?"

"I am as fit as a fiddle. It is a little too warm to suit my senior constitution this morning, so I have decided to read one of my favorite books that I found years ago in our library. My great grandfather once owned the book and signed his name in it along with many comments in the page margins as he read it. He is the one I told you about. I found him with a smile on his face as if he had looked upon the face of his dear old mother who was long departed before I came into being. What is on your mind this morning that troubles you, Brenda? I get the impression that you are about to ask me a question." David once again is amazed at these powers or abilities that Mr. Zeb seems to possess that most mortals know nothing of, at least, in an experimental way.

"Yes, sir, Grandfather, I just wanted to ask you if you know who put those little statues on top of the mantle above the fireplace in our bedroom?" Mr. Zeb looks up with a sober look.

"Brenda, I will assure you that there are no statues on the mantle in your bedroom."

"Grandfather, both David and I were looking and touching them only about thirty minutes ago! I know that there are little statues of fairies, goblins, giants, and other creatures of darkness and evil on that mantle!" Mr. Zeb looks up again and speaks:

"Why don't you two go back upstairs and double check? I am sure that there is nothing, but that huge old windup clock." Brenda replies to her grandfather somewhat frustrated about the situation.

"Alright, I will go back up there, but..." Mr. Zeb held up his right hand, palm facing Brenda, to let her know that she should cease speaking and just do as he suggested. Mr. Zeb looks up again from his book and speaks:

"Trust an old man. Go back up there, you two, and see if I am right or wrong." David speaks:

"I don't know what is going on around here, but I believe that we need to just go up to that bedroom immediately!" David and Brenda leave the presence of Mr. Zeb as quickly as possible with some dignity. When they get inside the house, they scramble up the huge flight of stairs as fast as they can. When they got to the door, both of them go through at the same time headed to the other side of the huge bedroom where the mantle stood above the fireplace. Where were the statues? They were nowhere to be seen! This can't be, no way! They were glued hard fast onto the mantle, but there was no evidence to indicate that anything had been glued to the mantle and it was a known fact that no one had gone up to the bedroom while Brenda and David were absence. Immediately David and Brenda have flashbacks as they recalled the moment they ran off the huge winding ramp back of the carriage house. When they turned around to look back up the ramp, they realized that the statues were gone! David speaks:

"Brenda do you suppose that....?" Brenda stops her husband in mid sentence and cautions him:

"Honey, maybe we need to forget it. I believe that we have just crossed a line that should have not been challenged!" David speaks:

"Brenda, how did your grandfather know the figurines were not to be here when we came back upstairs?"

"Who knows, he is indeed a man of mystery!"

Eighteen

David Meets with the UNCW Science Department Two Days Later His Family Drives Back to Boston for a Wonderful Visit

The next morning after a wonderful breakfast, David prepares to leave the Plantation and go to UNCW. He is scheduled to meet the faculty at the cafeteria at 11:00 A.M.. The meeting will last about an hour. All science classes were cut. The students were not troubled by the occasion because they would have more personal time to use at their own discretion. Assignments were posted on the electronic bulletin board notwithstanding the fact that all instructors had announced that there would be no classes for the next two hours due to a special department meeting.

David drives directly to the cafeteria complex and prepares to get out of his SUV. He recognizes several members of the science department as they quickly walk up the steps to enter and sit down at the tables already prepared for them by cafeteria staff. Doctor Fletcher, David's boss, drives up. Both men exit their vehicles and shake hands while expressing the usual greetings people normally convey to friends, family, and associates.

"Good morning, Doctor Fletcher, what a nice day we have to have our little get-together!" Doctor Fletcher smiles and replies:

"Yes, I believe that we will have everyone here today. No excuses to not be present based on poor weather conditions!" Both men walk on into the large building and go behind the heavy duty temporary wall panels that were slid and locked in place to create a nice sized room within the facility for the meeting. People exchange customary greetings and a wonderful banquet style meal is rolled in on fancy carts. Minutes later everyone; except David, has filled his or her plate and are seated. Doctor Fletcher informs David that if he wanted to speak while the rest listened and enjoyed the meal, he was welcomed to eat once he finished speaking. David gets up facing everyone and speaks:

"Doctor Fletcher has just informed me that I can eat after I talk. I believe that this is a big incentive for me to be as brief as possible. Thank you all for coming over here this morning. I am sure that all of you are aware of who I am, and it is probably a fact that everyone has read my bio. By the way, I did not write my bibliography. I paid someone big bucks to make me look really good, so just take it with a grain of salt." Most of the faculty is in a good mood and everyone either laughs out loud or chuckles a bit. "I am sure that all of you can read very proficiently and I have taken advantage of this fact by providing everyone here with the details on the changes that will take place around here. I also have more information posted on my website. You will even see a typical day under the new program to begin January the first. I realize that some of you are already proficient in the use of DSVs, and I am sure that you guys look forward to using the new DSV. The new DSV will accommodate more passengers. This will help relieve the old schedule by us not having as many dives scheduled as your old sub demanded by default.

"I want every instructor to learn how to pilot the new submarine. Now I know that some of you will not hug my neck because of this new change. You didn't have to learn how to use the vehicle in the past. I promise you all that I will be very easy on everyone who has never been in charge of a dive. Before it is all said and done, everyone will be certified to pilot our new DSV. I will relieve some of you before you have a panic attack, that there will always be two certified instructors in charge of a dive. I will try to schedule the more experienced people with the less experienced people. The DSV we will be using is much more powerful and it has a lot of new computer equipment on board that will assist you. The sub can even abort a dive and get you back to our mother ship." Doctor Hardin raises his hand:

"I don't mean to be a trouble maker, but some of us are getting along in years. I must be honest with you that I must include all of us faculty that are on the same mindset that we are most comfortable with our current arrangement." David speaks:

"I can appreciate what you are voicing and I will try to make the new changes as painless as possible. Hopefully after next year is history, everyone will be comfortable with their new duties and schedules. I hope that I can demonstrate to all of you the value of more hands on research. Text books and computer programs are wonderful and I support them; however, it is most practical to have hands on experience with our trade. Students will be able to learn how to operate the DSV. They will be able to use this knowledge in securing future jobs." Doctor Hardin once again raises his hand:

"Doctor Smith, I am all in favor of the use of the DSV, but I feel that we would be the wiser to support our famous technical institutions we have in our region and allow them to train DSV pilots. Our university is more geared and oriented around academia. There are plenty of people who are better suited at taking film of marine life. These people are shown on television daily. They have the mindset of a Nineteenth Century explorer hacking himself or herself through the jungles making their livings off of sensational finds, discoveries, and encounters with the wild." David sifts through what Doctor Hardin is trying to say before he answers:

"I understand what you are saying. I can appreciate your thoughts, but I am afraid that the day of the great white hunter type is mostly over with or the individuals who explored and discovered new ocean life on their own. At one time, and especially in the Nineteenth Century, there was some separation or a line of demarcation between the halls of academia and the professional explorer. In the past it was customary for explorers to spend their energies on knocking something in the head or trapping their prizes in cages so that the explorer could bring creatures of interest to civilization and the halls of great scientific learning where their catches were sold to be examined, classified, and entered into our text books." Several instructors whisper into each other's ears. Doctor Fletcher the head of the science department speaks:

"Excuse me people, is there a problem or something that we need to bring out into the open?" Doctor Joyce Brown who is a supporter of David's new program speaks up:

"I for one am very excited about the new future schedules and opportunities that will challenge us. I am no spring chicken, but it would be great to be able to get out of the classrooms and personally explore a world that I have lectured about for decades. I have been on several deep dives, but most of them took place when I visited Woods Hole Oceanographic Institution off of Cape Cod, Massachusetts, years ago. I would not like to do it all of the time because I am better suited for the classroom environment, but I do have enough confidence in Doctor Smith here that he will not over burden us with too much work in the field to coin an ancient expression." Another instructor speaks:

"So I understand that there will always be two instructors in the submarine on a dive. I can live with that. I just would not feel confident to be alone and responsible for the lives of my students." Several more members of the faculty were in favor of the changes to take place. One of the instructors, who no doubt was under the influence of Doctor Hardin, actually gave his notice. He had been offered a job as head scientist at a large local private school. He did not trouble his fellows that the new job had been arranged by his now good buddy Doctor Hardin.

After the meeting was over with, David and almost everyone is on their way to offices, classrooms, or perhaps home. Doctor Fletcher, the chairman of the science department speaks to Doctor Hardin:

"Doctor Hardin, I realize that you are not overly satisfied with the new opportunities that will require our faculty to participate in a new environment, but I hope that you will not feel led to undermine my new assistance's position. We need to improve our offerings around here and I feel that Doctor Smith can provide the experience, knowledge, and the type of leadership we need for the future. He is smart, full of energy, and has a solid track record. Please try and give him a chance to prove himself worthy of your respect." Doctor Hardin speaks:

"Doctor Fletcher, I like you am not a spring chicken. I have seen a lot of people come and go around here. I will not undermine your new man's position. His bio makes him look like boy wonder. I just hope for all of us sake, especially yours, that you will not be left with an empty bag of tricks and dreams to haunt you. It is not a pleasant road to walk down to Doctor Julia DeVann Corbett's office suite when she is not pleased by a less than brilliant performance achieved by one of her lieutenants." Doctor Hardin pauses a brief moment before finishing his suggested warning to his superior. "Undermine your new man, no, I am like an oyster. I have the patience of Job. Time will reveal all, good day sir!"

Our story now takes a leap in time and place. Two days after David's meeting with the faculty at UNCW, David, his wife Brenda, and the two children are on the road headed to Boston. The children have not seen their other grandparents all summer and they are naturally very excited. This is the longest period of time that they have not shared their lives with their father's parents. The children are also eager to knock on the doors of their old friends. The ties of love and friendship associated with their early childhood friends is as strong as a good weld on heavy steel! The children can't wait until they share their new life with the children who grew up with them! These friends will be amazed at the new world the Smith children have found.

Two days later, the Smiths are back in their old neighborhood. The children are almost uncontrollable as the SUV they occupy rides past the homes of their friends! Some of the children are seen in their yards in front of their homes, sidewalks with skate boards, bicycles, and just walking together sharing some childhood adventure enjoying their growing up years together. By the time the big SUV parks in front of David's parents home, a small army of children surround the vehicle, excited that their dear friends are back home at last to share their new found world.

Brenda calls the house and her husband's parents step out onto the huge porch of their most impressive old three story mansion. They patiently wait and give the neighborhood children the opportunity to visit their grandchildren and to allow David and Brenda time to speak to the many familiar and excited young people. These were their children's first friends. Most of them have spent many hours in David and Brenda's former house sitting at their dining room table eating, or perhaps in a bedroom with their children playing a game together. Often David and Brenda would invite their children's friends along when they visited the many historical parks, museums, or even offering the children the chance to go fishing with them on board the Smith's sixty-five foot luxury motor boat.

Twenty minutes later, the neighborhood kids respectfully leave realizing that the grandparents of their friends are patiently waiting on the porch. The Smith children turn around facing their grandparents and immediately rush up the stairs onto the extensive porch into their grandparents loving arms. Many eyes are moist with tears of love! My how the children had grown; a sure indicator that they had been absence! When the children had been sufficiently loved, Brenda and David get their turn. David is somewhat embarrassed by the arms of his father who usually shakes his hand, but this moment was special! Mrs. Smith Senior hugs Brenda's neck and tells her that they have been away much too long! The Smith's have only one child, David, and only two grandchildren; therefore, the older couple had sorely missed their family!

Just as David and his wife Brenda and their children prepare to walk into the house, natural instincts and the presence of their old family home on the other side of the street directly across from David's parents house, compel, David, Brenda, and the children to turn around and look at their former home. Flashbacks of days gone by explode in the corridors of their mind, such as the day they first purchased the home from the Jeffersons. Fond memories of birthday parties when friends and family were invited to celebrate the happy occasion, or perhaps the film taken of their children's first steps, trips to a park, and the momentous occasion documented on film of a fishing trip on their big boat when their son caught his first fish. Mrs. Smith speaks:

"Come on in and let's eat. There is plenty of time later for us to help you guys get the luggage out of the SUV."

It was good to have everyone back at the dining room table! What a pleasure it was for Grandmother Smith to share her considerable culinary skills on a meal prepared in love for her family! Doctor Smith said grace, which was more than a custom at his home, but a choice rooted in his

Christian upbringing and faith. The children could not wait to be served and their parents were not far behind them!

On the table was a feast fit to suite mostly any palate. Huge hot moist dinner rolls piled high on a platter rested beside a small dish of soft butter. A platter of seasoned stuffed baked chicken was on the table that was so tender that it practically melted in hungry mouths. Seasoned baked red potatoes in a fancy dish with a glass cover rested beside a dish of hot moist herbal rice. There were other favorite vegetables on the table such as spinach casserole, and broccoli wedges covered with herbal seasoned cheese sauce. Piled high in a large fancy glass salad dish was one of the Smith family's favorite dishes, a Waldorf salad, which was created from such things as fresh cut up apples, broccoli, raisins, celery, chopped walnuts, and sweetened apple vinegar to name some key ingredients contained in the mix. For desert, Mrs. Patsy Smith prepared an over sized plum pie, cheese cake, and one of David's favorites, a German chocolate cake generously covered with pecans and red moist cherries. When the meal was completed, the Smith's were stuffed!

Two hours later, the luggage is inside of the house in the bedrooms. Brenda and David will sleep on the third floor in David's old childhood room. David can't wait until he has opportunity to go up to the widow's watch above the roof of the mansion to look through the huge telescope he used hundreds of nights when he lived with his parents when he was a child. David and Brenda look at the many interesting things in the room before they leave it and walk down stairs. On a very large heavy duty table is David's two hundred and fifty gallon fish tank. He is naturally compelled to look at his old familiar friends swimming around the inside of the tank looking at him. The fish are very excited and are in a bunch together obviously excited at seeing a human face, probably not because they recognize David, but because they want to be fed. David picks up some fish food in his hands and sprinkles it on top of the water just to watch the fish scramble for the food.

Brenda leaves the fish tank because she is interested in looking at David's impressive rock collection. His extensive collection of natural crystals, rare gems, and unusual rocks with ancient fossils embedded in them are worthy to be displayed in a science department at some college or perhaps even a small museum where fossils are regularly displayed to educate the public.

Directly, David walks over to one of the many large windows that line the bedroom. He just stands near it and stares across the street at his former home. It was more than just a house, but a home where families are reared and nurtured physically, mentally, and spiritually. Brenda eventually joins David as they both just looked and remembered those wonderful days they enjoyed their stay in the old mansion. David speaks:

"I miss my house over there! I have admired that old mansion all of my life. I watched the Jefferson kids grow up there and then go off to school and depart their separate ways." Brenda looks up at David and speaks:

"Billy and Debbie Jefferson were older than you, right?"

"Yes, they were older than me, but I still realized that they were just older kids. I have always admired Billy. He was a boy of great convictions and he once helped me get up off the road when I fell off of my bicycle. I was not very old, and I lost my balance and fell down and skinned my arm. See, there is the scar near my right wrist. He got me up and checked me to see if I was alright and he picked up my bike and walked me back to my parents' house. He rang the door bell and my mother realized that he was helping me. Mother cleaned the wound and put antibiotic spray on it that also helped relieve the pain. Daddy purchased Billy Jefferson a large book about famous missionaries in Africa long years ago like William Carey, James Chalmers, David Livingston and Adoniram Judson." Brenda speaks:

"Didn't you tell me that Billy Jefferson is now in Africa working full time as a missionary?"

"Yes, I did. I have often wondered if that book had any influence on Billy's decision to become a missionary."

The next day was Saturday. Doctor Daniel Smith, David's father, was not working in his private clinic and decided to spend all day Saturday enjoying his family. On Sunday, everyone went to the old Presbyterian Church that the Smith's have attended for nearly three hundred years. Naturally the church family was delighted to see the Smiths with their son, his wife, and the two children, Dan and Betty. The sermon the minister delivered was about the Prodigal son. David almost felt that the sermon had been preached just for his benefit. David even joked with the minister about his feelings. Doctor Dobson the senior pastor assured David that he had plans to deliver the sermon months before he learned from David's mother that David was scheduled for a visit.

Monday and Tuesday were devoted to fishing. David and his entire family went fishing in the ocean. David owns a small sixty-five foot yacht that was especially designed to accommodate the needs of a nice size group of humans devoted to the sport of catching fish. There were so many Atlantic Cod, Herring, and Halibut caught that David's parents filled up over half of the room available in the large chest freezer located in a side room in their spacious walk in pantry. Many photos and hours of film were taken of the kids as well as the adults proudly displaying their prize catches.

On Wednesday, David goes over to visit the science department at the University of Boston. Once again he feels goose bumps forming on his body as he enters the extensive main science building where he was captured in stone. He honestly felt that he was too young to have his likeness and work history in such glowing acclaim for all to see. When Ann Davis, David's old secretary, looked up from her desk and sees her old boss walking into her office, she could not help, but get up and give David a hug.

"Doctor Smith, it almost feels like old times around here again with you here! What a joy to have you back! Doctor Miller will be back in about ten minutes. How long have you been in our fair city of Boston?"

"We have been here since this past Friday. Since then, my family and my parents have attended church and Monday and Tuesday were spent on the ocean fishing. We caught tubs of fish and I have enjoyed them immensely! We took lots of pictures of all of us proudly displaying our fish. We even cooked fish on board my boat. My wife and mother prepared the meals for us." Mrs. Davis speaks:

"How is Brenda? I have not seen her since you all moved to North Carolina."

"Brenda has many wonderful friends in Boston that will always generate warm feelings in her heart when she thinks about them, but now, she is home. She is living very much like she lived before I met her. We all have had a most blessed time with Brenda's parents, grandparents, and all of the wonderful childhood friends who come by every week to share their time and lives with us."

"I understand that Brenda's parents own and operate a huge plantation."

"Yes, it is the most amazing place I have ever experienced! I would love to write a book about this most unusual place and the wonderful people who live and work there, but the Pridgens do not want to be exposed to the world at large. I do understand why. With all of the people hungry for sensational stories and prepared to challenge property rights now days, I don't blame them for keeping their lives as private as possible." Doctor Dennis Miller walks into the office and excitedly shakes David's hand. He was aware that David was dropping by. David was in his department to meet with the faculty. Several hours after sharing with the science department the changes of schedule and the new opportunities that would take place in January, David departs for home satisfied that everything was on track. Everyone was excited and looked forward to the new adventures awaiting them in the newly delivered underwater living lab once controlled by the University of North Carolina at Wilmington.

Thursday morning found David and his excited family in downtown Boston. The plans of the day were to walk the three mile long so named Freedom Trail. David wanted to impress on his children the importance of their native city, Boston, lest they forget. Freedom Trail is a physical testimony of our beginnings as a nation. Along its path are many of the important sites of historical interest to anyone wishing to learn why the Colonies broke away from Great Britain and joined into thirteen colonies to eventually develop into the United States of America. There along the trail, David's children learned about the Colonist protesting unlawful taxation without representation, the Boston Massacre, where British troops fired on civilians and the Old South Meeting House where angry colonist gathered before the famous Boston Tea Party.

For several weeks, the Smiths tour Boston. The children learned that the Puritans from England founded the city in 1630. It is considered the Cradle of Liberty because this is the city that set the fires of liberty in the hearts and minds of the Colonies, and where the Revolution was actually born. Many churches such as the Old North Church and homes such as Paul Revere's house were visited and one of David's favorite historical icons floating in Charleston Harbor; the *USS Constitution* or affectionately called *"Old Iron Sides"*. Naturally David had to board the ship and he walked around the entire vessel reminiscing about by gone days when he was a boy visiting the old ship and the familiar names and faces he grew fond of. People who were in charge of keeping the old ship in top notch condition ready to sail at a moment's notice by the admiral of the fleet to defend not so much our property from physical attack by an enemy fleet, but to defeat as a reminding symbol, the enemies of indifference, and neglect to our founding principles, those basic ideals and foundational beliefs that provide us with the bedrock of freedom and human enterprise we enjoy.

For three weeks the Smith's stayed in Boston. Much quality time was spent with David's parents. Often the family would go to the beautiful garden back of David's parents house and spend time under the beautiful gazebo. The children delighted themselves feeding the large goldfish in the beautiful heated pool. All earthly pleasures must come to an end, so the time ran out that provided David and his family the pleasure to visit his parents and the city of his nativity. Now they must turn their attention and direction of movement to the fair State of North Carolina where the mighty Pridgen Plantation geographically hugs the sleepy little village of

Atkinson. Everyone had mixed emotions about going back to Atkinson. No one wanted to leave Boston, but at the same time, they sorely missed the Plantation and their elders and Brenda's parents and grandparents, and Mattie, who was always so much fun to be around. David's parents promised to visit in about a week. Oh what a joy it will be to have the best of both worlds in one location, if only for a little season!

Two days pass and Brenda and her Boston family are driving on the main road through the plantation heading toward the mansion. Once again the Smiths drive onto the third bridge one needs to cross before reaching the mansion. It was Déjà vu all over again. This was the longest period of time the Smiths had been away from the plantation since they had first taken up residence in North Carolina. Six young black teenagers were on the bridge fishing. In fact, one boy was actually pulling a nice sized perch onto the bridge to take the hook out of its mouth. When they recognized the huge black SUV, they went crazy with excitement! This time; however, things were different than the first time the Smiths crossed the bridge for the first time. Brenda was not the only person to recognize the young people on the bridge. Familiar faces looked upon each other. It was such a joy to be home again! The boys proudly displayed a cooler that was half full of mostly perch and a couple of black fish. Roy Henry's youngest son John spoke:

"Miss Brenda, we have plenty of fish to share, why don't you get a mess of them and carry them back up to your house and fix them for supper?" Brenda speaks:

"I believe that I will take you up on your offer if you are sure that you guys have plenty for your parents and the rest of your families." John speaks again:

"Yes, Ma'am, we have thirty eight fish in this cooler. One cooler is already full and you can see that this one is nearly half full. Why don't you take this cooler and I can pick it up sometime tomorrow. We brought along three coolers and we should have this one full before we get ready to leave. Ma is probably going to scale and clean our fish as soon as I get back home with them." Brenda pauses and looks at all six of the young people before speaking:

"Well, then, if no one objects, I will take the half full cooler." David speaks:

"Honey, I will get out and get the fish." Moments later David received the large cooler from, John, Uncle Roy Henry's youngest son." David speaks:

"Fellows, I thank you all for the fish! I will see you guys later." Brenda calls her mother, but says nothing about the fish. Fifteen minutes later, Brenda's family parks inside the huge twelve vehicle garage. Brenda and David grab the cooler and walk to the kitchen where Mrs. Lillian Pridgen, Brenda's mother, has just arrived to cook and warm up something for supper. Brenda has already called her mother and informed her that she was going to the kitchen. The door opens and Brenda and David come walking in with a large heavy cooler half full of ice and fish. The children follow their parents from the porch through the foyer into the kitchen where their grandmother stands in anticipation of loving her daughter, Brenda, and the children.

The children naturally rush to their grandmother who grabs them both and gives them a big hug that only a good godly woman can do! Brenda and David put the cooler down and the eyes of her mother naturally take an inquisitive look at the cooler. Mrs. Lillian speaks:

"Brenda, what is in that big cooler?" Brenda opens the cooler up and reveals the many fish fresh out of a local creek. Mrs. Lillian speaks:

"Now don't tell me that you guys stopped at one of the creeks to catch supper before you came on up to the house?"

"No, Mother, John gave us the fish. He and the other boys have already filled one cooler to its capacity and they have plans to fish until the third cooler is full before going home." Lillian speaks:

"Well, I sure didn't expect you guys to bring in supper, but a nice fish meal will be just perfect! We will have slaw, carrot salad with raisings and pineapple and walnuts, cornbread fritters, and your grandmother's pound cake. I just might have some pecan ice cream in the freezer on the porch." The children are very pleased to learn about the cake and the homemade ice cream! Three hours later, the entire family, including Brenda's brothers, are gathered around the table. It was good to be back at the table together again! The children as well as Brenda and David missed the love David's parents had for them. They all looked with great anticipation for the day that David's parents from Boston will come down from up North for a nice long visit!

Nineteen

David's Parents Visit the Pridgen Plantation

Our story takes a leap in time to target and share the arrival of David's parents from the big City of Boston. Everyone was aware that the Smiths were pulling up into the yard driving their dark blue Mercedes Benz SUV. The moment Doctor Smith and his wife exit their impressive vehicle, they are surrounded by the electricity of excitement and joy! The children go ecstatic! If Brenda's parents and grandparents were made from ordinary clay, they would have probably felt the spirit of jealousy tugging at their heart cords, but these people who were rich and generous in heart had no room for envy. David speaks after he shakes his father's hand and hugs his mother's neck.

"Father, Mother, let me introduce you to Brenda's grandparents. This very fine figure of a Southern Planter and gentleman is Zeb Pridgen and this lovely lady is Lilly Pridgen, a true Southern Bell who can whip up a cure to fit mostly any ailment acquired by man or beast." After everyone exchanged words, the luggage is carried up the east steps of the mansion. Mrs. Patsy Smith, David's mother, speaks to Brenda's mother:

"Lillian, this place is more beautiful than I expected and I will assure you that I arrived here on location with high expectations based on the information provided by Brenda and David about this grand house! May I ask why the house was built so high off the ground?" Mr. Zeb, the patriarch of the Pridgen Clan over hears the question and volunteers to answer the question directed to his daughter-in-law, Lillian.

"Well, I am sure that the most practical explanation is to be above flood water. We call them freshets around here. Most of them are caused by hurricanes. We have had several feet of water in this yard after a bad storm even though the old mansion sits high on a bluff that is about fifty feet above the surface of the river at high tide. Back in the late Twentieth Century, we had several bad storms that really dumped a lot of water on our state. I remember Fran, Bertha, Floyd and even Hurricane Hazel in 1954. Now that was a super storm. Such a powerful storm taking advantage of a high tide like Hazel did would now days do billions of dollars in property damage and take scores of lives as populated as our beaches have become in the last forty years or so. Such events can also cause a lot of property damage and create a lot of inconvenience for folks near rivers and low lying areas such as are common up and down our coastal plain. I am sure that there are other reasons this house was built on twelve foot pylons made of cut stone and cement. Snakes will usually not climb steps to hide on porches this high. They have a tendency to go to lower levels like holes or crawl through doors that are near ground level. I was watching a program on television this past year that showed snakes crawling in people's houses because the houses were not off of the ground." Patsy Smith speaks:

"Mr. Zeb, where did they say that snakes were crawling into people's houses?"

"The program was centered on Cobras and other dangerous snakes crawling into people's houses in India. The snakes crawled inside the ground level homes and got into bed with these people who slept on the floor. I understand that the federal government there is trying to encourage its people to sleep in Western style beds that have legs." Doctor Smith's eyes open wider as he enters the huge entrance foyer on the East Wing of the mansion. Doctor Smith speaks:

"Now this place is practically a palace! I feel sure that you folks are mighty proud of this house. It is no doubt the crown jewel of the South! I thought that my old mansion once owned by my grandfather was large at twenty thousand square feet, but I believe that one floor of this house must be near thirty thousand square feet." Lillian Pridgen speaks:

"Yes, we are mighty privileged indeed to live in such a place! I understand that the inside of this three story mansion is exactly eighty-four thousand square feet. If the two porches were included in the tabulation, we could add an additional sixteen thousand square feet to the equation. I had not laid eyes on this place until I started courting Beard here. The first time I saw it, I thought that I had died and gone to Heaven!" Doctor Smith speaks:

"I am surprised that this place has not been featured in the national registry of our greatest historical homes, or a television program!" Zeb speaks:

"We try to keep the lid on top of the pot so to speak. We do not want to make the same mistake that King Hezekiah made when he shared his knowledge to the king of Babylon's emissaries about the gold and silver in the House of God in Jerusalem and the fabulous wealth in the palace." Doctor Smith speaks:

"I understand and I do see the great wisdom in your philosophy, sir!"

After the bags and suitcases are carried upstairs, the family goes out into the bottom porch facing the north. Mrs. Patsy Smith, David's mother, looks like she is in a trance because she is over whelmed by the magnificent two hundred acre yard surrounding the great house. She is compelled to speak:

"Oh, my, I can't believe this place! What a glorious yard you folks have here! I have never seen anything like it. How do you keep up these gardens of flowers, shrubs, and trees?" It must take an army of workers to maintain this place!" Mrs. Lilly, Brenda's grandmother, speaks:

"Not an army, but about thirty young men and women who do little more. It is a task that I believe even old Hercules himself would think twice about before he made a challenge that he could work it. Lillian and I spend about a third of our time working and seeing to it that everything is in order around here. We also have a huge green house with all kinds of experimental plants from all over the world. We have about thirty young men and women who help us keep that house up. Zeb here has an herb garden he maintains all by himself. I believe the secret of success is all about being organized and having the right tools to do the work with and a back that is not shy around old fashioned work and hands that don't mind being soiled by the good earth." David speaks to his father:

"How long are you and Mother going to stay with us, Father?"

"That all depends on the Pridgens. I didn't tell you, but I have retired. I still own the clinic and I will keep an eye on it for a number of years in the future until I have the notion to sell it to someone who has the same philosophy that I have about the value of a good clinic that puts people before the almighty dollar. There are, of course, people out there that have this belief system, but they are not financially able to take on such a task. Now, I will have the opportunity to spend a lot of time with my family and old friends. Life is simply too short to burn all of the candle wax up working. I want a good reserve to enjoy it for many years to come, the Good Lord willing." Beard Pridgen speaks:

"Well, I believe that it is a little too late to show off the place, but I was told by my wife Lillian and my mother to say that we need to wash up and get ready to eat." The Smiths look at each other and Doctor Smith speaks:

"Well, Patsy, I believe that you and me have been invited to a meal on a Southern Plantation, let's not slow things down!"

Fifteen minutes later our characters are sitting at the small dining room table which will seat twelve guests. The hot food smells wonderful and everyone is blessed with hungry. Mr. Zeb agrees to say grace, a practice that has been mostly turned over to Beard his son. The children are so excited because they now have both sides of their family present. The warm love generated by the family is a gift no doubt from Heaven itself! Everyone is encouraged to fill their plates. Mrs. Patsy Smith is especially delighted by the wonderful chicken she is eating and wanted to know the recipe. She speaks:

"This chicken is the most tender chicken I have ever eaten! It has such a flavor to it! I am going to have to ask for the recipe before we leave!" Lillian Pridgen smiles at Beard her husband who is sitting across the table from her. Lillian finally answers:

"Mrs. Patsy, I am afraid that you are not eating chicken. I will admit that it does taste somewhat like chicken. I have the opinion like you that it is very tender, and I do love the rich wild flavor. You are eating Black River snapping turtle. Uncle Preston, the general manager of the plantation brought over this nice snapper that he had in his holding pond for about a year. He catches them in the creeks and the river and cages them and feeds them good food." Doctor Smith's face turns a little red and he started laughing very low. Tears are coming down from his eyes and he wipes his face with a fancy white handkerchief. He speaks to his wife:

"Honey, you have eaten turtle soup in fancy Boston restaurants with me several times."

"That is true. I just was not expecting such exotic food." Mrs. Lilly Pridgen frowns a bit and speaks:

"I have been told that we eat a lot different than city folks, but I rather believe that we just have a larger variety of selections to choose from that are not commonly available at a city grocery store. Before anyone is embarrassed, let me take a few minutes to put names on the platters of food we are eating. Over in that large covered dish is coon hash. You folks probably call it raccoon. It is delicious and a common meat on our table. The large dish that Zeb is now taking meat from is not beef, but bear meat. It is delicious and very similar to beef. We do not allow bear hunting on the plantation, but a few of our neighbors do hunt them and don't mind sharing it with us. We also have deer stew mixed with potatoes, carrots, celery and onions. Our main leafy vegetable is collard. We love them and I could not imagine living without them. Try some. I read a piece in the paper years ago that said they have over twice the nutrition that spinach offers." Doctor Smith speaks:

"Well, I am pleased to be able to sit down and partake with you folks a wonderful meal prepared by such excellent cooks! Now, do you ladies ever prepare Opossum for your table?" Lillian speaks:

"No, not very often, no more than one or two have been prepared for our table since I married Beard. Now, I have eaten Opossum. If they are properly prepared, I see nothing wrong with the meat. It is a little greasy, but I have never heard of anyone getting sick on an Opossum meal. Many of our plantation folks do eat Opossum on a regular basis, but they do not just shoot one and cook it. Opossums will eat just about anything and it is best to cage them for two or three months so that they can be fed food that will not harm us humans. Now if you would like the opinion of an expert on Opossum I will advise you folks to consult your son, David. He just might be able to fill in where I have been a little weak on my description of the pros and cons of an Opossum main dish." Brenda and David smile and say something to each other. Brenda speaks:

"What Mrs. Pridgen is alluding to is a recent supper David and I were invited to at the home of James Henry." Doctor Smith speaks:

"You mean that the plantation people invite you Pridgens over for meals?" Zeb speaks:

"Usually not inside their homes, but at parties held outside their homes. James Henry is usually the man who invites his plantation friends over. This has been going on for over two hundred and fifty years around here." Doctor Smith speaks:

"Well, that was during the days of slavery. You mean to tell me that slaves invited their Pridgen masters over to their homes for a social?" Zeb speaks:

"We, I say, we, because that was way before my days on this Earth, have always treated our black people like human beings should be treated. Yes, we had slaves in those days before the war. Black folks were actually captured and sold to Dutch traders by powerful black tribes. Slavery has been officially declared dead by most of the so called Western Powers, but look at what is going on all over Africa and other parts of the world even as I speak. Our so called slaves are also our friends down to this day. Of course, we have no papers on anyone and no one is required or forced to live here. Few have left here. We live very much like a big extended family around here. We share our lives together and we have always seen to it that everyone is well looked out for. Every person on this plantation has good health insurance, a decent place to live, and land to use as they see fit. Everyone has fishing right, hunting rights, and the list goes on and on.

It has been a number of years since Lilly and I have been invited to one of James' parties, but I would go at the drop of a hat if invited! There food is as authentic and as Southern as it gets. I enjoy fellowshipping with the folks who share this big plantation with my family. We go over old times together and bring back memories of yesterday that bring tears to our eyes and laughter that cleans the soul and fills our hearts with joy and appreciation. Now talking about having a good time, just you get invited to one of James Henry's parties. They will entertain you with ghost stories that will be sure to make a believer out of you. Hard times and significant events such as weddings, catching your first fish, hunting tales, all kinds of peculiar events taking place and strange aliments the old folks had and how they remedied themselves by all kinds of cures is both amazing and funny." David smiles and nods his head before he speaks:

"I am sure that everyone knows that Brenda and I were invited over to Uncle James Henry's house. About fifty other people were also invited. The food was delicious. I did eat Opossum. I was compelled to eat it, I believe. It is as Mrs. Pridgen said earlier, a bit greasy, but otherwise not bad. They served a large pork shoulder that was barbequed. We ate all kinds of wild dishes like the ones we are enjoying now. We also ate what they call chit lings, C loaf, souse meat, hog head cheese and other dishes while we sipped rich full flavored wines.

"Some of the tales or stories we heard have been passed down for generations. Even some old African Wise Tales were shared with us. I am of the opinion that these stories need to be recorded and published. Brenda and I also listened to thrilling accounts of bear hunts, so called coon hunts, and stories about wild cats or black panthers screaming out like women. These cats used to attack live stock centuries ago around here, I understand. The folks at Uncle James' place told us about the Indians that once lived around here and their superstitions such as the belief that humans can turn into animals. We listened with great interest about a young fellow who fell into a freshly dug grave after he was trying to make his way back home one night after work. We also heard the ghost story about Miss Cary Lamb appearing at her old house when James Henry's grandfather plowed up some of her favorite shrubbery."

When David stopped talking, Mr. Zeb turned toward Doctor Smith and his wife Patsy and spoke:

"Tell me about Boston. I believe it would be too much of a culture shock for an old man like me reared up to such a life as I have come accustomed to, but I do read and enjoy learning about other countries and how folks live in other parts of our fair land." That night at the supper table, David's parents told Mr. Zeb and his wife Lilly about Boston and their way of life. After the meal was over with and the cleanup work was history, everyone goes to the huge north porch. The sun was set and the temperature was around eighty degrees Fahrenheit. A nice breeze was blowing to provide clean fresh air, and to stir up the fragrances of the multitudes of flowering plants that surrounded the mansion. It no doubt smelled very much like the Garden of Eden itself!

In the distance, the sound of tens of thousands of frogs of different species filled the night air. It almost sounded like a huge frog choir out near the fishpond with the high pitched voices of the smaller varieties of frogs backed up by the deep calls of the large male bull frogs. Bats by the scores constantly flew above the yard with great speed and agility snatching mostly Lunar Moths and other big juicy insects out of the sky. The Smiths were amazed at the hundreds of fireflies blinking their tiny amber colored lights off and on. Dan, the ten year old son of David and Brenda, runs down the twelve foot high north steps to go out into the yard to capture a firefly to show it to his Boston grandparents. A huge Owl flies past the mansion and grabs up a large rat that had been running around the yard with its deadly talons. The full Moon starts climbing in the sky adding mystery to this place of enchanting beauty and suggestions of secret unexplored trails once walked only by the red man, the aborigines of this last remaining island of untamed wilderness.

David's parents are relaxing on a large porch chair together that is constructed from Wicker. The bottom of the chair has been padded with a very thick multilayered cushion. Their faces look like the faces of people who are on a much needed rest such as a long waited for Caribbean cruise, or other exotic vacation spots sought by the weary traveler. The night sounds and the soft cool breeze is just perfect to keep one at a most relaxed state of body and mind and has subdued any notion of our subjects to move any unnecessary muscle or entertain an unpleasant thought about tomorrow. They almost felt like children in the warm tender bosom of a loving and protective grandparent singing them to sleep by sharing old favorite bedtime lullabies like *Rock a Bye Baby in the Tree Tops*, or perhaps the tune of *Edelweiss* sung to a sleepy little one to sooth the spirit and too gently close his or her eyes for a nice long sleep in a soft bed. Mr. Zeb Pridgen speaks:

"Doctor Smith." David's father spoke back.

"Mr. Zeb, just call me Daniel. I am giving up my practice in Boston. I told David that I would like to keep the clinic and see to it that it serves the community that I built it for nearly forty years ago. I am not so old, but old to young people. I will be sixty nine years old in a few months. I have always been of the opinion like my father and his father before him that a man needs to have something to live for. I am satisfied that I have fulfilled that phase of my life's duty. I want to devote the rest of it to my wife, family, and many friends while I am blessed to enjoy theirs."

"I see nothing disagreeable about your plans. I turned over the operation of the Plantation to Beard when I became sixty-two. Now don't get me wrong, I stay plenty busy. I devote my time to taking care of the herb garden, reading good books, and collecting things I store over in our barn we call our museum." Doctor Daniel Smith speaks:

"I have a small museum in my clinic. It is a collection of several hundred old medicine bottles, tools and machines of my trade. I have it all in chronological order so that people visiting can see the advancements made for their benefit." Zeb speaks:

"I know that you are a board certified doctor, but what field have you specialized in?"

"I went off to medical school and became a general practitioner. I felt that I could provide more service than focusing on only one problem or only a limited area of the human body. A few years later, I went back to school and became an emergency room specialist. I can now do a little of it all including surgery if necessary. I do not transplant organs, or attempt to reconstruct a disfigured face or perhaps brain or spinal surgery, but I have been able to put my knowledge to practical use throughout my nearly forty years of practice. I now have eighteen doctors who work at the clinic for me and scores of nurses and medical secretaries. My work continues through them."

"Daniel, if you have no other plans for tomorrow, why don't you spend the day with me. I will show you the herb garden and fix up a cup or two of nice herbal tea for you and show you what we do to our herbs. After that, we can spend time just walking around the outside of this great big house looking at the many interesting things we have here."

"I would be honored and privileged to have the patriarch of the Pridgens to show off his place to me! I would love to!" Mrs. Lillian speaks to Mrs. Patsy Smith:

"Patsy, if you have no plans already finalized for tomorrow, I would love to take you around for an introduction to my life around here. We have hundreds of gardens of all different kinds. The size of our gardens and the many varieties of flowering plants, shrubs, and trees, have multiplied down through the centuries. We try to maintain what is here. Occasionally we add our touch by planting something different that we believe is special. Our greenhouse is a biotical wonder that is actually a miniature tropical jungle. We have all kinds of experimental plant varieties and the so called more common varieties are much larger and healthier than normally seen in nature. We have Venus Fly Traps that are large enough to catch a large wood boring bee. We have Pitcher Plants that are four feet tall, Sundews, Cobra Lily's Butterwort and newly discovered plants that look like something from a science fiction movie." Mrs. Smith speaks:

"Lillian, I would be delighted above measure to see and learn about all of these wonderful plants! I understand that you and Lilly make your own medicine around here."

"Yes, ma'am, it is a trade that has been passed down throughout the centuries around here. I knew more than the average person knows about herbs and how to use them for most common ailments before I married Beard, but my mother-in-law is privy to generations of this knowledge. It was all written down by hand and more recently entered into our medical journals. We have collected scores of the best books of herbal remedies and have old medicine books that go back for centuries in what we call our medical library in our main library."

Now our story goes back to touch bases with Brenda and her Boston family who are planning a day at Wrightsville Beach. David speaks:

"Brenda, I talked to my mother and she told me that we are free to go to the beach and stay as long as we wish. We have promised our children all summer and it is now September." Brenda speaks:

"David, your parents have just arrived. I would feel bad if we leave tomorrow without them!"

"Don't worry about it. Father told me earlier that he has retired and will be able to spend a lot of time with us. The kids have not seen the beach and I don't believe that this is right!" Brenda speaks:

"OK, you are right. How long are your parents going to remain in North Carolina?"

"I would imagine a month. Of course, all of the time will not be spent on the Plantation. I understand from mother that they want to spend a week at the beach to enjoy the water and do some sightseeing on their own."

The next morning at six o'clock, everyone is up and sitting around the table. The electricity of excitement and anticipation is almost beyond belief! The children have been told that their grandparents from Boston will be on the plantation when they are finished with their beach adventure. It is simply too much to be true! Mrs. Lilly and Lillian are prepared to give David's mother a tour of their vegetable garden and the huge green house that is full of exotic plants. Mr. Zeb will carry David's father to his herb garden and will top off the day by showing off the great barn the original living quarters of the Pridgens and the Lafayettes, Captain John Henry Pridgen's in-laws. Mattie is away visiting her family in Berry Hill, N. C. about fifteen miles from the plantation. Mrs. Lillian Pridgen always worries about these visits even though they are not frequent. Mattie's father is long gone, but Mattie is still taken advantage of by her nephews who have apparently inherited bad blood through their no count grandfather. Mattie is due back in a week.

Everyone is packed and ready to go, and Doctor David Smith, his wife Brenda, and the two children, Dan, and Betty climb into the big SUV. Little Betty reaches into a pocket in the seat in front of her and pulls out a brochure about the new Henrietta 1V, a two hundred and fifty foot riverboat docked on the Cape Fear River at Wilmington. She is unable to read all of the information about the big boat, but she is smart enough to recognize that a trip on it down the Cape Fear or Black River would be something worth remembering! Betty had heard her parents mention something about the big boat when they saw it going by past the mansion. While the kids were looking at the river boat, David their father is looking at a multi page pamphlet featuring the battleship the USS North Carolina. David speaks:

"Honey, we need to carry the children to the battleship. I am sure that we could spend three or four hours walking around the big ship!" Brenda smiles and replies:

"David, or you sure, that the kids would like to go and see that big ship?" Betty is still a small girl. I am not sure she would be able to climb up and down all of those steep steel stairs safely?" David speaks:

"That is true; I guess that we will have to wait several years before we can visit the ship." Brenda speaks:

"David, I will look after our little girl, if you and Dan would like to visit the big ship. If our daughter wants to visit the ship, I could assist her. I am sure that there are many places on the ship and the visitor's center to explore." David speaks:

"Brenda, have you read the brochure on Orton Plantation?"

"No, but I have been there about three times. I understand that it was a rice plantation. The original house is still there. I understand that the house is not on the tour, but is actually a private residence. The first time I went there was when I was in the fourth grade. Later, I went there with a bunch of my old school buddies when I was in the last year of high school. The last time I went there was when I was in college. We went as a class on a big bus. I am sure that we as a family would enjoy a trip to that beautiful place one day! There are lots of places around our several counties I would like for us to visit. I don't understand the mentality of some of our older local folks that take these places so lightly." David speaks:

"What you are saying is that they seldom visit." Brenda speaks:

"Something like that. I am thankful that my family has always taken an interest in our history. I have read about the history of the city of Wilmington many times, and I have learned something new every time I took the notion to read once again. The city was visited by George Washington himself. Ronald Reagan the fortieth President of the United States was the host for the 1959 Azalea Festival." David speaks:

"I am sure that Reagan was not President when he hosted the festival." Brenda speaks:

"Yes, you are right, he was involved in radio, acting, and I believe a spokesperson for General Electric. Honey, why don't we remain in the area for four or five days and take out time to enjoy some of the historical sites? I don't believe a rush job is the way to go about it, especially for the children. They need time to seriously reflect on each place we visit so that they will have real meaning in their lives."

In the main time, while Brenda and her Boston reared family read tour guides out loud to each other and are making plans to visit as many places as possible, including walking tours, horse drawn carriage, and trolley tours, Mrs. Lilly Pridgen and Lillian are walking down the north side of the huge mansion to the late summer garden which is about five hundred feet from the house. Lillian and her mother-in-law Mrs. Lilly continue to walk down the brick path with Mrs. Patsy Smith, David's mother. She is completely over whelmed at the stunning varieties of trees, shrubs, and literally millions of flowers in the two hundred acres yard. Up ahead she sees a large stone enclosure that surrounds about five acres of exceptionally rich soil. The wall is about six feet high and is capped on top with beautiful long stones that are joined so close together that the human eye can barely detect that the top of the stonewall is made from thousand of individual capstones. There is a large double gate made out of black iron. The gate was not just a simple gate, but a work of art on a grand scale. It is a tapestry of fine craftsmanship designed to delight the mind and soothe the spirit. Hundreds of beautiful flowers made of iron were skillfully and cunningly inlaid into the gate to strengthen it and to add much beauty to the effort. Patsy Smith speaks:

"This heavy gate is magnificent! Where did you purchase it?" Lilly speaks:

"No, it was actually designed and fashioned right here on the plantation by French Black Smiths. I am sure that they were handsomely compensated for the labor because the gentlemen normally worked for the parents of Captain John Henry's wife." Patsy speaks:

"Now, I believe that John Henry Pridgen was the original owner of this plantation." Lillian speaks:

"Yes, ma'am, we have statues of these people near a huge barn that is about five hundred feet from the house. One day Lilly or I will take you to the building. We call it our family's museum. You will not believe what you will see over there!" Patsy speaks:

"I look forward to seeing that place! I can't get over this wonderful place you folks live on! You have been blessed beyond measure!"

Zeb Pridgen, patriarch of the Pridgen Clan has showed his herb garden to Doctor Smith Senior. Doctor Smith was surprisingly familiar with the herbs Zeb grew for medicine and tonics. After trying some special blends of herbal teas, Zeb and Doctor Smith, David's father, decide to tour the grounds around the mansion. There was something interesting everywhere they went. The plantation was a living breathing fossil.

"Zeb, these are the most impressive magnolia trees that I have ever seen. They are so enormous and I can't believe the size of the leaves! How old are these trees?" Zeb answers:

"I was told by my grandfather that they are about two hundred and fifty years old. Now the huge live oak trees that are farther out from the house were here centuries before the house was built. Other than the trees my brother owns at his house, these trees you are looking at are probably the oldest and largest live oak trees in North America and possibly the world; I don't know for sure. Now you asked me yesterday about the gas lightning system in various places in the house and in the other main buildings around here. Here is one of the several generators we have around here that produces Carbide Gas. We could use diesel generators I suppose, but we are rather old fashioned around here, as you, I am sure realize. Just because something is old does not render it useless or inferior to so called modern devices." Doctor Smith speaks:

"Yes, I must concur with you. I like you still rely on the past. I have prescribed simple remedies such as warm salt water for a sore throat or a mustard and onion poultice for a really bad chest cold or perhaps a good bowel cleaning laxative to cure an ailment." Zeb speaks:

"This little building we are looking at houses one of our Carbide Generators. As you can plainly see, this generator was manufactured by the J.B. Colt Company. The generator is a two hundred pound capacity generator." Doctor Smith speaks:

"Where did this old generator come from?"

"I was told that this one came from Chattanooga, Tennessee. Look over here on the wall of the house and you will see the original instructions that came along with the generator." Doctor Smith speaks:

"So this is a Colt Model S Pit Generator! How old is this generator Mr. Zeb?"

"It is about one hundred and sixteen years old. My great-great grandfather purchased the gas producer and it works as well now as the day it was purchased. We keep all of our generators out of the weather and make sure we keep the outside clean and painted with good stove pipe paint." Doctor Smith reads part of the instructions out loud.

1. Never recharge except by daylight. Keep all artificial lights or fire away from generator.
2. Never recharge with carbide until the generator has been pumped out and refilled with clean water.
3. If water in any chamber should freeze, do not attempt to thaw it with anything but hot water.
4. Never pump out the sludge and water from the generator chamber L, until you have first removed the gas bell B, and the Carbide hopper V.
5. Lubricate vent plug O of well...

"I should not be reading all this out loud, I am sure that you have read it many times." Zeb speaks:

"Yes, I have read it a thousand of times. In fact, I read it every time I recharge the generator, because gas is dangerous if you break a rule. I once came close to walking into one of our generator houses to clean and recharge one of our generators and had a lit cigar in my mouth. I realized the careless mistake and got rid of the cigar. No artificial light including an open flame to a flashlight can be brought in here while recharging a generator. Now some of those chemical lights that you shake a few times are probably safe. We use these old generators as a sort of backup system. We do use them in a limited basis just to keep the generators and the pipes and the gas lanterns and stoves in good order." Doctor Daniel Smith looks all around amazed at the many interesting and ancient machines such as the windmills to pump up freshwater out of the ground, portable steam powered saw mills, old tractors, corn harvesters, and planters. Zeb speaks:

"Come on over here let me show you our soap house." Doctor Smith speaks:

"What is a soap house?"

"Oh, just a place we make our own soap." Zeb opens the door to the fancy little red bricked building and both men walk inside."

"This place smells wonderful! So you folks make your own soap in here. I did not realize anyone made their own soap now days!"

"Yes, we have been making it for centuries around here. Many of the soaps we make are hard to find on the market. We have soap for washing dishes, cloths, regular hand soap, and soap made for extra greasy hands and ground in dirt. We use all kinds of oils, roots, flowers, and minerals to make our soap. These large labeled jars on the shelves here contain many of the things we add to our soap, like coconut oil, palm oil, sweet orange, peach, mint, honey almond, Sweet Betsey, which is a flower that comes from a shrub, and the list goes on and on as you see. For hand soap we add powder from crushed volcanic lava, or mica. For antiseptic soap, we use such things as pine oil, camphor, and things like palm oil, aloe Vera, milk weed, papaya, and so on. Now, I usually use plain soap for my hands or as a body wash, but the ladies love soap to make them smell good and to make their skin baby soft. I use some of these skin softening soaps in cold dry weather. We even add vitamins like oil of vitamin E to some of these body soaps." Mr. Zeb grabs a cloth bag and hands it to Doctor Smith. "Get what you want and put the soap in this bag. We have little fancy cords to tie the bags up with." Doctor Smith placed about fifteen different kinds of soap into the bag before he tied the bag with a square knot. Doctor Smith speaks:

"Mr. Zeb, these huge oak trees around here are a natural wonder! I have never seen trees this big around except for the giant sequoia trees in our Pacific North West, such as the General Grant Tree or the General Sherman Tree. Of course, these trees are not near as tall, but I could spend days just looking at these magnificent giants!" Zeb speaks:

"Daniel, as you can see, we have windmills all over the plantation. Some of them were ordered by us from old Farm Bureau Magazines over a hundred years ago. Still other windmills were originally installed by Captain John Henry Pridgen himself a long time ago. Of course, each generation of Pridgens have maintained and replaced worn out parts. We have even paired these windmills so that one is responsible for pumping out the ground water where the water is directed into a large ground level holding tank. The water is next pumped from the holding tank to a water tank that is over a hundred feet above the ground. This is how we supply our house and other areas around here with fresh running water." Doctor Smith speaks:

"In other words, the water is pumped above the house and it runs down pulled by gravity when a faucet is opened up."

"Yes, sir, really nothing very complicated. Daniel let's go to our museum. We will go to the front and I will show you the statues of the first owner and his father-and-mother-in-law." Doctor Smith speaks:

"Were these folks from around here?"

"No, sir, they were originally from France. When my ninth grandfather married, he convinced his wife's parents to join him on his huge tract of land he had just recently acquired. They agreed and his first residence on this piece of land was actually in what we call our family's museum. We will pause at the statues and from there go to the back of the building where we have stored and collected things for centuries."

Our story now takes us back to the huge vegetable garden that is surrounded by a heavy stonewall to help protect the vegetables from animals. Mrs. Patsy Smith speaks:

"This is the most beautiful and most organized vegetable garden I have ever been privileged to see! What a sight this place is! What kind of fertilizer do you folks use on these plants?" Mrs. Lillian speaks:

"We use all natural compost. My father-in-law makes tons of it every month in twenty four large drums that can be turned by electrical motors. I do believe the natural animal compost plus the green compost we use makes all of the difference in the quality and the taste of our vegetables. In fact, even the color of the corn and some of the other vegetables like potatoes is not the same as store bought vegetables fertilized with manmade chemical fertilizers. I guarantee you that no manmade chemical fertilizers can create the wonderful taste our crops have, or the vitamin and natural mineral content." Mrs. Patsy speaks:

"I have never seen so many varieties of tomato plants. They are actually beautiful! I believe that I recognize some of them like the rows of Better Boys and Girls. I do realize that those over there are a variety of tree tomato. They must be around nine feet tall. This garden, I believe, would challenge even the first garden mankind was placed in!" Mrs. Lilly speaks:

"We probably don't have all of the various kinds of vegetables in that first garden, but I would wager that we would come in second or third place with any garden. We are, of course, only growing about five acres of vegetables, not hundreds or even thousands of acres, but we delight ourselves by selling many a pickup truck load of fresh sweet corn, squash, tomatoes, watermelons, cantaloupe, cabbage, and sweet potato. Now we do not tend all of the food crops for human consumption around here. We have a huge pecan farm of hundreds of acres of trees. We grow large truck loads of strawberries. The other crops are what we call our field crops such as corn for animals, soybeans, cotton, and peanuts." Mrs. Smith speaks:

"I heard about that cotton. How many acres do you grow around here?" Mrs. Lilly speaks:

"We grow about two thousand acres of the stuff. When it matures, and produces cotton balls, the field is a sight to behold! We have been pressured to produce more. My husband Zeb told Beard that it was up to him if he wanted to increase the acreage. We would have to hire outside help or give up something else or cut back on other money makers. I don't believe that even cotton can compete with the money we make on the cabins. I say this with humility, and a thankful spirit, that we do not need the money. We live on a very small portion of our cash income because we eat off of the fat of the land, and I must say it suits me just fine thank you!" Mrs. Patsy speaks:

"Well, I must say also with a thankful heart that Daniel and I could have lived a life of no work and all play, but I couldn't imagine such a existence! We have always believed that people need to work, not just for the cash, but the anchor hard honest work offers. Work if properly understood and embraced is one of the greatest blessings a human being can have. Honest work is one of the bedrocks of human existence." Mrs. Lilly is somewhat surprised by Patsy Smith's strong conviction about the duty people have to share their time and skills with their fellow creatures. Mrs. Lillian walks into a beautiful little stone garden house and comes out with six large baskets made out of white oak strips. Each basket has a hoop handle to carry it with. Mrs. Lillian speaks:

"Mrs. Patsy, would you like to help us girls gather a few vegetables for the table?"

"I would be delighted! Just tell me what and how many."

"OK, if you don't mind; we need about twenty nice big tomatoes for the table. Those Better Boys will do just find. We need about twenty or thirty tender squash, and a quarter of a basket full of nice tender okra. Now here is a vegetable knife to assist you. While you are working on your project, Lilly and I are going over to the pole beans and the speckled butter beans. We will cook them together after we shell them on the east porch." An hour later, all of the beans and other vegetables have been harvested and Lilly, Lillian, and Mrs. Patsy Smith are sitting in work chairs on the east porch shelling the beans and working up a wonderful appetite! Brenda and her family will be gone for about a week, but there were still six mouths to feed.

Mr. Zeb and Doctor Daniel Smith continue to walk toward the enormous barn that was also the living quarters of Captain John Henry Pridgen and his lovely wife Madam de Lafayette Pridgen and her parents the Lafayettes. The first thing that Doctor Smith focused on was the two enormous platforms in front of the French side of the so called barn. Each platform is actually several huge slabs of polished granite over twenty-five feet high. One platform included the life like statues of Captain John Henry Pridgen, the original owner of the plantation, and his beautiful wife

Madam de Lafayette Pridgen. Each platform is surrounded by a black iron fence with an entrance gate. People can walk up the platforms via steps carved into the stone. A stone table and chairs are included in the scene so that people can walk up and sit at a table and relax. The life like statues of both the Pridgens and the Lafayette's are standing back of the tables. Farther back of the table and sitting area of the Pridgen monument are the likeness of several of the huge live oak trees. Still farther back is the carving of the mega mansion that Captain Pridgen and his wife once occupied. The Lafayette platform was very similar except that the huge house was not a Southern Mansion, but a French Château. The very one that David Smith and his lovely wife Brenda had visited some weeks ago where they had a most unusual experience! Doctor Smith is stunned. He holds out his hands over his head and in front of him.

"Mr. Zeb, this is truly one of the grandest works of art I have ever seen! I have been overseas to France, Rome, London, and you name it. These lifelike statues of your folks and the magnificent detailed carvings of the mansions in stone, with trees included in these carved scenes is truly a treasure! I must say that you do look similar to your ancestors; except, of course, they were much younger at the time these carvings were cut out of stone." Mr. Zeb laughs and speaks:

"I do believe that I am dressed somewhat differently than my ninth great grandfather." Doctor Smith looks at Zeb and nods his head with a smile on his face and gives Mr. Zeb a head to toe glance.

"Yes, sir, I do agree with you about the difference in your grandfather's attire. He is dressed better than a modern king or president now days. The cloth is probably too heavy for our taste and temperament today, but a suit worthy of a man of enormous wealth and refinement back in his day, I am sure." Mr. Zeb speaks:

"Daniel, let's not go through the front of the building today. There is not much in there to see anyway. The furniture was taken over to the chateau centuries ago. I suggest that we walk back of the building where my people stored their wagons, passenger coaches, old cars, tractors, and a multitude of all kinds of interesting things. I keep my collection of anything from old newspaper clippings, machinery, books, and documents of historical significance in the barn." Doctor Daniel Smith speaks:

"Oh, my, now this is a large place! What are its dimensions?"

"It is over three hundred feet long and over a hundred and fifty feet wide. You saw the front of the building, that it is French. That part is, of course, the French quarters. I made no comment earlier about it because I figured that you would realize that."

"Yes, sir, I realize that the architectural design is French. A very beautiful face on the front of this nice structure, I might add. I am sure that even the French of our day would like to own such a beautiful building to show off to their many tourists." Zeb speaks:

"Yes, sir, I understand that it represents the front of a great house in Paris, France about three hundred years ago." Zeb and Doctor Smith walk to the back porch. From the porch, Zeb pulls open a huge door and our gentlemen walk into the so called museum. Doctor Smith speaks:

"Oh, my, what a sight to behold, no wonder your family calls this place their family museum! Doctor Smith walks up to a 1950 model Ford four door sedan and hits the driver's door with his closed hand to test the metal. "This car is all steel; they sure don't make cars like this these days! What a beautiful old car! The paint is such a rich dark blue. I believe that this old car is now about eighty years old. Do you mind if I get into it?"

"No, go ahead and knock yourself out! I was about six years old when this old car was purchased. I had it restored to mint condition about thirty years ago. It runs as good now as it did the day it was sold." Mr. Zeb speaks once again after Doctor Smith sits in the driver's seat of the old Ford for about ten minutes. "Come on, I have many more things to show you, Daniel." Doctor Smith speaks:

"I don't believe that I am familiar with this Make of station wagon or whatever it is, Mr. Zeb." Mr. Zeb speaks:

"This, sir, is a Willys Station Wagon. Zeb pops the hood to allow Daniel, Doctor Smith, to look at the engine. "This engine has 7 4-1 compression. It is a four cylinder F head engine with valve in head intake and valve in block exhaust. I come out here about every two weeks and open all of the doors and start the vehicles you see in here just to keep them in good working order. Now the truck back of you was one of my father's favorites, a 1950 Model F1 Stake. It has a hardwood platform or back bed that is steel framed. The engine is a V8. We used several of these trucks when I was a boy to do a lot of utility work around here such as working the orchards and hauling equipment around the plantation like small or medium engines, tractor parts, or whatever needed hauling that a horse and wagon would be impractical." Doctor Smith speaks:

"I am very impressed by these rugged small trucks. They built them to last back in 1950." The next truck inspected was a 1950 one half ton Studebaker. Zeb speaks:

"As you can see the next section of old antiques are old tractors. Most of these you see here were used on the plantation. My father and grandfathers before him loved to collect them as I do." Doctor Smith speaks:

"I was under the impression that you folks did not use tractors."

"We have used tractors for several generations around here, but we still depend on our big horses to plow the fields around here. Tractors have their place when you are in a hurry and when you need their power take off systems to run machinery with. Now this is a Ferguson Tractor on the wall here. This is an old advertisement taken from an old Farm and Ranch Magazine. I found it in my father's papers and have framed it behind glass. It is a good medium size tractor that has a lot of modern conveniences built into it." Doctor Smith speaks:

"Yes, sir, I am not very expert on farm tractors, but I see what you are referring to." Doctor Smith reads the old advertisement out loud.

1. Built in Hydraulic System
2. Automatic Implement Protection
3. Finger Tip Implement Control
4. Automatic Steering Alignment

"Now I really like the looks of these three tractors, Mr. Zeb!"

"Thank you. I am very proud of my three Farmalls. This little tractor is called the Farmall Club. I have been told that it can do the work of a team of regular size horses. I do not use it because it is so rare now days. The larger tractor next to it is a Farmall H. It is a two plow tractor. The next tractor is a three plow tractor. We had one years ago that had steel wheels. We used it to pull heavy logs out of the woods." Doctor Smith speaks:

"I don't believe that I have ever seen such a strange looking farm tractor! I see that it is a rear engine model G Allis Chambers. Now why would you purchase this strange tractor?" Zeb speaks:

"I didn't, my great grandfather purchased it about eighty years ago. It was mainly designed for such jobs as moving or planting seed. It is cheap to operate and was used to do jobs that would normally tie up much larger tractors. I have all of the attachments that were originally purchased for the tractor like planters and grass mowers. Who knows, our horses could all come down with a disease and we might have to use tractors around here." Doctor Smith speaks:

"I have a feeling that most of these tractors will never be used again."

"Yes, sir, I would not want to work these old tractors. Not that they couldn't do work, I just feel that they serve us better as part of our history." Doctor Smith continues to look around and to admire the old tractors and is compelled to speak.

"Now these are very old tractors! No rubber tires on these machines I see! The McCormick Deering Tractor, what a nice old farm tractor! Does it still run?" Zeb speaks:

"It is not running like I would like it to. I am going to see if I can ask a fine gentleman who lives on the plantation to have a good look at it. It is a little slow, but is heavy and could do a lot of work. This is a 15-30. It is equipped with a power take off. As you can see, it has a drawbar, and a belt pulley. It was actually ahead of its time. This tractor beside the old McCormick-Deering Tractor is an old EB Tractor. It runs on kerosene. I found this old tractor at an antique tractor show about twenty years ago in Raleigh, North Carolina."

"Mr. Zeb, what kind of horse power does it have?"

"It has twelve horsepower at the drawbar and about twenty at the belt. The tractor is a little slow, but was useful in its day." Doctor Smith Senior speaks:

"Now these old machines look like machines from the Middle Ages. I have never seen such old farm tractors before! I would imagine that many a museum would like these old tractors!"

"Yes, sir, these old tractors are some of the first tractors ever used around these parts. My great grandfather purchased these old machines. This first one is a 1928 Advance Ramely Oil Pull Model W201 30. It has about thirty six horse power. It uses oil not water to keep the engine cool. The next old mechanical beast as you can plainly see is an Allis Chalmers Model U. This is the very first American tractor sold on the regular market equipped with pneumatic rubber tires. As you can see, the tractor is very ruggedly built and still can do an honest day's work."

"If they built tractors like this now days in America, the average farmer would not have to purchase, but one or two tractors in a lifetime!" Mr. Zeb speaks:

"Yes, sir, there is no thin metal on this old iron workhorse. Everything is extra heavy and was built without all of the fancy gadgets on tractors now days that require a lot of tending to. Now, sir, this huge old iron monster is a 1913 Case Steamer. It is slow, but could pull like two full grown bull elephants."

"Why did your people buy such a monster, Mr. Zeb? What good is the thing? It looks very much like a small steam locomotive to me." Zeb speaks:

"Yes, it does at that. It runs the same; it is only outfitted with a different set of wheels that allows it to be used on the ground as opposed to a rail system. I understand from my folks long years ago that they used it to pull huge logs out of the woods and any job that required enormous power. It has a boiler just like any steam engine and I believe can run on wood or coal. I have never used it. There is not a thing wrong with it. It has been in this building for about seventy or eighty years. I may see what it can do one of these days just to make sure that it is in running order. It is much more valuable if it is in good running order." Doctor Smith speaks:

"What kind of horsepower does it have?"

"It only has about a hundred and ten horses, but with the eighteen tones of weight and the way this old mechanical wonder is geared down, that is a lot of pulling power! Now it is not as powerful as a heavy tracked tractor construction companies use for pushing rock, but it would give mostly anything moving or pulling a run for its money to coin an old saying. Daniel, let's go back to the car collection. I want to show off some more of my collection. I really did not purchase any of these old vehicles. My people have been storing cars, trucks, and you name it in this great big building for several centuries. I just happen to be the current owner; that is my wife and I. When we pass from this life into the next, my son Beard and his wife will take over where I left off. Now, sir, this is a 1908 Model T. It has a four cylinder in line cast iron block and cylinder head. In other words it has two valves per cylinder. It is very powerful and at twenty horses was the terror of the roads for a season on the great American freeway. Of course, back in the day this old gal was rolled off the production line there were few hard surfaced roads in this fair country of ours. It does have an advantage over most modern road vehicles in that it can go through mud like a charm. Most regular modern cars would never make it through the muck and mud this old gal faced on a regular basic in the early days of American motoring."

"Mr. Zeb, does this old car run?"

"Yes, sir, I have even driven it in Wilmington when they had their Azalea Festivals when I was a young man with my family. Beard and Lilly used to accompany me every year for about twenty years. Some years I would show off horse drawn carriages and leave the old cars like this in the barn here. People never knew what my family might drive in the parade. I kept them guessing from year to year. They say variety is the spice of life and I see no harm in spicing it up a bit, it makes it a lot more interesting, don't you think?"

"Yes, sir, I do lean heavily in favor of your opinion, Mr. Zeb. Life is what we make of it."

"Now this next automobile as I am sure you recognize is a much improved vehicle over the simple Motel T. This 1935 Model A can go about sixty miles an hour. I have read that the Ford Motor Company sold fifteen million of these cars. They are much heavier and provide more luxury and ease of driving than its simple cousin the Model T. Not a bad car to drive even now days. As you may have noticed, I have it inspected every year and there is a plate in the back. I do take this old gal out for a spin every once in awhile just for the joy of driving it. You and I need to take off one day and go down to Wilmington and just amuse ourselves at all of the eyes that will be looking at what we will be sitting in. I once had a policeman to stop me. He even had his lights on and let me know that he wanted me to pull over. When he got out and came over to me, he introduced himself and told me that he just wanted to see the old car because his great-great-grandfather owned one. He told me that the car was long gone, but he had an old photograph to prove his story."

"What did you tell the officer, Mr. Zeb?"

"I surprised him by getting out of the car and allowing him to take about twenty minutes behind the wheel. He eventually got a call and had to leave, but he thanked me for the experience. I got his phone number and called him one day and he met me and we drove this old car all over the place. We drove out in the country where we could enjoy ourselves and not get into a wreck, and I taught that young man how to operate the car. He actually comes by once in awhile just to see the cars and to talk. He loves to talk about how things used to be. He does a lot of reading and I am able because I am very much an antique myself to entertain him and provide him with a lot of practical knowledge about the past. He told me that he appreciates me taking up time with him because he never had very much contact with his family. I understand that his folks all died of one thing or another before he was twelve years old except for an older sister he gets to see every few months who lives in Raleigh, North Carolina. I understand from him that she is a nurse who is married to a building contractor. Well, I believe that we have seen enough of this place for today. Maybe we can come back here another day and spend half a day or so in here. There is enough in this building to keep a body interested for several months or perhaps even a lifetime."

"Yes, sir, thank you so much for showing me all of these wonderful old cars, tractors, and other interesting antiques. I have never seen such a private collection on this scale before. I am truly impressed, sir!"

"Thank you, sir. Now I believe that we should direct our attention to going back to the house and seeing what the gals have fixed up for supper. I do have a good appetite for an old boy my age! It is a wonder I am not carrying all of that good food around my waist, but I manage to work most of it off tending the herb garden and projects I find myself in either by my own design or what my wife or daughter-in-law conger up for me."

Twenty

Professor David Smith is Now Teaching at UNCW as the Second in Command of the Science Department

Our story must take a leap in time and place for the Smith family. The Smiths are now in their large home near Wrightsville Beach. The summer, fall, and winter months of the year 2030 are a fond memory now. Many days were devoted to the swimming hole in the creek on the plantation and the great fishing lake that will always be part of the history this family will have with them in their collective memories to share with their children and their children's children. David's parents were back in the big city of Boston at their impressive old mansion enjoying their retirement years or home away visiting friends or on some exotic vacation of their choosing. As promised, David's parents visited David at his new home near Wrightsville Beach and have plans to go back to North Carolina as much as possible. Back on the plantation the children's grandparents and their great grandparents sorely missed Brenda, David, and the children, but visit as much as reasonably possible because there is always a lot of necessary work that needs to be done on the big plantation. The children especially missed Mattie. She was always so much fun to be around and seemed to understand the children from their view point as children like no one else could. She took no offence at their pranks and was always around to cheer them up and put a little sparkle in their eyes.

Our story now takes us to a large classroom in the science department at UNCW. The new man that everyone was expecting either with joy or grief is now teaching in one of his classrooms. The discussion was centered on natural occurrences in nature such as earthquakes and huge waves commonly called tsunamis often generated by earthquakes. Doctor Smith speaks:

"In your handouts you will see listed a history of earthquakes in the continental United States. Notice the increase in the number of earthquakes from 1872 to 1885. In 1872, for example, you will notice that there were 18 quakes recorded. Every so many years you will notice that the number of earthquakes has gradually increased. This does not mean that as each year rolls by it will experience more earthquakes than the previous year, but there is an overall increase over a span of years that is very obvious.

"For instance, from this record, we notice that there were 27 earthquakes the following year after 1872. Note, however, that we have record of 20 earthquakes in 1874. In 1875 we have 33 earthquakes. Strange to say, but not a complete mystery. In 1876 you will note that there were once again 20 earthquakes. We see a back and forth pattern almost like a swinging effect on our charts, from a high year to a lower number of quakes. We will also note with interest and some alarm that the higher numbers continue to get bigger.

"Now there are some people who try to prove that there are no more significant earthquakes in recent times as in all of the known history of earthquakes. I do not beg to disagree. I do not offer that courtesy to such willful distortion of the facts. I am afraid that we scientist are not totally immune to political persuasion or to a little suppression of the facts of science, so that we will not brush the so called hair or feathers of certain groups and interested parties the wrong way. This is life, but I trust that you people will always allow the facts to speak for themselves regardless of whose feathers you may ruffle." A student raises his right hand to ask a question.

"Doctor Smith, I remember my pastor, Doctor Merrill McCoy, telling his church that earthquakes are mentioned in the Bible. I understand that they are to increase in number and strength. Do you find this to be accurate?"

"Indeed I do. Not because the Bible predicts earthquakes increasing in numbers and magnitude, but because the record speaks for itself. This is not a classroom in a church. I don't teach religion, but like it or not the Bible is dead on target on this one. Records reveal that from 1700 B. C. to 96 A. D. which covers a period of 1,796 years, there were only sixteen quakes. We have records from 96 A. D. to 1850 A. D. that there were 204 earthquakes or that is one every eight years. We will not take up more class time by me reading the entire record. You people are capable of reading this information while not in class.

"Certain earthquakes are worth knowing about because they have historical significance and unfortunately resulted in the death of a lot of people and caused a lot of property damage. In 1811 an earthquake was experienced along the Mississippi River from the mouth of the Ohio River all the way to Saint Francis a three hundred mile distance. The tremor was felt all the way to the Eastern Sea Board of the United States. The last shock occurred February 1812 thus covering a period of two months before the earth relieved itself of the pressure buildup. I have information for you people to read about the famous so called San Francisco earthquake, and the Charleston, South Carolina earthquake of 1886.

"Now let us get up and leave this classroom and walk down to the earthquake lab I had installed. I realize that some of the things I will show you today are new on the table of scientific knowledge. That is perfectly alright. I do understand that certain individuals' eye brows have been raised as a result of my work. I will not waste time justifying my work by pointing out the names of scientist and inventors who have experienced the same treatment by the so called establishment and were found to be correct and who remembers their opponents anymore or their outdated and useless theories and methods that were once considered science?" Minutes later the twenty nine students who were all working on at least a master's degree in geology or oceanography walked into a large room recently built and equipped with some unusual experimental equipment. Powerful computers were located in various places in the huge room along with models of the earth's crust.

"As you people can see, we have actual working models of the plates of the oceans and the continental plates created on a rather large scale of a number of sites knows for their high seismic activity. These working models represent reality as much as possible. The material the continental crust is represented by is made of a lighter material that floats on a semisolid mantel. The ocean plates are thinner and are forced by hydraulic pressure to go under the continental plate of the North American model you see here. There is even artificially created heat between the continental plate and the divergent ocean plates of the various models in this lab. As you can all see, we have working models of California, Hawaii, Oregon, Washington State, and the USA East Coast." A young man questions Doctor Smith after making a comment.

"Doctor Smith, I have never seen actual working models of these regions of our continental plate where the ocean plates slide underneath, this is fantastic!" What kind of material are the oceanic plates and the continental plates made of?" Doctor Smith answers:

"The oceanic plates are made of a silicon based material. The continental plates are composed of a combination of clay and a special rubber. Of course, there is rock of various grades in the material. Underneath the oceanic plate is a thin, but very strong rubber belt similar in material makeup of a rubber conveyer belt. This belt is moved ever so slowly to act very much like the real oceanic plate as it is pushed against the continental plate. Of course, we cannot push the ocean plates or they would buckle up, so we pull them. Tiny GPS sensors are positioned at various locations on this moving belt. The continental plates on the models are made in such a way as to resist the oceanic plates as they try to bury themselves or submerge beneath the continental plates. Tension builds up along the artificial shoreline of the two plates. The computers you see here constantly monitor the movement, the pressure, and the hot spot activity just like the real thing. Now these devices above the models that looks similar to the satellites that orbit our planet, are very similar to the real thing. The entire surface area of these models is marked off so that one square inch of the surfaces of these models represents one square mile of plate surface.

"Earthquakes do have some predictability as to time and place. The whole system of plate movement on the lithosphere of our planet represents one grand complicated machine in operation. We know, for example, how much the plates are moving. There are seven huge plates or slabs that move about and that makeup the surface of the Earth. This outer shell is, of course, named the Lithosphere. There are about twenty smaller plates that are positioned or squeezed between the larger plates and get pushed around. We know the direction of these plates. We had a fairly accurate understanding of this even before the age of ground positioning satellites. Could any among the scholars that surround me name a few of the plates that move on our lithosphere?" A young man raises his right hand and speaks:

"I am sure that anyone among us could name and point out where these plates are located on our globe, but I will name a few to keep a dialogue between you, Doctor Smith, and your class. North American Plate, Caribbean Plate, Juan de Fuca Plate, the Pacific Plate, the small Cocos Plate and the..." Doctor Smith indicates to the student that he is satisfied that his student has a grasp of the names and the locations of the plates on our earth's surface. Doctor Smith continues his lecture:

"Now just as these plates float on top of the semi molten layer of the upper mantle, so my models are designed in a similar fashion. The layers of material you see representing the ocean plates and the continental plates are very realistic, which allows the models to function very much like the real thing." Doctor Smith continues to lecture to the class explaining the design of the models and how they are all embedded with tiny wireless sensors that detect the slightest pressure buildup, heat buildup beneath traditional hot spots and the occasional tremors when a plate relieves itself by moving."

In a classroom in another science building Doctor Hardin lectures his senior undergrad students on tsunamis.

"Folks, I would encourage all of you to stay in school long enough to earn a double major in science. I am, of course, referring to a BS in both geology and oceanography. These degrees can work together or they can complement each other. Today we are going to talk about giant waves. Please don't everyone speak at once, but who among the bright young faces I look at can give us a little history of giant waves causing a lot of destruction and loss of human life?" Doctor Hardin looks around and speaks again. "I am still waiting. I will not punish you or cause anyone who dares to speak up any embarrassment. After all, we are all students of oceanography and geology unless I have accidentally walked into the wrong room this afternoon." A few students laugh as low as possible and a young man speaks:

"I didn't speak up because I wanted to give someone else a chance to speak up." Doctor Hardin smiles as he turns his head slowly toward his students and speaks.

"How noble of you, I am sure your fellow scholars are much relieved that you are now prepared to share your pantry of knowledge with us." The young man speaks:

"Yes, sir, I can't go all the way back and recite the record, but I do know about some of the major events of our time. There was a huge tsunami that formed in the Indian Ocean in 2004 that I understand was responsible for killing at least 150,000 people. I have seen film of this disaster, but I was not born in 2004 because that was about twenty six years ago. I understand that this fault zone moved upward about fifteen feet causing a huge rise in the ocean for about six hundred miles." Doctor Hardin indicated for his student to stop talking.

"As you said, this earthquake was caused by one of the plates of the earth's lithosphere to push itself below another plate. Now I ask, since we are primarily talking about huge waves that have often done great damage to humans, what other events can trigger these huge waves?" A young man raises his right hand to the simple question which was a question not so much as to really probe the depth of a senior science student's knowledge, but rather asked to get the academic ball bouncing in the classroom. That is teacher student interaction. The same technique is used by ministers when they feel like they need their audience to pay them more attention or attempt to control the excitement level of their congregation. It also unnerves some speakers to have a silent audience watching them.

"Doctor Hardin, I believe that we are all aware that earthquakes in certain locations near vast oceans or other large bodies of water can cause huge waves. I have learned that the largest wave in recorded history occurred off the State of Alaska in Lelurya Bay. I was told that the wave was over 1700 hundred feet high. It was caused by a landslide." Doctor Hardin speaks:

"Very good, who else would like to contribute to our discussion this afternoon? I am sure that many of you are struggling inside, just bursting with knowledge and excitement ready to say something that most of us have not thought about recently." A young woman raises her right hand in the back of the classroom. The professor recognizes her hand.

"Yes, ma'am, Miss Black."

"This may sound silly, but I was watching a science fiction movie that featured an enormous wave that was created by some evil people. They used a huge amount of very powerful explosives to create a wave that did some major property damage and killed a lot of people on a certain beach."

"Yes, ma'am, you are right. I am sure that hydrogen bombs sent in by missiles directed off the shore of the, let's say, the Eastern Sea Board of the United States, since we live near the ocean, would indeed cause a very large wave that could do hundreds of millions of dollars in property damage and kill a lot of people living near the beaches. It would really be a disaster if such an act was perforated during the height of the summer when tourism is at its peak. How many of you scholars know about the eruption and explosion of the volcano Krakatoa in the Sudan Strait near Indonesia?" All of the students lifted their hands. The professor continues. "How many of you have seen the old movie based on the eruption of Krakatoa?" Three students in the class of thirty raise their hands. Doctor Hardin continues:

"I would encourage all of you aspiring scientist to watch the old movie very carefully. It is very realistic and portrays a lot of destruction, loss of life, and the great fear that was experienced by a lot of human beings as a result of that natural disaster. We cannot go back in a time machine and witness the terror those people experienced or the enormous power of that terrible day in human history, but the old movie will be shown next class. If we can't finish all of it, don't worry because we will see the rest the following class."

Classes are over with for Doctor Smith and Doctor Hardin and they go back to their offices and complete their work there. While going to his office suite, Doctor Smith sees Doctor Hardin coming his way. He stops and speaks to him.

"Good evening, Doctor Hardin, I trust that you have had a rewarding day!" Doctor Hardin replies:

"I can't complain. I have worked here for many years and a lot of schools around the country have my former students as instructors. I feel almost like a car engineer who designs cars and trucks or boats. I try to make the best Makes and Models possible to last a long time and do a lot of honest hard work during their working years." Doctor Smith comments:

"I have never thought of our jobs as a factory, but your illustration and philosophy has a lot of merit. Have you been by the new earthquake lab, Doctor Hardin?"

"Yes, I went by there four days ago with several other instructors. It is very impressive. I have been to movie sets of miniature cities or natural landscapes and your lab reminds me of them. You must have been in a lot of creative projects when you were a kid to have such an imagination."

"Doctor Hardin, I realize that you do not consider such a lab very practical, but I have one also at Boston University. We have used it for years and I have found that it is very useful in teaching my new discoveries in earthquake predictions." Doctor Hardin speaks:

"Well, have fun. I really must go. I have an appointment with a friend of mine at Wrightsville Beach. He is mayor there. We have been fishing partners for over ten years now." Doctor Smith speaks:

"Well, if you are going fishing, don't catch them all. I might just get a chance to go fishing one of these days just as soon as I can go to Boston and sail my boat to Wrightsville Beach at the Masonboro Marina. I have purchased a slip so that I can permanently dock my boat." Both gentlemen say goodbye and depart their separate ways.

An hour later, David calls his wife Brenda at their beautiful mansion in the Wrightsville Beach vicinity across from the waterway and sound.

"Honey, I hope that you and the kids had an exciting day today!" Brenda speaks:

"Yes, we all had a very rewarding day at school. Our last teacher, a young gentleman whom the kids call Mr. Mets, was here for the first time." David speaks:

"Is he the new math instructor?"

"Yes, and his résumé informs me that he is from a small village called Kelly in Bladen County not very far from Atkinson. The small village has grown considerably since I was a child. Mets told me that a lot of outsiders have moved in because of the new factories recently built in the area. I am sure that some of the old timer farmers I used to know, when I was very young, would roll over in their graves if they knew what Mets described to me. I can't imagine Kelly having a population of over five thousand people now! A lot of old family farms no longer exist."

"Brenda, what kind of degree does the guy have and what courses will he teach?"

"I understand that Mets has a masters in mathematics and a BA in business and that he is qualified to teach basic math and modern math. He is very good at Algebra, Trigonometry, and Geometry."

"Does he have an assistant?"

"The assistant Miss Register was hired first. She is a senior student in education. Everything is on schedule. We have all of the legal rights and privileges necessary to teach up to high school. My goal is to eventually offer basic college accredited courses so that the brighter students will be able to start out as sophomores at any local college or university in North Carolina. Now, David, I will expect you to come over occasionally and lecture to our Introduction to Science Class." David speaks:

"What are you talking about? I teach graduate classes in geology and oceanography."

"Yes, dear, I realize that, but you can still drop by as a guest speaker for the kids and teach a few science classes. You could explain what scientists do and what kids need to do in order to prepare for a career in science. In other words, your job will be primarily to inspire them to work hard with real goals in mind."

"I have never taught grammar grades or high school kids, but I suppose I could do some fill in work if a teacher is out provided that I can be available, of course. In fact, I may talk to several other instructors under me to see if they would be interested also. Who knows, I may even convince some of the older instructors to spend some of their post retirement years teaching at your school. When I was in the fifth grade, I remember several adults coming over and sharing their jobs with us kids. One person was a fireman, another was a policewoman. I remember the manager of a large local grocery store talking about the grocery business and how they run their business, but I never had someone in my profession to speak to us." Brenda reflects on David's comment and speaks:

"Well, there is nothing wrong with being a first timer. Besides, I hope that you will be able to inspire the students to excellence so that they will put forth their best effort in getting the best education possible before going on to an institution of higher learning." David speaks:

"Enough about school, can you have the kids ready? I would like to take us to Eagle's Island. I promised myself to visit famous local stores and tourist attractions once we moved to our new home."

"I think it would be wonderful, David, to take a trip to the place. It is a little cold today, but we can still enjoy the place and maybe even purchase some of their wonderful ice cream. I am not sure that there will be a lot of vegetables offered in January. I am sure that there will be plenty of Collards. We all love them! They have a fish market and the inside of the place is a classical country store glorified. It has been fifteen years since I have had the opportunity to see the place. I wonder if they have expanded the facility after all these years." An hour later, the Smith family is on their way to Eagle's Island which is on Highway 421 not many miles from the Cape Fear Memorial Bridge which crosses over the Cape Fear River, North Carolina's largest river. The children become excited because they had heard of the old country store, but had never seen it. Brenda was also excited about visiting the store because she remembered her grandfather selling vegetables by the small truck loads to the owner. Brenda never really met the original owner because he had long passed this life's journey before Brenda was born. Mr. Flowers would be very proud if he could come back and see the place he had worked so hard to make a success out of.

When the children first saw the store just off of Highway 421, they said that the place reminded them of a glorified vegetable stand with a roof over it because when they walked under the shed outside the front entrance, there were huge green Collards piled high. Brenda commented that they were as nice as the Cabbage Collards her family was growing on the plantation. People were everywhere taking advantage of the situation because the prices were much lower than grocery stores and the collards were fresh and crisp not loose leaves bundled together like in most grocery stores. Beautiful oranges, tangerines, apples, and a dozen other kinds of fruit were on display. Back of the fruit were bins of all kinds of nuts such as pecans, walnuts, peanuts, and Brazil Nuts. David looks at Brenda and speaks:

"Honey, with a place like this in our area, I see no reason in us having a large garden this year. I believe that I had rather enjoy the warm months by fishing in our big boat, visiting local tourism attractions, and spending a lot of time enjoying the beach life. We can grow a few vegetables and herbs if you want to, but I say let's get vegetables here unless we happen to visit your parents." Brenda speaks:

"David, I do recall you saying before we moved to Wrightsville Beach in our new home that you wanted a big garden, but I can see your point. We could, as you suggested, have a few hills of some of our favorite vegetables, but I don't believe I would want to spend hours in a garden every week while life goes swiftly on its merry way. Let's go inside and get some ice cream, David. This place is famous for its ice cream. It is delicious and much cheaper than what you see available in town." While the Smith's enjoy their ice cream, the children were excited by all of the unusual items for sell or to delight anyone interested in an old fashioned country store that reminded many of its customers of a frontier trading post. There were just so many interesting things to delight the imagination of people of all ages. While musing around the store, David can't help noticing the shelves loaded down with canned and pickled vegetables, sausages, pig's feet, pickled eggs and all of the country delights that most people in the year 2031 had never seen except in old movies or books and magazines picturing a time mostly gone when people in our land of plenty were more self-reliant and homemade cooking was still queen on mostly any respectable dining room table. David speaks:

"Honey, this section of the store with these several thousand mason jars remind me of another place I have seen."

"Yes, I would assume that you refer to the huge pantry near the kitchen in my folks' house." David smiles while commenting:

"Brenda, just look at all of the wonderful handy work displayed here. Some people have sure done a lot of work to have canned or pickled all of these individual items! Let's see, I see Hot Sala, Sweet Baby Corn, Hot Pepper, Lemon Pepper, Black and Blue Mixed Berry, Elderberry Jelly, Apricot Jam, Apple Jelly, Corn Relish, Old Fashioned Pickled Beans and Corn. Pickled Eggs, now I love them, and this one is a favorite. My mother always cans Marinated Mushrooms." Brenda speaks:

"Yes, and other old favorites, Bread and Butter Pickles, and Chunky Sala." While Brenda and her amazed husband continued to take a mental inventory of the myriads of delightful and eye pleasing displays of good old fashioned farm products, the children in the main time were not idle, but were delighting themselves with a wall display of talking fish that were mounted like they were real fish. The children's giggles were innocent and loud as they expressed their pleasure while they watched very realistic looking mechanical fish move about and sing. David and Brenda left off looking at the jars of canned vegetables and meat products and walked to where their children were. Before the Smith's left Eagle's Island, they purchased all kinds of healthy favorite food including a big Red Snapper fish that would be prepared for supper.

Saturday found the Smith family at their new mansion off of Airlee Garden Road not far from the sound and the Intercoastal Water Way. They were fortunate in that they were able to find an unusually large Spanish style mansion that was surrounded by nearly ten acres of mostly large live oak trees. Fortunately, the spacious dwelling was sold by an older couple who had no children or heirs of any kind at a very good price. In fact, most people would consider it a giveaway. The large three story dwelling was over twenty seven thousand square feet of one of the most beautiful and interesting dwellings in the South.

Surrounding this European style mansion is a massive white ten foot high cut stonewall created from large blocks of granite shipped on rail from the Wilmington Port on the Cape Fear River. The Ocean White granite was originally purchased from a large company located in South India that sells high quality stone of many beautiful colors and patterns. The wall is adored on its top with a very heavy duty ornate black iron fence that is about three feet high. Beautiful carvings are engraved every hundred feet into the wall that are the official coats of arms of the houses of the kings of Spain and the important nobles who ruled Spain in her glory days. It is nothing unusual to see people outside of the wall standing on the public sidewalk looking at the very beautiful and educational wall that surrounds the ten acre estate.

Two separate entrance roads and gates serve the owners of the mansion. One gate is the entrance gate and its identical companion is, of course, the exit. A beautiful very ostentatious double arch stands above both the entrance and the exit for the estate. Standing in life like pose above each arch way are lifelike figures of important people in Spanish history. These statues are modeled after paintings done by famous artist of mostly soldiers and sailors who were already the talk of the town in their day as being note worthy explorers and conquistadores. The inquisitive eye of one hungry for knowledge and the arts will be constantly fed by endless myriads of breath taking paintings, beautiful frieze made of imported Greek veined marble, statues, and ornate carvings in every direction a sharp eye is directed. The Smith family in their lovely new home is literally surrounded by the dazzling glory of the once mighty Spanish Empire. Dan the Smith's only son questions his father.

"Father, who are those people on that?" Young Dan Smith pauses as he struggles for the proper words and then allows his father to supply the words he lacks in his ten year old vocabulary.

"Dan, this large structure is called an entrance arch. These lifelike statues of men dressed in armor and helmets carrying swords and shields are famous Spanish explorers and conquistadors. Remember Mr. and Mrs. Bartolomeo who sold the property to us?"

"Yes, sir, they are nice old people. They are almost as nice as our grandparents."

"Yes, son, they do not have children or any family of their own. This is the reason they almost gave us this property. They own several palaces in Toledo and Venice, beautiful cities in Spain and do not need the property or the money this place would normally cost." Dan continues to question his father:

"Father, how much is this place worth?"

"Son, now you asked me about the statues; which of the questions do you want answered?"

"I guess the one about the statues."

"Son, I am sure that you know what an explorer is; for example, Christopher Columbus."

"Or, Marco Polo, Father!"

"That is correct, son. Now if you get the opportunity, and I am sure that you will, since we now live here. Walk into one of the gatehouses and there you will see beautiful busts of these important people positioned in cutouts inside of the stonewalls. Below each bust is a history of these individuals. Take a look at them and then step outside and look up at the full life-size statues and you will recognize who these people are. There are also many paintings and murals depicting these people in their life's work in the house." Doctor Smith stops the car at the double arch leading into the driveway and points up at the figures above them. "Son, starting on the left, yes that guy, son, I will try to name the people these statues represent. That guy is Lope de Agirre. I understand that this soldier explored the Amazon River looking for El Dorado, a city the Indians told the conquistadors about that was legendary for its gold. Of course, the Indians were not telling them the truth. The Indians just wanted the greedy and blood thirsty Spanish to leave their territory so that they could get on with their lives." Becky the Smith's eight year old daughter directs a question to her father. She no doubt feels left out of this important family discussion and wants to impress her parents and her big brother that she also is able to participate in this seemingly important intellectual discussion.

"Father, what is a conquistador?" Her parents cannot believe the big word a child only eight years old submits to her father. Her mother smiles, but has an amazed expression on her face.

"Honey, did you hear what our daughter asked you?"

"Yes, dear, I am not swept over with a wave of intimation by the question, but by the shock of hearing our eight year old correctly pronouncing such a big word. Betty, a conquistador was a man who traveled to other parts of the world like South America, and by force takes over other peoples' property. Often the people who once owned the land were forced into slavery and made to work for nothing on the property they once owned. These conquistadors were usually Spanish military men who were of high rank. Now until you get into a higher grade level in school, I would not worry too much about this complicated stuff. Your mother will see to it that you get an good understanding of Western Civilization. In the main time, you are privileged to live in a huge house that is surrounded by Spanish history. David Smith quickly continued his conversation with his son about who the incredible life-size statues represent on the huge ornate archway that guards the entrance to the estate. "Son, next to Lope de Aquirre is Hermon Cortes. He is the man who conquered the mighty Aztec Indian Empire. Near Cortes is Francisco Pizarro. The plaque inside informs us that he is the conqueror of the once mighty Inca Empire in Peru. The next fellow is Hernando de Soto. This man explored the plains of Eastern North America and discovered the Mississippi river and the Ohio river."

Up ahead a huge circular entrance and exit road serves the mansion. Between the mansion and the driveway is a beautiful ornate stone banister that looks very much like a heavy duty banister on the porch of a palace. It is constructed from reinforced steel and concrete. This work of art not only is present to serve an ascetic purpose, but provides a strong protective barrier for the front of the great house because it prevents vehicles from being able to drive up directly to the mansion to inflict damage. Situated on the other side of this protective barrier is a sidewalk that goes around the concrete banister on both sides toward both gatehouses that serve both the entrance and exit roads. This sidewalk also goes back of the mansion. An automatic heavy duty security arm lifts up and allows the Smith family to drive back of the mansion. The sensor on the post reads an electronic security script that is secured on the windshield of the car. The bar code is scanned, and the security computer instantly recognizes that the car is authorized to enter the backside of the mansion where the six vehicle parking garage is situated. This beautiful structure was not an afterthought by the architect or the original owners of the estate, but is never the less a separate structure from the mansion. A beautiful enclosed covered walk goes from the garage to the house. This structure is constructed from blue granite imported from France and heavy duty tinted glass panels to allow people using the walk to see what is going on outside around them.

Our story will leave off of a description of this wonderful house for now except to say that the three story mansion is shaped like a horseshoe. In between the two wings of the house that face each other is a huge courtyard full of statues, flower beds, and an Olympic size swimming pool that is surrounded by blue and black granite tile for its patio. It is now Tuesday afternoon and Doctor David Smith is standing in a classroom of sixteen excited young people. The students had been told that Doctor David Smith a very famous scientist who works at the University of North Carolina at Wilmington and the husband of their principal Doctor Brenda Smith and father of two favorite classmates Dan and Betty Smith would be paying them a visit.

The beautiful international wall clock reveals that it is nearly two o'clock in the afternoon, and that would mean that it is almost time for the sixth grade class in Introduction to Science to begin. The discussion today will be centered on planning for a career in science. Mr. Simpson a senior student in geology at UNCW introduces David.

"OK, students, everyone please give Doctor Smith your full attention please. You will not be graded on what will be said this hour by Doctor Smith, but do not take this to mean that what Doctor Smith shares with you students is of little importance because it just may be that this will be one of the most important classes you will even attend while a young person in middle school. I am sure that all of you are aware that Doctor Smith is Doctor Brenda Smith's husband and that their son is present with us. I also believe that all of you guys are aware that Doctor Smith and his wife own this great big house that includes our school. I will probably be a student myself one day in class under Doctor Smith if I am accepted into the program that leads to a Ph.D." Mr. Simpson looks over at Doctor Smith with a fake sheepish grin. Doctor Smith was not a stranger and considered Mr. Simpson a very good candidate for the doctorial program. In fact, Doctor Smith had talked Mr. Simpson into pursuing the program once he completed his masters. Doctor Smith had even provided employment for Mr. Simpson by bringing up his name as a person he felt would be a good science teacher. Brenda Smith took her husband's advice and hired Mr. Simpson, who is a twenty three year old young man reared in the small town of Wrightsville Beach. The young man had spent his entire life on the ocean or in the sound. His father was a successful commercial fisherman who owned two large one hundred and twenty foot boats. One boat was used to catch fish while the other big boat was a shrimp trawler. Doctor Smith speaks:

"Thank you for that fine introduction, Mr. Simpson. I am sure that it will aid you in pursuing that Ph.D. in geology that you and I have talked about in the next few years." Doctor Smith smiles at Mr. Simpson who realizes that Doctor Smith is teasing him a bit. The children catch on to what is going on and laugh. Mr. Simpson sits down while Doctor Smith takes over the floor.

"I want all of you guys to tell me your names." All of the students look at Dan, Doctor Smith's son. Doctor Smith speaks:

"OK, I realize that I already know one name. I will now need to only remember fifteen names instead of sixteen. Let's start on my left. Young lady please tell me your full name." After all of the students state their full name, Doctor Smith starts with the first young lady on his left and recites back everyone's name. The students are most intimidated by such a memory demonstration. He definitely got their full attention! Doctor Smith continues:

"How many of you young people have decided what you want to be when you enter the workforce?" All of the students, except one young boy, tell Doctor Smith that they want to be scientist when they grow up. Doctor Smith speaks to him:

"Young man, what do you want to be when you grow up?"

"I want to teach history, sir." Doctor Smith speaks:

"I think that is a wonderful choice! I did not decide what I wanted to do until I was seventeen, and by then, I had already earned enough college credits to complete a degree. It is alright to take a reasonable amount of time to decide. Just don't wait until you are living at a retirement village or something." Everyone laughs:

"There are a lot of interesting fields to go into. Some people choose just that. They want to literally work in fields of corn, cotton, beans, and you name it. Farming does have its rewards. Being a good physician is very important or perhaps an engineer, or a landscape designer. The business world can be an exciting career. It is not uncommon for a person to be involved in several fields to fulfill their goals financially and interest wise. For example, many medical doctors sit on the boards of pharmaceutical companies. Farmers often are involved in more than one business. Many successful farmers are expert landscapers and own their own landscaping companies or perhaps own a business that offers fertilizer, seed, and farm equipment, and tools to other farmers. People who own restaurants often own a nearby motel. Doctor Smith continues:

"I know that I am asking a silly question, but how many of you guys go to the movies?" Almost all of the students raised their hands. One boy said that he did not watch movies at movie theaters because he could get all of the movies he wanted to see with cable television and that he had several thousand movies on disk. Doctor Smith continues:

"I watch a movie occasionally myself. I am very careful as to what I watch because I do not have idle time to waste. I love to watch old movies especially movies like *Ben Hur, The Ten Commandments, Gone With the Wind* or some of the older science fiction movies like *Ten Thousand Leagues Beneath the Sea* or other old movies about the ocean. Most movies will last no more than two or three hours. We are all amazed at the action, suspense, and thrill we see and experience as we watch a favorite movie. I used to watch the old movie *The Ten Commandments* in which Moses raises his hands up above his head and spread them out toward the Red Sea. Instantly, as if by magic, the sea is divided into leaving a dry valley for those millions of people to walk across the Red Sea. When I was in my early teens, I played that scene over and over again just amazed wondering how they did it. You guys would be amazed at all of the scientific discoveries and knowledge required and used to give us the ability to sit down in our rooms and watch a good movie, an event now days as common as turning a water faucet in a modern kitchen and getting yourself a nice cool glass of filtered water.

"There is an old wise saying that warns that familiarity breeds contempt. This is simply a way of saying that we should not become indifferent or to take for granted all of the wonderful things that surround us on an everyday basis. Of course, that included the people you are with almost every day of your life. It is good for us to occasionally take a few moments to reflect on all of the wonderful things that other people worked very hard on to benefit all of us. I like to listen to very old people in remote parts of our country that tell me that their parents did not have electricity in their homes. No gas or electric stove to cook with. That meant that someone had to cut down trees and saw them up so that they would have wood for the heater and wood for the stove so the lady of the house in those days could cook a wonderful meal for her family. Can you imagine life before the invention of the telephone, or the refrigerator? There was a time, young people, when there were no computers, no televisions, no airplanes, no cars or trucks and no cell phones. In terms of history, it really was not that long ago when all of these wonderful inventions or scientific discoveries were put into practice.

"Early man had little to comfort or give him aid in the hostile and primitive environment he worked to survive in. Today when most of us walk into a dark room, the first thing that we probably do is flip on the light switch. I don't even have to do that in the part of this house that my family lives in. I walk into a dark room I need light in and I simply say the words, light please. If I fall asleep in a comfortable chair and wake up in a large dark room, I need not stumble across the room trying to find a light switch. I simply ask the lights to turn on. If I miss the 6PM news report on a local television channel and I know that they were covering an event or reporting a story I want information about, I do not concern myself. I have a program in my television that can retrieve that news hour for me.

"I need to communicate to a friend or business associate about some important news. I don't have to send the message by Carrier pigeon, smoke signals or drums or even the mail now days. I understand from some of the old people who live near or on the plantation my wife's people own, that centuries ago in the Black River and Cape Fear River region, that men were employed to carry messages, medicine, and other important things by foot. They called these men runners. Unfortunately, there were no bridges across the rivers in those days and no roads to travel, only animal trails and a few crude paths cut out by the early people of that region. It would be unthinkable for someone back in those days to pull out a cell phone and talk to someone many miles away. In fact, if I could go back in time and have the ability to call someone in another part of the country and have a conversation with them while standing in a crowd of people four hundred years ago, they would burn me at the stake for being a warlock!" The young people in the class laugh as they consider how things have changed in our world. "I hope that all of you understand why I am telling you these things. I could spend the entire year on the subject, but life is too short for that even if you guys all average around ten years old. Now, since almost all of you young people feel sure that you want to be scientist, could any among you give me a description of what science is, after all, if you are planning on going into science as your vocation, it would be wise to know what science is." One young lady raises a hand and Doctor Smith recognizes her hand:

"Yes, ma'am, Nancy?" The girl is startled with amazement that Doctor Smith has not forgotten her name.

"Doctor Smith, I believe that science is about discovering things about nature." Doctor Smith comments:

"Not bad, it is not a complete definition, but you have a basic grasp of the subject. Scientists have special methods of going about their business or learning about the physical world that surrounds them. It is not complicated at all, but the way a person goes about discovering information is critical if anything of value is to be discovered in a reasonable amount of time. We are all scientist. There is not a person in this room who has not discovered something important. Now that does not mean that others have not also discovered the same thing. For example, most of us know that liquid water will turn into a solid if the temperature goes to 32degrees Fahrenheit. Most of us also know that water will turn to steam if the temperature rises to 212 degrees Fahrenheit at sea level where the atmospheric pressure is about 14.7 pounds per square inch. If you go to a tall mountain and try boiling that same water at 212 degrees Fahrenheit, you will discover that the temperature needs to be higher because the air is thinner and the atmospheric pressure is less in the mountains.

"All babies are scientist. They are constantly discovering scientific things. Not things that might get their discoveries chronicled in a scientific magazine, but never the less very important things. A hot stove in the days of wood or coal burning stoves is in a room where a two year old is learning about his world and the baby unfortunately touches the stove and is burned. His mother treats the burn and hopefully the baby now knows that a hot stove will hurt him. Now you may say that is not scientific discovery, but some of the simplest experiments have been done in so called scientific laboratories by scientist. For example, we were talking about water. You would be surprised at the importance of those early simple experiments centered on boiling water and freezing water and what this has to do with the possibility of life on our planet or the operation of a steam machine or many other industrial applications. Did you know that life in the oceans and any body of water would not be possible as we know it unless water floats when it freezes? If it did not float and instead sank to the bottom of the ocean or lakes, most plant life would not be able to survive because they get their nutrients from the soil just like your yard grass. I am sure that you realize that the animals that are in the water mostly depend on plants for survival; if not directly, most certainly indirectly. Could anyone give us an example of this fact on land?" A young lady speaks:

"Yes, sir, I realize that lions don't eat grass, but the animals they kill and eat do live off of grass and other plants."

"I am very impressed, Janet. Now water floats when it freezes. I will allow Mr. Simpson to explain this natural occurrence. Why does ice float in liquid water? Did you know that ice that is super cold cannot float? I will once again allow Mr. Simpson to go over this with you one fine day. How many of you young people own chemical sets, magnets, rock, mineral collections, and electronic kits where you learn to put together simple radios and computer components?" Only four of the students in the class raised their hands. Doctor Smith comments:

"How many of you young people own computer games?" All of the kids raised their hands.

"I think that is very sad. Now there is nothing wrong with good computer games. I am sure they have their value, but don't spend all of your time on computer games. Learn to work with your hands. Learn to enjoy discovering how things work in nature: Mr. Simpson." Mr. Simpson speaks:

"Yes, sir, Doctor Smith?"

"If I order chemical labs, rocks, and minerals, and electronic experiment kits for the class and kits to experiment with magnets and various types of optical lenses and cubes for refracting light rays, would you have time to introduce the students to these fundamental or foundational concepts, skills, and discoveries made by scientists?"

"Yes, sir, I would also assume that you would want me to talk to the principal about this?"

"Yes, I would. I will also bring up the subject. By the way, do the kids have access to good scientific magazines, like Popular Science or Popular Mechanics?"

"Yes, sir, I brought some to this class a few days ago." Doctor Smith speaks:

"Why don't you order enough magazines for each student and make sure they read the articles. I realize we are not now in high school, but the students could at least go over some of the topics discussed in the magazines in our school. Now do we have some nice microscopes available?" Mr. Simpson is amazed that Doctor Smith has taken such an interest in his science class and answers.

"No, sir, we are planning on ordering them next year."

"Well, speak to the principal about this. I will even help you get the microscopes. Now do you have any telescopes?"

"No, sir, but one of the students has a nice telescope."

"Would that be my son?"

"Yes, sir, he has allowed us to use it once."

"I would then suggest that four or five nice telescopes be ordered. I realize that we do not have a night class, but the Moon could be looked at during the day. You can also get planetary kits for all of the students that will teach them about the night sky. I also believe it would be good to have a couple of field trips at night to UNCW's planetarium. I know a gentleman who teaches astronomy there." Mr. Simpson speaks:

"Yes, sir."

"Have any trips been planned to the NC Aquarium at Fort Fisher, Mr. Simpson?"

"Yes, sir, we are scheduled to be there in a week." Doctor Smith continues:

"Wonderful, now do you have plans to have a nice aquarium here? I believe that it would be good if there were two of them. One should be a salt water aquarium, and the other should be a freshwater tank. The students could capture local fish for the aquariums rather than purchase fish at a hobby shop. This way they would become familiar with our local aquatic life. I have two nice printouts provided by our state that display and identify both our local salt and freshwater fish. Lastly it might be good to have a terrarium. This would allow the students to create a self contained tropical jungle of a sort full of all kinds of plants and animals. If it is large enough, a miniature lake could be included." Mr. Simpson speaks:

"Yes, sir, I will talk to our principal about all of your suggestions." Doctor Smith continues:

"I realize that the time will run out in about twenty minutes so I will try to talk no more than ten more minutes to allow Mr. Simpson time to talk to you guys after I depart. I need to wrap up my talking because I will need to go home." All of the students laugh because they are all aware that Doctor Smith lives nearby. "Here is a working definition of what science is. The word science comes from the Latin word, scientia, which means knowledge or the systematic search for knowledge. A long time ago, it was called natural philosophy. This is one of those words that you can break down so that you can get a better understanding of what the word is all about. It is like the word Philadelphia. There is a big city in the State of Pennsylvania that is called Philadelphia. Phil means love, and adelphia is a Greek word that means brother. This city is called the city of brotherly love. Philosophy can be broken down also. Phil means love and sophy means knowledge. Therefore we know that the word's basic meaning is to love knowledge. Now who in here can name at least three important scientists that are currently alive or were very important because of their discoveries?" The class continues for about ten more minutes as Doctor Smith wraps up his first class and promises to come back in a few months to check on the progress of the science class.

Twenty-One

The Smith Family Enjoys Their New Mansion
Earthquakes Start to Rock the Neighborhood

That evening David and Brenda Smith are out on the patio in deluxe chairs enjoying watching their children in the huge heated pool. The children are not allowed to use the pool unless their parents are present because of the size of the thing. Brenda speaks:

"David, I never dreamed that we would be so blessed. I just can't believe that such a house and estate is located here in Wrightsville Beach. I am sure that the Bartolomeos spend at least fifty million dollars on this house and the grounds. I have heard nothing about the construction of this place."

"Yes, Brenda, we have been blessed beyond our wildest dreams. I can't get over the number of massive paintings. There are statues and all kinds of eye catching carvings, murals, and friezes that probably were shipped from Spain. I doubt any company in this country makes such authentic replicas of the glory that Spain once enjoyed and her mother, Ancient Rome. I believe that the Bartolomeos said that most of the paintings and other works of art are not very old, but identical to the beautiful things that are in their palaces and other buildings in Spain. You know, I believe that we should visit those people one day. I would love to learn more about those wonderful people, but we will need to wait until school is out. I have been to The United Kingdom, France, and Germany, but never Spain."

"Don't forget about China, David."

"No, I have not forgotten China. I did not mention China because I was thinking about Europe. Brenda, do you have a lifeguard to look out for the children when they are swimming?"

"No, David, I have not offered our private pool to the school. I was not sure if that would be a wise decision. I do not want a child to get hurt or into trouble in this huge pool."

"I see your point, but knowing how to swim is very important. Maybe we should offer swimming lessons. We could get a couple of young people at UNCW who are experts at swimming to look after the kids and to teach them to swim. The children would have to be separated. I don't believe that the younger kids need to be taking swimming lessons while the older kids are taking their class. Sixteen kids swimming at one time will be a big responsibility for someone."

"David, I will look into it, but I don't believe it wise to have only one instructor present. I believe that we should always have two qualified people present. I don't expect trouble, but I believe that we need to be extra careful seeing that we will take upon ourselves such a big responsibility with other people's children. I would want not only good qualified instructors, but young instructors who have current Red Cross certificates."

"Yes, Brenda, I go along with that. Did Mr. Simpson talk to you about the suggestions I made to him about things that I believe should be purchased for the science class?"

"No, David, I will not see Mr. Simpson again until Friday."

"I will not go over all that I suggested for the class, but just remember that I will pay for anything that I have suggested. Not only will both of our kids eventually benefit from the things I will offer, but all of the kids as they grow older. I realize that Betty is just eight years old, but I know that one future day she will also be in a science class at our school. I make these suggestions because I personally had all of the things I suggested when I was growing up. I can tell you that I greatly benefited and would not be the scientist I am today had I not had those experiences."

"David, I promise you that I will implement all that you suggest. I am very thankful that you have taken such an interest in the school! I am very proud of you!"

"Brenda, some of these boys and girls that attend this school will likely major in science when they are college age. I will probably see them one future day walking down a hall. I look forward to that!"

"Honey, I have not thought about these young people as students at UNCW under you. You do open up my mind. I now realize that our school is like a greenhouse where young tender plants are nurtured until they are big and strong enough to be transplanted in the fields where they will grow up. I believe that the fields here would be institutions of higher learning like UNCW."

It is now Monday morning and Doctor David Smith is in a classroom teaching his students. The class has been going on for about thirty minutes. The topic today is tsunamis threats. Doctor Smith speaks:

"Students, I believe that the study of tsunamis threats is more than an interesting academic hobby, it is most practical in its application. If I came to the conclusion that our work as scientist was of little more value than providing technical information for people who write novels or science fiction movies, I would have gone into another line of work years ago. Hundreds of thousands of people throughout the centuries have perished for lack of knowledge about these huge waves and the signs nature provides to give us in most cases ample opportunity to remove ourselves from danger zones.

"Unfortunately, when volcanoes explode out in an ocean basin where there is deep water, people, animals, and everything else are often in danger of total or severe destruction. Earthquakes of non-volcanic origins such as when the huge plates that make up the earth's crust struggle against each other, or an extraterrestrial body hits our planet can generated tsunamis." A young man raises his hands and is recognized.

"Yes, Jason, what is your question?"

"What kind of threat do we have from meteorites plunging into an ocean or other large bodies of water?"

"I am not an astronomer. I am aware that large meteorites have struck our planet and there is abundance evidence that a lot of plants and animals were destroyed not only by the initial force that creates huge craters on the surface, but the atom bomb like heat and pressure wave that occurs immediately after the impact. How many of you people are aware of the meteorite that exploded in the sky in the Tunguska region of Siberia?" Everyone raises their hands acknowledging that they are aware of the incident that took place in 1908. "Now I am sure that all of us are naturally concerned about such an event occurring over a major city, but scientists have come to the mathematical conclusion that such events are very rare. You would not want to wager your money that such an event will take place in your working years.

"Now in passing, I will tell you that there was a near miss in 2029 by the asteroid named Apophus. In April 13, 2036, Apophus, whose name means the destroyer who dwells in eternal darkness, will visit us again and will pass closer to our planet than our communication satellites are. I understand that if it did hit our planet, it would strike anywhere from the Pacific Ocean somewhere near California to Central America. Now even such a close visit will have a slim chance of actually striking our home planet. There is only about one chance out of forty five thousand for contact. Like I said, I am an oceanographer and a geologist. I am confident that my two degrees will aid me in identifying and predicting more likely sources of danger for mankind than my friends who worry about a large rock hitting our planet. I am not minimizing their profession.

"There are over three thousand volcanoes worldwide. Many of them are under the oceans. We should all be aware of them and where they are located and why they are there. We should also have a good handle of history making volcanoes. Their names, geographical locations, and their track records. We have all heard of the ancient Roman Cities of Pompeii and Herculaneum and the volcano Vesuvius which destroyed these beautiful cities. I have been to both sites and I would love for our school to help sponsor a working trip to these sites for a group of grad students. I believe it would be a life changing experience that will help the students to take their future professions as a most serious occupation. The volcano Krakatoa not only exploded and destroyed most of the small populated island it had created, but it generated a epic size wave that killed a lot of people and wildlife. Mount Saint Helen exploded in 1980 and many others around the world are active and have been active for the ages.

"Anytime and anyplace an active volcano is near or surrounded by deep water it has the potential to cause huge waves to develop. Many of these volcanoes have created islands in the ocean. The magma rising to the surface can cause earthquakes which in turn cause huge landslides to occur. Sometimes the islands break apart and huge blocks or chunks fall into the ocean abysmal with Biblical or epic destruction being a most certain probability.

"I have a listing which includes maps of all of the known volcanoes on both the surface of our planet as well as those underwater. Now I don't expect you to know all of them. I have listed about fifty volcanoes that are of noted interest. All of you will go into the field of oceanography or geology, I understand. Not all of you will spend your working careers climbing the summits of volcanoes to take samples or be involved with mapping or monitoring the ocean floors. I am thankful for that because our profession is far broader than that.

"Many of you will spend your future working time diving or living in underwater labs. You will work in land based facilities. We all have to eat and many of you will probably be working to stabilize commercial fish populations, oysters, clams, lobsters or whatever. Some of you will eventually work for a state or the Federal Government. You may be working to enforce and control manmade as well as natural pollution. Still others here will labor to discover new cures for human diseases, unknown food sources, and industrial applications. Your work will increase incrementally as world populations continue to rise and food and disease control becomes a most serious issue.

"Today's discussion is centered around tsunami threats, not earthquakes in particular or even volcanoes. Both of these events, of course, in the right place, time, and magnitude can change history. In passing, how many of you have visited Crete in the Mediterranean Sea?" One young man raises his hand. Doctor Smith continues his lecture. "I have been to the island of Thera to look at the Volcano Santorin. This monster is a must see site if you plan to specialize in volcanism. However, there are now live web cameras and live satellite pictures of the volcano available if you can't make it to the place physically. I have a listing of volcanoes that can be seen on line. Now days with our sophisticated computers and web cameras, we can explore these sites without actually going there. Several significant tsunamis have also been filmed along with lots of information about these events. Getting back to the Volcano Santorin, I can speak from experience that the site is very sobering and thought provoking because this monster changed history when it exploded.

"This natural wonder was probably not only the major contributor for the fall of the very high Minoan Culture, but there are ancient cities all around the Mediterranean that are now underwater as a result of this volcano exploding. The event was ultimately triggered by a massive earthquake. Some scientists believe that this event was what resulted in the destruction of Atlantis. This event was caused by plate tectonics. The eastern part of the Mediterranean is the plate that Africa rides and struggles against the Aegean Plate. This subduction zone is mapped and explained in your handouts. Remember that all of this information can be looked at via my website. Everything is presented for farther explanation and real time illustration. The African Plate pushes in a northerly direction. Part of this plate is sliding beneath the Aegean Plate. The explosion of the Volcano Santorin caused a huge tsunami that killed a lot of people and destroyed a lot of property around the Mediterranean Sea. We will not discuss the wave size or path because it is all on the website you have been directed to. I am sure that none alive today will ever have a full picture of or the ramifications that fateful day brought forth. I have listened carefully to people who were present on the beaches that day when the Tsunami of 2004 was born in the Indian Ocean. I have seen very good film as recorded by many present that day from many locations around the Indian Ocean, but there is nothing comparable to a real life experience.

"Now you may say to yourself, 'what has this event to do with me personally,' "I will then ask you a rhetorical question; are you aware of the super volcano under Yellowstone National Park? I would suggest that all of you look up the information on my website. You will not be tested on this for now, but one day I promise that this topic will take up a great deal of your study time because we have a growing problem under Yellowstone that is definitely going to change history in a very bad way one of these days, and we currently know of nothing that we can do about it.

"Now back to tsunami threats. Significant tsunamis do not happen every year, but you would not want to be taking a stroll on a beautiful beach enjoying the sun and the beautiful location and notice that the tide is fast becoming unusually low. I trust that you as an alert junior scientist would suddenly put it all together and come to the unhappy conclusion that you should leave the beach and forget about the chair, the drink cooler, and whatever comforts of civilized life you brought along with you to aid you and make a quick exit from the beach to your vehicle and leave the area as quickly as you can without crashing into other vehicles occupied with other bright people out of harm's way. Unfortunately, believe it or not, a lot of people do not run away, but remain often dumb to what is taking place until they suddenly see a black wall of water coming at them. In your text book are about twenty pages devoted to infamous tsunamis that changed human history or were destructive enough to be listed in our history.

"I will not have to go over their history because you can read for yourself. If you are really interested in oceanography or geology and plan to work as a scientist, I suggest you make this information a part of your way of life. If you are going to be worth your salt in any profession, you need to eat and breath mentally your profession. This does not mean that you don't or will not have other interest, but to illustrate, how would you like to go to a physician and he did not take his profession very seriously? I am sure that you would find someone else. My father is a physician. He has recently retired, but he put his heart into his work. Put your passion into your work. Don't study just to make good grades. We need people who are as serious about their life's work as famous people we have all read or heard about who were consumed with their way of life.

"Now for you young scientist who believe that history making tsunamis are over with and that you need to be more of a knowledgeable historian than an alert scientist, I tell you that there are places all over our planet, including the continental United States, that are ticking time bombs. We need people who will be capable of understanding the great forces that cause these killer waves and who will develop and discover new ways to give people the time to evacuate danger zones. Biblically speaking for you who attend church, we need watchmen who will blow their trumpets to warn us of impending danger. Governments around the world are at last seriously listening to our warnings. Huge waves cannot be arrested like terrorist caught trying to blow up a city, but they can sure do a lot of damage and if we get the necessary funds to develop and implement studies and set up warning systems both on land, sea, and via satellites, we can and will provide a great service to billions of human beings.

"Governments cannot afford acceptable risk factors or literally gamble that these waves will not suddenly become realities when and where scientists are waving red flags. The 2004 Indian Ocean tsunami was probably our latest major wakeup call. We have lots of very good film showing people standing looking like dumb cows waiting and looking at that wave while it rushed toward them. I have seen lots of film of the event ever since I was a kid, just dumbfounded, wondering why those people are not running for all they are worth. A lot of equipment has been put in place around the world to monitor and warn officials so that they can hopefully evacuate these danger zones.

"Now we will discuss our East Coast tsunami preparedness." A young woman raises her hand and is acknowledged. Doctor Smith speaks:

"Yes, ma'am, Julia?"

"Doctor Smith, how long would it take to warn people on the coast about a huge wave coming for a visit?"

"We will go into this question in more detail before the class is over with, but to answer your question, it will take only about four or five minutes to run people off the beaches if all goes right. Of course, warnings can go out, but people have to obey them and people have to have time and road space to exit danger zones. A crowed beach at the height of the summer would prove a big challenge for officials because small beach towns do not have enough law enforcement people to control huge crowds of people who will be very much concerned about survival. There will be traffic jams, wrecks to move out of the way, people acting hostile toward other people because of fear. We need more bridges across our Intracoastal Water Way, but that is not an easy goal. Money is not as plentiful as it once was. It is hard enough just for our country to keep up the roads and bridges we currently have in service.

"As I said, the 2004 Indian Ocean tsunami which killed several hundred thousand people was the biggest wakeup call in modern times alerting officials and citizens alike that we need to take the tsunami business seriously. It took this tragedy to get the wheels going. There was a similar incident in the Twentieth Century that caused the Powers That Be to change and enforce new regulation to save lives. Someone please try to guess what I am referring to." A young man raises his hand.

"Sir, I believe that you are referring to the Triangle Shirtwaist Factory incident in 1922 when hundreds of people were burned to death in New York City. The Government made new safety rules regarding doors that push out rather than those you have to pull open from the inside to exit a building."

"No, I was thinking of another incident. I am impressed that you bring up another incident that changed laws and forced officials to do what should have already been done. I was thinking about the H M S Titanic tragedy that forced maritime countries all over the world to see to it that enough life boats were provided for everyone on board a commercial ship or boat. Of course, now days that law has been extended to any large private boat. The U. S. Coast Guard routinely stops vessels in our harbors and makes sure the life boats or rafts are available and in good repair. Our government, like all governments before 2004, did not provide the necessary funding because it was basically gambling like insurance companies on the numbers.

"We are aware that seventy percent of our tsunami problem is a Pacific Ocean generated phenomena. For that very reason far more is known about this area than our East Coast. That is understandable. However, we need to increase our knowledge about potential tsunami threats regardless of where in the Atlantic these waves might be born, and that includes off our own continental shelf. Huge waves have in fact come our way. Ancient evidence here in North Carolina is everywhere. This is why we have so many sand hills. That wave came ashore before recorded history according to some scientist. One huge boulder has been located in the Bahamas that was deposited by an enormous wave. That boulder is at Port Stephens. It is estimated to weigh two thousand tones. It was picked up by the tsunami and deposited five hundred meters inland, eleven meters above sea level. A wave came ashore near Grand Banks, Newfoundland, Canada, in 1929 that killed people and did property damage. If a wave of that same size would hit the same area, it would potentially kill a lot more people than the 1929 wave because of the huge population increase. More structures would be destroyed.

"All earthquakes, even very large ones do not always produce tsunamis. The key word is location. Research has revealed, for example, that earthquakes near Cape Anne in1755 or near Charleston, South

Carolina, in 1881 were not and will not breed significant waves." One student asks a question:

"Doctor Smith, where would an earthquake need to take place to cause a tsunami on our East Coast?" Doctor Smith responds to the question:

"I would say about a hundred kilometers from the shore where the continental slope usually starts. If a really large quake took place where a huge underwater landslide sent billions of tons of the shelf into very deep water, we could expect a dangerous wave. Before anyone asks, scientist and that includes me, believe that a 7.5 earthquake is the maximum size quake we will ever expect. Now this has nothing to do with the size of waves that could be generated off of islands near Africa or other locations.

"It has now been twenty five years since NOAA completed its first series of deep ocean buoys off our coast. Since that day, several more have been added to our early warning system. They have all been ungraded every so many years as new technology is available. DART stations are installed with two way satellite communication which allows scientist and our officials and all concerned coastal regions the ability to be on top of anything coming our way.

"In the years 2005 and later in 2006, NOAA received seventeen million dollars and six million prospectively. Years since 2006, more money has been given to NOAA because citizens are demanding more. Now before anyone asks me, I will tell you if you don't already know that Norfolk, Virginia, was the first large East Coast city to be so called tsunami ready. This happened back in 2006. This program is called the NOAA National Weather Service and it helps our communities to prepare evacuation plans in case of a real need to get the public out of harm's way. Also classes are held for the public designed to train and inform so that we will not be caught off guard.

"The West Coast of the United States is in good shape when it comes to tsunami warning systems; in fact, all of the major countries bordering the Pacific Ocean are provided with accurate warning devices set in place and monitored by twenty six member states. Can anyone tell me why the United States is interested in working closely with these other countries?" A young lady raises her hand. Doctor Smith calls her name:

"Yes, Natasha?"

"Doctor Smith, I am from Hawaii, need I say more?" Everyone laughs realizing the question has been answered because Hawaii is just about in the middle of the Pacific Ocean. Doctor Smith continues:

"Earthquakes, or anything that could create a huge wave is of concern for Hawaii. In fact, the main Pacific warning center is stationed at Ewa Beach, Hawaii. Now students, I believe that all of us realize that there are other places in the Pacific that we should be concerned about tsunamis such as Australia because over fifteen percent of that country's people now live in low areas near the ocean. These people need to be tsunami educated. There is New Zealand, studies have been done in the Bay of Plenty for years now to determine how many underwater folds are dangerous. At one time only six were known about, but after the 2004 tsunami in the Indian Ocean, which killed nearly two hundred thousand people, scientists have double timed their research in the area. We now know about one hundred and sixty six folds where continental plates converge that are of interest and concern. We could spend much time about the Philippines or New Zealand, but this will have to wait until another class.

"Many of us have been taught or have assumed that destructive waves are all natural occurrences and as a geologist and oceanographer, that assumption is what I work with, but be aware that the United States and I am sure other powerful nations have considered creating their own mega tsunamis as weapons of mass destruction just like other weapons designed and used to fight with. I am sorry to say that experiments have actually been conducted by scientist to create huge waves. This knowledge was kept top secret for a very long time. Tests were conducted in New Zealand off the coast of Chuckland. Huge bombs, probably nuclear, would be timed to go off at the right sequence, time, and location to create the most destruction. I am sure that a high tide at night off the coast of a nation we were fighting during World War II would have been disastrous and without warnings nature often provides us to give some prior notice of danger." A young man raises his hand to ask a question:

"Yes, James, what is your question?"

"Sir, why didn't they use this technology against the powerful nation of Japan?" Doctor Smith answers the question:

"James, it was not because of a change of heart, but because the ability to create the necessary waves to cripple Japan was not fully developed before the war was over with in 1945. You do remember what event in history aided Japan in making its decision to surrender?"

"Yes, sir, the atom bombs."

"Do we have a history of tsunamis in the Atlantic? Yes, and I have a listing of these events. I will mention a few, but will not go into all of the details. I have highlighted what you need to know. I do not expect you to remember all. I am actually more interested in students having the necessary skills to monitor these danger zones and to accurately predict imminent dangerous possibilities that we all need to be concerned about. On page 32A you will see listed the 1755 Lisbon, Portugal, quake. Look at the factors that caused the almost 9.0 magnitude quake. You will see the convergence zone in red where Africa and the Eurasian Plate are located at a ridge named the Gorringe Bank. Get the science down, look at the history so you will realize that these places generate people killers and history altering events. On page 37A you will notice an earthquake which occurred in the Aneganda Trough. Notice the size of the wave. In 1918, there was a 7.5 quake near the Puerto Rican Trench which is the deepest place in the Atlantic." A student raises his hand and is recognized:

"Doctor Smith, I live on Wrightsville Beach. I have lived there for about a year. I am now wondering if it is a good place to live. I consider this class a wakeup call for me. Should I relocate?" Doctor Smith answers his student:

"No, I would not leave if you are happy, and the rent is reasonable. Look people, no matter where we live on this planet, there is always a chance that you will suddenly be faced with a natural disaster. I have even read where one man years ago was sitting in his house watching television and a small meteorite from outer space went through the roof of his house and landed between his legs. Go to California and the hill that your luxury house sits on slides suddenly downhill with you in it. Or perhaps a huge wild fire sparked by dry lightning rushes through the neighborhood you are living in. You go out to our mid-western states and you walk out the door and a huge tornado sucks you up and your tragic story is material for television news. Live here on the East Coast of the United States and if you live here for ten or more years, there is a very good chance you will experience a large hurricane that you will hopefully survive.

"Could we experience a tsunami here in our area? Of course, we could. I would not gamble on the odds in favor of such an unlikely event, but the unexpected is what we are usually concerned about, right?" Let's go over the tsunami history. If I was considering hiring you for a job, I would require a resume or a verifiable track of your job history. This record would hopefully inform me of your qualifications. How you treat other people, and your criminal history which is usually an addendum to a complete resume. In a sense, we can look at the resume of a tsunami threat for our neck of the woods. Some scientists believe that a tsunami washed into the shores of North Carolina before recorded history and created the so called Sand Hills of the state. I may be wrong, but I believe that the hills were created by ocean levels at various times and place. The main sand hills that people think about are near the Piedmont area of

North and South Carolina. These sand hills are now valuable because they naturally help filter our water supply that makes its way from the mountains. I do believe that the coastal plains were much lower about eighteen or so thousand years ago or the land has risen. The Atlantic was probably not hugely deeper in those days if the land rising theory is incorrect.

"I mentioned earlier about a tsunami that hit the East Coast of the United States in 1929 near the State of Main which was caused by an earthquake in Newfoundland. It did not affect us here, but was never the less an East Coast tsunami." A young lady raises her hand and is acknowledged and asks a question:

"Doctor Smith, when did the so called Sand Hills first start forming? I find this subject interesting because I have an aunt that lives in Moor County. I used to collect all kinds of sharks teeth, whale bones, and shells from a huge sand hill back of my aunt's house." Doctor Smith comments:

"Yes, it is very interesting walking and digging around those sand hills. Once when I was a boy visiting some of my father's distant cousins, who still live in Southern Pines, North Carolina, I went fossil hunting. My cousins owned a large sweet potato farm. A series of hills ran through the backside of a large field they owned. My cousin and I dug holes into the sides of the hills looking for shark teeth. I found dozens of Megaldon teeth. I still have them in a glass display case at my parents' home in Boston. These sand hills are now located where the ocean once stopped just like on our beaches today. These sand hills are not the only ones in North and South Carolina and they can be easily spotted from a low slow moving airplane. Most scientists believe that this sand was deposited by the Atlantic about twenty million years ago in what we call the Miocene Age which is indicated by the type of fossils found in these deposits.

"Now students, I am going to pass out some old information done back in the early years of our century about tsunami threats. This information is still valid and scientifically correct. We have not had a tsunami since these studies first came out. Mother nature is very patient and human life is very brief, even the life of major civilizations in the scheme of things. Sometimes nature surprises us unexpectedly and suddenly with history making events. These are the ones we need to worry about and become wise to. A volcano starts rumbling, smoke comes out of its top and this goes on for months providing all of the warning anyone or any city would need to have the native intelligence to realize that people should seriously consider the possibility that they need to pack and leave as soon as possible. I am not so worried about these events as far as human life is concerned. The cost potential in huge damage to nearby cities, or valuable forest is an almost certain. We scientist are still keeping a careful eye on the Canary Islands." Doctor Smith turns on a fancy projector connected wireless to a laptop computer and displays the Canary Islands out in the Atlantic off the West Coast of Africa not far from Morocco. He directs a laser pointer onto the Island of La Palma that is displayed on a huge motor controlled screen. He next magnifies the active Volcano Cumbre Vieja for a close up. "Students notice that the summit is cracked in a star like crescent pattern. The volcano has more than one vent. In 1949 a large portion of its western flank suddenly dropped down four meters into the Atlantic. The volcano was also active back centuries before 1949, but this event was witnessed by more modern scientist and the fact that the western wall slipped down got people to thinking about a future potential disaster. This large chunk of rock is now moving ever so slowly, not because of seismetic activity, but by gravity. It would take thousands of years for gravity to carry all of this rock into deep water. In fact, most likely it would break up into hundreds of smaller pieces. This is what many scientists believe.

"We now have in 2031 GPS systems all over Cumbre Vieja that keep track on verifiable movement occurring. No one can dispute this now. The debate still goes on as to how much of the volcano will plunge into the Atlantic at once. Gradually, in little chunks, as some believe, would not result in a history making event. If the entire western half of the island suddenly plunges into the deep trench, a major disaster would undoubtedly take place. In 1971, the volcano had another eruption. That has been sixty years ago, so we are expecting another eruption of significance any year now." A hand is raised:

"Yes, James?"

"Sir, if the entire western half of this volcano would suddenly plunge into the Atlantic during a major eruption, how high would the wave be and how soon would it reach Wrightsville Beach?" Doctor Smith speaks:

"A lot of lab as well as computer generated models have been worked to determine the height of the tsunami. Remember that scientist must know what they are talking about and have a proven track record before the authorities will take them seriously. We are like prophets in the Bible. We read about bad prophets giving out wrong information to the people and those in authority and cause a lot of trouble. For example, a prophet predicts that an imminent invasion by an enemy nation is a sure thing. The king orders people to stop what they are doing, such as farmers planting crops so that the nation can eat. Also, all other kind of industry is suddenly halted so that everyone can prepare for war. People will have to be evacuated and provided for. Cities are locked down and all domestic commerce as well as international trade must cease while waiting for the huge enemy armies to arrive.

"Now just suppose the enemy never shows up? That prophet is out of a job or missing some body parts such as his tongue or perhaps his head. We as scientist must be careful also. Most of our funding that pays our salaries for instructors, staff, and all equipment comes from government sources. If we as a community predict that a huge wave is on its way to visit and tens of millions of people's lives are disrupted so that they will not perish, we had better unfortunately be on target.

"Twenty seven years ago the once director of the famous Benfield Grieg Hazard Research Center at University College London sounded the trumpet and predicted that one day the entire western half of the volcano on La Palma was going to suddenly and with little or no announcement plunge into the deep dark waters of the Atlantic creating a mega tsunami that would cause immense lost of life and property in all of the North Atlantic basin. When he made this domes day prediction, a lot of people were considering the worst possible situation. Doctor McGuire said that the mega tsunami would travel at the speed of a commercial jet back in his day, which was nearly six hundred miles per hour, crossing the Atlantic to arrive nine or ten hours later with a height between twenty and fifty meters.

"If you happen to be in the vicinity of a harbor or an estuary, you really will be in big trouble because the wave will be even higher and will rush in with greater force. In a worst case event, the continuous wave front could force its way as much as fifteen miles inland depending, of course, on the height of the land in a particular area above sea level. Remember that this is not just one wave making a big splash and that is it. These waves move in continually similar to a storm surge for as much as fifteen minutes before they stop their advance onto the land.

"We are fortunate in that there is far less volcanic and plate activity in our local ocean than the Pacific. Our continental plate on the Atlantic side is considered a passive zone or margin. This simply means that we have no plate collision or plates moving past each other as far as we know." A student raises her hand for a question:

"Doctor Smith, how far inland could a wave travel in a worst case situation?"

"In a worst case situation, as I said, the wave front could travel as far inland as fifteen miles depending, on the height of the land above sea level. Of course, the half trillion tones of rock would have to plunge into the ocean in a minute of time to produce such a transfer of energy. Some lab results have this wave to be vastly taller than my conservative estimate.

"The Mid-Atlantic Ridge is moving outward as fresh molten rock comes from deep within the mantle. There are a few hot spots of concern in the Atlantic that you should be aware of. Remember you need to know only the information I have indicated in your handouts. The dynamics of each area of interest, volcanoes of concern, or famous events like earthquakes that changed history are all illustrated on my huge website. As I said earlier, you don't need to be a historian at this point in your educational development. I would be much more impressed if you know the twenty five or so events and places I have underlined and the dynamics or science behind what caused the events of interest, or perhaps current activity taking place. I am more interested in the practical application of our profession. A simple illustration, but not a hard comparison; some people can tell you all about cars. These people have memorized automotive history and all of the features of the engine and the manufacturing process, but I would never allow these experts to work on my one hundred and fifty thousand dollar SUV. I would trust an old boy or girl who has spent their lives under the hood. A person that has to use lava soap every day to cut the grease and grime off their strong seasoned hands." A bell rings and class is about to end. Doctor Smith speaks:

"Students, I will see you all next Wednesday, that is, if a tsunami does not wash all of us away before then. Have a nice weekend!"

The Smith family is home. Supper is over with and the children are playing inside. They have been very much entertained by the huge new house they are living in, school activities taking place, and their summer plans to enjoy many a day with their new found friends in the Wrightsville Beach Community. Brenda and her husband, Doctor David Smith, who will be referred to as David Smith outside of school or formal functions is with his wife walking around their huge Spanish style home admiring every inch of it! The walls are formally and tastefully decorated with huge oil paintings of Spanish history such as the hall they are walking through which is decorated with a history of the royal families of Spain. While David and Brenda continue to walk, they cannot help, but to notice the beautiful painting of Ferdinand and Isabella not long after they were married. Below the painting was a plaque that read, "In union is strength."

On the other side of the same hall is a huge oil painting of the famous explorer Columbus. Columbus was in a very important conference in a beautiful room inside a palace. On a fancy table he had maps of the known world. Sitting before the table was the King and Queen of Spain earnestly listening to Columbus as he explains his plans to the royal couple. Columbus sought financial help to purchase ships and secure crews and needed supplies to make an attempt to sail to the Far East to India to develop business relations with the merchants of India who were wealthy with valuable spices so desired in Middle Age Europe.

At the head of the great hall David and Brenda were slowly walking down, they pause to admire a hand painted mural on the wall just ahead of them. The mural was a reproduction of the famous painting of the landing of Columbus and his ship's crews on what he thought was India. The scene is very striking as Columbus kneels down on one leg with sword in hand looking up in a prayer like state of mind. Surrounding the explorer are scores of men, some praying, others holding flags and staves in their hands. Beyond them in the woods, probably unseen by Columbus, are native Indians watching and wondering who these strange and interesting visitors are.

The Indians, so called, who are recognized as natives of San Salvador received Columbus and his men with open friendship. During later exploration of the vicinity, the islands of Haiti or as some call it, San Domingo, and Cuba were discovered. David speaks:

"Honey, I would like to visit your parents tomorrow. We have not been on the plantation for a couple of months. Your parents may feel that we have forgotten about them." Brenda speaks:

"I would love to visit them. We have been so busy. You have just started teaching at UNCW and I have just opened up our home school. I am sure that my parents understand. David, you never did get around to exploring the blue hole in the fishing lake."

"As you said, Brenda, we have been very busy. I talked to Dennis Miller about it. We only talked about the hole for a minute or two. No plans have been finalized to explore that hole."

That night everyone was awaken; except for Betty, who was deep asleep as only a child her age could normally experience. David is immediately awaken and realizes that a jet or an explosion did not shake the ground or the sound barrier. A few seconds later, another jolt takes place. The next morning on Channel 6, WECT, a news reporter reports that local residents were alarmed that an explosion had taken place or that the military was shooting large guns off the coast. While watching the television and eating breakfast, David comments:

"That was not an explosion, I am sure of that, but a small earthquake!" Brenda looks at her husband with concern on her face and speaks:

"Honey, are you sure about that? I have never heard of an earthquake taking place around here!" David speaks:

"Actually earthquakes do take place in North Carolina, but not very frequent. Most of the fault margins are old and very deep. The majority of earthquakes felt in North Carolina actually began in other states." Brenda quickly cleans up the table and puts the few bowls and utensils into the dishwasher while David makes sure the children are prepared to stay a few days at their grandparents' home. Small suite cases are packed and are in the family's big SUV. Fifteen minutes pass and the Smith family is leaving their exit gate excited about going back to enjoy a few days on the plantation. David will not teach until next Wednesday. David's class will be conducted by a substitute instructor. The first twenty minutes of Monday's class time will be devoted to taking a twenty minute test. The rest of the time will be devoted to watching a scientific film about fault lines underneath North Carolina and the history of earthquakes in the region.

It was good to be back on the plantation again! The children were very excited about the visit. Brenda could not, but to become a little emotional the moment she saw the great house beyond the ancient trees. How blessed above measure she felt! It was truly a place where the ladder of love and joy went all the way to Heaven itself! David felt a great weight lift from his mind as he just sat for a minute in his SUV seat after the vehicle was turned off. What a place of mystery and beauty this great big plantation possessed! He could not even imagine how life would be like if he had not married Brenda. Brenda's parents and grandparents were in the yard just waiting for the doors of the SUV to open. The moment Brenda steps out of the SUV, her mother, Lillian Pridgen, hugs her neck. Grandmother Lilly also grabs Brenda and gives her a big hug. The children run to their grandfather who was near them. The ladies hug David and Beard his father-in-law shakes David's hand and pats him on the left shoulder affectionately. Mr. Zeb holds his hand out to David and speaks while shaking his hand.

"Well, son, it is mighty good to have you back! I wish that school was just outside of Atkinson so that all of you could live right here with the rest of us." David speaks:

"Yes, it would be nice, but it would be a little difficult to arrange that. I don't believe that we would have much luck in persuading the Atlantic Ocean to move about forty miles inland." Mr. Zeb looks a little serious before he comments:

"I just hope that great big lake will just remain where it is at. I don't believe it would be a welcomed event. Say, what do you think about that earthquake two days ago?" David speaks:

"It was only a little one, about a magnitude 4 on the Richter Scale. The only thing that surprised us was that it was located about one hundred miles almost directly out from Wrightsville Beach. I may go out there one day and check the situation out. It may have been caused by a simple underwater landslide." Great Grandfather Zeb smiles and speaks:

"Well, I am sure everything will be alright. It will probably provide a little adventure for you." David speaks:

"Yes, we will, of course, check the situation out. That is what we are in the business for." Mrs. Lillian speaks so that all can hear her:

"Come on into the small kitchen everyone; let's sit at the table and drink some hot apple cider we put up last year and have some of that pound cake my mother-in-law baked yesterday. I may just be able to find a little strawberry ice cream in the porch cooler." The children are especially excited about the prospect of sitting down with their grandparents and enjoying a big snack. Lillian speaks:

"Mattie, is that cider hot enough yet?"

"Yes, Ma'am it is ready, nice and hot!" Cinnamon sticks are placed into each mug to add a rich flavor. The cake is cut and beside it in each plate is a generous helping of homemade ice cream. The children soon learn that their bedrooms have not been changed and that the train set and the doll house are still out and ready to entertain them on a cold winter morning. Brenda speaks:

"Mother, are they holding the farmers market in Atkinson today?" Lillian answers:

"Brenda, I would imagine a few hardy souls are faithfully serving their customers, but it is a little too cold for me. When I was younger, I would be there, but there is always plenty to do around here. Your grandmother and I are going to spend a few hours in the greenhouse. If you care to join us, you are welcome to come along. We will just walk through it to make sure everything is OK." David spends a few hours with his father-in-law who seems to be very interested in David's work at UNCW. This is the first time he has expressed so much interest. Mr. Zeb has most of his morning in his herb garden preparing herbal teas he will later bring to the house to share with David to take back home with him so that his granddaughter's family will have plenty of rich natural tea to enjoy during the cold winter season.

While David and his father-in-law are having a nice conversation in the sunroom facing the east next to the east porch, they see a buckboard come up pulled by a single large brown mule with a sort of coat or wrap to keep the animal warm. Beard looks at David and back toward the front of the mansion's front lawn wondering what Roy Henry wants. He gets up to go outside to see what was up. David follows his father-in-law outside. They both grab their heavy coats and winter caps before going outside to face the thirty five degree weather. Beard speaks:

"Top of the morning to you, Roy. What news do you bring our way?" Beard knew his old friend well enough to know that Roy did not come by to find something to do or engage in small idle talk. Roy recognizes David's presence and reaches down from the buck board to shake David's hand. Roy's face wrinkles up as he considers what he is about to share with Beard Pridgen, a man he respected and had fished with and played with when they were children.

"Beard, I have not been drinking, or smoking anything I don't have any business with, but what I am about to share with you, I would not fear to say in church as anything, but the Gospel Truth." Beard looked surprised, but he patiently listened. Roy speaks:

"Last night I saw a huge hairy animal on my front porch about twelve at night. I have never heard such a racket in my born days! I thought that the windows were going to fall out! My wife and three boys slipped out the back and stood next to the house just a firing their shotguns at that thing. There was no way to miss their target and they all had OO buckshot in their twelve gauge guns. I have never seen the likes of such a beast. It looked like a huge dog. There was something mighty queer about that animal. I have seen all kinds of critters around these parts. I know that a varmint's eyes will shine when a light is shinning on them, but there were no lights shining on them! That thing must have come from Hades itself because no mortal or earthly animal has eyes that glow in the dark like that! I am almost afraid to say more." Beard is stunned by what Roy shares with him. He knows that his old friend is not one given over to foolishness or made up tales. Beard speaks:

"You may as well share the rest of the story, Roy."

"That creature suddenly disappeared. It exploded into a great big ball of light going every which a way. We were blinded a moment after it exploded." Roy stops talking while looking a little disturbed." Beard speaks:

"I don't know what to make of it, Roy. I have never seen a creature like the one that visited you. I am sure that you are living right and that this occurrence was not some kind of warning or something."

"What do you mean by that, Beard? I ain't perfect, but I try to live by The Good Book and you know that my boys are not slipping around doing something they ought not to do. I do remember an old white fellow who I overheard while at one of the stores in Atkinson when I was a young fellow telling his neighbors that he believed in omens. He told them that he was fishing one day long ago with his father with cane poles and up comes a black crow that lands on the end of his father's pole. It was the queerest thing heda ever witnessed. When his father shook the bird off his pole, the thing flies back and perches on his pole again as big as you please just a making a fuss like you know crows make. He said that his father turned and looked at him and told him that bird was a messenger announcing that someone had died that they had to immediately head back home.

"When they got back home, a small crowd of neighbors had showed up. Their horses and early model cars were near the porch of the old house. The man walked into the house with his son who shared this story with us at the country store. He realized that his wife was crying and several older sisters from the church they all attended were comforting her. The man soon learned that his youngest daughter had fallen into the well and drowned." Beard just shook his head taking it all in. David had never heard of such a strange tale before, but was; however, troubled by the thoughts of an incident he and his wife had experienced together last summer at her great uncle's huge chateau, and experience that he and his wife have not talked about since, hoping they could just forget all about it. Beard continued to listen to Roy Henry while slowly shaking his head right to left, unable to come up with an acceptable explanation for Roy's unusual experience. Beard speaks:

"Roy, I do recall that years ago when I was a young boy while in grade school, one of our neighborhood school teachers spoke about a strange incident that his great grandparents shared with their people. He said that his great-great grandmother was very sick in bed while family was gathered around her bedside. It was certain that her journey on this earth was fast coming to a close. Family members were praying and the old preacher from their home church near Atkinson was there with the family to comfort them as best as he could. He was doing what preachers do. He was doing a little praying and Bible reading. It was in the late fall of the year and the fog was rolling in on their little estate out in the country before the days of modern outside lights. It was getting late, but the minister was determined to remain until the end. He was reading favorite passages out of the Bible about Elijah and Elisha. I am sure you have read it or heard it many times how old Elijah was caught up in a chariot of fire pulled by horses not from this world. Now I understand that while the parson was reading, the old woman who was about to pass from this life to the next, threw her hands up into the air and shouted for all to hear, 'they are here, they are here!' Outside, heard at some distance, rapidly on its way, was the sound of a rushing chariot or some kind of wagon pulled by what sounded like horses.

"The door of the old shack suddenly opened aided by an unseen hand. Moments later the door closed and the sound of a chariot was once again heard moving away to parts unknown with unnatural speed. I understand that everyone in the old house was frozen with terror and awe. One of the folks near the old woman immediately announced to all that the matriarch of the family was no longer with them. When they all looked upon her face, they could see that it was frozen in a smile."

Our story now takes a leap in time and place to Wednesday afternoon at UNCW. There are many professors lecturing in the science buildings or working with students in labs and field projects here and there, but our story focuses on Doctor Hardin's class because he is a person of interest. Doctor Hardin speaks:

"I teach both oceanography and geology. Today most of you in class will specialize in oceanography. How many of you are working on double majors?" Eight out of thirty three students raise their hands. "Good for you! I hope that the rest of you guys will consider pursuing a double major or will come back and get a second degree. It will take you two extra years to get the degree. Some people find it easier this way and seem to be able to concentrate better on one major at a time. I say this because I can promise you that your scientific understanding and your job opportunities will almost double. Jobs are not always easy to get. You don't want to be put in a position of having to work in another field, perhaps a nonprofessional job unable to breakaway and get the job you went to school for. Do you folks realize that most college graduates do not work in the fields they were trained in? That is not good. Lots of companies will hire you just based on the fact you graduated with good grades in college. Go to the employment agencies or read the job listings in any newspaper and you will prove my point for me.

"We need lots of people who will be able to help our country develop its natural resources both underground as well as under the oceans. Our oceans are hurting because of overfishing. We need people who are trained and empowered to work on this problem. Coastal ecology is very important and our rivers are not near as healthy as they should be. New natural drugs need to be discovered and developed that will open up hope for people suffering from all kinds of diseases." While Doctor Hardin is lecturing to inspire his students, the room is shaken by a strong jolt sufficient to get everyone's attention! Hardin speaks: "It looks like we might be experiencing a minor earthquake." A few moments later a second jolt shakes the classroom. "Students, there is nothing to be alarmed about. That was a minor earthquake that I am sure will be discussed in tomorrow's newspaper."

That night at the Smith residence, Brenda and her husband are in bed getting ready for a nice winter night's sleep. It is Wednesday night. Brenda speaks:

"Honey, if I am not mistaken, we had another earthquake. What do you think?"

"Yes, Brenda, I have checked on it, but I don't believe that we have anything to worry about. The epic center was like the last quake about one hundred miles off our local beach. We scientist know of no active faults in the region. I will be going out to the site where the earthquake took place and take a look at it. I would imagine that what is taking place is some minor continental shelf failure, a simple landslide."

It is now Friday afternoon and Doctor David Smith is teaching a class about earthquakes in North Carolina. Class has just begun. A young man raises his hand and is acknowledged. Doctor Smith speaks:

"Yes, William?"

"Doctor Smith, what is causing the recent small earth tremors we have experience here lately?"

"Doctor Smith speaks:

"I don't know. I will be investigating the site in about a week. I am guessing at this point that we are having some minor landslides. I am sure that it would be hundreds of millions of tons of rock, but that is not hugely significant. If it took place on a mountainside, in close proximity to a small city, it would be serious. A slide that many miles out hundreds of feet under the ocean renders it a minor event at this point in time.

"I have taken advantage of the web page hosted by our state. The Geological Hazards Earthquake in North Carolina. You all have copies of the eight pages I printed off. Keep this file as a reference, especially if you plan on working here in this state. In fact, all of you will be required to participate in field trips to study and to familiarize yourselves with places of concern. We are not going to look at everything. Up at the top of the page you will notice landslides, sinkholes, old mines, and the heading of earthquakes at the top. Be aware that all fifty of our states have official websites about geological hazards. So, if you want to do study on a particular state or simply are visiting a state on vacation, it would be interesting to look up the information. Perhaps you would want to see some of the so called geological hazards personally.

"Earthquakes are part of North Carolina history. I emphasize this state because we can take advantage of what is here and not have to travel all over the world. The same or similar forces that create earthquakes taking place in the state of our residence or quakes felt that were generated in nearby states like South Carolina, create earthquakes all over the world. Before the nineteen sixties, most small earthquakes were not recorded because there were not enough seismograph stations put in place. Earthquakes are known to have taken place as early as 1698. We learn about these early quakes when we read historical accounts. Scientist can only estimate their size based on the amount of reliable damage reported.

"Now, I am not going to waste classroom time reading and lecturing about every earthquake that North Carolina has experienced. Turn to page two of the handout sheet and you will see where in our state the earthquakes took place and the magnitude on the Richter Scale. Notice that we have had four magnitude three-four quakes and you can add two more to this history. Notice that we have two types of scales or measurements to tell us about a quake. A comparison of the Modified Mercalli Scale and the old Richter Scale is very enlightening. If you hear that a 6.0 quake has taken place going by the Richter Scale, you can look at the Modified Mercalli Scale and get an idea of the potential damage that may have taken place and people's reactions. Get very familiar with this chart, memorize it, it will be on a test. If you are serious about what you are here for, you will make sure you do not forget it. Need I say more? These are the tools of your trade. The signs and symptoms your patient is manifesting and experiencing after an earthquake of significant size. Our patient will probably never be a human being, but planet Earth.

"If you were a physician confronted with a patient who has a terrible disease that you know could spread and kill many people, you may realize that you cannot save your patient, but you can enforce immediate measures that have been put in place by government and the authorities in your neck of the woods to halt the spread of the disease. The same holds true for us scientist who study the earth. We can do our best to predict an earthquake or perhaps the eruption of a volcano and if appropriate, a possible tsunami and its size and direction.

"Most of you people will probably not teach. Your work will require you to work for local and state governments and large construction companies. The Powers That Be will not allow the construction of large buildings, bridges, water towers, huge smoke stacks, roads, and you name it unless they secure the help of a type of geologist. You can't build large structures just anywhere or disaster will take place. My wife's family owns a large plantation at the junction of Bladen, Sampson, and Pender Counties, about three miles from the small town of Atkinson. If you don't know where Atkinson is located, you can go to your computer and download virtual road trips or even plane trips to fly over Atkinson. On the plantation there are people who do hardly anything, but make pegs, which are basically wooden nails or perhaps roofing shingles. As simple as it might appear to you, these folks take their jobs very serious. They take pride in their work. Need I say more?"

Our story once again takes a leap in time and location. Doctor Smith and dozens of students have been assembling a working model of Wrightsville Beach. Every house and commercial structure is included, even the now two bridges that go over the Intracoastal Waterway. The purpose of the project is to determine property damage done by tsunamis of various heights. Another working model that is on a much larger scale includes the entire region out to the continental shelf drop off. This project is not complete because more data is needed to make sure the working model is a true reflection of actual current conditions. Doctor Hardin walks into the lab with several of his fellow teachers to see what is going on. He is very aware of the work taking place, but has not been required to participate nor has he volunteered himself to help his boss, Doctor David Smith.

Twenty-Two

Doctor Smith Carries a Team of Scientists Out to the Continental Shelf and Learns that the Shelf is About to Collapse

Doctor Hardin walks up to a large working model of Wrightsville Beach with several of his, shall we say, disciples? Doctor Hardin has been working hard for some time now gathering up his forces. Nearly a third of the faculty have been influenced by his magnetic personality. Doctor Hardin speaks to Doctor Smith:

"I see that you have filled out an NURC/UNCW Cruise Plan for next week. I assume based on your objectives that you are going to determine the source of the recent minor earthquakes we have experienced here lately."

"Yes, I believe that we should try to determine what is going on out there."

"I just hope that you will not be led to sound the trumpet and announce an imminent tsunami threat."

"No, Doctor Hardin, I like you don't expect a tsunami, but who knows. I do know that something unusual is going on out near the continental shelf or we would not be experiencing so many earthquakes as of lately."

"So, I assume that your models here of Wrightsville Beach and the continental shelf are being designed to help you make a tsunami prediction."

"That is correct, Doctor Hardin. I don't have enough information about the continental shelf disturbance until I go out there with a team and see if there is something going on that we should be aware of." Doctor Hardin continues to walk around the huge lab making comments to his associates. He eventually leaves and goes back to his office to grab his coat and briefcase before he drives home.

Our story once again takes a leap in time and location. Doctor David Smith is on board the Sea King, a two hundred and fifty foot so called mother ship. The purpose of the mission is to determine why there have been so many earthquakes just off Wrightsville Beach about a hundred miles out where the continental shelf slopes into much deeper water. On board are three professors and eight senior students all working on their doctorate in marine science. Everyone had been informed of the trip a week in advance so that personal commitments and appointments would be attended to before the trip. On board helping Doctor Smith is Doctor Joyce Brown, Doctor Jerry Skinner, and Doctor James Highsmith, who has not been introduced. It is March the tenth and the temperature is sixty degrees with a slight breeze coming out of the North West. The water is smooth and just perfect for such a mission. Our team has plans to stay for three full days if necessary to fully investigate what is going on.

While Doctor Smith and his team are preparing to explore the continental slope disturbance about a hundred miles off of Wrightsville Beach, Doctor Hardin is in class talking about methods and equipment UNCW works with to explore the ocean with.

"Students, I hope that all of you have enough background to appreciate all of the advancements made over the years and tools to aid us in our work. I illustrate, no matter how good of a mechanic one might be, it would be very hard if not impossible to work on a car engine if one did not have the right tools and electronic equipment. In our business we need more than our eyes, hands, and a few things like buckets, pickaxes, and shovels, and some primitive scuba gear to aid us. If we are going to do any serious study of our environment, we need boats and ships to carry us to the places in our rivers, lakes, and oceans. We need to be able to navigate or travel without getting lost. Instruments such as microscopes and chemical labs are important. We have to have the ability to accurately record our findings and make professional sketches or film of the plants and animals we are studying. Have any of you students looked at the findings of the H.M.S. Challenger Voyage that lasted for several years?" One student raises his right hand.

"I would encourage all of you people to take time to look at the Challenger collection. It is very impressive. Remember that this ship sailed not long after the American Civil War. That is 1873 to 1876. We can still learn from those volumes of books and from the thousands of specimens of plants and animals they preserved. We have learned more in the last hundred years about the oceans than of all of the people of antiquity combined. It is not that we are smarter than they, but we stand on their shoulders. We are blessed here at UNCW because we have so much going on in our favor. Our scientist travel the world over learning more about our oceans and other major bodies of water than Neptune himself could have known about."As you can all discern from a cursory glance at the information before you that the opportunities to learn and expand as individuals and as an institution are almost unlimited. Today we are able to use government or big company vender leased subs, ROVs, and AUVs almost every day." A student raises her hand:

"Yes, young lady?"

"Doctor Hardin, how deep will our submersibles go?"

"We have many that routinely go more than a thousand meters. Woods Hole Oceanographic Institution's DSV Alvin has been used a few times, but not often. It will descent over six thousand meters. I have never gone on such a deep dive and don't see a practical reason for us to be going down thousands of meters. I do most of all of my research in a hundred meters or less because that is where most of the fish, plants, and shell creatures live." A young man raises his hands:

"Doctor Hardin, don't we now have an exploration submarine that can go about four thousand meters down?"

"Yes, The Sea Explorer was brought from Boston University's facilities. We traded the Sea Wise for the submarine. The Sea Wise is an underwater living facility equipped with a lab and all kinds of scientific equipment. I have printed off a sheet from a website that is very old, but is informative and useful for this class. The sheet, as you students can see, is a comparison of DSVs and two other machines underwater research is done by. Of course, anytime we use DSVs we have the risk of human injury or death. It is very rare, but is always a possibility even if you send a team of scientist in scuba gear only twenty or thirty meters underwater. This is the reason we use DSVs because people are surrounded by steel and composite material. Of course, DSVs can go to depths no human could possibly survive in. I am not going to read all of the advantages and disadvantages of each unit. I do expect you students to read the material and have a decent understanding of these systems." A young man raises his hand and is recognized:

"Doctor Hardin, I understand that you are not in favor of the exchange of UNCW's underwater living lab for Boston's DSV. Why do you consider this a bad decision on UNCW's part?"

"We got, the Sea Wise, which is over a hundred feet long and capable of housing ten people almost indefinitely at a depth of over forty meters for a third of what it is worth. We obtained the Sea Wise from a Japanese company that farms oysters. Now we have a similar facility off the coast of Florida. UNCW exchanged the Sea Wise, which we housed off Wrightsville Beach, for a very advanced DSV that is primarily designed to go on very deep dives. Most of our research is in much shallower water not thousands of meters down. We can borrow such a DSV from Woods Hole Oceanographic Institution if we need one. I am speaking about Alvin 11. Most of the information about NOAA's Undersea Research Center concerns students getting their masters or above in oceanography. Of course, every field now days is like a tree with branches going in many directions. I want all of you scholars to look at the website listed on the handout. Read over it and have some basic understanding of what is going on over at the facility. For example, if you want to know what kind of research opportunities are available, simply go to the website. If you plan to continue your education in this field, I would encourage you to become as familiar as possible about this facility. In fact, by going over this site you may even see what your future will be like." A young lady raises her right hand and is acknowledged:

"Doctor Hardin, you said that UNCW has access to an underwater laboratory somewhere in Florida. Could you expand a little on your statement?"

"Thank you for asking. Folks, as long as you stick to what we are discussing, I have no problem with questions. In fact, I encourage them as long as we are able to move along and not spend too much time doing so. The name of our underwater laboratory is called Aquarius. At one time it was the only laboratory like it in the world where scientist could live and do their study. Of course, that is no longer true. The people who first worked on the Aquarius are no longer with us or they are retired. The Aquarius has been raised many times and repaired or upgraded." A student raises his hand:

"Yes, Benjamin, what is your question?"

"Does the university own the Aquarius?"

"No, Benjamin, it is actually owned by the Federal Government. It is under the control of the National Oceanic And Atmospheric Administration, commonly referred to as (NOAA). Our school manages it. The underwater laboratory and living facility asked about is located about 4.5 kilometers offshore from Key Largo, Florida." Another student makes a comment:

"So this means that UNCW no longer owns its own underwater laboratory!" Doctor Hardin speaks:

"You have got the message! Now if you people want to learn more about our program, go to the website listed on the handout. I believe that is the bell. I hope that all of you will study hard because I will test you on the material I have indicated on the handout and our lecture. The test will only last about thirty minutes. It will be served Friday. You people have the rest of the week to study."

Our story takes us to the Sea King, a two hundred and fifty foot research/mother-ship owned by UNCW and donated to UNCW by The Department of the Navy. Most of the team is now inside the command room except for the captain and a few utility deckhands. Several earthquakes have taken place in the vicinity. The epic center is almost directly one hundred miles off of Wrightsville Beach. It is not unheard of for minor quakes to shake Wrightsville Beach and its neighboring towns and the city of Wilmington. In fact, an earthquake was reported in 1884 and a second quake occurred on March 5, 1958 in the same spot. Nothing major took place. Houses were rattled and a few people reported that they had been rolled out of bed.

Several students are looking at a map of North Carolina where the counties are indicated. The purpose of the map is to show where earthquakes have taken place in N.C. Several of the students are looking at a blocked off region that covers New Hanover and Brunswick counties and extending out into the ocean. The students note that four quakes have taken place in the immediate area not counting the most recent quakes. They are minor, all being in the 4-5 magnitude range according to Richter scale measurements. Doctor Smith speaks:

"I am aware that our three instructors know and probably all of you students, but I will not assume without saying that our state is not known for a huge amount of seismetic activity. Our greatest danger is for a large earthquake to take place in a neighboring state sufficient to cause us grief. Our neighbors, for example, South Carolina, Georgia, and Tennessee do have active faults. Ours are much older. A major earthquake near Charleston, South Carolina, could cause areas of our state major problems.

"Our trip is not primarily to discover a major unknown active fault off our coast. I rather believe that we are going to be finding that our outer shelf has some significant structural weakness that should concern us. If the shelf is weaker than we previously understood it to be, it would not take history's largest quake to cause a major shelf collapse resulting in a tsunami. This tsunami would split in half. One wave would race toward Europe and the other wave closer and on the shore side would race toward Wrightsville Beach and arrive in about twelve minutes. We would have no practical warning time for this first and probably the larger wave. I say probably because when the wave bounces off Europe and comes back our way, it could cause even farther shelf collapse. I am, of course, thinking about the worst situation.

"Most of you know, or should know that cracks were discovered off the Virginia, North Carolina coastline over thirty years ago. The area of concern is about a hundred miles offshore. If indeed this approximately twenty-five mile stretch of our outer shelf suddenly plunged into much deeper water, our two states could experience a lot of destruction. The wave would come in very quickly and with little or no warning. If such an event occurred at the height of summer when a lot of people are living on the beaches, a lot of people would drown, including people in boats and yachts because a tsunami of at least thirty feet high would suddenly rush in. A wall of water that would continue to come in until all of its energy was dissipated." A student comments while looking at a monitor:

"I did not realize that there were so many canyons out here! I saw five large canyons in a book. I remember that one of them is the Wilmington Canyon. Doctor Smith, why haven't all of these canyons been mapped?"

"Most of them have been mapped, but are not significant for most people to be concerned about. Most books about the continental shelf only feature major canyon features. Most all of these major canyons have names that indicate their location to major rivers or cities. A few have even been named after sunken ships." Doctor Jerry Skinner speaks:

"My old college professors could only dream about this new all electrical hybrid ROV/AUV. I can't get over its speed, diving range, and its many functions. In the old days, we would use several vehicles and tools during a research project to achieve what the Octopus can do! Look at those high definition pictures coming in on our monitors!" Doctor Joyce Brown speaks:

"Yes, I remember us dragging or towing our side scan tow fish up and down the coastline or perhaps places like Northern Puerto Rico and the Virgin Islands." Doctor Smith speaks:

"I have used tow fish, but I feel that we need to get as much information as possible about the situation. We may only get one shot at the situation." Doctor Joyce Brown speaks:

"What do you mean by that, Doctor Smith?"

"I am under the impression that what we are doing is not politically correct. I have heard that it is rumored that I am trying to create a crisis." Doctor Jerry Skinner speaks:

"I am not sure what we will find. I don't expect anything earthshaking, but I would like to believe that what we are doing is appreciated and in line with our objectives." Doctor Smith continues:

"Look at all of those huge cracks. They are miles of them! Look at those sink holes. They are huge! We will determine the thickness of this structural weakness and continue to travel north so that we will scan the entire affected area. We can then start to determine the cubit volume of the material likely to collapse into the deep." Our team of scientists continue to survey and to access the possibility of a major continental shelf collapse. The shelf appears to be in peril for over forty miles from just south of Wrightsville Beach and north all the way to Browns Inlet just outside of Camp Lejeune, Marine Corp Base.

Friday afternoon finds Doctor Smith back at UNCW discussing his findings and showing running film and still pictures of his recent trip.

"All of you can plainly see how unstable the outer shelf has become. We also found the presence of a huge amount of semi-solid methane gas. In fact, enough to power the entire country for years. As you can see," Doctor Smith points with a laser pointer at the now still picture frames, "the sediment appears to be under pressure from water coming from the continent. We went much deeper with our ROV/AUV and discovered several large underwater landslides that are layered on top of each other. I am sure that the recent earthquakes are responsible for the slides. Before anyone asks, we have determined that about five cubit miles of debris has so far slid off the continental shelf into deep water." A young man raises his hand and Doctor Smith pauses the film to respond to the student:

"Doctor Smith, I do not take classes under you. I am only a second year student, so please forgive me if I ask a stupid question." Doctor Smith smiles and is somewhat surprised at the student:

"Sir, I was under the impression that we are living in a dead zone as far as seismetic activity is concerned. Are you concerned that a small earthquake like the ones most recently experienced could cause a massive landslide that could generate a significant size tsunami?"

"Yes, I am concerned because the sediment is under a great deal of hydro-pressure. In fact, the trigger to start the whole problem next time may not be seismic activity. Gravity or a combination of gravity and a sudden burst of hundreds of billions of tons of sediment along the forty mile area of concern could potentially create a tsunami. I am not saying it will take place. I am only concerned. The word concerned probably should be highlighted or underlined. I have predicted many earthquakes or killer landslides. All I know at this point in time is that I see smoke, but not the fire.

"There are other places on the East Coast that have a similar problem. In fact, this knowledge is over thirty years old. I have handouts about some research a certain Doctor Peter B. Flemings did years ago off the coast of New Jersey. It appears from his findings that water is trapped in sediments under dangerous pressure. In fact, his findings warned of the possibility of enough shelf collapse to generate a tsunami. He said that a large earthquake would not be necessary. Think of a huge underwater cliff of trillions of large water filled balloons piled on top of each other. The mass of balloons is obviously unstable and is found to be under pressure from the source or where the water originates from. In other words, someone forgot to turn off the water hose that continues to apply pressure to the balloons. The whole mass will be shaken by a minor earthquake, not a huge one, but just large enough to cause the whole make believe cliff to suddenly collapse displacing whatever medium it falls into. Of course, we are talking about rock and mud-sediment, plants, animals fossils, sand, and all the material that makes up the continental shelf falling down into deep water." Doctor Smith continues to deliver his findings to students, faculty, and some interested members of the public.

Our story once again takes us to another location and time frame. The entire Smith family is downtown Wilmington. It is April the eight and excitement is in the air. David, Brenda, and the children are all present prepared to enjoy the beautiful floats and all of the wonderful entertainment that will take place in downtown Wilmington and other sites for the next several days. The entire Pridgen Clan is comfortably seated on a bleacher on Third Street waiting for the Air Force ROTC Drill Team NCW to march by. The children are naturally excited because this is the first parade of any kind that they have been to. Cotton candy, popcorn, boiled peanuts, candy, hotdogs, and all kinds of drinks are offered by walking vendors to the excited crowd. Great Grandfather Zeb Pridgen speaks to his family:

"I have been coming here every year. I have seen it all and I can tell you all that things have changed beyond belief from that first parade I saw back in 1948 when Wilmington had its first Azalea Festival! I can still remember the old mayor back in the sixties. He was a very powerful and respected person I have been told. I remember seeing Mayor OO Allsbrook at the festival and every significant event that concerned Wilmington. I believe those were the most important public event to take place in North Carolina. The Governors usually showed up, important senators, high ranking military officials, big business people, and famous movie stars. General George C. Marshall himself, General of the Army, came once. My father, George W. Pridgen was very excited about General Marshall coming for a visit because my father was a spy during World War 1I." Brenda speaks:

"Grandfather, was he stationed in Morocco?"

"Yes, Brenda, he remained there a year." Zeb continues to talk:

"Our family visited Orton Plantation one year. Ronald Reagan himself was there that day getting his picture taken with an actress. The gentleman who took the photographs was a famous North Carolinian named Hugh Morton. I believe that his grandfather gave Wilmington Hugh MacRae Park. While we were at Arlie Garden, we dropped by to see W A Corbett the owner of the place. He is a cousin. Of course, he has left this life many years ago now." Brenda speaks:

"Mama, did you get a copy of this year's North Carolina Azalea Festival?"

"No, Brenda, we didn't have time."

"I purchased a copy for you and Daddy." Brenda's mother speaks:

"Actually, Brenda, I have never purchased one of the event books. We did try to participate in the parade every year up to about ten years ago. Beard and I drove old cars in the parade along with other folks from the plantation. When your grandfather was much younger, he would drive those huge passenger coaches pulled by eight draft horses each. Zeb told us that the hard pavement was a little too much on the horses' hoofs, so we decided to just drive our old cars. Some of those old coaches were from England and France. They are probably far too valuable to ride in a parade. Zeb said they were the type of passenger coaches kings and nobles used to ride around in." Dan Smith, Brenda's son speaks:

"Mama, can we visit Greenfield Lake and go to the Street Fair?"

"Honey, I will have to ask your father." While the Pridgens sat, band after band marched by playing their commanding music. Beautiful floats advertizing and representing scores of businesses, schools, and branches of the military, continued to pass by. The floats were covered with beautiful azaleas and beautiful young ladies dressed in gorgeous white costumes that were once the formal attire of Southern Belles. The daughters of wealthy Southern families. The children were very excited and amazed at the huge elephants that walked by under the watchful control of their trainers. Clowns were everywhere with their funny faces riding little cars and running into each other and getting into make believe fights.

While everyone in the huge crowd was immersed in all of the excitement of the moment, a young newspaper reporter spots David and realizes that he is the famous new scientist from Boston. The reporter also is aware through the grapevine that Doctor Smith is famous for accurately predicting earthquakes and huge waves called tsunamis. The reporter has learned that Doctor Smith and a team of scientist have gone out to the continental shelf about a hundred miles out from Wrightsville Beach to try to discover what is causing the several earthquakes the region has experienced recently. The reporter from the Wilmington Tribune, a new newspaper in town, speaks while holding a mike.

"Doctor Smith, I hope that you are enjoying the festival."

"Yes, thank you. I am very much enjoying the parade and have plans to enjoy several days of events that are scheduled during the Azalea Festival."

"Doctor Smith, I understand that you have gone with a team of scientist out to our continental shelf about a hundred miles out to see if you could determine the cause of the recent earthquakes."

"That is correct. I felt that it was my duty to learn what is causing the quakes."

"What did you learn, sir?"

"I learned that our shelf is much weaker than expected and that there has been some significant shelf failure."

"Do you believe that the public should be concerned about this finding?"

"I see no reason to alarm the public at this point in our analyses of the situation. It is much too early to say. I have some models back at UNCW that we are working on that will help me and those who work with me to make a scientific judgment on the situation."

"Do you believe that we are in danger of having a tsunami?"

"Like I said, until we complete our study in the lab, I am not prepared to make a prediction. If I feel that I need to announce a tsunami, I will do so. At this point I simply must reserve judgment."

"Sir, I believe that you are credited to have developed new computer software and more advance working models that are over ninety percent accurate in predicting earthquakes and tsunamis. In fact, you are responsible for saving millions of lives in your career."

"Yes, that is true, but I don't let this success cloud my judgment or alter my simple lifestyle. I take my work very seriously. I am not interested in fame getting in my way. My work is my calling. I consider my work more important than my name becoming a household word."

"I take it then that you do not rule out a tsunami?"

"No, but I am not predicting one either."

The next morning after the Smith family has enjoyed the azalea parade downtown Wilmington, the family is at the table enjoying their breakfast. The news is on and the reporter announces that a famous scientist, a certain Doctor David Smith, from Boston, Massachusetts and now the second in command at the UNCW Science Department believes that there is a possibility that the recent minor earthquakes could generate a tsunami due to a weak continental shelf. The reporter informs the public that Doctor Smith and a team of scientist had recently gone out to the area of concern about one hundred miles out from Wrightsville Beach to investigate the continental shelf and found that the structure is much weaker than assumed. The reporter spoke about the tourist industry and the importance this influx of people are to the local economy. The reporter said that the mayor of Wrightsville Beach, a prominent businessman, and other business and civic leaders were not happy about the statement Doctor Smith made.

The next day Doctor Smith is in a two o'clock class working with his students and assistant instructors on the models of the Wrightsville Beach area extending beyond the continental slope. The new data that was acquired as a result of the recent expedition to the continental slope area some weeks ago was being intergraded into the computers in the lab and physically incorporated into the working models. Already there was enough information added to the program to reveal some potentially disturbing future events. The computers not only were able to calculate the mathematical probability of a tsunami, but were capable of controlling the action of the two models of Wrightsville Beach and its neighboring towns and cities for a forty mile stretch mostly north of Wrightsville Beach. In short, the computers actually had complete control of the models and the ability to transform the models exactly like the actual conditions along the continental shelf both on the surface and below the ground.

The process is accomplished similar to the way industrial printers are programmed with software and various hydraulic pumps, hoses, and heads with reservoirs filled with various metals or composites to create gaskets and all kinds of tools by a continuous process of laying down a thin layer of the shape or outline of a gasket or tool on a medium or foundation; back and forth until a three dimensional working gasket or tool or part for a car or truck, for example, is created. In fact, some engineers are currently working on huge "printing units" that will one day actually print out houses from raw material their electrical pumps will draw or suck out via heavy duty rubber hoses from tanks of hot liquid material and print this material out through their printing heads. Layer after layer of material is thinly printed on a concrete foundation the completed house will stand on. The giant printer head goes back and forth from one end to the other while it is automatically raised ever so slowly to be able to accommodate the new height of the hardened material that will eventually become a dwelling place.

The models of Wrightsville, except for the realistic human structures such as houses, commercial buildings, and the two bridges across the Intracoastal Water Way, were all the handy work of the computer software and the printers stationed over head the huge models. The material was the actual material gathered or rather cored at the edge or slope of the continental shelf. This material was arranged or separated according to where the material was taken from by the scientist. Out under the ocean there is not one solid layer of the same kind of material, but layers of various type of material on top of each other. Any experienced scientist could look at the material in the marked off reservoirs positioned around the models and tell you approximately what depth and location the material was obtained, its age and its composition. The computers had stored in their memory banks extensive knowledge of the makeup of the continental shelf structure and knew exactly where the material was to be "printed" on the floor of the huge glass/steel structure that would look similar to a Holly Wood version of Wrightsville Beach above water and under the water out near the end of the continental shelf. In other words, the model would look and act exactly like the real thing including the realistic layers of sand, rock, mud, fossils and whatever is out there. The models were filled with water to represent the ocean. Even the waves were created in the blue tinted water to wash up on the sandy white beach in a realistic manner. The models are so large that the scientist do not walk up to them and look down at a realistic working model of Wrightsville Beach.

Tiny cameras are arranged at various locations on the models that constantly monitor the beach and out into the "ocean." This scene is observed via the monitors. Underwater actual working models of tiny hybrid ROVs/AUVs continually scan the continental shelves of both working models. They can be programmed to do a continuous battery of various images of the weak structures created in the continental shelf. It is so realistic that even a scientist of long experience would be fooled if he or she were looking at the images constantly coming in on the monitors. All kinds of sophisticated sensors and tiny cameras of various kinds are installed on these machines. The water is kept at the same temperature it is found at the various depths of the water. The scanners can "see" on or below the surface of the seafloor. Even special supersensitive audio equipment is installed to pick up the slightest noise in the closed containers. Doctor Smith has discovered that earthquakes are often announced by very high or low sounds humans are not able to hear.

Twenty-Three

Doctor Smith is Relieved of His Administrative Duties by Doctor Fletcher, His Boss
A Tsunami is on its Way

Our story takes a leap in time and location. It is the month of May. Doctor Hardin has just finished a much anticipated two day fishing trip with a friend of his. Doctor Hardin was able to find a qualified instructor who was willing to take his place in class for several days. Hardin is with a long time friend the now current mayor of Wrightsville Beach, Mayor Ricky Evans. Mayor Evans looks and acts very much like newspaper Chief Editor Perry White in the old Super Man Television episodes in the days of black and white television. Mayor Evans speaks to Doctor Hardin:

"Sam, what in Hell in going on in the head of that new instructor you folks have out at the University?" Doctor Sam Hardin speaks:

"I know without asking what is on your mind, Ricky. I have tried my best to get Doctor Smith to change his mind about a possible tsunami hitting Wrightsville Beach."

"Well, you had better try a little harder. His statement has caused a lot of trouble for the town. I met with the Wrightsville Beach Chamber of Commerce last week and they tell me that our town is off nearly ten percent from last year. My office has received several hundred phone calls from people who live in other parts of our country who own cottages, houses, or businesses down here expressing their concern. I understand that some of the insurance companies are considering a serious rate hike. Several of my friends are foolish enough to believe that young scientist and have actually moved their yachts from the area.

"I know that you realize that our town is mighty proud to sponsor UNCW's Marine Science Center. We have given generously to the school for over twenty years now. The effort UNCW has done to increase the oyster, clam, shrimp, and fish stock is a miracle, but that young man is about to ruin us. Can't you do something about it?" Doctor Hardin speaks:

"I will express your concerns to the department head. He is already aware of my feelings about the situation. I would also suggest that you and the Wrightsville Beach Chamber of Commerce write the department head and the Chancellor expressing your concern and outrage. Tell them that you all need Doctor Smith to recant his statement so that business this summer will not be ruined."

It is Friday and Doctor David Smith has finished his classes for the week. He is gathering his briefcase and some other personal belongings and has plans to drive home and enjoy the weekend with his family. He receives a summons from Miss Blankenship, Doctor Fletcher's secretary. The phone rings and David answers realizing that the call is from Miss Blankenship's desk.

"Hello."

"Doctor Smith, I have a message from Doctor Fletcher, he would like for you to swing by his office before you go home."

"No problem, I will be there in a few minutes." Doctor Fletcher was behind his desk when David walked into his office as directed by Miss Blankenship. Doctor Fletcher was on the phone. He hangs up and welcomes Doctor Smith.

"How are you doing today, Doctor Smith?"

"I am doing good, thank you. I trust that you have had a rewarding day today also." Doctor Fletcher was more reserved than usual and David could sense that he was somewhat distressed.

"Doctor Smith, I appreciate your enthusiasm and devotion to your profession and your loyalty and commitment to both our department and our people. You have more energy than anyone I have ever worked alongside of. Your outstanding leadership and commitment of keeping our profession at the cutting edge of scientific discovery and advancements are known by not only most professionals in our field, but by millions of people who look up to you. Now this all said, I now am required to continue my laudation of your remarkable career with words of caution.

"It has been voiced on radio, television, newspapers, and even the Internet, that you are predicting an imminent tsunami. I have studied the report you and your team of scientist obtained while exploring our continental slope. I agree with you that the structure out there is much weaker than previously thought. I know that you are aware of the two other sites, off the coast of New Jersey where water is trapped in sediment and is under pressure and off the Coastline of Virginia and North Carolina where studies were done years ago by Doctor Neal Driscoll that revealed twenty-five miles of dangerous cracks that indicate a unstable continental shelf out there. In fact, Newfoundland, Canada, experienced a quake in

1929 that generated a tsunami when an underwater landslide occurred in the region.

"I appreciate your concern, but you must remember that we as scientist need to be very careful about sounding the trumpet. We just may shoot ourselves in the proverbial foot trying to kill the rattlesnake that we fear is going to bit. I have just gotten off the phone with our chancellor Doctor Corbett. Her office has had to hire two extra people just to answer incoming phone calls and calm people down about a tsunami washing all of us away. As you know, our region and especially small towns like Wrightsville Beach depend on tourism. Already the mayor's office has been inundated by phone calls from concerned people from all over the country. A few shop owners have actually closed their businesses. Local mariners are complaining that several hundred big boats have been relocated by their owners because they fear a tsunami. I have been told that you have actually relocated your fishing yacht back to Boston. In short, I have been told to ask you to retract your statement that there is a possible tsunami on its way. Tens of millions of dollars are at stake including threats by local people and powerful organizations to cut back on their private donations."

"Doctor Fletcher, I did not say that a tsunami was on its way. I did not make a prediction one way or the other. I simply did not altogether rule one out. I explained that I did not have enough data to make such a statement." Doctor Fletcher speaks:

"Very good then! I am sure that we can clear this misunderstanding up in a week or less when the announcement is made by you that you do not expect a tsunami, that you were simply misunderstood." David is now put into a very difficult position, but he is a man of principal and is not intimated.

"Doctor Fletcher, I am sure that such a quick statement would indeed relieve the situation very much like half a teaspoon of baking soda often relieves a bad heart burn, but I don't have the nerve to make such a quick assumption believing that it will be OK. It is like putting a bandage over a malignant melanoma cancer on my arm to cover up the problem fooling myself that it will simply go away if I pretend it is not there." Doctor Fletcher is somewhat angry and frustrated by what a man who is under him says.

"Doctor Smith, as the department head, I must insist that you go to our media center Monday afternoon or as soon as our local television stations can show up and resolve this problem!"

"I am sorry, sir, but I must respectfully stand by my statement. I am sorry that it has caused you and others grief, but I have been this way before. Give me a few days to make my decision. I am going to revisit the data our scanners obtained and if I can honestly announce that there is a very rare possibility of a tsunami, I will gladly say so!" Doctor Fletcher's face is very serious and David realizes that he is considering his options very carefully. While looking directly at David, he turns his head away from him searching for the right words. He directly speaks:

"Doctor Smith, I hope for both of our sakes this problem can be quickly resolved. I pushed very hard to get you here. I firmly believe that you are the best of the best, but I also have a boss and I told her that you would retract your statement or even better put the matter to rest. I see that I have failed and you have put both of us in a very bad spot indeed! I am going to have to have a very convincing argument when I see Doctor Julia DeVann Corbett in about forty minutes. Do I tell her that you refused to do as I have instructed you and that I was forced to relieve you of your position or do I tell her you understand the delicate situation we have been placed in and you will resolve the issue once and for all?" David speaks:

"Tell her that I request a few more days to go over the information and work with the models. People's lives, not just their money, may be at stake. If I find in three or four days that I am even more convinced that we are definitely in danger or at least the area closer to the beach, I will make my announcement to you and you can relieve me of my position if you feel that you need to do so. I will not protest, but I will consider making a public announcement on my own. I hope that I will be able to announce that all is well." Doctor Fletcher speaks:

"OK, I am going to present your decision to her as fair and balanced as I can. I will call you tomorrow and let you know her decision. There is really nothing else I can do. If she asks me if I believe there is a greater than a fifty percent chance a tsunami will come ashore in the next hundred years or so, I will tell her that in my opinion I don't expect such an event. I hope I am right!" David gets up and shakes Doctor Fletcher's hand to let him know that he has no hard feelings, that each must do what he feels is right.

It is Friday night and the Smith family is home and in their beds. David and Brenda are talking about the conversation that David had with his boss in the science department at UNCW. Brenda speaks:

"Honey, what are you going to do if Doctor Fletcher is ordered to dismiss you?"

"Well, I could just go over to the media center and announce that I was wrong, that there is no serious possibility of a major tsunami washing over Wrightsville Beach. After all, my superior, who was a scientist when

I was in grammar school agrees with me that no tsunami will come our way. There are several problems I have thought of that trouble me."

"What problems are you talking about?"

"I am sure that Doctor Fletcher will not allow me to use his name as a person who agrees with me that a tsunami is not in our future."

"Why is that?"

"Very simple, if there is a tsunami, he will get as much or more fallout than I, resulting in his dismissal and reputation damaged. Law suits could occur. Now I am sure that Doctor Hardin would not cry too much over the affair because he would probably be the new department head after such a power vacuum has occurred."

"I thought that you told me that he very much disagrees with your concerns about a tsunami."

"He does, but he will not be in the spotlight. He has voiced his opinion to instructors and students alike and I would imagine the mayor of Wrightsville Beach and our Chamber of Commerce, but he will not be blamed. He will not be respected as much at school, and I am sure his friends will look at him from a different perspective, but they will not demand his blood or his dismissal."

"David, that is not right or honest!"

"Life is not fair, Brenda. Doctor Hardin is a very smart politician. He will simply confront his problem by saying that he did not go out to the continental shelf and do study. He only had my word and his superiors, Doctor Fletcher, that all was OK."

It is now Saturday. Breakfast has been eaten and Doctor Smith and his wife Brenda and their two children are out on the patio at their huge pool having a blast. David takes his time with his family very seriously. He also realizes that he is not dependant on a job for a living. Doctor Smith knows that his options as to how he will spend his creative time is almost unlimited because he is constantly inventing computer software related to commercial fishing or computer software programs for AUVs, ROVs or DSV technology. He is a highly paid consultant for many governments, oil, and mineral companies. He also helps several large insurance companies to accurately and fairly adjust rates for their customers based on David's predictions concerning natural hazards such as earthquakes, volcano eruptions, tsunami threats, or weather changes. Both private companies and universities also consult Doctor Smith about improving employee training and course offerings or production issues. The phone rings and David answers the expected phone call.

"Hello."

"Yes, David, this is Doctor Fletcher. Our chancellor called me about ten minutes ago. I did my best to express my opinion that you are a scientist of very high standing in your field and that you are also known for being an individual who stands by your convictions regardless of what others believe. Now this all said, I have the unfortunate duty to inform you that you have been relieved of your administrative duties until this affair can be resolved. I asked Doctor Corbett to allow you to work with your models and allow you a week to recant your statement or to resign. She will not directly fire you because of the contract we have between Boston and Wilmington. Now, David, I mean, Doctor Smith, I would have never dreamed that I would be put in a position to have to tell you these things, but I know that you are very resilient and resourceful. I would imagine that you or your family will not suffer any financial setback as a result of this unfortunate development. This makes it much easier for me to say for our community at large that I sincerely hope and pray that you are dead wrong on your belief that we could face a dangerous tsunami. Such an event is almost unimaginable." Doctor Fletcher says goodbye and David puts his phone back up. Brenda looks at David with a concerned expression and speaks:

"David, I could hear every word of that conversation. What are you going to do? We have never faced such a crisis!"

"Brenda, I am going to call Doctor Dennis Miller at Boston University and ask him to fly to Wilmington as soon as possible. I am also going to borrow an AUV/ROV and go with him to the fishing lake on the Pridgen Plantation and check out a hunch I have. I have come to the conclusion that that underground river is one of our problems." Brenda cannot believe what David tells her."

"David, what are you talking about?"

"Brenda, I have a feeling that the river that supplies the huge fishing lake ends its journey under our continental shelf miles beyond Wrightsville Beach. It does not have a natural mouth like a surface river such as the Cape Fear our major surface river. In fact, I have not seen a cave opening under the Atlantic that serves as that underground river's outlet. I am afraid that this river is the dynamists behind the weak shelf structure and it is super saturating our shelf out there. The sediment out there is almost bursting it is under so much pressure. Most of the water probably filtrates upward through the continental shelf material. We found the presence of a huge influx of freshwater mixing with the ocean's water all along the shelf where there are huge sinkholes and cracks. In fact, there are miles and miles of cracks just south of Wrightsville Beach and about forty miles north of our local beach."

"David, that underground river that supplies the water for the huge fishing lake on the plantation has always been there. Why is there now a problem out on the continental shelf? Has something changed things recently?"

"Yes, Brenda, the earthquakes have apparently caused the underground river's natural outlet to collapse. Pressure is building up. We can actually see the underground river with our sensors. It looks blue. Now if a huge landslide does take place out there as I am coming close to predicting, which will create the tsunami, the huge displacement of nearly half a trillion tones of sediment will open the river's natural outlet once again. It will take a hundred million years to roll by before enough sediment will accumulate out there again to cause the conditions we are seeing out there presently. A major landslide out there will relieve the problem for a very long time, but for us living around here that knowledge is of little comfort practically speaking. This information provided by the sensors we dropped off along our continental shelf is transmitted to satellites that are over the earth. These satellites in turn share what information they receive from our sensors out there to my computers in the laboratory that control the conditions in the models. In other words, our models are realistic miniatures of what is actually taking place out about forty to a hundred miles from our local beach." Brenda is astounded!

"David, I never realized that such was possible. This means that if a tsunami is about to take place, you will see what triggers it and know it is on the way!"

"Exactly, Brenda, if I feel that there is nearly a one hundred percent probability that an earthquake will take place out there or a massive landslide caused by gravity and a burst or almost explosion of billions of tons of material due to it being under hydro-pressure caused by that huge underground river that I suspect has had its mouth closed by a collapse of it outlet because of the recent earthquakes, I will call local officials and express my concern, and if they refuse to believe me, they will then be responsible for not warning the public."

"David, should we pack our things and leave our home and go back to the plantation?"

"Yes, I believe that we can all use a nice break. I do suggest that we move back to the plantation until this crisis is over with. I have the computers at the laboratory setup on a secured Internet service. I will be able to know what is going on via my laptop computers that I will carry with me to the plantation."

Two days pass and Doctor Dennis Miller, head of the science department at Boston University arrives by plane. There at Wilmington International Airport, Doctor Miller is picked up by Doctor Smith his former boss. The two men naturally engage in conversation about David's predicament with the science department at UNCW and the controversy he inherited when he told a newspaper reporter that a tsunami could possibly slam into Wrightsville Beach and the many coastal towns mostly north of Wrightsville Beach. Doctor Miller speaks:

"Well, you know you are always welcomed back at Boston. I am sure that we could find a full time job for you next semester." Doctor Dennis Miller smiles waiting for David to reply:

"No, I don't believe that I would like to look at my statue in that hall every time I went to work. No, I will take my stand and try to prove my theory and maybe, just maybe, someone might believe my findings if they prove to be conclusive about the tsunami." Doctor Miller trying to lighten the otherwise difficult and sad state of affairs comments:

"Haven't I heard that statement before about taking a stand. Oh, yes, I remember, it was George Armstrong Custard!" David comments:

"I know that you are just trying to tease me, but I do believe that before long I will have enough data about my theory that I will be able to say with an almost certainty that a huge wave is on its way. I told Doctor Fletcher, my old boss, that I would announce on television and local newspapers all over the region that a wave is on its way."

"You will be taking a huge risk making such an announcement, but I know your track record and I would be nowhere near that beach or any other beach forty miles on either side of Wrightsville Beach! If you indeed make such a prediction, I will back you up publically."

"No, Dennis, not that I don't appreciate your statement and the trust you have in me. I would not want to put you in such a position because I could be wrong, and if I am, law suits could be on their way to plague us. You would also find it very hard for a working relationship with UNCW. I can be replaced. I have set up models, computer programs, and I have laid down a good workable program for UNCW and Boston University to work together in achieving my goals and theirs. I will be OK. I will be a little bruised up reputation wise if no tsunami takes place, if indeed I predict one, but I would rather be wrong than right because no telling how many people will drown if I am right."

An hour later David drives his SUV into the Pridgen mansion's carport. David's wife, Brenda, and their two children are already there. It is about four o'clock in the afternoon. The plans of today are to have a good time at the mansion with the Pridgen Clan. Tomorrow David and

Dennis will drive out to the great fishing lake and get into a boat and carry a small, but well equipped AUV/ROV out to the great blue hole in the lake that David believes will help him make a final decision to predict an imminent tsunami threat or to announce that he was mistaken and to apologize for the inconvenience he caused people. Many people have closed shops at Wrightsville Beach and moved their expensive yachts to other mariners many miles away from danger. Over ten percent of the summer business is gone. People fishing on the several piers purchasing bait and tackle, ice and coolers, beach balls, and floatation devices, motels, restaurants, and service stations to name a few businesses normally booming this time of the year are hurting because people are afraid to be near the beach.

When David and Doctor Miller walked onto the huge porch, Brenda and her family were sitting in various porch chairs and couches enjoying the nice breeze coming from the trees and watching the beautiful yard where birds were singing for all to hear. Doctor Miller is absolutely amazed at the size and beauty of the mansion, but was even more impressed by the Pridgens! He could not recall meeting people so warm, friendly, and down to earth, despite their enormous wealth. Later on before supper, David and his father-in-law Beard Pridgen carried Doctor Miller on an hour tour around the gigantic two hundred acre yard. Dennis could not get over the magnificent oak trees. They are almost unequaled on the Earth. Garden after garden was visited including a quick walk to the museum where our characters had only time to allow Dennis the privilege to admire the beautiful statues of Captain John Henry Pridgen, his lovely wife, and his father-in-law and mother-in-law the famous Lafayettes from Paris, France. Doctor Miller appeared to almost be in a trance he is so over whelmed by the wonderful things he is allowed to see.

That evening at six o'clock, the Pridgen Clan had their supper with their guest Doctor Dennis Miller. The children were all excited because they had been knowing Doctor Miller for years. He had eaten many a meal with David, Brenda, and their children at their old Boston home. The supper was exciting and was a big experience for Doctor Miller. He expected to eat a little differently than what he was used to, but not this different! When Grandmother Lilly Pridgen introduced Doctor Miller to the various meats on the table, he was almost in shock. He felt very much like David felt the time he ate at Uncle James Henry's house when Henry invited David and Brenda over for a plantation party, an experience David will not likely ever forget with vivid details the rest of his journey in this life.

What a spread of exotic foods that Doctor Miller was forced at first to eat out of a sense of courtesy and out of loyalty to his friend and old boss's family. Great Grandmother Lilly Pridgen speaks before everyone starts to fill their plates.

"Now, I will put a handle or name on our many dishes here, Doctor Miller, because I don't want to insult or to panic you. I have been told that we eat rather different than folks from big cities, but I have always been of the opinion that our table is simply spread with a lot of dishes or cuts of meat that are not normally available at big city supermarkets. Someone once said that variety is the spice of life and we plantation folks are great proponents of that philosophy. Now on your left, that large covered glass container with the handle that resembles a catfish is in fact fresh catfish harvested from our private catfish pond. In front of you with the sweet potatoes and Vidalia onions is Opossum. Try it. We have not served it for years, but it has a good rich taste that is very moist. Now my son, Beard, is taking Bear meat from that pot of stew meat. It tastes somewhat like beef. Surrounding the meat are vegetables like potatoes, onions, and carrots. We have Venison or deer meat and Black River snapping turtle. Now over there is a plate of..." Doctor Dennis Miller enjoyed a supper on a real Southern Plantation that evening, an adventure that will be shared with family, friends, and associates as long as he lives! Our story continues the next morning.

Breakfast is now over with at the Pridgen mansion. David and Doctor Dennis Miller are prepared to go to the great fishing lake and get into a large fishing boat with the portable AUV/ROV and direct it into the blue hole to explore David's hunch. Magnetic detection equipment shows that a huge river is coming from the continent and is going out about forty miles off the coast of Wrightsville Beach. It appears that the natural outlet has collapsed as a result of the recent earthquakes. There has got to be another outlet farther north of this outlet that has not collapsed. If it had collapsed also, the great fishing lake would already be overcome with a significant rise in the water level.

Once the AUV/ROV is released into the water, it will be controlled via special computers David has with him. The high tech batteries powering the AUV/ROV are fully charged and will last for many weeks before they need recharging. The project David and Doctor Miller will be engaged in should last no longer than two or three days. They will remain at the great cedar pavilion situated out on the fishing lake and will use the facility as their home base once the AUV/ROV is launched and inside of the huge cave at the bottom of the lake.

The rest of the family stays away and do not even call David via his cell phone because the men will take turns operating and looking at what is being discovered via monitors receiving information from the AUV/ROV. While David sleeps, Doctor Miller will work. The purpose of the trip is to take film footage of the collapsed outlet. If successful, the film will up the ante on David's prediction of an imminent tsunami threat. David will not go to bed until his regular bedtime since both men have slept all night.

In the main time our characters are out on the pavilion's porch enjoying the scenery. Doctor Miller feels very much like David felt the first time he saw the huge oaks, pines, elms, gum, and the granddaddy of them all, the ancient cypress trees that surrounded the lake. Doctor Miller speaks:

"David, have you noticed or heard any members of your family talking about the lake's water level being unusually higher now or in the past?"

"No, I have not and I don't believe it has happened before. I know why you ask. If the lake overflowed and spilled over into the Black River, it would have left a huge path on its way to the ocean. I believe that this river is as large as the Cape Fear River." Doctor Dennis Miller speaks:

"I have come across mounds here and there above previously unknown deep faults." David speaks:

"Yes, I am aware of the mounds. A deep fault with water pressure or perhaps steam pressure opens up cracks to the surface here and there along its route as a result of an earthquake and spews up sand and ancient fossils. I have not looked for any such mounds in North Carolina. They are used to trace deep fault lines, but I don't believe they are around here. I am also aware that caves like the one we are currently looking at now are very important in the understanding the history of earthquakes. I have done research in several caves. Not very complicated science, but very important. Most underground caves filled with water have stalagmites growing or forming in them. I realize that stalagmite growth or rather where old stalagmite growth is broken off as a result of a major quake can help us scientist determine very accurately when the last great quake took place. I have cut off stalagmites and have marked where I broke them off with a special dye. I go back a year later and measure the growth rate. I don't expect a huge earthquake in this part of the world. A small one can do the job because that continental shelf is structurally unstable. I simply need to certify that the cave to one of the underground river's outlets has collapsed." Doctor Miller speaks:

"Yes, I have gone over your findings when you and your team went out in the Sea King. I like you am fully convinced that we have little time left before disaster will strike the local coastline."

Our story must take a forward leap in time and location. Doctor David Smith and his friend Doctor Dennis Miller from Boston University have their evidence. The outlet has indeed collapsed as theorized by Doctor Davis Smith. The water pressure is simply going to force its way out and when it does, the entire East Coast from just south of Wrightsville Beach all the way north about a forty mile distance is probably going to almost instantly slide off the bedrock into the deep dark cold waters of the Atlantic Ocean with an energy release that will no doubt birth a giant wall of water that will roar louder than any lion and forever change the history of the region.

Four days go by and Doctor David Smith and his friend Doctor Dennis Miller are standing by appointment on the extensive front porch of Doctor Tommy Carr's old mansion. Doctor Carr was once the chairman of the science department at UNCW. A man of great fame and accomplishments. The door bell is pressed by Doctor Smith and the butler answers the door and invites our characters into the beautiful old mansion which is located near Fourth and Orange in Wilmington. David and Dennis Miller follow the butler through several hallways where they eventually are directed to Doctor Carr's study and private library. It is a very impressive room of about fifteen hundred square feet. On a wall back of Doctor Carr's very impressive desk encased in the wall are many ornate shelves filled with thousands of books. Many are very rare and valuable volumes about oceanography, geology, and related sciences. There on the middle shelf David and his friend are amazed to notice the complete copies of the extensive Challenger Expedition created between 1873 to 1876.

The men are formally introduced to Doctor Carr by the butler and the butler excuses himself. Doctor Tommy Carr speaks while he grabs his hat.

"It is so good to meet you fellow! David, when this crisis is over with, I want you to please drop by as occasion permits. Of course, that goes for you also, Doctor Miller. I have looked at all of the data you have collected about the situation and I like you fellows am firmly convinced with great alarm that we are very close to experiencing a horrible disaster on our coastline. I have lived here in Wilmington all of my life. In fact, my people have lived here for over two hundred and fifty years. This old house was put up by one of my ancestors on my father's side of my family in about 1843. Gentlemen, let us get over to the science department as fast as the law allows and talk to Doctor Fletcher. I just hope that he is right!"

Doctor Tommy Carr the former head of the science department at UNCW along with his new friends Doctor David Smith, and Doctor Dennis Miller, walk down the hall of the main science building with plans to catch Doctor Fletcher in his office before his second class which will be in about an hour. Doctor Carr asked David to not call Doctor Fletcher about their plans to attempt to persuade him to change his mind about the tsunami situation. A surprise visit by the most respected former head of the science department along with Doctor David Smith and the now head of Boston University's science department will hopefully surprise and wakeup Doctor Fletcher to the dire situation.

When our scientist reach the center of the huge building where the three main hallways come together, Doctor Miller, who has never visited UNCW or met Doctor Tommy Carr until today, sees a large bronze bust of Doctor Carr in the foyer on a polished marble platform. A very impressive plaque made of nickel steel etched in very fancy lettering shares the impressive history of Doctor Carr's scientific career. It reads that Doctor Carr had the longest stay at UNCW as a department head. Many of his most important contributions to the local science school he labored in, as well as the world wide community, benefited as a result of his impressive career. Doctor Miller is allowed a few minutes to look at the bronze bust and time to quickly read Doctor Carr's work history. Doctor Miller is most impressed and he turns and looks at Doctor Carr with a look of a hero worshipper or perhaps like a thirteen year old boy who is standing next to his favorite sports hero. Doctor Miller speaks:

"Doctor Carr, I never realized you were responsible for so much foundational work done by our profession!" Doctor Carr smiles and speaks:

"I just hope my fame is still big enough around here to influence Doctor Fletcher to listen to reason. Perhaps we should carry this bronze bust with us when we walk into Fletcher's office and put it onto his desk as a reminder." David and Dennis Miller laugh. "Of course, I am only joking. I am sure that an old pyramid builder like myself will not shake up Doctor Fletcher too much. He is a good scientist and may also see his statue or bust erected in this building or maybe at the junction of one of our university streets for all to admire. I just hope that all three of us will weigh enough around here to influence him to change his mind. People's lives are literally at stake here if we fail on our mission."

Our three gentlemen walk into Doctor Fletcher's office suite and stand before Doctor Fletcher's executive secretary's impressive oak desk.

402   *Robert B. Corbett*

Miss Blankenship immediately recognizes her old boss and is shocked to see him with David and another young man who like David looks important. Miss Blankenship jumps up from her chair all excited and cannot help, but to hug Doctor Carr's neck. A practice that would not have taken place during their years of professional relationship together working at the university. Miss Blankenship realizes that something is up, but out of professional courtesy does not question Doctor Carr about why he had showed up with David and Doctor Miller. Miss Blankenship is introduced to Doctor Miller and she speaks:

"I have heard some wonderful things about you, Doctor Miller! I am sure that you know the source." Miss Blankenship looks at David with a smile. "I realize that you gentlemen have not dropped by here today to chat with me, but to talk to Doctor Fletcher. I will go ahead and page him for you." Before Miss Blankenship can press the pager button, Doctor Fletcher opens his office door into Miss Blankenship's office. He is visibly surprised to see not only David with a young important looking gentleman about David's age, but the former head of the science department. Doctor Fletcher is nobody's dummy and he instantly guesses why the three men are present, but he does not say it. Doctor Fletcher speaks:

"Come in, come in gentleman into my office!" Doctor Fletcher extends his right hand out to Doctor Carr and he is quickly and formally introduced to Doctor Dennis Miller by David.

"Have seats and make yourselves comfortable! Is there anything that I can get for you fellows, perhaps some hot coffee or some bottled water?" All three men say, no, that they were in no need. Doctor Fletcher speaks:

"I am sure that you guys did not come by my office this afternoon to pass the time away. What is on your minds?" Doctor Fletcher has a firm, but pleasant smile on his face. Doctor Carr speaks: David and Doctor Miller had appointed Doctor Carr to be their spokesperson.

"Doctor Fletcher, I did not come by here to magnify myself or the impressive accomplishments of my two younger companions here. I am also aware that you have looked over the data obtained by the team of scientist that recently explored our continental shelf. I know that you are a very capable and wise man. I am not saying these things to sugar coat you or to influence you by pampering your ego.

"I am here along with, Doctor Smith, who is on administrative leave due to his firm convictions based on sound science and his own experience with tsunamis and earthquakes. He represents the future. I do not consider his work to be peripheral in nature, but it represents new technology and I believe pure genius. I know that Doctor Smith would never tell you that he has one of the highest I Q's on record because he is a very humble man who takes advantage of his considerable mental powers to benefit his fellow creatures. Doctor Smith can testify that we have never met until today.

"I say this in his presence not to embarrass him. I was aware of him even when he was a student. I read news reports of his almost supernatural abilities. He has already saved several million people by warning officials of incoming disaster. The frightening thing about it is that he has been right every time. I would not gamble against him. Doctor Miller here," Doctor Carr makes eye contact with Doctor Miller, "is no minnow himself. He was chosen to take Doctor Smith's place because he is a very exceptional scientist himself. I will speak for him at his request that he is also firmly convinced that a disaster is on its way. Doctor Miller worked under Doctor Smith for several years. He has added Doctor Smith's knowledge to his own plate so to speak. He is Doctor Smith's best disciple. He has been a witness to Doctor Smith's predictions being present under Doctor Smith learning first hand his methods and standing amazed at his computer models designed to accurately predict earthquakes, volcano eruptions, tsunamis, or whatever." Doctor Fletcher speaks:

"I understand your concerns and I do appreciate the work Doctor Smith has done here and at Boston University." Doctor Fletcher looks at Doctor Smith. "I have gone over the data provided including your recent findings about the collapsed outlet for that underground river system and I..." Doctor Tommy Carr, Doctor David Smith, and his friend Doctor Dennis Miller continue to advise as concerned members of the local community, except, Dennis Miller, and as responsible scientists and friends that it is not Doctor David Smith that needs to recant his statement about a possible tsunami on its way, but Doctor Fletcher, the UNCW department head. David closes the conversation between the men.

"Doctor Fletcher, like you, I would have never dreamed that we would be on opposite sides. I continue to respect you as a person who is recognized as a scientist of considerable standing. We have worked together now for nearly seven months. The experience has been a joy, and privilege except for this last five weeks. I hope that I am wrong! I can say that so far I have not been wrong about my predictions. I hated to make them. It is not easy to convince the mayor of a major city or even the president of a country to evacuate a major metro area, but I have done it several times. The people believed me and saved their lives by doing so.

"I am now forced to go public and announce that I firmly believe that I am correct in my understanding of what is going on out on our continental shelf. Of course, you have the privilege to publically disagree with my findings. If you are right, I will probably have to consider working for myself full time." David extends his right hand out and shakes Doctor Fletcher's hand to let him know that he is not angry or disrespectful. David and his two distinguished companions leave Doctor Fletcher's office. Doctor Miller is driven to the airport and David sees him off. He is going back to Boston expecting to hear some bad news in a few months or even weeks."

The following morning Doctor David Smith is in the studio of a local television station. A reporter asked him to explain to the public his findings about a dangerously weak continental shelf off Wrightsville Beach and extending north for about forty miles. The interview lasted about thirty minutes. Doctor Smith even has charts and pictures of the continental shelf where huge cracks are shown and sinkholes. The reporter speaks:

"Doctor Smith, I understand that you have been relieved of your position as the second in command at UNCW's Science Department." Doctor Smith speaks:

"Yes, that is true. I must stick by my findings. I am very convinced by the working computer models that I talked about earlier on this interview and my trip all along our local continental shelf that disaster is most imminent." The reporter Doug Jackson speaks:

"You are taking a very big chance if your prediction is incorrect!"

"I realize that, of course, I am sure lawsuits will take place if I am wrong. I have tried to protect myself and my family in a financial way because several large insurance companies back me. I am not alone. I have saved these companies billions of dollars in the seventeen years I have worked as a paid professional. Often I am able to help these companies by helping them in lowering their premiums. When they do so, they are able to get a lot more customers than their competitors. Look, I realize the economic impact my statements have made on the local economy. The beaches up and down our coast for many miles are not near as active as normal years. A lot of business owners and officials are not happy with me. I have been relieved of my job. I have received dozens of threats from law firms and private citizens that they are going to sue me." Doug Jackson speaks:

"I am sure that there are many people out there that do appreciate your willingness to put your reputation and possible financial health at risk. I understand that business is down fifteen percent and is getting worst because people are afraid to visit the beaches or to run their businesses. I am sure that you are a very responsible guy that takes your work very seriously, but I will have to admit that I hope that you are wrong and that the people will simply forgive you for being mistaken. Now you say that a huge tsunami is going to wash onto shore. When do you believe this event will take place?"

"I believe that it will take place sometime between August and the end of September of this year. I hope that I am wrong. I am not going to go over my track record again, but I say again that I have so far not been wrong about a disaster." Doug Jackson speaks:

"We appreciate you dropping by today and expressing your professional opinion about our continental shelf. I will take your advice and stay off the beaches. Of course, I may now be sued or fired for making this statement, but you have convinced me." Several weeks have passed and David has been interviewed over a dozen times. One prominent newspaper even has a time chart counting off the days before the big wave will wash ashore. The information they feature every day in their paper about tsunamis and other disasters, plus several interviews a week with David has greatly boosted their sales. Many of the other papers are running articles that strongly disagree with Doctor Smith's prediction.

David's prediction that a huge tsunami is on its way has now been published in most of the major newspapers across the United States and the world. His story is plastered everywhere news stories are featured, including the Internet. Even late night talk shows are commenting about this development. Some show host poke fun at the situation and David and others are taking it with a serious note. Government officials of all ranks are investigating David's prediction. All of his scientific findings about the tsunami threat have been shared in detail. No one in big government has spoken against David's prediction because they are all aware of his reputation.

Our story takes us back to the mighty Pridgen Plantation. David and Brenda are in bed taking. Brenda speaks:

"David, what are you going to do with your time now that you are not working at UNCW?"

"I will continue to work on my many projects. I have several new computer software programs and some new equipment I am trying to design for oil companies that use my products. While I am engaged in my usual peripheral activities, I believe that I just might give Uncle Roy Henry a visit and learn how to build log cabins. I need to keep physically active."

The next morning bright and early, the Pridgen Clan is at the breakfast table enjoying a wonderful Southern meal. Every one is a little less talkative because David is out of a job. Everyone is aware that David is still making a huge amount of money on his own, but he takes his work as a scientist very seriously. He has never faced such a situation before. Dan, the Smith's ten year old son, speaks:

"Father what are you going to do now that you are not working at the school this summer?"

"Son, I am going to build log cabins."

"Father, have you ever made log cabins?"

"No, Son, but I believe that I am capable of learning the trade. What do you think?"

"Yes, sir, I know that you will learn to build log cabins." David gets into a pickup truck he borrows from his father-in-law Beard Pridgen and goes over to Uncle Roy's shop. Henry notices David the moment he walks under the huge shed.

"Well, look ahear who has done come by old Uncle Henry's shop! Good morning to you, sir, and how is the Misses and the youngins doing?"

"They are doing very good, and how about you and your family Uncle Henry?"

"Couldn't be better. We are mighty blessed! What can I do fer you this morning?"

"I have decided to learn how to build log cabins. I have some extra time on my hands now. I no longer teach at the university. We could not agree on a problem I believe is about to take place near our coast." Henry speaks:

"Yessa, I heard about the predicament you have found yourself in as of here lately. I believe that those folks should listen to you, but they didn't listen to old Noah either, I understand." David speaks:

"I have never compared myself to, Noah, but I am sure that a disaster is on its way. Not a worldwide one, but one that will destroy a lot of property on our local beaches and one that will probably drown a lot of people unless they heed my warning."

Over a month passes and David is working nearly every day with the men who are engaged in manufacturing log cabins. Uncle Roy Henry is amazed at how quickly David learns the trade. His unusual intelligence and dexterity are shinning forth! He is formulating plans to get up a team of people and start putting together log cabins himself. He knows a lot of people of considerable financial resources that would be interested in purchasing a log cabin for their own use or could be persuaded to purchase cabins for commercial use. Brenda and the children are not idle and find everyday an adventure to engage in. The older folks around the plantation are sorry that David lost his job, but that sorrow is offset by the fact that the children and their young parents are living with them once again. Fishing at the great fishing lake, visiting Paradise Island, crayfish parties, and going all over the region visiting historical sites such as Orton Plantation is an everyday experience.

One morning while everyone is finishing up at the breakfast table the Pridgens are startled by a huge noise outside. It sounds like hundreds of horses are running pass the mansion. Something was frightening the creatures. It took all day and part of the next day for the Pridgens with the help of over a hundred plantation people to drive the animals back into the huge two thousand acre pasture that is surrounded by a fence. The extensive wooden fence is soon repaired. Many stories are going around the plantation that something is not right. The chickens are not laying eggs and yard dogs that have never been inside a dwelling are barking at the doors of their masters' houses wanting to come inside.

Newspapers and television stations have already reported that there is no sign of seabirds on the coast. Tens of thousands of them have left the coastal area and have taken residence in Pender County or even farther westward. People in the area are reporting a phenomenal increase in their dogs and cats missing. Fish by the tens of thousands are washing up on the shores of Wrightsville Beach dead. The authorities are trying to determine what has caused the fish kill. Several large ships and smaller private fish trawlers and shrimp boats have reported that they are seeing a strange light hovering over the ocean miles from the shore. Wrightsville Beach is now practically a ghost town.

It is eleven o'clock in the morning and Doctor Sam Hardin and his long time fishing partner Mayor Ricky Evans are driving up and down the streets of Wrightsville Beach. Naturally they are engaged in conversation. Mayor Ricky Evans speaks to his long time friend and fishing partner Doctor Sam Hardin:

"Sam, I have never seen anything like it! Business is down below the water table. Most of our citizens are gone. I have threatened to fire several members of my staff and even some of our police officers because they have refused to show up for work. This morning I stopped at our local bridges to chat with the tenders and learned that they did not report for work. Of course, they will lose their jobs and will probably be fined. What in the dickens are these people thinking! I believe that people have about gone crazy watching too many fantasy movies or smoking more weed than I suspected around here. Perhaps I should have pushed for more arrest around here for suspected drug dealers!" Doctor Hardin speaks:

"I believe everything will be alright in a week or so when people realize that Doctor Smith has cried wolf, perhaps for the last time! I am not one for all of that strange new equipment and those so called working models of Wrightsville Beach he uses to predict disasters with. Have you been by the science center and looked at his models?"

"No, I do not have time, but I understand that they look like something from a Holly Wood movie set. Perhaps I should have a look at them. I have a buddy that works on movie sets and has actually produced a few movies of his own. I am sure that UNCW will soon make plans to dismantle those so called models of our local beach as soon as they realize that it was all a big mistake. I would imagine that they would be very cheap."

"Yes, I will talk to Doctor Fletcher about them. Doctor Smith actually made two models of our local beach. One of them is a sight to behold! If you don't get them, perhaps a local attraction around our area would purchase them as a curiosity. People would pay to look at them." Both men laugh and they continue to drive around the almost abandoned town. They will soon be getting out of the mayor's car to take a look at the beach and perhaps walk on the shore as they continue to complain and poke fun of Doctor David Smith.

In the main time we are back on the Pridgen Plantation. It is Friday and the children are upstairs playing with their friends. There is almost nothing like a huge train set for young boys to play with! Little Betty is enjoying her time also. Six other girls are in her bedroom playing with the huge dollhouse that her mother owns. It is amazing to watch the lifelike dolls walk around and talk to each other and engage in normal activities like eating dinner at their dining room table or perhaps on the telephone or watching the tiny televisions. Mattie, Mrs. Lilly Pridgen, and Brenda's mother are on the porch shelling field peas. They have many bushels of them and lots of time on their hands to work. Brenda almost feels like a girl again as she sits with her mother, grandmother, and Mattie on the huge porch doing something that she had not done much of since leaving the plantation years ago.

Mr. Beard and his father Zeb are with David on the porch in another location engaged in conversation. Mr. Zeb speaks:

"I have not said a word to Lilly about this, but my brother Gregg visited me last night." Beard is amazed because he had never heard of his uncle visiting the mansion before. In fact, he had only seen him a few times when he was a small boy. He was a man of great mystery! Beard speaks:

"Where did he meet you, Papa?"

"I was on the porch about two this morning. I slipped out of bed. I have seldom done such, but I just could not sleep. I dreamed that I was drowning. It was so real that it woke me up! I am surprised that I did not wake Lilly, but she was sleeping like a baby in a crib. I was not on the porch over fifteen minutes when I realized that my brother was standing in front of me. I nearly jumped out of my skin, but I controlled my emotions." David could not believe what he was hearing! He was aware that Zeb's brother was a man of great mystery. A legend of a man. Many unusual stories of strange unexplainable happenings surrounded this man that few cared to meet in person! Beard speaks:

"I have never seen him here at our house, what did he want?"

"He told me that all of the fountains at his château were spewing mud and little fossils high into the air. He said that something strange was going on below us. He said that a disaster was on the way." Beard speaks:

"How long did he talk to you?"

"Oh, I don't believe that he stayed over five minutes before he left my presence. I am fearful that he knows what he is talking about. I don't know. I have been told that my brother and I are possessed with a gift. I hope we are wrong!" While David, Mr. Beard, and his father, old man Zeb Pridgen continue to talk about what Zeb's brother said, the earth is shaken with a strong jolt. Not one that could damage a strong structure, but one strong enough to get everyone's serious attention. The children are a little frightened and run down stairs to where the adults are located. While they are running down the stairs another quake is felt. One child almost falls down the stairs. The children find the adults and naturally want to know what is going on. David's face turns white because he is almost certain that his prediction is about to take place. He goes upstairs where he has his computers. These computers are on a secured line that allows him to know what is taking place out many miles off the coastline of Wrightsville Beach and up and down the coast for many miles.

What he sees is most disturbing! It appears that a massive landslide has taken place and that a huge wave is on its way! He immediately calls the mayor's office at Wrightsville Beach and learns that the mayor is out riding around with Doctor Hardin. David asks the office manager to call Doctor Hardin and tell him that the quake that the entire region has experienced has unfortunately caused the continental shelf to collapse and that a wave is on its way! The mayor is informed that the wave will wash ashore in about ten or twelve minutes. Mayor Ricky Evans is very displeased at what his office manager tells him and he demands Doctor Smith's telephone number, but no one answers because his office manager and several other employees are on their way outside preparing to get into their vehicles as fast as humanly possible and get as far away as time will permit from the beach before the wave comes ashore. Doctor Hardin and Mayor Ricky Evans are in a parking lot near a pier looking at the ocean. Mayor Evan speaks:

"Doctor Hardin, I am going to have to law that young man! Even my office is not answering me! Has everyone gone crazy or what!" Minutes pass and Doctor Hardin notices that the tide is receding. He looks at his watch to check the time of day and realizes that it is not time for the tide to change. He picks up the powerful binoculars he always carries with him when he is on the beach and steps out of the mayor's car to take a look at the ocean. The mayor speaks:

"Well, I hope that you are not now under Doctor Smith's spell!" Doctor Hardin speaks:

"Ricky, I would suggest that you step out and take a look!" Mayor Ricky Evans notes something in the tone of Doctor Hardin's voice that alarms him. He gets out and tries to make light of the situation.

"Well, I guess that we were wrong. Oh, well, you lose some and you gain some. I probably will not win next year's election." Doctor Hardin says nothing. About eight or nine miles out, by their estimation, the men can see a huge black wall of water headed in their direction. If only they had believed! They only have about seven and a half minutes to try to distance themselves from death. It will take them that long to make it to the bridge that goes across the waterway and the sound. There will be no time to cross it, but they will try! When they get to the nearest bridge, they realize that there is no use trying to cross the Intercoastal Water Way because there has been a wreck. A large gasoline tanker and a trash truck have crashed into each other. A fire is raging blocking traffic from crossing. Several people see the mayor when he and Doctor Hardin exit the car they are using. Several people make threatening words to him expressing their angry and fear. Why had they listened to him! Now their chances for survival were minimal. The mayor and his friend, Doctor Hardin, realize that they need to climb as high on the superstructure of the bridge as they can. They are followed by dozens of the citizens. Many people are not capable of climbing the tall structure and no one volunteers to help them because it is now every rat for himself or to be nice about it, every man for himself.

Back at the Pridgen Plantation our characters are still on one of the porches talking and deciding if David and his Father-in-law and perhaps

Mr. Zeb should get into one of their heavy duty four wheel drive pickup trucks and go to David's mansion not far from Airlee Gardens to check on the damage done to the property. Brenda and David love their beautiful mansion. They were above measure blessed to get it from an older couple from Spain who practically gave it to them.

While most of the adults were talking, Brenda and her mother slip into the small kitchen and turn to a local television channel. They are alarmed by what they see and call the rest of the family into the kitchen so that they can see what is taking place. A reporter is standing on Oleander not far from Saint Andrews On The Sound Episcopal Church, which is less than three miles from Wrightsville Beach. Ocean water is waist deep covering the church's lawn and the surrounding streets. Debris from fallen trees and manmade structures is everywhere. The reporter says that rescue workers are unable to reach the beach because of the high water which is rapidly receding back to the ocean sucking away everything that was not initially washed down by the impact of the huge wave. Beard speaks:

"Pa, let's get into a truck and get to our private airport and use one of our planes to fly to the beach." Zeb speaks:

"Beard, call Mr. Charles Sidbury out at our airport and tell him to get our two choppers into the air. Tell him to get plenty of good heavy rope and some good strong volunteers to get into each chopper. We need to offer our service and see if we can rescue any of those folks that might have found something high like a bridge or whatever to get away from that wave when it washed over." Beard and David are impressed with Mr. Zeb's quick thinking. Thirty minutes later, David, his father-in-law Beard, and, Mr. Zeb, Beard's father, are in a plane high in the air on their way to look at the damage done to David and Brenda's beautiful mansion. David was hoping and praying that he had a house left to go back to. He was hoping that the huge extra heavy duty solid stonewall did not collapse under the force of the tsunami as it came through the region. His father-in-law realized what David was thinking and told him that at least he had the plantation to fall back on in the event their home was damaged beyond reasonable repair. David told his father-in-law in so many words that he appreciated the offer, that he felt at home living on the plantation.

Our characters being about half a mile up over Wilmington not far from Airlee Road, which is about a quarter of a mile from the Wrightsville Sound and the Intracoastal Waterway, can see the destruction from a distance. David is naturally apprehensive because he is concerned about his beautiful Spanish style mansion that he and his family are so proud of. Trees and power lines are down for several miles on the West side of the Intracoastal Waterway and the Wrightsville Sound. Building debris is everywhere. Large shopping centers a couple of miles from the beach are ruined. The wave smashed through the huge glass windows and all the water rushed inside of the buildings with some considerable force ruining food supplies, electronics, and anything that is commonly displayed for sale in commercial establishments. Beard speaks as the Pridgen plane passes over David's huge house on Airlee Road.

"David, I believe that your house is OK. The original owners were very smart to have put up that huge wall around the mansion. I am sure that they did not put it up expecting a huge wave to come out of the Atlantic, but probably for security and privacy considerations." David gets a pair of binoculars he sees hanging in the plane and looks down as the plane he and his family are in is lowered a few hundred feet above the mansion.

"I believe that I will have to spend a lot of time cleaning up the yard and getting that salt water out of my pool and flushing my yard with fresh water so that the salt will not kill the trees and smaller plants. Otherwise, I am so thankful by what I see so far!" Moments later as the plane flew over the sound where the now two bridges crossed, David, his father-in-law, and Great Grandfather Zeb realize that a lot of people are high on the bridge. Most of the water from the huge killer wave has receded, but it is still nearly seven feet above the island. The entire island is flooded. Few homes are left standing. They just could not withstand the force of the nearly twenty-five meter wave that came crashing onshore.

David and his companions are amazed and sober as they see such destruction! No doubt thousands of people were drowned all up and down the coastline for over forty miles, especially north of Wrightsville Beach. Huge ten and twelve story hotels that were standing not many hundred feet from the water's edge were no longing standing, but had crashed onto the smaller buildings and private dwellings surrounding them. The pier was missing most of its concrete flooring, but most of the concrete pylons were standing and appeared to be OK. People were on roof tops everywhere waving shirts or whatever they had to get attention directed to them so that rescue workers and volunteers could find them. Beard flew the plane over the beach for over an hour calling in to the Red Cross the locations where he saw people stranded and waiting for help to arrive.

Beard and his companions saw the Pridgen Plantation helicopters lowering down ropes and bringing up people from the roofs of all kinds of structures including the bridges. One chopper pilot reported with some humor noted in his voice that they had just rescued Doctor Sam Hardin and Mayor Ricky Evans while the men were high up in the superstructure of the bridge they used to escape the wave. Both men were shaken and much humbled by the experience. Mayor Evan's political career was over with. He would not now be considered a good candidate for a prairie dog town after this event! Doctor Hardin just knew that he would probably have to go down to the unemployment office. His boss, Doctor Fletcher, would probably be dog meat when judgment was pronounced upon his refusal to believe Doctor David Smith who had never been wrong about predicting imminent disasters on their way to kill and to destroy.

A week later after the huge tsunami crashed into Wrightsville Beach, the public was not allowed to visit the beach town. It was far too dangerous because of all of the power lines down and some large structures on the verge of collapsing! The water tower was leaning badly and sewer pipes were exposed with their unpleasant contents spilled all over the area. Large barges, yachts, and commercial fishing boats were washed on shore on top of houses, trees, or whatever was in their path as they were hurled ashore. It would take the passage of two or more years before all infrastructures were repaired or build again as they had been before the disaster. At the present time in our story, such things as hard surface roads, power lines above and under the ground, the water and sewer plants, shops of all kinds, grocery stores, and gas stations were no longer in existence or unusable. Thousands of large cottages and homes will need to be built before Wrightsville Beach is a corporal place again and not just a legal entity marked on the map. Some people will not be back. Many are no longer with us because they were killed by the wave or indirectly killed as a result of the wave. Other people are afraid to build on the island again because they no longer feel safe from what might come from the mouth of the Atlantic.

Doctor Smith spent many a day on television and radio programs explaining that there would be no more tsunamis on their way due to the continental shelf collapsing because it would take a hundred million years for enough sediment to be deposited from the continent out near the shelf drop off to be able to create a large wave. He explained that there were other dangers out in the Atlantic that were capable of birthing a tsunami, but the sources of potential disasters was far enough away to allow people many hours to evacuate low lying areas of our coastline. People were much relieved when this famous scientist shared this information to the public.

As expected, Doctor Fletcher is no longer working at UNCW. In fact, he is not working anywhere. He was allowed to retire with at least the outward trappings of dignity. David is now head of the department of science at UNCW. A position not sought or wanted, but he is a smart man and will use his new found position and the powers he now has to better his profession and to benefit all of mankind. Let us now briefly step back a few weeks in time to learn about the change of powerful positions at UNCW.

Our story takes us back just minutes before the huge tsunami washes ashore at Wrightsville Beach and other coastal towns. Doctor Fletcher is in his office going over some paper work when the news of the tsunami reached UNCW. When Miss Blankenship heard the dreadful news she could not control herself and rushed into Doctor Fletcher's office without knocking. She finds Doctor Fletcher at his desk looking like a man who knew that he only had a few minutes to live. Miss Blankenship speaks:

"Doctor Fletcher, I apologize for not knocking on the door, but I have some dreadful news to share with you!" Doctor Fletcher speaks:

"I know, the tsunami that Doctor Smith predicted has become a reality." Miss Blankenship looked very confused because there was no radio or television in Doctor Fletcher's office. Miss Blankenship speaks:

"Did someone call you and give you the bad news, Doctor Fletcher?"

"No, Miss Blankenship. That earthquake we just experienced told me. I suddenly realized like a flash of light what had happened. I put it all together in my mind. I should have known, but I was mentally missing part of the puzzle, I reckon. Well, I am sure that I will now need to prepare myself for my retirement. I should have already retired and I would not be facing this predicament today. I have made our school look very bad and I am sure that Doctor Julia DeVann Corbett will have my hide manufactured into a nice lampshade for her office suite as a warning to others who would like to replace me."

"Doctor Fletcher, surely you don't mean those things!"

"Yes, I am afraid that I will soon be summoned down to Doctor Corbett's office minutes after she gets word about the tsunami. I am sure that my bronze bust, that was never displayed publically, but was reserved for display after I retired, will be ground to dust and served to me at my going away party." Miss Blankenship tries to lighten the gravity of the situation:

"Well, Doctor Fletcher, perhaps it will not be as bad as you imagine. You will still receive your retirement benefits. They can't take them away for an honest mistake. You will now be able to go back up North and once again be with your family a little sooner than you had made plans to do so." Doctor Fletcher speaks:

"Yes, I probably need to look at the bright side of the situation. I feel like I am a loaf of bread. One side is burnt black and the other side is perfect. I just will have to not think about the burnt up side." A week after the tsunami washes onto Wrightsville Beach, Doctor David Smith is asked to meet Doctor Corbett, the famous chancellor of UNCW. When David arrives, he is directed into Doctor Corbett's huge office suite. We will not have the privilege to attend the entire meeting except that we learn that Doctor David Smith is strongly urged to consider taking Doctor Fletcher's job. Doctor Smith is informed that Doctor Fletcher has already been relieved of his position and that he will be moving back to his home town in a few months. Doctor Smith speaks:

"Doctor Corbett, I respect Doctor Fletcher enough that I would never consider taking his job. I do understand; however, that he no longer holds his position and that someone must be hired to take his place. With this said, I hope that he will leave his office with his head held up high. I do respect him as a person of noble qualities and do personally consider him an outstanding scientist. He is not a light weight. He simply made a mistake. If his head is so called chopped off, who among us will face the same treatment in the future? I will accept the position provided that he is treated with all due respect for a scientist of his standing. I also would like to keep Doctor Sam Hardin. I realize what he has said about me around here and to his friends at the former mayor's office at Wrightsville Beach. I am sure that he expects to be disgraced and fired. I would like to surprise him and allow him to continue his stay here as the second in command. He is a very smart man and I will bet money on it that he will soon be my best disciple and will back my program around here with as much enthusiasm as my former lieutenant Doctor Dennis Miller at Boston University who is now the head of the science department there. I am aware that you know who he is." Doctor Corbett speaks:

"Doctor Smith, you speak with great wisdom. I have met few with your forgiving attitude. I had better be careful because you may just replace me one of these days!" Doctor Corbett smiles. "You do what you want to do with Sam Hardin. He has been on my hit list for years, but I just could not catch him. He is a slick operator, but I am also aware that he is very good at his trade and is probably our most talented instructor in your field. Students love his classes and I must admit he has been responsible for training some of the best young scientist in our country. Go over to his office and have a talk with him. If you want him to be your number two man, let it be so. If you want to fire him, you have my permission. You just may be the man who will rope him, put a saddle on his back and make him the scientist he should be. He will just have to give up his so called political career around here and stick to business!" Doctor Corbett shakes David's hand and tells him good luck.

Doctor Smith walks to his old office suite across from Doctor Fletcher's old office suite. He walks in and his former secretary is pleased, but very surprised that David walks into her office. Mrs. Baxter speaks:

"Doctor Smith, I am surprised to see you! I hope that you are doing good!" Doctor Smith speaks:

"Yes, I am not complaining. Now, I would like to see Doctor Hardin. Would you page him for me and tell him I would like to speak to him?" Doctor Hardin is informed that Doctor Smith would like to see him. Doctor Smith is invited into the office.

Doctor Hardin has a very sober look on his face when he sees Doctor Smith. Doctor Hardin had just received the news from the chancellor's office that Doctor Smith is now the head of the science department. He is fully convinced that Doctor Smith had come into the office to have some unpleasant words with him and to fire him. He knew that his goose was cooked! Doctor Smith asked Doctor Hardin to have a seat and to relax and hear him out.

"Doctor Hardin, you probably have the office keys nearby so that you can give them to me so that I can give them to your replacement. Well, you are wrong. I want you to be my second in command." Doctor Hardin could not believe what he was hearing. He is for the first time in his adult life, speechless. Finally, he regained his composure and was able to speak:

"I don't understand. Why would you want me around here? I did everything I could to undermine your position around here. I honestly felt that I deserved your position. I was dead wrong about that tsunami and a lot of people are dead now because I influenced the former mayor of Wrightsville Beach to consider you a charlatan." Doctor Smith speaks:

"Doctor Hardin, I am convinced that he had already made up his mind. You became his yes man. I am sure that you would not have risked your life even for your friend by being on that beach if you did not believe it safe to be there. You were wrong, but honestly wrong. Now if you had made it a practice to avoid the beach after I announced that a tsunami was on its way, I would consider you a false prophet, just pretending that a tsunami was not imminent just to please your friend and other powerful business people in the region.

"Now, for the remainder of the years we will be working together as a team, I am asking you to learn about my computer models and the working models of Wrightsville Beach so that you will add what I have discovered in my seventeen years as a scientist to your plate of knowledge. I asked Doctor Miller at Boston University to do the same things before I hired him. He is so far my best disciple. I consider you to be a very smart man and you are capable of being more flexible in your work assignments. You will learn to pilot our new exploration submarine and I want you to be our best operator. Help me to achieve my goals around here and try to incorporate them into your goals. There is no room or time for hurt feelings or jealousy in our business because people's lives are at stake. Not only by natural disasters such as the one we have recently experience, but by diseases we need to try to help cure and the food and water shortage on our planet that needs to be addressed because things are getting worst every year. Will you help me? We will not solve all of mankind's problems, but we can surprise even ourselves if we all work with a new vision in our hearts and minds." Doctor Hardin humbly accepted what Doctor Smith offered him and promised to work with him with renewed interest and a spirit of cooperation.

Our two characters are now on the road to success as never before and have ended their conversation as this story must also end. Good luck to you and I hope that you have enjoyed my story. It may just be possible that you also are now inspired to write a story. It may be fiction as my story is or a true life event that will uplift and inspire others to not give up. I have heard it said that everyone has a book in them. It is not always an easy task to take up pen and paper or perhaps a computer program and start recording your thoughts in writing. A long journey on foot must always begin with that first step. When you are published, let me know in your dedication that I had a little influence in your decision to write your book. I would be very much inspired to continue my work no matter how humble it may seem to some. Good luck and God bless!

CPSIA information can be obtained
at www.ICGtesting.com
Printed in the USA
LVOW04s1747040816

499079LV00023B/844/P

ML   9-14